THE FLASHING LIGHT INDICATED A CALL FROM STONY MAN FARM

"We were just put on yellow alert," Barbara Price stated without preamble when Hal Brognola picked up the phone. "The Man wants to put a team in the field."

"Where's Striker?"

"The Philippines. From the time we reach him, he's only a few hours from our target."

"Good enough. I'm on my way to see the Man." Brognola cradled the phone and glanced at the carnage on the television. The tape was already being shown again. No matter how many times the news media played the recording, he wouldn't buy it. Commander Conrad was known to him through reputation as a stand-up guy. And none of his SEAL team was the sort to shoot at shadows.

Something had gone badly wrong with the operation, and with the President calling for the Stony Man teams, the stakes were still on the table. Brognola knew from long experience that the buy-in ante would have to be paid in blood.

DON PENDLETON'S
MACK BOLAN®
STONY MAN™

VIRTUAL PERIL

A GOLD EAGLE BOOK FROM
WORLDWIDE®

TORONTO • NEW YORK • LONDON
AMSTERDAM • PARIS • SYDNEY • HAMBURG
STOCKHOLM • ATHENS • TOKYO • MILAN
MADRID • WARSAW • BUDAPEST • AUCKLAND

First edition September 1997

ISBN 0-373-61914-6

Special thanks and acknowledgment to
Mel Odom for his contribution to this work.

VIRTUAL PERIL

Printed in U.S.A.

CHAPTER ONE

Korea Bay,
North of the Yellow Sea

Sudden death approached in long, cool whispers across the surface of the sea, creeping under the fog-shrouded moon.

Commander James R. Conrad knew the routine well, and it burned at the back of the primitive warrior's brain as he swam toward the North Korean fishing trawler now less than a hundred yards away. As the leader of the handpicked team of U.S. Navy SEALs, Conrad had seen action in a number of ports during the past seven years. He was twenty-nine, but had been blooded several times over. No doubt remained in his mind that it would happen again this night.

Altering his stroke, he surfaced for just a moment to study the trawler. She was the *Dragon's Gate*, a government-owned fishing vessel. Blunt and ugly, the trawler showed the hard years of fighting the sea. Looking like gray webs cast against the night sky, the rigging didn't appear strong enough to weather the approaching storm. He figured that was why the skipper was using the diesel engines.

Conrad submerged, satisfied that his group was on track. With the trawler's speed, they'd only have one chance to make the interception. The long swim through the chill water from the Swimmer Delivery Vehicles three miles back was beginning to tell. His muscles cramped slightly, and he knew the payback on the mission the next few days was going to be rough.

Activating the UTEL built into his face mask, Conrad said, "Manta Leader to Manta Squad, give me the quick count."

"Roger, Manta Leader, this is Manta Two. We're showing clean and green. Picking up no sonar."

The rest of the team quickly counted off, assuring radio contact and position.

Ahead of his group, the SEAL commander was the first to intercept the approaching trawler. He fought against the wake to touch the hull of the vessel with a gloved hand and glanced up at the railing as he broke the surface. No one was there. "Manta Three."

"Here."

"Secure the line."

"Aye, sir." Less than ten feet away, Manta Three rose to just below the surface. Conrad couldn't see the man, but he knew the instructions he'd given.

A silvery sheen of bubbles left from the compressed air of the speargun was the only thing visible. The trail ended suddenly when the spear impacted against the wooden side of the *Dragon's Gate.*

"Tie on," Conrad ordered. "Count it down when you're secure." He swam strongly, kicking out hard with his fins. The trawler pushed through the water at a speed faster than most of his team could maintain for long despite their training and conditioning. The window of opportunity for target lock was shrinking rapidly.

The SEAL team commander touched his face mask and dropped the modified infrared lenses into place. The ocean took on a whole new look. Behind him, coming up with speed, a red glowing line snaked through the water as it dug into the vessel's side. The infrared lenses picked up the specially treated line easily.

Conrad grabbed the line without difficulty, submerging quickly and holding on. The line was knotted every two feet and made gripping even easier. His team counted off raggedly, but every man was on.

"Move it," Conrad commanded, pulling himself up the line. Until then, the ocean had been a friend, buoyant and supple. Now it became another enemy, shoving and pushing against them as the trawler continued on its way. Hand over hand, Conrad hauled himself along the line. His arms ached with the effort, but he made himself go forward.

In a long minute, possibly two, he reached the side of the trawler, then took a small, collapsible grappling hook from his chest pack and shook out the line. He touched the release button, and the four flukes popped from the sides. He spit out a mouthful of salty water and the rebreather mouthpiece. "Four."

"Ready, sir," the man's voice called out behind him.

"On my mark."

"Aye."

Conrad spun the grappling hook over his head, cresting the waves expertly. "Go." At the apex of one of the waves, he let it fly.

"I'm away," Manta Four called out.

Cast well, the grappling hook dropped over the trawler's side. Conrad held his breath and submerged, quickly drawing up the slack as he slid along the umbilical. The grappling line drew taut with enough force to tug fiercely even though his falling weight was almost negated by the water.

He released the umbilical and swarmed up the grappling line. When he broke the surface, he saw the heads of some of his group already gathered around the ascension point. "Four."

"I'm on, sir."

"Let's go."

"Aye, aye."

Climbing the rope was difficult, but the trawler's motion and the spume of the waves made the situation even worse. Still, Conrad went up it steadily. When he had one arm over the railing, he worked the zipper on a pouch holding his silenced Heckler & Koch MP-5 SD-3 and drew the deadly little machine pistol into the open. He flipped off the safety, then threw his other arm over the railing and hauled himself aboard.

The deck was worn, with piles of nets secured around the bow. Two men stood near the mast, working with the sail rigging. One end of the canvas had come loose and was flapping haphazardly. Both men scrambled to secure it.

Conrad kicked free of his flippers and out of his rebreather, dropping them on the nearest pile of netting. If a fast evac was indicated, he could grab them on his way over the side. If he couldn't, he could make do without them, and none of them could be traced back to the U.S. government.

Water dripped from his black balaclava as he quickly slipped on a pair of black joggers. By then, six of his team had joined him on the deck. He slid the headset radio into place and switched it on.

He waved two of his team toward the men working with the canvas, then headed toward the wheelhouse with two more men to back him up. The remaining two went aft, their H&K MP-5s canted across their chests.

Suddenly a harsh voice rang out, followed a second later by a blast of gunfire.

Conrad whirled in time to see one of the SEALs he'd assigned to the men working on the rigging stagger backward. The SEAL leader lifted the machine pistol and cycled a dozen rounds, knocking both of the deckhands off their feet. Tapping the transmit button on the headset, he said, "We're blown! Move in now!"

He raced for the wheelhouse, pausing at the door as the two men with him separated. One lined up behind him while the other took up a position on the other side of the door. At the prow of the vessel, the downed SEAL commando got to his feet, letting Conrad know the bullet had been stopped by the Kevlar vest.

More gunfire broke out around them, and muzzle-flashes slivered the night. The trawler was a floating hardsite, which was no surprise. Intel had reported through CIA channels that the *Dragon's Gate* was bringing in a load of fissionable material to Pyongyang, North Korea, from an undisclosed source, probably a free agent in China. With the advent of capitalism and the confusion during the retaking of Hong Kong from the British, a variety of players were actively taking their cut of whatever profits were available.

Conrad turned his attention to the door. "Manta Two, this is Manta Leader."

A jagged streak of white-hot lightning slashed across the dark sky, sprouting two flickering tongues. A crack of thunder followed almost immediately, creating a burst of static on the communications frequency.

"Two copies, Leader."

"Your sit rep?"

"Working it, Leader. Give me another minute, and we'll have this tub wired for sound and true destruction." If recovery of the fissionable material wasn't possible, they'd been ordered to drop the trawler and its cargo to the bottom of the bay.

Conrad signed out, then lifted his leg and kicked the door open. He whirled around the door frame, the H&K MP-5 thrust before him. He had only a second to realize that too many people were crowded inside the wheelhouse, then a hail of bullets smashed into his chest and left thigh, knocking him back out of the doorway.

Outside Nampo, North Korea

"CLEAR UP THAT STATIC, dammit!" Dixon Lynch bellowed as he watched the half-dozen monitor screens on the long table in front of him. "I don't pay you for static!"

The computer operators struggled with their equipment, offering no excuses. They were a crack team, the best money could buy, or they wouldn't have been sitting at those consoles.

Lynch knew the approaching storm was causing problems with the satellite feeds from the cameras on board the *Dragon's Gate*. To his left, a separate monitor showed the sweeping advance of the storm system overtaking the trawler, imaged into a whirling white spiral that jerked with digital reproduction. Silently he cursed the weather. In a world that could generally be reduced to a collection of logic, where people could actually be shot out into space then recovered quite easily, he hated the chaotic.

"The American spy satellites are locked out of visuals on this?" Lynch asked.

"Less than a minute ago," the man confirmed.

"Are our cameras getting all of this?" Lynch asked.

"Yes, sir," a young blond man responded. "We're enhancing as we need to."

"How much of this is going to be in infrared?" Lynch

shifted his view to a monitor on the right. Green figures ran madly across the blackened outlines of the trawler. It was easy to discern humans from the surrounding structure, but not so easy to know which side was which. Both were firing their weapons now, the bullets showing up a hotter green than the body-heat readings, the digital tracking showing them almost floating across the screen.

"I don't know." The man rapidly tapped the keyboard in front of him.

"Mr. Arno, I need as much of this as possible in color, in black-and-white at the very least." Lynch gripped his hands behind his back. At six-four, built like a tennis player, and wearing a gray pin-striped Armani suit with an authority that seemed innate, he was an imposing figure. His complexion was a smooth consistency, like butter mixed with chocolate, reflecting his mixed heritage.

"I'm working to salvage as much of the transmission as I can, sir."

Lynch glanced around the prefab building. The space was limited, but his team had made the most of it, nudging the North Korean military into the support tents that surrounded the building.

General Chai-Song Sym stood less than six feet away, looking complacent. He was an iron bar of a man, well into his fifties. Barely an inch above five and a half feet and weighing perhaps 130 pounds, he was the epitome of the North Korean fighting man. The uniform was crisp and clean, and worn with pride. His hair was flecked with gray, as was his Clark Gable mustache.

"I have my team standing by," Sym said in English. He purposefully didn't look at Lynch.

"I'm well aware of that, General," Lynch said in Korean. Languages had always come easily to him. So did a position of command. He felt the friction between himself and the North Korean general, as strong as it had been a few weeks ago when they'd first met, but ignored it. As long as Lynch had the Communist government in his pocket, he didn't have to worry about Sym.

A half-dozen soldiers stood at attention behind their commanding officer. They were sharp counterpoints to the T-shirt-wearing civilians Lynch had assembled to man the computers.

Despite Sym's objection in front of his men, Lynch had invoked his authority, and the general backed down. The earlier argument had deepened the schism between the two units, but Lynch didn't give a damn. He had his own agenda here, and he knew he was only safe as long as the North Koreans needed him.

Judging from the amount the Communist party had paid him, Lynch knew they thought they needed him badly. But when it came to computer espionage and political sabotage behind the scenes, he was the best money could buy.

"The sacrifices of those soldiers don't have to be made," Sym said.

Lynch pinned him with a hot gaze, then let a sardonic grin cover his lips. "General, you don't give a damn about those men on the *Dragon's Gate*. You'd just like to claim your pound of flesh now and show the president what a bully good soldier you are."

Sym's gaze narrowed, and he tried to pierce Lynch with his stare. "I warn you, Mr. Lynch, your insubordination will not long be tolerated."

Taking a step closer to the man, Lynch spoke in Korean, loud enough for everyone in the room to hear. Those that didn't understand his words would get the gist of his reply. "It's not insubordination. There's no one at this site that I'm subordinate to."

Wisely Sym refrained from making the situation worse. He kept his gaze fixed on the computer monitors.

"The SEALs are pulling back," a woman's voice said in a clipped, upper-class British accent.

Sliding smoothly once more into the command situation, Lynch scanned the screens. The storm was on top of the fishing trawler now, and the satellite relays were picking up the torrent of rain lashing across the deck. He walked over to stand behind Gutter Razor.

During their three-year association, Lynch had never learned the beefy Australian's real name. Inches short of six feet, Gutter Razor was balding and blond, thick and heavy rather than fat. He had a round face and peered at the world with baby blue eyes behind round-lensed glasses. Despite being short and stubby, his fingers played the computer keyboard like a virtuoso. There was no one better at interfacing with corporate and political ICE, and getting past the security measures to access whatever data was being hidden.

"They know they've been set up," Lynch said.

Aboard the *Dragon's Gate,* the infrared images of the SEALs were scrambling now, trying to establish a holding position against overwhelming odds. The trawler had become a death trap.

"Yes." The woman stood at Lynch's side. She was tall and slender. Her platinum white hair was worn cropped close, allowing the delicate lines of her skull to show. Long earrings from a popular science-fiction television series depended from her ears. A cosmetic diamond comprised of a triangle of blue meeting a reversed triangle of green lay over her left eye. A ruby earring flashed on her right nostril. She wore black leather pants, hot pink pumps and a black leather vest over a hot pink tube top.

Her name was Kalico, and she was probably the most

dangerous woman with software Lynch had ever had the opportunity to meet.

"How's the video coming?" Lynch asked.

"I've laid out the parameters," Kalico replied in her quiet voice. "It'll look good."

"How long?"

She flashed him a winning smile. "Minutes. We already shot the blue-screen stuff. And I've just completed the palette changes that'll bring everything together."

"What about seams?"

"Come on, Dixon, you've seen my work. If seams were needed in this production, they'd be as artistic as those in fishnet stockings. Are you getting antsy?"

"No." When he'd found her, Kalico had been working with a prominent California-based CD-ROM gaming outfit that was raking in millions every year. His investment in Kalico to get her away from the gaming company had been considerable, but Lynch knew her special effects were nothing short of magic. "I do know the rain and the lightning are going to throw off the shadows and light sources."

"It's taken care of. I used a flicker-image program I wrote. Which, if I were back in the colonies, would net me a rather handsome infusion of cash, I might add."

"But without all the subterfuge allowed by using it here."

She smiled at him. "Touché, love. There is something delightfully wicked about this particular orchestration that satisfies somewhat of an erotic nature."

Lynch shifted his attention to another man. "Jon, how's the ID coming?"

Jon Cameron was as lean as a rake and had a cocaine habit that coincided with the intensity of the computer security systems. The more risky the gig, the more he leaned on the blow, but Lynch had to admit the drug did seem to enhance his performance. "I've got three of them so far."

"Show me."

Cameron worked the keyboard. His monitor cleared, then a computer-enhanced image still from the *Dragon's Gate* took shape rapidly, pixel by pixel, like a puzzle falling into place. The hacker hit the keys again, shrinking and shifting the picture to the upper left corner. A window opened on the screen and revealed two more pictures of the same man in more ordinary full and profile shots. Text sped across the bottom of the screen.

"Meet Commander James Redmond Conrad," Cameron said, "leader of special SEAL Team Knock-Knock. Twenty-nine years old. Been in the Navy since he was eighteen. A SEAL the past seven years. Took his first ops mission in Panama during the Noriega fiasco. I can also tell you his birthday, inseam size and favorite color as of his last psych eval two months ago."

"Set it up and shunt it over to Kalico's machine."

"Done, boss. If I get any more, she'll have those, too."

Lynch nodded and turned to Sym. On the computer monitors, interrupted only for brief flickers by the storm, the deadly combat continued to take place. It was easier to distinguish the Navy SEALs now: they were the ones taking a savage beating. Still, they were holding their own, running up the North Korean military casualties.

"You see, General," Lynch said, "that's why your government contracted me for this job. In one evening, I'm going to give you more ammunition against the United States than all those fissionable materials will do. This is a black eye that's not going to go away easily."

"Still, you've not said where the fissionable materials are," Sym replied.

"They'll be along," Lynch said, turning back to the

monitor. "Getting them here was even easier than orchestrating this play. But I trust my intelligence circles more than I trust the North Korean military's." On the screen, more of the North Korean soldiers disguised as fishermen were moving against the SEALs. He reached for the radio handset. "Razor."

"Yeah, mate?"

"Secure a com line to the skipper of the *Dragon's Gate.*"

"Done."

Lynch pushed the handset at Sym. "They're your people. Tell them to back off. We need as many of those men alive as we can get."

Reluctantly Sym accepted the handset and barked the orders.

"Now," Lynch said, "you can send in your birds." He stepped back and glanced at Kalico. "Let's see what you've got."

She nodded and walked back to her machine.

"Arno," Lynch called out.

"Yes?"

"Bring up the media outlets we have on the dissemination program."

As Kalico brought up the footage of the actual raid on one half of the split screen and the preprogrammed work she'd done on the blue screens on the other, Lynch glanced back at the images Gutter Razor had showing on his monitor.

The disguised North Korean soldiers had slowed down their rate of fire. During the brief lull, the SEALs were trying to reestablish their position and care for their wounded and dead.

"That's beginning to look like the massacre at the Little Big Horn," Lynch snapped.

"Don't worry about it," Kalico advised smoothly. "By the time I get through with this footage, it's going to look like those soldier boys took a trip down an unarmed Hogan's Alley."

Lynch looked down at the beautifully curved neck and felt suspicion dawn inside him. So far, his operation had never been infiltrated. Still, it wasn't paranoid to pay attention.

Kalico's fingers never faltered on the keys. "I worked on some of the FBI virtual-reality simulation for Quantico's shooting range, love," she said. "Remember?"

"Sure. Now show me what we're going to do with this footage." Lynch noticed the smile she was wearing and knew the earlier comment had been designed to needle him. "You're a very deceitful little bitch."

"Thank you. Coming from you, I know that's a professional compliment of a very high caliber. Now watch."

The Dragon's Gate

IGNORING THE THROB in his wounded thigh, Conrad rammed a full clip into his H&K MP-5, then wheeled around the lifeboat and fired a 6-round burst into the North Korean who'd broken cover in an attempt to gain ground on the SEAL team. The 9 mm parabellum slugs turned the lunge into a death dance, the corpse tangling in the lines of a fishing net as it went down.

"Colder than a dead mackerel," Chief Sebastian Warnicke cracked as he readied an HE grenade. He was a grizzled twenty-year veteran, and possessed a black sense of humor.

Conrad felt a cold grin slide into place across his lips as he looked at Warnicke. The SEALs knew they were the first in on an operation, and reinforcement, if any, was usually too far back to do any good. In the present situation, there was no backup at all.

Warnicke held the grenade for a brief count, then tossed it into a small knot of North Koreans huddled near the wheelhouse. The bomb went off with a loud explosion and a flash of blinding light. Two North Koreans were thrown to the deck and didn't move again.

Swinging around the lifeboat on the other side, Conrad held the machine pistol low and fired controlled bursts into the reeling survivors. Three of the enemy went down as he rode the rising recoil. He tapped the transmit button on his headset. "Three, this is Leader."

"Go, Leader."

"Give me a count."

"Three wounded. Two dead." The radio connection was clear, but the staccato reports of autofire sounded like static.

"Do we have possession?" Conrad had never left a man behind, alive or dead, and he didn't intend to be the first to foul the SEALs' record. Still moving, forcing the leg to take the weight and hold firm, he fired another burst that raked a man from the top of the wheelhouse where he'd set up a sniper's nest.

"Aye, sir."

"Abort the mission," Conrad ordered. The words sounded as if they were coming from someone else. In all his years commanding his SEAL team or being part of another, he'd never failed to reach an objective. But there was no choice. Whoever had sucked them into the raid had succeeded with a vengeance.

"Aye, sir."

"Two, this is Leader."

"Go, Leader."

"Keep your finger on that detonator. On my mark."

"Aye."

Conrad scanned the deck. His team had pulled back to the starboard side of the trawler. With no one at the wheelhouse, the vessel was starting to founder in the water. As if sensing their retreat, the North Koreans redoubled their efforts to put down the American special-ops team. Conrad finished off his clip with a blazing figure eight that chopped a man from the partial cover provided by the forward mast. The grenade the North Korean had been preparing to throw erupted in sudden destruction that sent his flaming corpse spinning.

"Six," Conrad called, fitting another magazine into the H&K.

"Go, Leader."

"Our satcom?"

"Dead and gone, sir. They took it out in the initial blast."

With the miniature satellite dish gone, Conrad knew they had no way to relay the situation to the waiting sub. The support teams wouldn't know the mission was a failure until the SEAL unit went over the allowed time frame. Or didn't come back at all.

"Over the side," Conrad commanded. "Call out the numbers when you're clear. Chief, you're with me."

The unit responded like the well-oiled machine he'd trained it to be. The only discrepancy was the two numbers that were called out by the men carrying the bodies of their teammates.

Recognizing the withdrawal, the North Koreans surged forward, forcing Conrad into deeper cover as he and Warnicke tried to defend the retreat. Then a PA crackled across the sound of gunfire, and orders were given in Korean.

"Chief?" Conrad glanced at Warnicke, dropping the empty H&K to hang from its shoulder strap as he drew his SIG-Sauer P-226.

"Telling them to back off us," Warnicke said, readying another magazine. "They want us alive."

Two men came around the wheelhouse in the stern of the *Dragon's Gate* as Conrad tried to fathom the reason for the orders. Responding on instinct, he raised the SIG-Sauer and fired a dozen rounds at the soldiers. The first target crumpled from the hail of bullets, but the second tried to face Conrad, lifting his AK-47. The SEAL commander squeezed off his remaining four rounds into the man's upper body, punching the dead man backward.

"Shit!" Warnicke said in a strangled whisper.

Wheeling, Conrad saw the man stumble to the side and raise a hand to his throat. Bright blood covered the chief's forearm.

Warnicke tried to say something else, but he was drowning in his own blood. He went to his knees, and the light dimmed in his eyes. Death took him before he hit the deck.

Conrad kicked the spent magazine free of the 9 mm pistol, plucked another from his webbing and shoved it home. Then he seized the chief's body and ran for the trawler's starboard side. The rest of the team had already made the evac. The slippery deck eased towing the corpse. Two rounds hit Conrad in the back, were stopped by the Kevlar body armor but still staggered him. The harsh Korean voice cracked out again, and the gunfire died away as the North Korean soldiers rushed his position.

Conrad slid Warnicke's body under the railing and over the side, then grabbed his flippers and the LAR V in his free hand. Spinning, he brought up the SIG-Sauer and emptied the clip at the nearest enemies. Five men stumbled and fell, tangling up the men behind them.

The SEAL team leader sprinted toward the starboard railing and hurled himself over the side. He released the flippers and rebreather, intending to retrieve them when and if he could. Below him, Warnicke's body was already sinking into the depths, and he concentrated on it, not wanting to lose visual reference. In the dark water, the corpse would be almost impossible to find. The other SEALs were swimming away from the trawler.

He tapped the transmit button on his headset. "Two."

"Go, Leader."

Hitting the water hard and slightly off balance, Conrad went under immediately. He twisted and stroked, coming back to the surface in heartbeats. Water drained from the pencil-thin microphone looped at the side of his mouth. "Blow it, Two."

He glanced up at the trawler as the explosives on board went off with a rolling, thunderous series of roars. Orange-and-yellow flames spread in sheets, venting clouds of smoke that looked gray against the coal black sky.

The North Korean soldiers lining the starboard rail were blown away, ripped to shreds by the antipersonnel bombs that had been set to clear the decks. The demolitions crew had taken their target by the numbers.

As he tucked away his pistol and dived for the rebreather and Warnicke's body, Conrad thought his team might just make it out of the situation with most of them alive. But when he surfaced, Warnicke's bloodstained shirt knotted in one fist and the LAR V in place, someone yelled out a warning over the UTEL.

"Choppers! Coming this way!"

Conrad looked up into the sky in the direction of the North Korean coastline and spotted the trio of warbirds streaking toward the *Dragon's Gate*. Flaming debris from the trawler was scattered all around the site. There was no mistaking the approach pattern of the helicopters, and Conrad knew there was no way the choppers were friendly.

"Get under!" he ordered his team. "Stay down. We'll

go as far as we can." He dived, pulling the corpse after him. All of the team members were rigged for neutral buoyancy, so the body followed easily though slowly.

He swam, using his legs and fins expertly, cruising as silent and sleek as a shark almost ten feet below the surface.

Harsh white light spilled across the ocean's surface in elliptical pools, probing the murky water. Dulled by the liquid medium, the throbbing of the whirling rotors slapped concussive waves through the brine. Abruptly a steady stream of machine-gun bullets interlaced with fiery purple tracers sliced through the water.

"Deeper," Conrad transmitted to the survivors of his team. He angled his body into a steep descent and pulled the corpse after him. Despite the odds, there was a chance the unit could escape.

CHAPTER TWO

"We've picked up some company."

Seated at the steering wheel of the Mazda RX7 with the crowded downtown streets of Tokyo all around him, David McCarter hit the transmit button on the headset he wore that connected him with the rest of his team. "I know it, mate. Gray Toyota van riding up close, and the Isuzu Trooper hanging back a little farther."

"Damn," Calvin James said. "If you already had them, why didn't you tell us?"

"I was about to. You blokes were there at about the same time." He turned on the car's wipers, sweeping away the light sprinkling of rain that continued to fall over the city. In the night, with the absence of a moon, the streets looked like glazed black glass.

"How do you want to handle it?" James asked.

McCarter cut his eyes ahead of them, taking in the long limousine carrying the men they'd been sent to protect. So far, none of the tails had closed in on the trade representatives, who were bound for the economic summit in Seoul.

"Let them play about for a bit," the Briton advised. "Then we'll see what they're up to." He was lean and fox faced, with green eyes and light brown hair. Once, he'd been with the SAS, and was a tough commando according to those he'd worked with. Lately, though, he headed up a team of warriors called Phoenix Force, working out of a covert counterterrorist hardsite hidden away in the Blue Ridge Mountains of Virginia.

"Something?" his companion asked.

McCarter flicked a glance over to Hisoka Ishii. "We're being followed."

The Japanese National Police officer smiled briefly. He was in his fifties, hair beginning to silver, but his body was still lean and hard.

"You," Ishii said, "watch too many movies. You Americans, you always look for the adventure."

McCarter took a moment to light a Player's cigarette, crank down the window and expel a cloud of smoke through the crack. "I'm not American, bloke. Want to watch me break out in goose bumps when I sing 'God Save the Queen'?"

"You work for them."

Nodding, McCarter said, "Quite right. But it hasn't affected my sensibilities, nor triggered any new juvenile fantasies."

"Who is supposed to be following us?"

"Gray Toyota van about four cars back."

"Not a good following distance," Ishii replied. "The driver could easily lose us."

"True. Let's find out, shall we?" McCarter tagged the headset's transmit button. "Calvin?"

"Go," James responded.

"Be a good lad and dissuade the van from following us."

"Direct or indirect?" Calvin James was lanky and black, and from the heart of Chicago. He eventually saw service with a U.S. Navy SEAL unit, then, after a stint in the police department, was invited to join the ranks of Phoenix Force.

"Indirect," McCarter said. "Who knows? Maybe the chap can take a hint."

"I'm on it," James said.

McCarter flicked his eyes to the rearview mirror and watched as James muscled his sedan farther up the line of cars, neatly cutting off the van at the next intersection and slowing deliberately to catch the red light. "Gary, do you copy?"

"I'm here." Gary Manning, a Canadian, was the remaining member of the team in Tokyo, and his specialty was explosives. Besides a military career, he'd also served as a demolitions instructor with the RCMP and West German GSG-9.

The two other Phoenix members were already in Seoul, South Korea, having finished up their present assignment of bodyguarding U.S.-sponsored Thailand representatives to the economic summit taking place there over the next few days.

McCarter watched, but the van appeared to have no problem waiting behind James. At the next right turn, James left the traffic, peeling off. The van was content to work on closing the gap.

"See?" Ishii said. "They're not following the representatives."

"I'm glad you feel so confident," McCarter said with only a trace of sarcasm.

"Cowboys," the JNP man said.

McCarter didn't think he was overreacting. During his career, he'd learned to trust his instincts, and right now they were reading off the scale. Because the representatives were known to be sympathetic to American economic needs, Phoenix Force had been assigned to protect them. With Hong Kong changing hands and the trade alignments and spheres of influence altering in the Asian countries, the

President had wanted to make sure terrorists who were anti-American didn't take the opportunity to target the representatives. America had been invited to the Asian economic summit, as well, but wasn't expected to get the chance to provide much in the way of influence.

"They didn't shake," James said.

"I noticed," McCarter replied. "Means that we're all wrong—"

"Or that they've got the limousine wired."

"Of course," Ishii said, his fingers steepled together before him, "it's not secret that we're taking this group to Tokyo International Airport."

McCarter grinned. "No, it's not. However, our precise destination isn't public knowledge. If they'd merely been wanting to see the representatives off, they'd have been waiting at the airport like the media."

"Perhaps," Ishii reflected, "your concerns do hold some merit." He reached for his own radio and started issuing orders in Japanese. Before he'd finished, the stalking group made its move.

The attack came from an unexpected quarter, in the form of a mass-transit bus. Evidently somewhere along the way, the attackers had stolen the vehicle, then locked on to the limousine's course through radio communications.

"Hold on," McCarter said, stomping on the accelerator. Skillfully, drawing on the talent and experience that had made him a good driver in the rallies back home, the Phoenix Force leader aimed his vehicle at the approaching bus.

The limo driver saw the danger and hit the brakes, flaring the taillights in bright ruby. Without hesitation, the bus suddenly crossed lanes, smashing into an oncoming car and sending it spinning away, narrowing the distance to the limousine.

"Calvin, Gary," McCarter called out over the headset as

he drew his Browning Hi-Power pistol from shoulder leather.

"Here," Manning said.

"Coming around," James replied. "Be there in a minute."

But there was no time to intercept the bus. It barreled down the street like a runaway locomotive, closing on the limousine as it tried to back away. Overtaking the luxury car, the flat front of the vehicle smashed up against it, knocking it out of control.

McCarter drew even with the limousine as it butted up against a light pole on the curb. Then the bus smashed into it again, driving it through the light pole and up against the front of a nightclub, scattering the patrons as they ran for their lives.

The bus driver shifted, then surged forward, using the bulk of his vehicle to pin the limousine against the brick wall of the building.

Three or four men inside the bus made a dash to get out, carrying automatic weapons. They fired at the limousine, not doing any real damage because the luxury car was bulletproof.

Stepping on the brake, downshifting and throwing the Mazda into a controlled slide, McCarter brought the car around to face the bus broadside. He opened his door and got out, shouting at the JNP man to stay down.

Bullets sparked across the Mazda and whined from the wet street surface.

Aiming coolly, making every bullet count, McCarter fired five times in rapid succession and put down three of the gunners, his accuracy bringing renewed effort on the part of the surviving members to take him out.

He ducked behind the Mazda, and a glance at the limousine told him the representatives inside weren't about to get out. A really bad feeling began to gnaw at him. He hit the transmit button. "Calvin, see about getting those people out of that bloody car. Gary, you're with me."

"And where are we going?"

"Into the bus. I don't like the way they've left it perched there. They knew the representatives would stay inside the car."

McCarter's premonition was given more credence when he saw the two tails he'd spotted weren't interested in doing anything more than picking up the survivors from the bus. The Toyota van and Isuzu Trooper made their pickups and turned around immediately, tangling with the Japanese police cruisers pulling into the area with whirling blue cherries.

"Set up a cordon around that bloody bus right now," McCarter said to Ishii, "unless you want a lot of bystanders killed, too." He pushed himself away from the car and sprinted to the bus.

Calvin James parked beside the limousine and started to beat on the driver's window. He was either being ignored, or the doors were jammed.

Running with the Browning Hi-Power in his fist, McCarter was the first man to reach the bus. Manning was at his heels. Palming a flashlight from his coat pocket, the Phoenix Force leader switched it on and played it over the interior of the bus.

"Shit," he said when he saw the arrangement of explosives in the aisle between the seats. An LED was counting down from one minute forty-seven seconds.

Manning had out his own flashlight and was walking toward the bomb. "It's not wired for a remote that I can see. Looks like it's just a timer detonator."

"Yeah, but the bleeding thing has enough firepower behind it to kill everyone in that limousine," McCarter said as he slipped into the seat behind the steering wheel. The ignition was empty of keys, and the windshield was thoroughly shattered.

Leaning underneath the console with his pocketknife, the Briton quickly stripped the ignition wires. Sparks flew when he touched them, and the diesel engine turned over sluggishly. Still, it caught.

Ishii stuck his head into the bus long enough to see the bomb as Manning was working on it.

"Clear the street," McCarter ordered, backing the bus off the limousine. "I need a place to put this."

"There's a parking garage a block up," the Japanese policeman said, "used only during business hours. It'll be locked up but empty."

McCarter nodded and got the bus under way while Ishii stepped off and started talking into his walkie-talkie.

"Gary?" McCarter said.

"What?" Manning was still playing the flashlight over the bomb.

"What are the chances of defusing that bloody thing?" McCarter rolled over the center median, barreling over trees, scanning the building signs.

"If I had three, maybe four minutes," the Canadian said, "it'd be a piece of cake. I'm looking at twenty-nine seconds here. Find the garage." He switched off the flashlight and walked forward. "When it goes off, there's going to be a hell of a bang."

"Let's just hope we're not around, mate. Now see if you can help me find that bloody parking garage."

"There." Manning pointed at a sign that had a picture of an automobile on it.

McCarter swerved for it instantly, cutting across a line of oncoming traffic and drawing a multitude of horn blasts. The steel doors were closed, but provided only brief resistance. They gave with smashing clangs, then the bus was inside the building.

Leaving it rolling, McCarter said, "Go," and followed Manning out the door. The two Phoenix Force commandos ran hell for leather, barely clearing the hanging steel doors when the explosives ripped the bus to pieces behind them.

The heat of the blast rolled over them as the concussive force knocked them to the ground. McCarter covered his head until all the debris had stopped falling.

"Cut it pretty damn close, eh?" Manning asked as he pushed himself up. The parking garage was a disaster area.

"Any closer, mate, and we wouldn't be here talking about it." McCarter jogged back toward the area where the limousine had been overtaken.

Police cars filled the area. Fire trucks were arriving, as well, and a cordon had been erected to hold back the flood of media that had appeared.

"Anybody hurt?" McCarter asked James.

The ex-SEAL shook his head, obviously disgusted. "No. Looks like everybody came through it okay. If you hadn't gotten that bus off them, I doubt any of them would have survived."

"So what's up?" McCarter asked.

James pointed at the dignitaries approaching Ishii. "Do you recognize all those people?"

"No," McCarter admitted. Most of them he recognized from the dossiers supplied by Stony Man Farm. Learning their identities hadn't been as important as keeping them alive. Interaction hadn't been a facet of the operation.

A slim Japanese man with hard features drew abreast of Ishii, then spit on the policeman's shoes and walked away.

"Not exactly a happy camper, is he?" Manning said.

"Not a camper at all," James said in a sarcastic voice.

"Notice the people that have obviously taken him under their wing."

McCarter looked. The man in question was being taken to a Mercedes, escorted by six young men in fashionable attire and severe attitudes. The dislike between them and the police officers was intense and immediate. Upon closer inspection, the Briton noticed that two of the men had colorful tattoos that could be seen on their chests and arms in the light issuing from the nightclub.

"Yakuza," McCarter said.

"I'd be willing to bet on it," James said. There was a click, and McCarter realized the ex-SEAL had palmed a miniature camera and was snapping pictures of the man who'd gotten out of the limousine with the representatives.

"Maybe," the Phoenix Force leader suggested, "this means that our little stay in Seoul isn't going to be totally without event."

"THEY'RE GETTING AWAY," General Sym stated.

Not looking away from the monitor reflecting the infrared satellite view where the SEALs were shown as duller green man-shaped images now because the water cooled their body temperature, Dixon Lynch said, "No, they're not." North of the SEALs' position, the *Dragon's Gate* was a writhing mass of pale jade with scattered pools of emerald around it. Lynch reached for the radio handset keyed into the satellite uplink. "Peregrine Alpha, this is Chiprunner."

"Peregrine Alpha reads you, Chiprunner."

"Bring out the hammer." Lynch put the handset away and continued watching as the satellite view picked up the helicopters. The sensors were delicate enough to discern the images of the men inside through the metal skin. Drums rolled down ramps in each helicopter and spiraled out into the ocean.

"What is that?" Sym asked.

"Depth charges," Lynch asked. He turned to the general and smiled. "Never underestimate me. I'm not without resources and cunning. They're set for forty to sixty feet. It doesn't matter how indestructible those SEALs are supposed to be. They won't be able to handle the detonations. Kalico, how are those news bytes coming?"

"You'll have them, love. They'll want trailers, too, for the evening and morning shows. I've almost gotten them all finished. That way, if necessary, I'll be free to work on other things as we need them."

Lynch nodded, satisfied. On the screen, sudden lime green mushrooms flared into shape, sending out concussive waves that caught the SEALs as they were swimming, buffeting them mercilessly. In seconds the fight was over, and so were any chances of the American special-ops team getting away.

The helicopters deployed life rafts at Lynch's direction, then patched his voice through the PA systems mounted on the undercarriage. "Commander James R. Conrad of the United States Navy, you are on computer lock. You are also under arrest by the North Korean government for spying and compounded hostilities. Surrender, or the next salvo won't be merely set to stun."

Cautiously the helicopters stayed out of range of possible small-arms fire. Other computer monitors showed differing views using the FLIRs mounted in the noses of the helicopters. None of them were as good as the satellite.

Showing obvious reluctance, the SEALs swam for the lifeboats. Escape was no longer an option.

Lynch put the handset aside. "Satisfied, General?"

Sym said nothing.

Lynch didn't care. He was working on his agenda, and things were moving along smoothly. Joining Kalico at her console, he said, "Break the story." Then he watched as lies were spun into truth.

Silver Springs, Maryland

"DAMN!" Harold Brognola swore when he accidentally poured hot coffee over his hand instead of into his cup. Automatically he put down the cup and ran his hand under cold water from the tap in the kitchen sink. His eyes never left the thirteen-inch color television his wife had mounted under the cabinets.

Routinely he watched CNN in the morning before leaving for work at the Justice Department, trying to get a leg up on the rest of the world. As special liaison to the President, he kept his eye on the world picture.

Today it had turned bloody.

He turned up the volume on the set as he studied the picture. He recognized the vessel as a fishing trawler and got a sick feeling in his stomach. Yesterday he'd been briefed on the SEAL-team infiltration only hours before it had been scheduled to take place. After a quick glance at his watch and calculating the time zones, he knew the 8:22 p.m. showing on the television translated to 6:22 a.m. East Coast time. Less than eight minutes ago.

"...joining the transmission in progress," the female anchor announced. "We don't have all the details yet, but we have verified that a covert unit of American special forces has been taken captive by the North Korean military after a savage attack on a fishing trawler called the *Dragon's Gate.*"

The scenes shown on the screen were from an infrared spy camera, Brognola knew. They were also brutal and savage. The American special-ops team clambered aboard the trawler and raked withering fire across the sailors aboard without warning, dropping bodies over the deck. More scenes followed, depicting further atrocities committed by the SEALs.

Brognola couldn't believe what he was seeing, and only hoped none of the team had been identified until things had been researched. However, that hope died with the next scene and the anchor's accompanying words.

"The team leader has been identified as Commander James R. Conrad, head of a squad in the nation's SEAL Team Six counterterrorist unit. Our anchors in Washington are trying to get further details at this moment. As they get that information, we'll switch to them so we can keep you up-to-the-minute with this fast-breaking story."

The anchor broke off for just a moment as more footage was added. The segment featured in-depth information on Commander Conrad from a military-type dossier. Onscreen the anchor cautioned viewers that the information was believed to be correct, but hadn't been verified yet. However, it was being broadcast from North Korea and was part of the news. Then the scene cut back to a close-up of three members of the SEAL team brutally shooting down a pair of unarmed fishermen.

"Hal."

Brognola turned at the sound of his wife's voice. Helen stood in the doorway, wrapped in her robe and wearing a worried look.

"I've got it," the head Fed replied. Together they watched the story unfold. After pouring a full cup of coffee, he washed down a couple antacid tablets. "Probably be a late night."

Helen nodded wordlessly.

The phone on the wall rang, and the flashing light revealed that it was the scrambled line from Stony Man Farm. Brognola picked it up and said hello.

"We were just put on yellow alert," Barbara Price said. As always, she was crisp and efficient. "The Man wants to put a team into the field."

"Who do you have available?" Brognola asked.

"I've put a couple feelers out for Mack," Price said, "but I've already planned insertions for Hawkins and Encizo. They're already in Seoul. The rest of Phoenix Force is with the Japanese economic representatives scheduled to arrive in Seoul by noon local time. They had some trouble there, but nothing they couldn't handle."

"Where's Striker?"

"The Philippines. From the time we reach him, he's only a few hours from our target."

"Good enough. I'm on my way to see the Man. Keep me posted." Brognola cradled the phone and glanced at the carnage on the television. The tape was already being shown again. No matter how many times the news media played the recording, he wouldn't buy it. Conrad was known to him through reputation as a stand-up guy. And none of the team was the sort who would shoot at shadows.

Something had gone badly wrong with the operation, and with the President calling for the Stony Man teams, the stakes were still on the table. Brognola knew from long experience that the buy-in ante would have to be paid in blood.

CHAPTER THREE

Southwest of Seoul, South Korea

"Sir."

Mack Bolan came awake at once despite the comfortable chair and the long hours he'd had behind him before making the contact with Stony Man Farm. The bit of business in the Philippines had turned nasty with a vengeance. He looked at the thin copilot. "You've got my attention, Lieutenant."

"There's a chance we're being followed," Navy Lieutenant Frank Edison said. "The captain would like you to come forward."

Bolan roused himself out of his seat and grabbed the equipment bag Price had arranged for, then made his way to the cockpit. The Lockheed P-3 Orion's four engines filled the plane's interior with noise and vibration. Equipped with a trailing magnetic-detection boom used in antisubmarine patrols, the plane was supposed to give the appearance of being part of the South Korean coastal-defense system.

However, if the side trip to the Philippines had been noted, that bit of camouflage was history.

Bolan dropped into the copilot's seat while Edison remained standing by the back wall. Dressed in a light blue cotton shirt, charcoal gray pants and hiking boots, the soldier gave his transport no clue as to his identity or order of business.

"Company?" Bolan asked, leaning forward to scan the radar image on a computer monitor.

Conley, the pilot, said, "I think so." He pointed at the monitor. "I wouldn't have noticed it if your people hadn't been monitoring us. They've got a satellite uplink peeping down on us. But I don't know if they know."

Bolan studied the green glowing blip on the screen. "How far back?"

"Ten, fifteen miles." Conley shrugged, his ham-sized hands steady on the yoke. "When it comes to accessibility, though, you're talking a matter of seconds."

"Yeah."

"And they've kept the distance pretty much the same for the last hundred miles," the pilot said. "The elevation, too. Probably means they've got a signature lock on us, as well."

"Could be from the tower in Seoul," Edison said.

"Those people'll be pushing a lot of traffic through those channels," Conley said. It wasn't disagreement, just a way of playing devil's advocate. "Ever since those Navy boys got picked up, every reporter that could jump a plane or boat has been coming into Seoul."

"Then whoever's following us has access to a satellite system, too," Bolan stated.

Conley nodded. "Better than even money on it, hoss." He flashed the warrior a mirthless grin. "Of course, when it comes to clandestine operations these days, that bogey could be one of our own and we're not supposed to know it."

"I'd rather be sure," Bolan said.

"You and me both," Conley admitted. "In my time, I've

weathered some heavy business. But this situation in North Korea is promising to be a shitstorm." He gave a sidelong glance at Bolan. "Whether you're involved in it or not."

Bolan didn't reply, instead turned his attention to the notebook computer that Price had included in the gear waiting for him in the Orion.

After bringing up the system, he connected to Stony Man Farm, which took a few seconds while it was routed through a series of cutouts. Scrambled and transmitted in bursts, the communication was made even harder to intercept.

"Identify," the liquid blue letters challenged.

Bolan keyed in a response. "Striker."

"Password?"

"Double-down."

"You've got Electron Rider." The code name belonged to Aaron Kurtzman, the Farm's cybernetics genius. "What's up?"

"Have you checked the kite lately?" Bolan queried.

"Last time I looked, you were on course."

"The kite picked up a tail."

"Give me a minute, guy. I'll get back to you."

Bolan glanced back at the radar screen. The bogey was still hanging tight. He looked at Conley. "Break four degrees to the east and lose five thousand feet. Let's give them something to track."

"You got it." Conley made the adjustments smoothly. The four engines growled more loudly, but the vibration seemed to fade out. "If we're hot, have they got any backup ready?"

Bolan shook his head.

"Kind of figured that," Conley said, "when everybody was being so hush-hush about picking you up. We get in a dust-off, we're going to be hurting. All we're packing is a .50-cal machine gun concealed in the nose. Got two thousand rounds of ammo. If they've finessed any sort of ground force between here and Seoul, that plane running the back door can light us up with a laser for a land-based missile and you can stick a fork in us because we're done."

"Then we've got to see that it doesn't happen." Bolan had already played scenarios out in his mind. None of them appeared very hopeful. The call from Stony Man had been placed with a message drop, and he still hadn't had time or privacy to talk directly with Price or Brognola to figure out why he'd been called in.

On the computer monitor, the bogey trailing the Orion made course adjustments. Conley tapped the keyboard, and for a moment glowing green numerals gave the bogey's altitude. The figures dropped rapidly.

"No doubt about it," the pilot commented.

"Also proves they're locked on by satellite," Bolan said. "They monitored the altitude deviation, too."

The notebook computer beeped as new lines of communication flowed across the small screen.

"Your tail's been tagged, guy, but I'll be damned if we know who it is. Want us to send in a welcoming committee from the *Thomas Paine?* They can make the rendezvous in less than ten minutes."

"Negative. If there are ground units working with the bogey, more aircraft are going to be sacrificed. In my notes for the Philippine mission, there's mention of an American Army contingent carrying out a series of war games about fifty klicks out of Seoul."

There was a brief wait.

"The lady says your Intel is right on the money, Striker."

"Brief me."

Kurtzman told him that the war games were supposed to

be a show of strength and confidence. With the economic summit taking place in Seoul over the next few days, the President figured it would be politically correct to flex a little muscle. He hadn't counted on the snafu a few hours earlier.

Bolan gazed through the Orion's Plexiglas windows at the dark sky outside. The numbers on the play he was putting together in his mind were whispering to him, counting down as the plane streaked toward Seoul. He asked Kurtzman how far the plane was from the war games' location.

The computer wizard replied that the aircraft's location was in blue, and the war games' was in red, and asked if the Executioner was thinking of dropping in.

When Bolan answered in the affirmative, Kurtzman supplied further instructions.

"At your present speed, you've got a forty-five-second window to put you down within a couple miles of the troops."

"Thanks. I'm going to need some kind of intro."

"The lady's already on it. By the time you get down, the CO will know to expect the colonel."

"I read you, buddy. I'll be in touch when I can."

"Right. In the meantime, we'll be trying to find out who your new playmates are."

The notebook computer's screen cleared with a ripple of white light and a small, liquid pop.

Bolan closed the computer, disconnected the phone and put the equipment away. Shouldering the bag in a chestpack rigging, he glanced at his watch. Just under two and a half minutes remained for his jump zone.

"Maintain your present heading," the soldier told Conley. "I'm getting out."

"No problem," the pilot said. "You have a care out there."

With the two-minute mark fast approaching, Bolan followed Edison back into the cargo hold, shifted the chest pack into position and shrugged into the parachute he was offered. He slid an altimeter onto his wrist, then accepted the SIG-Sauer P-228 Nightstalker pistol in a jackass sling that Edison offered.

"Got a silencer for it in the pocket beside the two extra magazines," the copilot said. "It's proprietary, so if you lose the gun, the silencer's worthless. It's a good gun. Dead-on at fifty yards."

"I appreciate it," Bolan said as he pulled the rig on and slid it under the parachute harness. His watch showed twenty-seven seconds and counting down.

Working the side door's latches, Edison pulled it in and slid it sideways. The wind whipped inside the opening. "Had it modified so we could ditch passengers or cargo as necessary," the copilot yelled over the noise. He stepped behind Bolan and did a final check on the parachute.

The second hand on his watch was sweeping the last eight seconds when Edison clapped Bolan on the back of the helmet, letting him know everything was go. The soldier glanced over his shoulder and tossed the man a small salute, then threw himself into the night sky.

The countryside was black and unforgiving below him. Even though he couldn't make out the details, he knew rough and broken terrain waited for him. Glancing up, he saw the stark T-shape of the Lockheed P-3 pulling hard to the left, veering out toward the coastline again.

"They've tagged you, buddy," Conley calmly reported over the radio. "The plane's staying with you, not us."

The cold wind ripped into the Executioner's face, numbing it in a hurry. "Roger." Without a flight suit, he couldn't control his descent and gain some ground by tracking toward the war games' area. He'd bailed from the Orion at twenty-eight thousand feet. By the time he reached twenty-one thousand feet, the bogey had caught up with him.

Limned by the sparse moonlight, the aircraft looked to Bolan like one of the Gulfstream business jets as it closed on him. For a moment, he thought it might try to shoot him down even though at his present rate of descent, success would have been a near impossibility.

Abruptly the Gulfstream heeled up, losing speed at once. Bolan guessed that it had slowed enough to risk stalling the engines. As it started to nose down again, obviously losing the war with gravity, three black specks separated from the jet, followed quickly by five more. The way they moved away from the craft let Bolan know they were a crowd of parachutists.

The fall from the heavens had just become a deadly race to ground zero.

Seoul, South Korea

GUIDING THE STRIPPED-DOWN military jeep into an unmarked space in the graveled parking lot at the side of the Blind Cobra Bar, Thomas Jackson Hawkins scanned the building with a jaundiced eye. Having spent most of his formative years in El Paso, Texas, he knew at a glance that the tavern wasn't just a watering hole for the locals.

The Blind Cobra was a two-story structure sandwiched between a ceramics store and a bicycle-repair shop. The ceramics store was closed, but lights were on in the bike shop. Hawkins doubted that legitimate business was keeping the owner working overtime and figured it handled whatever fencing of stolen property wasn't taken care of in the bar.

Still, it made sense that the man he was meeting would choose such a location. Hawkins's own presence in Seoul had started out as part of a security assignment for Phoenix Force, but with the activation from Stony Man Farm, he was standing in the twilight space between lawful and unlawful himself.

However, his business there was squarely on the side of right, and that was all that mattered to him. The Navy SEALs being held hostage were all the reason he needed. Stony Man Farm hadn't elaborated on all the details yet, but it was enough for him that Brognola and Price had agreed to the covert action necessary to attempt a rescue.

He uncoiled from behind the steering wheel and walked toward the front door of the bar, a lean and muscular man with light brown hair and flashing hazel eyes. He was dressed in cowboy boots, denim jeans and a hunter green brushed-denim shirt with the sleeves hacked off at midbiceps. A battered Texas Rangers ball cap shadowed his face.

At the door, he slipped a five-dollar bill into the beefy bouncer's hand and was waved inside. The interior of the bar was dark and filled with smoke. Three nude dancing women writhed on a chrome-and-mirror-finished stage to a heavy-metal beat.

Hawkins walked to the bar and ordered a beer from the tap. He leaned on the scarred Formica bartop and pretended to watch the gyrations of the women while he scanned the crowd.

A slim man with dark sunglasses walked up at the bar to stand beside Hawkins. He ordered a piña colada. After taking a sip, he turned to the Phoenix Force warrior and said, "You're Mr. Johnson?"

"Livingstone, I presume," Hawkins replied.

The man didn't crack a smile. "You don't appear to be carrying the cash we agreed on."

"I can get it. This didn't seem to be the place to carry a briefcase in."

"I have a table." Adroitly the man threaded his way through the thronging patrons as the DJ started a new tape. The man took a seat with his back to the wall. "You're alone?"

"Yeah," Hawkins said. He sipped his beer and used his peripheral vision to pick up the two heavies who'd vectored in on the table. Both of them looked Korean. Neither was any closer than eight feet, which was a long distance when considering the tavern's crowd. But Hawkins knew that a bullet could cross the intervening yardage in less than a heartbeat.

The meet had been arranged through Stony Man Farm, put together by a CIA section chief who'd thought he was helping out a Naval Intelligence Service operation working on a drug-supply ring inside the troops stationed in Seoul. Hawkins's connection was a munitions supplier for deep covert ops in the area. Barbara Price was already gearing up for the mission behind North Korean lines to free the captured SEALs if something couldn't be worked out through diplomatic channels.

It was that readiness to lay everything on the line to achieve a worthwhile goal that had drawn Hawkins into the Stony Man fold. However, on the present leg of the mission, the point team needed weaponry. Culling from the American stores was out of the question, though. The rescue effort was unsanctioned, and none of the weapons—in the event of a capture—could trace back to American or South Korean units.

"You have my order?" Hawkins asked. He could feel the other two men staring at his back.

"As you have the money you were supposed to bring to me," the munitions supplier said. "It is nearby." He reached under his jacket and pulled out a pack of cigarettes.

Extracting one, he tapped its butt on the tabletop to pack the tobacco.

"I'm operating on a time frame," Hawkins said. From what Price had told him and Rafael Encizo, Mack Bolan was due within the hour.

"Yes. Wait a moment, please. In this business, one cannot be too cautious."

The sixth sense that had seen Hawkins through action in Grenada, Panama, the Gulf War and Somalia tightened the skin between his shoulder blades in a cool prickle. He smiled. "True. But also true is that one can't take too long in this business."

The munitions dealer flicked open a chrome-finished lighter and ignited his cigarette. As he let out twin plumes of smoke through his nose, one of the bodyguards left his chair and approached the table.

Without looking at the bodyguard, Hawkins stared straight at the munitions dealer. "Back him off."

A contemptuous smile twisted the man's lips. "Or what?"

The bodyguard came to a stop just behind Hawkins.

"Or I'll hurt him," the young Phoenix warrior said in an even voice. "And maybe I'll hurt you, too."

"I'm supposed to fear an unarmed man?" The munitions dealer shook his head. "I don't think so."

"Your mistake. Where I come from, it's a man's duty to warn another man when he's about to take on more than he can handle."

"You Americans with your John Wayne attitudes." The man snorted, then expelled a cloud of smoke into Hawkins's face. "All this posturing aside, you're going to answer my questions."

"You're not the guy I was supposed to meet after all, are you?"

There was only a moment's hesitation. "No. He met with an unfortunate accident only a short time ago."

"I guess he wouldn't answer your questions, either."

"Not at all," the man said behind his black-lensed stare. "He was only too glad to answer my questions. The problem lay in the fact that you and your people lied to him about who you represented."

Hawkins digested that. If the man had access to people who could sift through the smokescreen Price and Brognola had set up to cover the operation, then he was heavily connected with military and political factions in South Korea.

"I know you're here as a result of the SEALs' capture," the man said. "What I wish to know is who your unit is, who you represent and what your mission is to be."

"Sorry," Hawkins said, "I can't tell you that for your own good."

The man released another cloud of smoke. "My own good?"

Hawkins shifted in the chair. Automatically the man standing behind him took a small, anticipatory step forward. "If I told you," the Phoenix Force commando said with a cold grin, "then I'd have to kill you."

The man looked annoyed. Unconsciously he flicked the lighter open and closed in his hand. The snapping noise was audible for only a few feet.

"On-Jook," the man said, then nodded at Hawkins. "A demonstration."

The big man behind the commando nodded, then lumbered forward like an automaton.

Hawkins guessed that the guy outweighed him by at least seventy pounds, and had a longer reach and probably a gun, as well. Even if he'd been so inclined, a fair fight wasn't in the offing. But that went either way.

Snapping into motion, Hawkins swiped a whiskey bottle

from a nearby table and brought it around in a vicious arc that exploded against the bodyguard's head. The bottle fragmented, and the contents spilled down the big man's clothes. However, the blow had only staggered him.

The bodyguard yelled with rage, loud enough to be heard over the crashing riffs of the guitar solo coming from the overhead speakers. His hand came out of his pocket curled around a .44 Magnum Charter Arms Bulldog.

Still in motion, Hawkins snatched the lighter from the other man's hand, snapped it to life and tossed it at the bodyguard's chest. As soon as the lighter bounced against its target, flames whooshed up the man's clothing, licking hungrily at the spilled whiskey.

The cries of rage turned to howls of fright and pain.

Patrons of the tavern sitting at nearby tables jumped to their feet and tried to get away from the burning man, unknowingly blocking whatever shot the second bodyguard might have had.

Hawkins delivered a spinning front kick to the man on the other side of the table. The guy went backward, stumbled over a chair and went down. As the human torch collapsed to the floor, the second bodyguard fought his way free of the crowd. A large, matte black automatic vented a foot-long muzzle-flash toward Hawkins.

The bullet missed the commando by inches and gouged a deep hole in the paneling. Reaching up, Hawkins ripped the mounted antelope head from the wall. He held it in both hands as he charged toward the gunner, catching the man before he could get off another round. One of the long, narrow horns sank deep into the gunman's chest. The other tore into his throat and turned his cry of pain into a wet, leaking hiss.

Hawkins slipped the Glock 17 from the dying man's grip

and palmed it expertly. He turned back to the contact man, who was scrambling in a tangle of chairs, trying to get up.

Dying flames lapped at the smoldering body lying on the floor.

Hawkins moved quickly, holding the Glock in front of him. The rest of the tavern's patrons seemed only interested in clearing the building. He was conscious of the time because the busted play was going to draw police and military interest faster than cowshit drew flies.

His mouth bloody, the man reached under his jacket as he stood unsteadily with his back to the wall.

"I wouldn't," Hawkins advised. He didn't stop advancing, but the Glock was locked on the man's forehead. "Now I'm going to ask you some questions. Turn around and put your hands against the wall."

The man did as he was told.

Quickly and efficiently, Hawkins frisked him, turning up a Beretta 92-F, and a butterfly knife sheathed along the man's wrist. Roughly, wanting to intimidate the man, the Phoenix Force warrior jerked his prisoner around to face him. He plucked the sunglasses away and dropped them to the floor.

"No famous tough-guy last words?" Hawkins asked.

"No."

The man's voice sounded too even, too sure of himself. Then Hawkins spotted movement reflected in the dark eyes. Before he could move, he felt the cool kiss of gunmetal laid across his neck.

"Koh doesn't need them as long as he's got me," a velvet voice said. "And make no mistake about it—if you even flinch, you're going to have a bleeding stump where your head used to be."

Reluctantly Hawkins released Koh and slowly raised the captured pistol to point at the ceiling.

"Good boy," the velvet voice said. "Now let Koh have the gun."

Hawkins did.

After retrieving the pistol, Koh backhanded him across the face.

Hawkins rolled with the blow as much as he was able. The gun pressing against his neck never wavered. He stared into the other man's eyes. "Touch me again and you'll have to kill me to stop me."

"Out the back way," Koh ordered. Wisely he stayed out of reach.

Turning, Hawkins faced a blond stripper.

She was undressed, wearing only a scanty scarlet G-string. Her green eyes were as cold and dark as the muzzle of the Ladysmith .357 she held.

"Do you moonlight as a stripper," Hawkins asked, "or do you moonlight as a hired gun?"

"Whichever way pays the most at the time, cowboy. Let's go."

A big man with a beard and a Special Forces tattoo showing on his right forearm stepped out from behind the back door with a cut-down double-barreled shotgun. His T-shirt advertised the Blind Cobra Bar, and Hawkins figured he was either one of the owners or a bouncer. "You people want to hold up right there till we sort this thing out," he warned in a whiskey-roughened voice.

Without a word, the blond stripper raised her pistol and fired three rounds that caught the man in the chest. A drink coaster could have fit neatly over all three bullet holes. He was dead before he hit the floor.

"You might want to keep in mind that I didn't even blink," the blonde told Hawkins.

"I will."

She put the .357 back on him. "Hands behind your head. Lace your fingers."

"Just like they teach you back in MP school," Hawkins said.

She pushed him toward the back door. "Wiseass."

The door opened into a narrow corridor leading back to another door that had to front the alley behind the club. The stench of rotting vegetables and sour liquids was also a clue. It was dark in the corridor, too, which helped him disguise his movements.

Quickly he slipped his thumb and forefinger under his watchband. Tripping the quick release he'd designed, he pulled the watch from his arm when the band slid apart. Gadgets and gizmos had always been a specialty of his while he was growing up. Each new James Bond picture had only fed an already fertile mind.

Walking into the Blind Cobra empty-handed hadn't sat well with him. The pistol he'd secured in the borrowed military jeep might as well have been in another galaxy. However, inside the watch was enough plastic explosive to tilt the odds in his favor even if only for a moment.

He pressed the button to initiate the fifteen-second delay detonator. Ahead of him, Koh was reaching for the door and talking on a cellular phone.

At six seconds, Hawkins dropped his watch. It clinked when it hit the concrete floor, still audible above the confusion echoing in from outside.

"What was that?" the blonde demanded. She knotted her free hand in Hawkins's shirt and pulled him around.

Hawkins didn't answer as he kept the measured count going in his head.

"Talk, you son of a bitch." The woman slapped him, cutting his cheek with her fake nails.

Ignoring the sting of pain that covered most of the side

of his face, Hawkins used the movement to scan the floor for the watch. He had to be standing almost on top of it, but the darkness in the corridor allowed little visibility.

"What is it?" Koh asked.

"He dropped something."

Koh pulled the door open. "Ignore it. There isn't—"

A brief flash of moonlight on metal was all Hawkins needed. Two seconds remained before detonation. He managed a short kick that sent the watch streaking toward Koh, then tried to concentrate on the woman just as a muzzle-flash erupted in his face in a fiery blast that blinded him.

CHAPTER FOUR

"You're being followed."

Rafael Encizo didn't react to the news as he stood across from the tall wooden counter in the Taiwanese curio shop in Seoul's main marketplace. He spread currency across the glass-topped surface. "How many?"

"Three," Hiu Kwan-jo replied.

Encizo shifted and let his lightweight jacket fall open so he could get to the Beretta 92-S snugged into shoulder leather. He wasn't surprised that he was being followed. The feeling had been nagging at him for the past hour, but he hadn't been able to confirm it. His tails were definitely good at their job.

He'd started looking for leads on the locations of the captured SEALs in the marketplace almost three hours earlier after splitting off from Hawkins. So far, he hadn't turned up any hard evidence of who had tipped off the North Koreans about the SEAL mission, or where the SEALs might be being held.

One thing Encizo was sure of, though: if the street sources had been cut out of the information link, whoever had ultimately been responsible for taking down the SEAL team had his own network in place. That no one knew of it for certain let the Phoenix Force commando know he was dealing with a deadly enemy.

"Do you know them?" Encizo asked the shopkeeper.

"No." Kwan-jo kept smiling as he reached into the display case and brought out another item of jewelry for Encizo's inspection. "I thought at first they might be American CIA agents."

"Why did you think that?" Encizo asked.

Kwan-jo shrugged. "All these years in this business, and you get a feeling for these things."

"They feel American?"

"Look it, too. I'll show you." The old man reached under the counter again and brought up a brocaded mirror with a gilt overlay that made it resemble a spider web emerging from the reflective surface.

Encizo reached out as if he were only getting the feel of the mirror but actually adjusted it so he could see the shop's front door behind him. He spotted two of the three men easily. The third he took Kwan-jo's word for.

Outside the shop, most of the businesses were closed. It was after 11:00 p.m. Only a few, like Kwan-jo's curio shop, offered small café areas to legitimize the late hours. The street was deserted except for occasional vehicles.

The two men Encizo identified were tucked into the shadows just beyond reach of the shop's lights. Both were of medium build and wore casual clothing that allowed them to blend in with the people who'd crowded the marketplace earlier.

"Were they there when I first walked in?" the Cuban asked the shopkeeper.

"I didn't notice them." Kwan-jo put the mirror away.

Encizo guessed they had a reason for closing in now, and their motives couldn't have intended any good for him. He pointed to one of the bracelets he'd been shown earlier as if deciding on a purchase. "So why tip me off?"

"You pay well," Kwan-jo said. "And I won't stand for

losing any customers inside my shop. Bad for business.''
He put the bracelet in a small paper bag and handed it to
Encizo.

''Where's the third guy?'' Encizo asked.

''Alas, I lost him.''

The Cuban's stomach tightened. He wasn't worried
about handling himself if things turned violent, but running
a high profile at the start of the mission wasn't good. Being
IDed tore the hell out of the element of surprise. ''Have
you got a back way out of here?''

The old man's eyes twinkled. ''If I didn't, I wouldn't
have lasted in this business as long as I have. The hallway
to your right, follow it all the way to the back. The door
is locked from the outside.''

''Thanks.'' Encizo kicked in another twenty percent to
the amount he had placed on the countertop.

''You probably won't have much time,'' Kwan-jo said,
making the money disappear with a sweep of his hand. ''I
don't intend to attempt preventing them from following
you.''

''No problem.'' The Cuban took his package and headed
nonchalantly for the rear of the curio shop as if he were
still interested in checking out more of the offered goods.
A glance at the front of the shop showed him one of the
men walking toward the entrance.

The hallway Kwan-jo had indicated was covered with
dozens of string beads interwoven with silver bells. Encizo
parted them with his hand and pushed through, setting off
a small cacaphony of tinklings. He deposited the bracelet
on one of the small shelves that covered the wall on his
left. Drawing the Beretta, he raced to the exit with the
sound of the small bells ringing in his ears.

He kicked the heavy metal door open, both hands gripping the 9 mm pistol as he took up a Weaver stance, then

sprinted into the alley. His car was parked four blocks down. If he'd been followed as long as he believed, the vehicle was no longer an option.

The glowing red dot of a laser sight sweeping across a broken and taped window ahead of him lit up his survival instinct. He went to ground automatically, a heartbeat before a bullet cored through the area where he'd been. Rolling to his left, he came up against the building fronting that side. The pavement was rough under his free hand and against his stomach as he took cover. He knew the laser sight indicated the unseen sniper probably had some kind of night-vision capability, as well. Another bullet slammed into the bricks only a few inches above his head, confirming his suspicions. Brick splinters needled against his exposed skin.

With the Beretta thrust before him, he scanned the storefronts above the exit from the curio shop. He detected the movement in his peripheral vision as he heard the snick of a bolt action being worked. Since there'd been no muzzle-flash, he knew the weapon was shielded.

He fired on instinct, starting where he guessed the sniper's ankles might be and riding the recoil up as he squeezed off a blistering eight rounds. Sparks jumped from the wrought-iron railing on the third floor where he'd seen the movement.

A pained cry echoed down the alley. Abruptly a shadow separated from the darkness pooling along the small balcony and fell over the side. The corpse hit the pavement with a meaty thud.

Encizo was back on his feet as the other two men came crashing through the back of the curio shop with Kwan-jo screaming curses at them in a handful of languages.

"There!" one of the gunners yelled, pointing at Encizo.

In the dim moonlight, it was hard to make out details,

but Encizo was certain the two men were now wearing night-vision goggles. They brought up their guns like well-oiled machines.

Stepping into a combat crouch, both hands slipping around his pistol, the Cuban targeted his enemies and squeezed off two rounds apiece, working from left to right. He saw the guns flare in their hands a second before his bullets took them, but he got lucky as both rounds passed him by.

He moved forward, keeping the men covered. When he was close enough, he kicked away their weapons and stripped the NVGs from all three dead men. Two of them were identifiable, but the 9 mm hollowpoint rounds had ripped the sniper's face into a gory mess.

Kwan-jo moved closer. A sawed-off shotgun dangled from one of his bony hands. He glanced at Encizo and broke the weapon open, extracting the shells. "In case they decided to attack me," the shopkeeper explained.

Encizo nodded, then knelt to go through the dead men's pockets.

"You don't have much time," Kwan-jo said. "I have an arrangement with some of the police officials. There's a button in my shop that alerts some of them who have a special interest in my business. I used it when you left my counter. They'll be here soon."

Encizo understood. Kwan-jo didn't just work the international scene; he also kept local authorities up-to-date in exchange for protection. There was nothing in any of the men's wallets that would tell Encizo who they were or who they might be working for. The Cuban took a small penlight from his jacket and played it over the dead men. "Do you recognize any of them now?"

"No." The shopkeeper removed his glasses, cleaned them and looked again, then shook his head once more.

A screaming siren cut through the air and kept up a steady banshee wail as it approached.

"But the clothes," Kwan-jo said, "definitely aren't domestic." He bent down, surprisingly supple for a man his age, and pulled at the backs of the jackets the dead men wore.

Encizo moved the penlight. He kept the Beretta in his other hand.

"The labels have all been cut out," Kwan-jo said. "Standard operating procedure for a number of agencies." He felt the material. A small smile lit his face in the gathering gloom. "Ah, but the cloth. I think it's British. One of their knockoff weaves."

"You'd know?" Encizo asked.

Kwan-jo nodded. "I'd know."

In the inside pocket of the sniper's jacket, Encizo found a magazine rolled up into a cylinder. When he unfolded it, he was looking at the cover of a current *Sports Illustrated* dedicated to all-baseball coverage.

The shopkeeper tapped the magazine. "No one else would be so interested in baseball. These men were Americans."

"In cheap British suits," Encizo said.

"Yes."

The police siren sounded as if it was almost on top of them.

Encizo kept the magazine. Maybe it was more than just something to pass the time while they'd been stalking him. He also took the rental-car keys he found. If his own transport was questionable, there was a chance he could use theirs. After saying a final goodbye to Kwan-jo, he jogged into the night. But he didn't put the Beretta away for almost two blocks.

Not many cars were parked on the street, but he got

lucky two blocks away. The rental car was parked in a marked fire zone. The small tag on the rear bumper announced that it was a rental.

His thoughts turned to Hawkins. If someone had made him, Encizo felt certain his teammate had probably encountered trouble, as well. He started the car and pulled out, keeping the speed at five miles over the posted limit, and arrived at the Blind Cobra Bar in ten minutes. Seeing the crowd of people out front, but not noticing Hawkins among them, the Cuban drove the stolen car around to the back of the tavern. If Hawkins wasn't there, he fully intended to go in after him.

Before he got halfway down the alley, a group of men spilled from a parked van. All of them had guns.

Without warning, the back door to the bar suddenly blew off its hinges and fragments of it scattered over the alley. Encizo rolled forward during the confusion, taking the time to put a fresh magazine into the Beretta. He had no doubt that Hawkins would be somewhere near the eye of the sudden storm of violence.

STANDING BEHIND KALICO as she tapped computer keys, Dixon Lynch studied the news footage as it played on the two computer monitors in front of her.

The American military and political machines were still reeling from the blow he'd dealt them by offering the doctored film to the various media. On the surface, they were disclaiming any knowledge of the SEAL operation in North Korean waters, but behind the scenes the covert troops were starting to put the pressure on various resources to gather information about the aborted raid on the *Dragon's Gate*.

Behind Lynch, the temporary base camp was a flurry of activity. A number of agencies were entering the fray, including the Chinese, British and Japanese. Keeping track of all of them was time-consuming but necessary. He wouldn't settle for anything less than a stellar success with the mission.

"Quite the party, eh, love?" Kalico asked as she leaned back in her chair to stretch for a moment.

"Expected nothing less from you," Lynch said. "You're a true artist."

"But a commercial one," she reminded pointedly. "I expect to get paid very handsomely for my endeavors."

"The moon," Lynch said. "If I could, the moon would be yours." He took her hand and kissed the back of it.

"Only," Kalico said sagely, "if you could be guaranteed keeping ownership of fifty-one percent of it."

Lynch laughed because he was in a good mood and because events were actually ahead of his timetable. The only fly in the ointment was General Sym.

For the time being, the general had decided to vent his wrath on his troops, and was pulling a surprise inspection. Occasionally his shouted orders could be heard through the doors when one of the cybernetics team entered or left.

Gazing at the left monitor with its identifying CNN tag in the lower right corner, Lynch watched as one of the committee heads of the House regarding American military involvement in the Far East was grilled mercilessly by the press.

"There's two obvious ways for the President to handle this situation," Lynch stated. He held up a finger. "First he can pick someone to be the scapegoat."

"True, but then you'd have to plan on whether he found a willing scapegoat, or simply picked one."

"Let's assume it would be a willing one."

Kalico showed him a doubtful smile.

"Or second the President can lie to the people and plead ignorance of the situation."

"Lies are such wonderful little things," she replied. "If done properly, of course."

"So you think he'll lie?" Lynch asked.

She nodded. "Especially if he's activated that covert squad you're sure he has."

"I'm sure he has them." Lynch watched the news footage continue across the screens. Barring a natural disaster somewhere, he knew the raid on North Korea was going to be the darling in the news media for hours. He intended to keep the pot stirred. "I think we've targeted two of them."

"Any IDs?" Kalico asked.

"Not yet." Lynch glanced around the computer nerve center. Gutter Razor and Jon Cameron were deeply involved in the programs they were running. "One man's been intercepted by Koh and Desiree while trying to purchase munitions. Another's been spotted making the rounds in the black-market district."

"What makes you think they're part of this phantom force you're looking for?"

"I've been hunting these people for over a year," Lynch answered. "They've been involved in several operations around the world. From what I've found out, they're multinational, but they operate on orders from the American government. These men fit some of the descriptions I've arrived at."

At that time, General Sym walked back into the room, looking perturbed.

Spinning in his seat, Razor got up and approached. He brushed hair out of his eyes as he spoke to Lynch. "The guy you told me to keep an eye on down in the black-market sector?"

"Yes," Lynch said.

"The bugger just blew away all three of the people you had on him and waltzed out one step ahead of the police."

"Where is he?" Lynch demanded.

"Haven't got a clue. The only thing I was left with to keep track of him was the police frequency. They don't know, and the description they're being given by the shopkeeper conflicts with what I know to be true."

"He'll turn up again," Lynch said confidently. "What about the other man?"

"Things got hairy there, mate. But Koh and Desiree have him in tow."

Lynch nodded and turned his attention to Sym, who was walking toward them. "Let's see if they manage to hold on to him." Personally he didn't think they could. The team he was hunting was extremely competent.

Razor noticed the general's approach, gave a dramatic sigh and returned to his workstation.

Sym came to a stop within arm's reach of Lynch and locked eyes with him. "My superiors wish to know about the delivery of the fissionable materials," he said without preamble. "These elaborate plans of yours are getting much too chancy, and your interest in the movements of the Americans is wasted. We have the SEAL prisoners. They will not do anything to jeopardize them."

Lynch shook his head and broke eye contact. "Wrong, General. Your superiors may be getting antsy, but the president and his staff are kept fully briefed on everything I'm doing. They're satisfied."

"This is a military matter," Sym argued, having no choice but to follow him.

Stopping and turning so abruptly that the general looked awkward as he came to a halt, as well, Lynch said, "Then maybe you should call the president and inform him that this whole operation should be under a military aegis and not trusted to him and his staff." He had to give it to the smaller man because he didn't immediately back down.

"Accepting delivery for the fissionable materials is my responsibility," Sym said. "I want to know when they're going to arrive."

Lynch glanced at his watch. "Three hours and twenty-seven minutes."

Calmly Sym checked his own watch. "How will they arrive?"

"I'll let you know." When the general started to interrupt, Lynch talked louder, barreling over the man. "When the time comes, I'll let you know. Until then, it's a closed house to you and your men. Your government is paying me because they know I can deliver. I'm not going to let you within an inch of fucking this up. If you can't handle the program, let me know. I'll suggest that you be replaced so fast that it'll make your head swim."

A cold, tight smile spread across the general's face but never touched his eyes. "At the moment, you are a guest of my country," he said in a low voice. "Perhaps you'll still be within its borders should that change."

"And maybe," Lynch said, "I'll ask for your head as a souvenir when I decide to take my leave. Until then, let me get on with doing my job."

Visibly stung, the general had no choice but to leave.

Lynch watched him go, aware he'd made an enemy that would last a lifetime. Of course, knowing that meant that Sym's lifetime would be appreciably shortened. It was foolish to leave someone as powerful as Sym standing somewhere he might need to return to.

He walked back to Kalico's station. "If the President decides to deny knowledge of the SEALs' actions, it's going to delay events. Get in touch with Wayda and have him drop the file on the mission to the media."

Kalico nodded and punched buttons on the cellular headset phone she wore.

Lynch walked around the room, conscious of the passage of time. He had planned so carefully, allowed for every kind of contingency, nothing could go wrong. Except for the handful of men he was certain operated behind the scenes for the American military to clean up problem areas.

They were a ghost force, as Kalico had called them, but their network was there. He'd bumped up against it during other business he'd done. But no one had any idea who they were or where their base was located.

Since he'd discovered them, Lynch had made it his mission to find out. His interest in computers and software had begun at an early age, and he was easily as conversant with them as any of the geniuses he employed. Others had their special talents or areas of interest, but Lynch preferred management of the systems. As a result of his involvement in North Korea, he was going to be able to put a deal on the table that would create a crime cartel the likes of which had never been seen before.

And the beauty of it was that he would be there as an enabler of that cartel, taking a percentage of everything he touched, but not getting too close to the front lines.

"Dixon."

Glancing up, Lynch looked at Arno.

"That transport plane you asked me to keep an eye on," Arno said, "just had someone jump from it."

"Parachute?" Lynch came over to the computer monitor as interest sparked inside him.

"I think so. It hasn't opened yet."

On the screen, the satellite picture showed a downward view of two airplanes. A lambent green blip was near the center of the monitor, trailed closely by a string of eight more. Pale red digital numbers skated across the computer monitor, decreasing with every second.

Lynch pointed at the numbers. "Descent?"

"Yes, sir."

"Have we identified this man?"

"No."

The numbers fell from a thousand to the hundreds as Lynch continued to watch. The string of blips behind the solitary one soared closer, but their descent rate wasn't as great as their quarry's. There was no doubt about who would reach the ground first.

"Are you in contact with the leader of that group?" Lynch asked.

"No," Arno replied. "But it'll only take a few seconds."

"Get it done." Lynch watched as the jumper hit eight hundred feet. There was still no sign of a parachute. Cameron had alerted Lynch to the special-ops transport that had been assigned to the pickup in the Philippines. When Kalico had traced the orders back, she'd found them to come from one of the military adjutants that he'd identified as being on the periphery of the covert team he was hunting. As a result, Lynch had staked a team on the flight, hoping to learn more about the passenger.

"I have them," Arno said a moment later.

As soon as the pale red LED readout hit four hundred feet, the first green blip suddenly sprouted a spray of lime green. It spread out, hovering over the blip like a jellyfish. Lynch knew the man had used his parachute.

Lynch took the handset Arno gave him. "Tarantula Prime, this is Chiprunner. Do you copy?"

The reply came back only slightly broken up by the distance and the overlay of the compressed covert-communications relays. "Tarantula Prime reads you, Chiprunner. Do your instructions stand?"

"Yes," Lynch said. A loss this early in the game would send a message to the nerve center supporting the covert-ops unit. From what he'd discovered, there were any number between ten and thirty men in the core group. But they had access to other resources at times. The whole North Korean gambit had been designed by him to cut those resources off.

Whoever those people were, Lynch was certain they were alone on the operation. No one would dare help with the wild-card play they were undertaking in the Koreas. Political backlash was a potent weapon in the United States, and the media would expose every mistake that was made.

"You're sure killing him is what you want to do, love?" Kalico asked at his side.

Lynch hadn't even heard her approach. "Yes. Following him now is out of the question. I want him killed and identified. Then I want to find out as much about him as we can. We can tie him to the U.S. government, and when we give that to the media, these people will take a direct hit."

"Won't it make them back off?"

"I don't think so." On the monitor, Lynch watched as his eight hired killers hit the ground and closed on the stationary blip they were tracking. He was surprised the man wasn't attempting to run. But then, the guy didn't know he couldn't hide. "These people are a last-ditch team. They're good. They won't give up."

"You could drive them into hiding."

"No," Lynch replied. "They can't be hidden any more than they already are. Success is the only chance at survival they have, and I'm sure they know it. But replacing this man—" he pointed at the blip on the screen "—is going to take some time. During that time, they're going to be more vulnerable. I intend to capitalize on that."

"You're awfully sure of yourself, love."

"Yes," Dixon Lynch said as he watched the green blips he controlled close in on the one he wanted to eradicate, "I am."

CHAPTER FIVE

The heat from the blast swirled over T. J. Hawkins like the fetid breath from some desert predator. He'd closed his eyes an instant before detonation, hoping to preserve his night vision. Now he opened them, searching for the woman.

Fire clung to the remnants of the door opening onto the alley. Thrown by the concussion of the explosion, Koh's twisted body lay just on the other side of the threshold. Hawkins knew the man offered no further threat.

"You son of a bitch!" Desiree screamed as she backed away, blinking furiously. The pistol was up and firing. She squeezed off round after round, blinded by the flash.

Hawkins had been partially deafened by the blast himself, so the gunshots sounded dulled, not really threatening at all. He bent his knees, diving to the side of the corridor, then springing for the woman like a big cat.

His greater weight and momentum brought them crashing onto the floor, sliding a handful of feet. Desiree continued to fire even after he had a hand around her wrist, until the pistol cycled dry.

Beneath him, she turned into a snarling animal. She raked the nails of her free hand across his neck, narrowly missing his right eye. The red-hot furrows bled, running quickly as the blood mixed with sweat.

He gave her a backhanded slap that rendered her unconscious.

Angry voices filtered in from the alley.

Hawkins figured Koh's people had been waiting for them outside and would investigate any second. He picked up the woman's pistol and confirmed that it was empty. With the way she was dressed, he knew she wasn't carrying any extra bullets.

Shadows drifted into the doorway.

Getting to his feet, Hawkins sprinted back along the corridor until he reached the dead bouncer's body. He picked up the double-barreled shotgun, then cut loose the bandolier of extra shells around the man's chest with his boot knife. A pair of bullets chopped into the door frame beside him. A third struck the dead man's foot and made it jump.

Hawkins wheeled with the cut-down scattergun, staying in a crouched position. His left hand was on top of the barrels to help control the recoil, and he touched off one trigger. Loosing a thunderous roar, the shotgun belched a widely spread pattern of double-aught buckshot that caught two men and flung them backward.

On the move at once, Hawkins drove himself hard, breaking through the irregular arrangement of tables and chairs like a linebacker headed through a scrimmage line. Bullets chased him, splintering the wooden furniture, scarring the bar and shattering the mirrors and bottles.

Movement at the door alerted him that someone was waiting, but more gunners had taken up position in the corridor. There was no way he could try to hold the middle ground.

Bullets pocked the floor as he changed direction and veered toward the latticed window fronting the Blind Cobra. He dropped the shotgun briefly in line, then squeezed the trigger.

The double-aught pellets ripped through the windows and thin boards easily, propelling a glass-and-wood maelstrom ahead of them.

Hawkins didn't hesitate about leaping once he reached the window. He went out, slightly off balance. Unable to get his feet under him, he went down in the gravel parking area. Rolling, the Phoenix Force commando managed to reach brief cover behind a car that had parked close to the building.

Autofire raked the vehicle. His back to the fender as he ejected the spent cartridges from the scattergun, Hawkins felt the car shift as bullets cut through the tires and deflated them. He took two more shells from the bandolier and shoved them into the 12-gauge, then closed the breech.

Running footsteps crunching on the gravel alerted him.

Hawkins scuttled down the side of the car as bullets continued to drill into it. When the man came around the rear bumper, he dropped one of the hammers of the shotgun.

The burst of double-aught took the man in the chest, lifting him from his feet and depositing him a couple yards back from his original position. The AK-47 he was carrying dropped into the gravel.

Hawkins broke open the shotgun and replaced the spent shell, trying to figure out how he was going to make it across the open ground to his vehicle.

The strained growl of an engine and transmission protesting abuse rolled out of the alley. It was a rental car, Hawkins saw as he lifted the shotgun into a ready position, but it had taken some devastating damage. The windshield was a tattered and webbed remainder of the original condition, and the back glass had holes punched through it. As it wheeled around the corner, streaking toward him, another burst of autofire ripped off the passenger-side mirror in a flurry of sparks and shrieks.

"Hawk!"

The Phoenix Force commando recognized Encizo behind the wheel.

Jamming on the brakes, the Cuban stopped only a few feet from his teammate. He pointed the Beretta in his fist through one of the holes in the starred windshield and fired rapidly at the collection of ragged shadows that appeared to consider giving chase from the alley. Two of them dropped in response.

"You waiting for an engraved invitation?" Encizo demanded.

"No." Hawkins gathered himself and leaped for the rear of the sedan. He landed across the trunk and stretched a hand through the broken back glass, grabbing the backseat. "Go."

The car's front wheels spun as they searched for traction. Then the rubber met the road, and the car shuddered into motion.

Hawkins held on tightly, rocking across the back of the car, his feet sticking out beyond the edge. A pair of gunners fired from the shadows in the alley, their muzzle-flashes highlighting their features. They didn't look Korean.

Shifting, Hawkins thrust out the shotgun and fired. He wasn't sure if he hit anything, but at the least it drove them back to cover.

Less than a mile farther on, traveling along the side streets away from the heart of the city, Encizo pulled over in front of a closed candy store.

Hawkins released his hold on the rear seat and got off the car, his arm aching with the strain of maintaining his grip.

"I don't think we were followed," Encizo said, abandoning the car.

"No," Hawkins replied as he concealed the shotgun under his shirt after pulling it outside his pants to hang loose. He hadn't seen anything. "But these guys knew about me. They took out the munitions dealer we were going to do business with."

"There are others," Encizo added. As they walked down the street, alert for anyone who might be unduly interested in them, he related his own story.

Hawkins digested it, then fleshed out what had happened at the Blind Cobra. "This isn't the North Koreans," he said when he finished. The abandoned rental car was almost a half mile behind them. They'd changed directions three times, heading for the safehouse Price had arranged.

"I don't think so, either," Encizo said. "But whoever it is, we know they're out there now."

"Only means one thing," Hawkins said with grim certainty.

Encizo looked at him.

Flashing his teammate a cocky, evil grin, Hawkins said, "They don't know it yet, but there's no escape."

Encizo was silent for a moment. "Hawk, there are times you worry me. You really do."

Outside Seoul, South Korea

THE SHROUD LINES of Mack Bolan's parachute had fouled and gotten caught in a tree that he hadn't seen until the last moment. He hung in his harness a little more than twenty feet off the ground, saddled with the extra weight of the notebook computer in the chest pack. In the quiet of the jungle surrounding him, he could hear the silence of the nocturnal animals. Part of it he'd caused, but he knew the rest of it resulted from the approach of his enemy.

Simply loosing the parachute harness wasn't an answer. The drop wasn't enough to kill him, but it was enough to twist an ankle or break a leg. In the end, the result would have been the same.

Instead, he unbuckled the harness and hung on. Slipping the Swiss Army knife from his pocket, he gathered the shroud line on the other side of the harness and sliced the cords. The parachute jumped in the treetop as the weight changed, but it remained stuck.

The soldier put the knife away, then worked his way down the shroud lines and harness. The extra lines cut the drop to something more than ten feet, which he managed without difficulty.

Night covered the terrain around him with a near impenetrable dark. He freed the SIG-Sauer P-228 Nightstalker from shoulder leather and moved out. There was a small compass in his chest pack, and he retrieved it. As he eased through the trees and dense underbrush, he plotted his course. The U.S. Army unit couldn't be far off.

Without warning, a small sapling on his right jiggled and sprouted a sudden white scar that blistered across the bark, and a ringing impact vibrated in his ears. There was no other sound.

Instinctively Bolan went to ground a heartbeat before the first loud cough of the sound suppressor reached his ears. More bullets clipped the tops of brush and grass around him as he scrambled for cover.

The gunner seemed to track him effortlessly, letting the Executioner know he was up against troops assigned to kill and equipped with night-vision capabilities. The man's voice carried to him softly, one half of a radio conversation.

"He's here," the man said with an American accent. "I saw the bastard and had him in my sights. If he hadn't been moving so fast, I'd have had him easy and we could be on our way home."

Thirty yards farther on, moving through a maze of trees,

Bolan halted and turned back to spot his pursuer. He had time for his peripheral vision to pick up a hazy outline of the man.

Then a ragged burst of autofire tore through the trees and ricocheted dangerously close.

Bolan gathered his feet under him and plunged on. He was confident the man hadn't tracked him to his hiding spot through normal means. His jungle skills had been honed in war, proved by continued survival.

"Man," the gunner said, shoving his way through the brush now, not even bothering to mask his approach, "this bastard's moving now. I've got him on the screen, but it's like chasing a ghost."

Bolan kept advancing on the high ground. He wasn't sure what he was up against, but controlling the high ground was part of every soldier's strategy. The thick brush worked both for and against him, scratching him and slowing him down while concealing him.

"He's coming around on you, Two. Coming fast." His pursuer's voice carried, but he just didn't care. "Fuck it. Use the damn thing if you've got a target lock on him. Nobody's going to come out here anytime soon to check out whatever noise we make."

Bolan heard the telltale *whumpf* of a grenade launcher. Breaking cover, he raced up the incline, vaulting over a fallen tree and taking cover.

The 40 mm grenade exploded against the leafy boughs twelve feet off the ground and just short of his position. Shrapnel ripped through the branches and brush, thudding into the tree trunk.

Aware that the burst of heat would work in his favor at least for a moment, Bolan got to his feet and ran. He knew he wasn't up against conventional night-vision equipment, and thermal imaging wasn't that good, either. The assassin team knew where he was by homing in on his heat signature—and they knew where each of them was, too. It added up to GPS gear. And that didn't add up to the North Koreans at all.

According to the maps he'd studied of the area, a creek meandered off to the east some seventy yards, cutting a path of least resistance through the hilly terrain. With the season and the rainfall, he guessed that it would be deep enough and cold enough to suit his purpose.

He sprinted, hoping the effects of the grenade would last long enough. It was possible that he could simply outrun the pursuit, once he'd established a sufficient lead, but that wasn't taking a ground crew into account.

Keeping to the trees and brush as much as possible, the soldier reached the final hill overlooking the stream just as a swath of bullets cut through the brush behind him. He didn't hesitate. As he went over the hill, more than a hundred rounds slammed into the trees and ground in his wake.

For twenty yards, he angled along the stream bank. Trees shrouded the area, casting a pall over the dark water that passed by with a steady trickle. He secured the chest pack and made sure the waterproof seals were zipped, then he waded into the water.

The chill it carried was a physical assault. Within two steps, the Executioner knew the stream was deep enough for what he had planned. He took a deep breath, then plunged under the surface and swam downstream so he wouldn't have to fight the current as well as the cold. Unable to see, he used his hands to guide him, pulling himself along the cold mud at the bottom.

Only when his lungs were burning did he surface. A glance at the ridge above the stream where he'd gone in showed him two figures scanning the area. Their voices carried into the small valley and across the water, but the words were indistinguishable.

From their body language, the soldier knew they'd lost him.

Reeds grew at the side of the stream, partially strangled by strands of wild rice and lily pads. Frogs jumped into the water at Bolan's approach. Using the Swiss Army knife while staying mostly immersed, his muscles aching from the unrelenting cold, the soldier slashed through one of the taller reeds, then cut off the other end. When he was finished, he had a serviceable breathing tube.

On the ridge, the two men turned in his direction hesitantly.

Bolan slipped the reed inside his mouth and went under again. Lying in the mud amid the wild rice, reeds and lily pads, he had a restricted view of the gunners' approach. He breathed slowly and evenly, trying to make the amount of oxygen work for him even though it was less than his lungs wanted.

His eyes hurt from the cold, but he kept them open. The SIG-Sauer was hard and angular in his hand. In his mind, he became another layer of mud over the streambed. He was certain that the team hunting him was tied into a satellite feed, targeting him through his body heat. And he was also certain that the cold water would serve to insulate him from its cybernetic gaze.

"You think the bastard went into the water?" one of the men asked as he walked along the bank.

"Maybe he just got wet," the second man replied. He'd split off, heading back upstream. "Got his clothes soaked enough to blind the satellite's sensors and ran like a bat out of hell."

"This rig doesn't work like that," the first man said. "If

he was up and running, the satellite would pick up his heat signature.''

''But with wet clothes…''

''Trust me, Junior,'' the first man advised. ''This is high-tech gear. If he was out there, we'd know about it.''

''Then he's in the water.''

''I think so, so watch your ass and don't get out of earshot.'' The first man waded deeper into the stream, less than six feet from Bolan's position. ''Shit, this is colder than a well-digger's ass on a January midnight.''

The gunner was in the process of calling in the rest of the team when Bolan came up out of the water. He caught the man's silenced Uzi in his free hand, then jammed the SIG-Sauer's barrel against the goggle lens over the man's left eye. His right eye was covered by a protruding NVG-like visor.

The Executioner pulled the trigger twice. The pistol's reports were harsh cracks that echoed across the running water. The corpse fell away from him even as he turned to deal with the second gunner.

Little more than fifteen yards separated the Executioner from his target, but the man was covered in Kevlar body armor and sported a bulletproof helmet. Unable to get off a clear shot at the man's face or neck, Bolan opted for the guy's forward ankle. The Nightstalker's laser sight touched the gunner's ankle, and the soldier squeezed off three rounds.

Unable to stand on a foot that was nearly severed, the gunner fell into the water.

Bolan charged through the water as the man flailed around and succeeded in bringing his silenced Uzi back on track. Dodging to the left, the Executioner narrowly avoided the stream of 9 mm manglers. He brought up the

SIG-Sauer and fired a pair of shots that took the gunner in the center of his face.

The corpse was hammered back into the water and floated toward Bolan.

"Hanks! Feldman!" the radio headset chirped. "Report in!"

The Executioner hauled the first dead man to shore, then grabbed the second one before the body could float by. He raided them for gear, knowing the other members of the team would be on him in seconds. When he was finished, he pushed the second man's body back into the stream. It floated away at once, captured by the current.

Using the first man's web gear, the soldier secured grenades and extra magazine clips for the M-16 the second man had been packing in addition to the Uzi. The GPS computer hookup was rigged for an over-the-shoulder carry. He slipped on the helmet, then snugged the chin strap.

When he pulled down the visor, the night retreated and his vision cleared. LED readouts chased themselves across the lower lenses of the visor monitor. He scanned the hillside as he settled the radio headset into place and secured the five-button keypad connected to the backpack PC.

He'd adjusted his load as much as he could, but the weight was still considerable. He took off at a jog, moving back into his enemy. With two of them down, there were six left. Now confusion was a weapon in his arsenal.

The battle gear was familiar to him. The keypad and menu layouts were much like the Army's Soldier Integrated Protection Ensemble he'd seen, but the portable PC was smaller than any that had ever been coupled with the system. Much of the available software was unfamiliar to him, too. The basics contained night-vision enhancers, GPS information married to a digital compass and a large data base that included first-aid instructions, maps, languages, distance finders and descriptions detailing the usage of a number of weapons. The SIPE system was going to change the face of land warfare, Bolan knew. He and John Kissinger had talked about it as the technology was developed.

Someone had not only managed to steal the Army designs, but had evidently improved on them, as well.

"Feldman!" the radio squawked in his ear. "Hanks! Do you copy?"

At the top of the ridge, Bolan unlimbered the M-16 and took a prone position. Tapping the menu select on the keypad, he changed the view in the visor to one coming from the satellite. The breeze that rolled over him brought a fresh wave of chills from the wet clothing.

When the visor changed, six green blips were shown closing in on his position, marked in ghostly lavender. Another was stationary behind him, while one more was in smooth, gentle motion flowing south along the stream. The soldier shouldered the M-16 and flipped back over to night vision after marking the positions of the men on his mental map of the area.

"He's making his way downstream," one of the men radioed.

From his vantage point, Bolan could look down on that end of the ridge as the land fell away. He picked up the first man easily. The infrared sight on the M-16 was good enough to identify targets 2200 meters out. The distance separating them was perhaps 170 meters.

Settling into a prone position, his weight resting easily on his elbows as he sighted in on his target, the Executioner took up trigger slack. He led his man slightly, then pulled the trigger. The assault rifle recoiled against his shoulder, but he rode it out easily and brought it back to his target in time to watch the man stumble and fall.

"Son of a bitch," someone said over the com link. "Someone just blew Chauncey's brains out."

Switching back to the infrared visor, Bolan located a second target, who'd taken up a position in a copse of trees. The visor's night-vision capabilities seemed to take away the forest. When he took up the M-16's scope again, Bolan noted the thick tree the man was standing behind.

The Executioner was aware of the man's body armor, so he settled the assault rifle's crosshairs just above a fork in the branches. He waited patiently as the team leader ran through the roll call, coming up three people short now.

"The bastard's infiltrated us," the unit leader said. "Do a visual confirmation."

Checking back with the visor, Bolan saw each of the enemy blips flare briefly, then die away. He didn't know how to access the software to maintain his illusion. Going back to the rifle scope, he saw his quarry's face appear between the fork of the branch. He let out half a breath, then squeezed the trigger through.

The man died between heartbeats, a bullet coring into his skull just above his left eyebrow and below his helmet line.

Bullets thudded into the trees and ground around the Executioner. He reached under the M-16 for the M-203's trigger and readied the grenade launcher. Expertly he placed a round almost on top of a gunman streaking for him from sixty yards out.

The man had been taking advantage of the tree line, but the antipersonnel grenade ripped that and his life away. The soldier recharged the launcher with one of the three remaining grenades he had.

"Pull back, dammit!" the leader snarled. "Get organized! He's just one man."

Bolan waited, watching on the sensor visor as the surviving three gunmen worked themselves into a point and two wingmen. Once they seemed to be moving in tandem and the assault on his position was more pronounced, he ripped a pair of incendiary grenades from the combat harness he'd liberated.

He pulled the pins, then lobbed the bombs into the middle distance about thirty feet apart. They went off almost together, filling the night with thunderous roars and blinding light.

Bolan pushed himself into motion at once, flipping back the visor. For the moment, he'd rendered his enemies' night-vision capabilities questionable if not totally ineffective. Flames from the incendiaries spread over the trees, then the grass caught.

The Executioner was up and running, skirting the flaming area as he circled in on the last place he'd seen the trio of active blips. He came up on them an instant before the left wing spotted him.

"He's here!" the man yelled, bringing around his machine pistol.

Raising the assault rifle, the Executioner loosed a deadly figure eight that hammered the man backward, catching him in the face and destroying the surprised look he had. A short burst from the other wingman sent Bolan to cover.

With the magazine empty, the soldier raised the M-16 again, framed the man in the sights and triggered the grenade launcher.

When the 40 mm warhead struck, fiery pieces of the corpse scattered throughout the jungle.

Bolan rolled and got to his feet just as the remaining man's rounds vectored in on him. He dropped the useless M-16 and raced behind a tree. Bullets tore into the trunk, and one of them ripped through his shirtsleeve as he drew the Nightstalker and whirled.

The guy was screaming incoherently, barely audible above the chatter of the unsilenced assault rifle in his hands.

Coolly Bolan stroked the pistol's trigger twice, putting the rounds just below the bridge of the guy's nose. He closed in as the man collapsed, holding the Nightstalker in both hands. The dead man's bloody face was bathed in reflected light from the bonfire.

The soldier took up the M-16 again and fed it a new magazine. After a brief recon, he resituated his gear, then checked the GPS readout.

Nothing was moving in the area.

He broke into a distance-eating jog that served to stave off the chill from the wet clothes. One and a half miles farther on, satisfied that he wasn't being pursued, he took the notebook computer from his chest pack and attached the cellular phone. He got Aaron Kurtzman on the second ring. "Me," he said simply.

"We were beginning to wonder," the cybernetics expert said. "Hawkins and Encizo ran into some trouble in Seoul."

"Phoenix is here?" Bolan asked.

"They are," Kurtzman replied. "McCarter and the rest of the team are en route with a convoy from Japan."

"The economic summit."

"The very thing."

"Can you get a fix on me?" Bolan asked.

"Already done," Kurtzman answered.

"How about a message through to the Army unit running maneuvers in the area?"

"Sure. We've negotiated authorization now. What do you want?"

"Transport."

"Give me a minute."

Bolan waited patiently. His clothing had dried some from

the wind and from his exertions, though some of the dampness had been replaced with perspiration from carrying the heavy load. A keyboard clacked hurriedly on the other end of the connection.

"Got it," Kurtzman said. "ETA's seven minutes."

"Thanks," Bolan said.

"No prob, guy. Barb was getting ready to send out a search party with a loud-hailer. With things getting dicey in Seoul, and not making any real sense as to who's involved yet, she's on a timetable from hell to get the three of you into play."

"Where?"

"North Korea."

"The SEAL team that got captured?"

"Yeah," Kurtzman replied. "There's more to the story than what's hit the news. She's getting a brief prepared for you, Hawkins and Encizo."

"What happened with Hawkins and Encizo?" Bolan asked.

Quickly, without a wasted word, Kurtzman brought him up-to-date on the assassination attempts. "Like yours, they don't appear to track back to the North Korean government. At least, not on the surface."

"Got a prize for you on this one, too." Bolan told the cybernetics specialist about the SIPE suit.

"Definitely not the North Koreans," Kurtzman said. "Too much money in high tech."

"Unless they're paying someone. The software on the SIPE database looks specialized, too."

"If Akira or I can get into it, maybe it'll tell us more."

Bolan agreed. In the distance, he heard the steady thrum of rotors. "How does the game plan shape up from here?"

"You get a straight shot into Seoul," Kurtzman replied. "Jack's meeting you there. He'll be flying you and the others into North Korea. Encizo and Hawkins scraped up enough gear from a couple other sources to make you operational for an extraction.''

"Do you know where the SEALs are being held?''

"Not yet. But Hal and Barb are working on it, and Katz is following up on another avenue. At any rate, we're in the position to make an educated guess right now. Once you're on the ground, hopefully something will break.''

Bolan agreed and cleared the link. He used one of the flares he'd recovered from his attackers' stores to mark his position for the helicopter pilot. It burned a bright red star in the cloudy heavens.

The helicopter was a fat-bodied Boeing Vertol CH-47D Chinook with dual rotors. Searchlights stabbed through the night, crisscrossing on the ground, then locking onto Bolan just long enough to let him know they'd spotted him. Then they flicked away, probing the ground for possible snipers. The Chinook was also outfitted with FLIR fore and aft.

The big chopper landed in the nearest clearing. The rotor wash whipped the grass and brush into a frenzy, and tore branches from the trees.

Bolan went forward, letting the assault rifle hang by its shoulder strap while he kept his hands out at his sides.

A trio of young infantrymen met him. Their weapons were at port arms, ready for instant action. "Colonel Pollock,'' the young corporal shouted above the din created by the Chinook.

"At ease, soldier,'' Bolan replied. "We're alone here.''

"Yes, sir. I need password verification.''

Bolan gave the password.

"Thank you, sir.'' The corporal saluted smartly.

Without breaking stride, Bolan returned it and stepped up into the Chinook. A moment later and the helicopter leaped from the ground, heading north-northeast.

"Sergeant Lasko," a thin, athletic man with a high forehead spoke up. He offered his hand. "I've been assigned to get you into Seoul."

"Pleased to meet you, Sergeant," Bolan said. "Have you got a topographical map of this area?"

"Yes, sir." Lasko pulled a map from an inner pocket of his BDU.

Taking the map, Bolan marked the area where the battle had taken place. "About two klicks south you're going to find eight bodies. I want them recovered and held. You'll be getting instructions regarding them later."

"Yes, sir."

"How far away from Seoul are we?"

"Fifteen or twenty minutes. We've already radioed ahead. You'll be met by your pilot at the base."

Bolan nodded and settled back against the bulkhead. He'd known from the time the story first broke on the SEAL team that not everything had been revealed about the mission. Looking at the helmet in his hands with its sophisticated visor, he didn't have a doubt that the covert action had been set up for failure.

The attack on him and the Phoenix Force members revealed that their unknown enemy had considerable resources and was willing to use them. The stakes on the play were obviously high, and the gauntlet had been thrown.

Bolan didn't intend to let it go unchallenged. The real front line was somewhere ahead of him, and he was going to find it and stake his claim.

CHAPTER SIX

Dixon Lynch stared at the monitor. The satellite link showing the ambush site was still on-line. On the screen, the helicopter was reproduced in a dozen different greens, the most brilliant of them the hot areas of the engines and rotor bearings. "He killed them all," he said. "He also has one of the SIPE units."

"Yeah," Jon Cameron said. "I've limited access to the channels available to the SIPE PC, but I haven't been able to cut them all."

Lynch was agitated. He'd underestimated the man. He didn't often do that, and there'd been a long list of conquests behind him who could testify to that. "Shut that unit down completely," he ordered.

"If I do that, we're going to lose some of the systems open to us."

"Only for a time," Lynch replied. "It's worth it. Get it done."

"Sure, boss." Cameron leaned forward and started opening windows on the computer monitor, calling down menus.

Lynch moved on, marshaling his thoughts. With the way he'd designed the campaign, he still had a lot of trump cards. "Razor?"

"Yeah, mate."

"Get me a patch through to the White House."

"Scrambled?"

"For now." Part of the campaign's success depended on the media getting the same amount of information as the American President. During his early years, while he was amassing his empire in Singapore and across Southeast Asia, Lynch had used the same tactics to scuttle competing entrepreneurs and to set up buyouts that had delivered companies and corporations into his hands at a fraction of their actual values. In the information age, knowledge was more than power; it was a weapon. And Dixon Lynch wielded it with a callous and sure hand.

"How do you want it sent?" Razor asked.

"Take it through the subroutes we've set up at the military base," Lynch replied.

"Dixon," Kalico called.

He joined her at her console. "What?"

"They made a phone call."

"You're sure?" Lynch peered more closely at the screen. Getting into the computer system regulating the undersea phone lines had been fairly simple. One of his companies had bought stock in the South Korean venture, and another had done some of the work laying it.

Figuring out some of the cutouts the American covert team used had been the difficult part. He'd labored for months developing sort software that would trace phone calls that had been made from international points that he'd tentatively identified as sites the covert team had hit. But the investment of time and bribes had paid off. During their last operation, he'd tagged many of their calls.

However, as yet he hadn't succeeded in getting past the scrambling techniques used on some of those communications or tracked down the hidden base. That was what Kalico was working on.

"As sure as I can be, love," the woman said. "They made the call from here." She tapped the keyboard in quick syncopation.

On the screen, the image shifted, becoming a street map of Seoul. Lynch recognized some of the street names. Abruptly a window opened up in the center of the monitor, and a crimson dot was placed next to a coffee shop downtown.

"The call originated here." Kalico tapped more keys, pulling down menus.

Lynch watched as a line sped from the pay phone on the street to a junction box for the South Korean phone company. As the line grew longer, the picture jerked and recalibrated, the dot getting smaller while the street map grew larger.

White letters formed on the screen, initialing the coastline where the call had moved into the Korea Telecom submarine cable. It also provided the time. When Lynch checked his watch, he saw that less than sixteen minutes had elapsed since the call had been traced. The time was well within the strike window he'd created in the software program.

The line continued on across to Hong Kong.

"After the trace reached Hong Kong, things got a little dicey," Kalico confided. "I didn't know if they were going to stay on the phone long enough."

The trace grounded out at a satellite-relay station in Hong Kong. Swiftly, while the line stalled, the clock started working against them.

"That's why we put so much pressure on them in Seoul," Lynch said. "By taking away their primary outlets and shutting down the munitions supplier, they'd have to alert their base and get a timetable change on the mission."

"I'm going to speed this up a little." Kalico worked the keyboard for a moment.

Three minutes twelve seconds into the satellite relay in Hong Kong, the blue line was on the move again. The monitor view changed even more, pulling back to a suborbital shot of space. The blue line looked like a small comet trailing iridescent cobalt fire as it arced toward a communications satellite, then bounced off five more satellites of various long-distance phone carriers. It touched down in North America.

"Canada," Kalico responded.

"Cutouts?"

Kalico nodded. "These people you're hunting, love, they're very, very good." Her slim fingers caressed the keyboard. "The signal ended up on a line in an independent film company called Hooper and Martin Video Heroics. They specialize in made-for-video feature cartoons about comic-book heroes. They do a lot with computer-generated graphics."

"So they have a lot of computer hardware."

"Exactly."

"And they do a lot of E-mail." Lynch could already see the tangle that was starting.

Kalico nodded. "Fax lines. E-mail. They even do some process serving on the side to subsidize their artistic efforts."

Lynch watched as the clock ran again. He felt irritable. He was so close to tracking them down, but time was working against them.

At seven minutes and twenty-two seconds, the blue line streaked out of Vancouver, slipping down the West Coast.

"It moved out of the movie studio on an open transmission line rigged for faxes to a special-effects place in Hollywood." Kalico wrinkled her nose in distaste. "I did some independent work for them. They were good at what they did, but they discouraged creativity.''

"It's a legitimate business, too?" Lynch asked.

"Sure. But before I could trace it any further, the phone conversation quit.'' The glowing numerals on the monitor showed eight minutes and fifty-three seconds.

"Can you trace it any further?''

"I'm trying.'' Kalico shrugged. "As I said, these blokes do know their business.''

"Can we restrict the location to the West Coast?''

"I think we'd be fools if we did. That could have been another jumping-off point. If we manage to get another phone call or two, it'll help triangulate the area.''

"It'll come.'' Lynch clapped her reassuringly on the shoulder. "You did good work.''

She nodded and went back to the keyboard.

Even though it was a setback, Lynch wasn't overly concerned. The covert assault force, whether or not it knew it, was dancing to the tune he was calling. There was an amount of latitude, but the targets would be his in the end.

They had to be. He'd never lost before.

"Razor," Lynch called. He noticed how Sym's posted guards tracked onto him when he spoke loudly. It was easy to reason that all of them spoke English as a second language. The general would be kept up-to-date on everything that was said.

"Yeah, mate?'' The Australian hacker turned in his seat.

"That line to the White House?''

"Up and running. I was waiting on you.''

"Then let's get it done.''

The Razor cracked his knuckles and turned to his console. "What are we sending?''

"Filename—Realdeal.''

A flurry of tapped keys later, Razor said, "We're set.''

"Burst transmission," Lynch directed. "In and out so fast they have nothing to lock on."

"Done and done." Leaning back in his chair, the Razor watched his handiwork in action as the computer signaled full transmission.

Lynch nodded in satisfaction. It was a definite shot across the bow of the Americans, and it would be interesting to see how the President reacted. The cellular phone he had clipped to his hip buzzed for his attention. The building had been outfitted with a satellite-and-scrambler combination to provide the computer network its own phone lines to work along. One of the secondary lines was his.

"Lynch," he said crisply. Only a handful of people had this number, and he wanted to do business with all of them.

"Mr. Lynch," the heavy Slavic voice said. "You know who this is?"

"Of course, Aleksei." Lynch slid smoothly into his business mode, shutting out all the disruptions around him. Aleksei Kandinsky was one of the most powerful men to emerge in the Russian Mafia. He was also the only man Lynch had invited who'd turned down the chance to be part of the network he'd organized. The rejection had galled him; he'd been very selective about whom he'd chosen and thought the Russian should have felt flattered. "How are you enjoying the show so far?"

"I must admit, my friend, you're a very convincing ringmaster."

"I appreciate your candor."

"One has to wonder if you'd appreciate it as much," the Russian said, "if you were faced with denigrating comments."

"Fortunately," Lynch said, "I've not often been faced with those."

"So I'm told." The Russian laughed politely. "Furthermore, I've been informed that you're very quick to render retribution when someone offends you.''

"Not offends," Lynch corrected. "Only if they cost me money, or betray me and cost me a profit.''

"I didn't think revenge was cost-effective.''

Lynch smiled confidently, knowing the Russian would hear the sound of it in his voice. "A man must have his hobbies.''

"I'm going to cut to the chase, Mr. Lynch," Kandinsky said, "because time is money.''

Lynch couldn't agree more.

"I'd like to be a part of the meeting you're staging tomorrow afternoon.''

Deciding to play hardball because he knew the Russian wouldn't be expecting it at this point, and partly because he was still incensed over the earlier rejection, Lynch said, "I'm afraid that meeting must be made in person. If at all. Are you, by chance, in Seoul?''

"No," Kandinsky replied. "Business here has kept me somewhat preoccupied." The Russian controlled most of the illegal activities flowing through the island of Aruba in the Caribbean Sea, including Colombian cocaine, Sicilian heroin and a dozen other profitable crimes spread across the globe.

"I'd heard the DEA was trying out a new paramilitary-type strike force down there," Lynch said.

"Doomed to failure, I assure you," Kandinsky said. "Still, I like to oversee these ventures myself. I assume you're on-site there in North Korea.''

"Yes.''

"I like doing business with a man who takes a personal interest in his affairs.''

"So do I," Lynch replied pointedly.

Kandinsky chuckled. "A man of few words, too. Since

I obviously can't be there, I thought we might arrive at a compromise."

"I'm listening."

"I took the liberty of placing an associate of mine in Seoul. On the surface, this person's there representing certain investments my company has made in Hong Kong. With things in a state of flux the way they are there, a number of opportunities have arisen."

"I know." Lynch had taken advantage of several of them himself over the last year.

"Make no mistake about it," Kandinsky stated. "My associate is very important to me. If anything happened to this person as a result of my decision to trust you, I would hold you personally accountable."

Lynch nodded, feeling good. If Kandinsky was going to roll over, he had the deal in the bag. Nothing was going to stand in his way. He glanced at the roving North Korean guards. Not even Sym and the missiles. "Believe me, I understand completely. Because if this associate of yours turns out to be a problem, I'll be knocking on your door."

"Of course."

"Does your associate know where we're meeting?" Lynch asked.

"Yes."

Lynch nodded, knowing it meant the Russian had checked him out thoroughly. "Is there anything else?"

"Not at the moment. I'm sure I'll have questions after tomorrow's meeting. Until then, however, I'm interested in what you're doing next with the Americans."

Staring at the computer consoles, Lynch grinned. "I'm turning up the heat, Mr. Kandinsky. Just turning up the heat."

The Oval Office, Washington, D.C.

"SO WHERE ARE Striker and the two Phoenix Force commandos now?" the President demanded.

"Minutes away from Seoul," Hal Brognola answered. He sat in a chair across the desk from the Man and leafed through the satellite photos Aaron Kurtzman's team had managed to relay from South Korea only a few minutes earlier. They were of the strike team that had tried to take Bolan out of the play. "Transportation's there waiting on them."

"Have we got something on any of those people?" The President used the remote control on the twenty-seven-inch television built into the wall across the room, surfing through the channels to pick up the news specials. Most of the footage was familiar by now. The only additional scenes involved the names of the SEAL team members who'd been captured or killed. Reporters were digging into the background they'd been given with a fervor.

"Not yet," the big Fed said. "We're working on it now. We should have something soon."

"I hope so. This is turning out to be a fiasco."

Brognola didn't say anything. He'd advised against the SEAL mission. A military operation left too many sources open to foreign intelligence agents. He'd felt it should have been a Stony Man operation from the beginning.

"Look," the President said in an undertone, "they're releasing another one."

Brognola focused on the television, an icy knot forming in the pit of his stomach. So far, the North Korean military leaders had given up the names of two dead SEALs. Both times the information had been released through a staged computer presentation.

"This just in," the CNN reporter said. He was bearded,

curly haired and on location in Seoul, standing in front of one of the downtown hotels housing the economic-summit representatives and the media. "Another of the SEALs has been confirmed by the North Korean government as killed in action."

The scene shifted, replaced in an eye blink by two rows of head-and-shoulder shots of the men that had been in the SEAL team.

Brognola could already recognize the faces. As much as they'd been shown on television during the past two hours, he was certain that most of America could recognize them, too.

Two of the faces had a crimson X across them.

The reporter went on in a voice-over. "The latest in the list of the slain is Ensign Luke Hamilton, the twenty-seven-year-old father of two."

Four men across on the lower row, Hamilton was a dark-haired guy with a sardonic smile and light gray or green eyes. A crimson X scratched across his face.

"Son of a bitch," Brognola growled. Wherever Hamilton's family was, the head Fed knew they were staying glued to the television. After the files had been released to the media, the military had confirmed the story to the families, asking that it be kept quiet.

It hadn't been.

Quietly Brognola prayed that the SEAL's children were in school or at a friend's house. Anywhere but near a television set.

A window opened up on the television screen. It was a casual picture, taken at Christmastime. In the picture, Ensign Hamilton had his arm around a vivacious redhead holding a small boy while a five- or six-year-old girl with hair like her mother's leaned on his shoulder. Presents sat around the tree in the background, and stockings hung from the modest fireplace.

"Ensign Hamilton leaves behind a wife and two children," the anchor said.

"Where did they get the picture?" Brognola asked, turning to the President.

The Man shook his head. "I don't know."

"Somebody has to," the head Fed argued. "See if you can get someone in NIS to look into it."

"I don't see your point," the President said. His tie hung at half-mast, and there were bags under his eyes.

"Those boys didn't take any ID with them," Brognola stated. "And they sure as hell didn't take any family photos. Finding out how the North Koreans got hold of them might help us figure out what went wrong over there."

Without another word, the Man lifted the phone and placed a call. His orders were short and definite. "Got it," he said. "Should be getting word back soon."

"They overplayed their hand." The head Fed reached into his pocket and took out a couple antacid tablets. He chewed them carefully, then washed them down with lukewarm coffee. "This proves they either knew about the operation before it went down and had time not only to identify each member of the SEAL team, but to ferret around in their personal lives, as well."

"Or?" the President prompted.

"Or they've got someone inside the military feeding them information." Brognola's words hung heavily inside the room.

The TV screen had switched to a young blond woman in a crowd of what looked like supportive family members. A man dressed in a Navy uniform talked briefly with her, then she collapsed into the arms of an older woman and started sobbing hysterically.

The President's face was grim. "Bastards are milking everything they can out of this. Everything they show about those families now is going to feed the information the people holding those boys will have.''

Brognola nodded in agreement. ''I still think you should make a statement. Let the public know what that team was doing over there.''

''I can't.'' The Man shook his head. ''If I tell them we were looking for fissionable materials in North Korea, we'll have the hawks in this country in an uproar, further confusing the issue. Certain heads of state in the United Nations wouldn't be exactly thrilled, either. Not to mention how angry the South Korean government would be at our involvement.'' He tapped a pen on his desktop, staring at the television. ''For the time being, we'll concentrate on the hostages. We'll either free them or we'll avenge them. And if those damn fissionable materials are to be found, we're going to take those, too.''

Brognola nodded. The Man was right about the political atmosphere. Too many self-interests were active there. ''At this point, without proof, it would also look like we were crying wolf after the fact to layer in some kind of justification,'' the big Fed growled.

As Brognola sifted through the satellite photos some more, a tattoo on one of the men's forearms caught his eye. He flipped back to the reference material Kurtzman had included with the packet, checking the notations against the picture number. So far, the tattoo hadn't been identified.

Sorting back through the pictures, he found the color photo Kurtzman had included. All the pictures had come in both color and black-and-white, for color and detail.

The tattoo showed a shapely woman in a green sarong with a black leopard curled around her protectively, its paw reaching out to strike. A banner with writing ran under her feet. Unable to make out the words, Brognola went over to the coffee service and picked up a thick-bottomed drinking glass.

He sat the picture on the edge of the desk, then placed the glass down over the tattoo. He moved the glass up and down, using the magnifying properties of the bottom, until the letters were in focus.

"Something?" the President asked.

"Graceful Mu Lan," Brognola read. He looked through the bottom of the glass again to confirm it.

"I wouldn't think it was his mother," the President said, studying the tattoo. "His girlfriend, maybe?"

"I don't think so." Brognola moved the glass over the man's other arm. In the corner of his elbow, the comical figure of a blue gray shark wearing boxing gloves danced on heavy fins, the dorsal fin jutting up over the rounded sleekness of the marine predator. "May I borrow a phone?"

The Man gestured to one of the phones that littered his desk.

Grabbing the nearest one, Brognola punched in his number for Stony Man Farm. When the call was forwarded to Barbara Price, she answered on the first ring. "I may have something," the big Fed told her. "Have you got copies of the pictures of the guys who tried to whack Striker?"

There was a pause, then she said, "Yes."

Brognola checked the back of the picture for the designation number. "Take a look at that one and see if it can be blown up. Have the Bear send pictures of that guy to the merchant marine and see if he's licensed somewhere. I'm betting he is, or was, listed as an able-bodied seaman somewhere. Those tattoos remind me of the time I spent walking a beat down at the docks. Graceful Mu Lan may be the name of a ship."

Before Price could reply, the intercom on the President's

desk suddenly buzzed. "Sir," a woman said, "there's an eyes-only coming through the satellite channel."

"Who from?" the President asked.

"I'm not sure. The source code isn't clear."

The Man glanced up at Brognola.

"Hold on," the big Fed said into the mouthpiece.

"Put it on," the President said.

On the other side of the room, the TV-VCR suddenly exploded into color, erasing the news footage that had been there. An olive-drab screen had a white banner running through the heart of it, then darker green letters spelled out "Realdeal."

Working the remote control, the President turned up the volume.

"What you're looking at is footage of an actual event," a calm, cultured voice said, "in case you're wondering if the North Koreans really possess the fissionable materials your people went after."

The rainbow static cleared and revealed a night scene, showing a train straining up the side of a mountain. Without warning, an explosion rippled along the narrow tracks and rolled the locomotive, the four cars following and the caboose.

Armed guards spilled out of the train cars in dazed disorder, and lightning flickers of autofire tore holes in the shadows draping the mountainside.

"This little raid took place less than two weeks ago outside Yongdingzhen, China," the voice went on. "The train was carrying plutonium. Only a few agencies knew about it."

"Barb," Brognola said, "get Aaron to track down this transmission. Now. Copy it, and find out about Yongdingzhen."

"Working it," the mission controller said.

The camera angles changed on the television, shifting from the aerial view to a ground perspective. Foot soldiers equipped in SIPE suits moved in. Their skills were deadly and telling. Men in Chinese military uniforms dropped in their tracks as the high-tech warriors rolled in for the kill.

The view changed again, taken from a helicopter, Brognola judged. It showed the attackers walking among the dead Chinese soldiers, mercilessly finishing the killing. A cargo net was lowered from another chopper. In rapid, orderly fashion, crews gathered canisters from the broken train cars and loaded them into the cargo net. There was a close-up of one of the canisters. The Chinese characters were painted in red, but a translation in English was printed out across the canister. Brognola knew the plutonium grade at once.

An LED readout flashed in the lower-right corner of the screen. In less than four minutes, the mission was over and the strike force had reboarded their aircraft. The last scene had been shown from the satellite view as three helicopters winged toward North Korea.

"As you can see," the cultured voice went on, "the raid was totally professional, and resistance was futile. Within a couple days, the deal was finalized with the North Korean government. Delivery is being made despite the efforts of your SEALs."

The suddenness of the picture exploding and melting from the screen was startling. Only the rainbow static was left.

"Do not lightly dismiss the danger the North Koreans represent, Mr. President," the voice went on. "The economic summit offers an internationally focused forum for them to air their grievances." The audio transmission ended with a pop.

"Tell me you traced it," Brognola said to Price.

"I don't know," the mission controller replied. "Aaron's working on it now. We didn't get a copy, though. That, I do know. But the CIA file I took a look at had rumors in it concerning a train raid in the foothills of the Ailao Shan. This looks legit."

Brognola thought so, too. The game board still held a lot of dangerous pieces, and the opening gambit of the play had cost plenty. It was hard to separate the actual moves from illusion. But the Stony Man teams had no choice about involvement. With the fissionable materials confirmed, they had to make the attempt to get them back.

CHAPTER SEVEN

Stony Man Farm, Virginia

With years of experience and millions of dollars worth of hardware and software at his disposal, Aaron Kurtzman had learned to keep watch over the world, protecting it from the predators. He sat at the horseshoe-shaped desk on the raised dais at one end of the room and scanned the three monitors before him as he worked the keyboard. Unaware of the movements his fingers made on the keys, he was totally submerged in the cybernetic processes of his machines.

He had a tenuous hold on the transmission signal to the Oval Office, then lost it somewhere in uncharted ICE. Before he had a chance to breathe even one of the choice bits of profanity he'd selected during the tracking effort, his systems warned him of the virus spinning back toward him.

He hit the Escape key to try to get out of the loop, but the virus continued to vector in on him, burning up the miles between them in seconds. Shifting to the trackball with one hand, he pulled down his ready menus, selected a virus buster he and Akira Tokaido had put together and sent it winging along the cybergrid to its target.

At the moment of impact, his computer shut down, hesitated, then rebooted itself and began running diagnostics.

He leaned in closer, watching the numbers spin, relaxing only slightly as they all fell within normal parameters.

"Did you get it?" Brognola was on the speakerphone.

"I don't know yet," Kurtzman answered. "There was a surprise package waiting at the other end. Before I access any information I might have retrieved, I want to make sure our systems remain clean."

Silently Barbara Price walked up beside him. Honey blond and still possessing all the natural beauty and grace that had allowed her to be a magazine-cover model during her college years, the mission controller was nevertheless a professional.

"The monitor here is fried," Brognola said.

"We would have been, too," the cybernetics expert said. He got into the DOS shell and checked out other systems, looking for damage where experience and cunning told him to. "Okay. Everything looks clean." He initiated the jump into the specialized software he'd created to run most of the Stony Man applications. A quick peek into the video-optical jukebox drive let him know that he hadn't been able to record the transmission in either audio or video, and he relayed that news to Brognola.

"What about tracing it?" the head Fed asked.

"Actually," Kurtzman said, uploading another program, "we might have had some luck there. Hunt and I were playing with some programs over the past few weeks and came up with an idea for tracking burst transmissions like this one."

The screen flickered and changed, becoming a map of the Blue Ridge Mountains where the Farm was carefully hidden away. A dot appeared on the screen in the topographical area where the Farm was, then radiating rings formed around it.

"Normally you can't trace a burst transmission back to

the source," Kurtzman said as a window opened on the upper-left corner of the screen and showed a power gauge. "What we did was incorporate an immediate send-receive E-mail file that we might be able to track back." He keyed in an adjustment. "Okay, I've got the signature. Let's see how far we get."

On the screen, a thin red line spit out from the Farm, speeding toward Washington, D.C. No news there, but the big man was hoping. The red line kept moving north and east.

"BUGGER ME!" Gutter Razor snapped, hunching back over his console. "Dix! Somebody has a lock on us, mate!"

"What?" Lynch demanded. He covered the ground quickly, joined by Kalico seconds later. "That's impossible."

"Then someone should bloody well tell them," Razor said. He typed rapidly. "I can't shut the board down. Son of a bitch, they're going to get the location in New York. Another couple jumps, they're going to have the satellite pinpointed, as well. After that, we might only be a couple minutes from having a Tomahawk missile shoved up our arses."

"Move," Lynch commanded.

In spite of his bulk, Razor jumped up from the seat as if it were electrified.

Ignoring the gathering of Sym's guards, Lynch seated himself and took over the keyboard. The board was locked, and he couldn't disengage.

"The trace is at New York," Kalico said quietly in his ear. "Seems to be having trouble making the transfer over to the satellite signal."

"What is going on here?" General Sym demanded. He came to a stop almost within arm's reach of the computer tactical group.

Lynch disregarded the question, thinking furiously. If the trace was having trouble making it onto the satellite grid, there had to be a reason why. The only possibility was that the transmission lines were crowded with the programs running through the New York CPU.

"Who's tracking us?" Sym asked. "Lynch, talk to me!"

"Stay out of my face," Lynch said as he began downloading software programming and kicking it into the signal. "Kalico."

"Right here, love."

"I need that hard-drive virus set up."

"We're going to crash and burn New York?" She was already in motion, racing back to her console.

"Yes." Lynch dumped the *Grolier Encyclopedia* on-line and sent it to the other computer station. With all the video bytes logged into the software, it would eat up available disk space, jamming the board even further. He knew it had to be the E-mail they were using to track him.

Sym took up a position in front of the computer monitor. Before anyone could move, he pulled his side arm and pointed it at Lynch's face. "Stop what you're doing or I'll shoot you down."

Lynch was grimly aware of his own dark reflection in the monitor. He looked up at the North Korean general. "You shoot me and you'll be killing yourself. This whole building is wired with enough explosives to put it into orbit." He smiled. "You won't have to worry about anyone finding you."

"You're lying." Sym took a fresh grip on his pistol.

"Am I?" Lynch reached into his pocket and took out a remote-control detonator.

Sym's eyes widened as he recognized it.

"I'm not the only person who has one," Lynch said. With a flick of his thumb, he armed the detonator. "I had the building mined in case we had to evacuate quickly. I didn't want to leave anything behind. But it'll work just as well for this.''

A nerve quivered in Sym's jaw as perspiration trickled out of the hollows under his eyes. The gun never wavered.

"If I stop what I'm doing here,'' Lynch said, "the Americans will find us.''

"How?''

"That's not important.'' Lynch kept his hand loose around the detonator.

"You were hired to do a job,'' the North Korean general said, "not to endanger our operation here.''

"I'm doing my job,'' Lynch responded.

"Dixon,'' Kalico called, "I've got the virus ready.''

Lynch didn't look away from Sym. "Send it.''

"Going.''

"Your move, General.'' Lynch didn't bat an eye. "Shit or get off the pot.''

For one frozen moment, Sym didn't move. Then he slowly eased the hammer down and flipped the safety on. "If you betray us, you'll never make it out of this country alive.''

"I wish you could believe me as much as your superiors do,'' Lynch said. "Because betraying you is one of the last things on my list.'' And it really was.

"Do what you have to.'' Sym stepped back, and a dozen soldiers stepped back with him.

"Okay, love,'' Kalico called out, "the virus has hit New York.''

Tapping the keyboard, Lynch accessed the infrastructure of the American relay, pulling the stats up on the screen. The trace had stopped dead in its tracks. Within seconds, fragmentation had begun on the other CPU's hard drive, eating away at all the files.

Lynch pushed back from the computer console and addressed Razor. "Stay with it and make sure nothing crawls out of that chaos."

"Right, mate." The big man seated himself.

Lynch went back to the center of operations and surveyed his teams. Everything was running smoothly even after the brief excitement.

"You're up against a very inventive mind," Kalico stated as she joined him. "They very nearly had us there."

"A good challenge will only make me rise to the occasion," Lynch retorted.

"I'VE GOT A LOCATION in New York," Aaron Kurtzman said. He stared at the blinking dot on the screen.

"Was that the source of the transmission?" Brognola asked over the speakerphone.

"I doubt it." Kurtzman flipped through programs, trying to reach past the ICE barriers. "More likely, it was a transfer point."

"Able Team's in Newark, New Jersey," Barbara Price said, "finishing up some business with the Chinese immigration ring we uncovered there. They can be in New York in a short time."

"Can you get a fix on that transfer location?" Brognola asked.

Kurtzman watched as the longitude and latitude degrees popped onto the monitor. He tapped the keyboard and brought up a topographical map. A heartbeat later, crosshairs formed on the screen, pinpointing the location. "Got it." He blew up the image and started accessing other records. "Looks like private property outside the Pepacton Reservation in the Catskill Mountains." He called over to Carmen Delahunt's console. "Carmen."

Delahunt was old-line FBI that Stony Man had lured

away from the Quantico offices. Short and red haired, she followed up an assignment with tenacious efficiency. "Yes."

"I'm splitting off a file for you," Kurtzman said. "See if you can find an address and a realty history on the area I've tagged."

She nodded, already at work as she surveyed the topographical map on her monitor.

"Can you get Able in there?" Brognola asked.

There was enough of a hesitation that Kurtzman glanced over his shoulder to see what Price was doing.

Only a few feet away, the mission controller finished up a cellular phone conversation and punched it off. "Able's already moving on it, and should be there within forty minutes."

"What about a support team?"

"I'm going to see if I can cut a deal with state troopers in the area," Price replied.

"Aaron," Delahunt called.

Kurtzman looked over to the redhead's workstation. "What have you got?"

"The address," Delahunt said. She tapped the keyboard rapidly. "I've tracked it back through one of the local real-estate agencies, but they show it was purchased by a company in Hannibal, Missouri, called Circus Hats."

"Can you get anything on Circus Hats?"

Delahunt shook her head. "I've got an address, but according to the information I have, the business bankrupted and everything ended up in probate court three months ago. None of it's been resolved."

"Was an executor named?"

"Richard Stanfill."

Kurtzman noted the name, asking for the spelling. Mentally he broke the information down into areas of attack. "Akira."

"Yeah, boss." Akira Tokaido sat in front of the huge screen that filled the forward wall at the far end of the room and carried images from the capture of the SEALs. A mini-CD player was strapped to his right thigh and led up the single earphone in his right ear.

"Get on the files Carmen has and see if you can break through the red tape surrounding that land transaction. It's probably a front for a holding company or companies. See if you can run it down through whatever garbage they've put up."

"You got it." Tokaido turned back to his console. A pink bubble spewed between his lips, then popped as it reached bursting point. The young Japanese American was unconventional and didn't appear to fit within the military guidelines of Stony Man Farm, but that was one of the major reasons he'd been recruited. He had a keen, incisive mind that could make creative leaps that weren't all that logical at times, but that often scored direct hits. Kurtzman regarded the young man as one of the most dangerous hackers he knew.

Kurtzman turned to the remaining member of his cybernetics team. "Hunt, I need a package put together that we can transmit to Able Team. Terrain, blueprints, satellite pictures if we can get them. Let's bring our guys up to speed as soon as we can."

"Right." At one time, Huntington Wethers had been a full professor of cybernetics at Berkeley. He always dressed for business, and the glasses, as well as the pipe he habitually chewed on but never smoked, enhanced his scholarly appearance. In seconds, he was assembling the necessary information.

"Carmen," Kurtzman said, "stick with Stanfill. Find him if you can. Find out more about him if you can't."

She nodded and turned back to her work.

Finished for the moment, Kurtzman looked back at his own screens. He pulled down another menu and routed another trace, this one an inquiry through other long-distance telephone carriers that might have leapfrogged the transmission burst further on. So far, he was coming up empty.

"Have we been able to target a search area for Striker and his team?" Brognola asked over the speakerphone.

"No," Price answered, putting her phone away as she returned to the desk. "However, Yakov is following up a possible lead with the Chinese trade lobbyist group in Washington, D.C."

"A lead?" the big Fed asked.

A small smile twisted the corners of the mission controller's mouth. "He assured me that Chunae Hwan wasn't your typical lobbyist."

From the sketchy background he'd been able to pull up on the female Chinese agent, Kurtzman had to agree. She'd been linked to at least two particularly bloody assassinations over the years. Yakov Katzenelenbogen was no saint, the big cybernetics expert knew, but approaching Chunae Hwan was like stepping into a dragon's mouth.

"MR. KATZENELENBOGEN."

The voice that spoke his name was quiet and earnest. Katz turned in the hallway, navigating the chattering crowd in spite of his broad shoulders. Dressed in the double-breasted pin-striped blue Armani suit, he easily fit in with the other lobbying groups jockeying for position in the hallway of the House of Representatives. His gray hair was neatly done, and his light blue eyes looked out of place in his craggy face.

A beautiful young Chinese woman made her way through the crowd and stopped just out of arm's reach. "Ms. Hwan sent me, and asked that you accompany me to her," the young woman said. A polite smile lighted her face. "Ms. Hwan suggested that you might be more moved to join a pretty woman than one of her other associates."

Katz smiled. "Ms. Hwan is correct. But why isn't she here? She agreed to meet me."

"Due to circumstances, Ms. Hwan is unavoidably detained."

"I see." Katz translated the statement as meaning that Hwan was currently running a high profile. "And where is she?"

"We're going to meet her outside."

"I could have done that," Katz said.

"It was easier to verify that you were alone and unarmed like this."

Katz nodded. "What's your name?"

"You may call me Rikki." She stepped closer. "Now I would like for you to give me a hug as though I'm a favored friend or niece you've not seen for some time."

Katz took the woman into his arms and found she fitted very well. Acting as though she was glad to see him, she hugged him back, but he was aware of the way she searched him with her body and her hands. There was even a quick dip between his thighs at his crotch to check for a concealed weapon. No one appeared to notice.

"You're unarmed," the woman said, breathing softly into his shoulder.

"I think you would know after that," he said.

"If you'll accompany me, then," Rikki said, moving away.

"You don't mind if I take your arm," Katz stated, "seeing as how we're such good friends."

She nodded her head, calmly, but she had to know that he was taking control of her to use as a shield against a possible setup.

Katz hadn't lived to his present age in his line of work by being foolhardy. He kept scanning the corridor as they walked toward one of the side entrances.

"This way," Rikki said, pulling him toward Independence Avenue once they were outside.

"We're being followed," Katz said.

"They're there for our protection."

"Besides the two men that picked us up as we walked through the corridor," the Israeli replied.

"How many?" Rikki turned her head as though to look at him and laugh at a remark he'd made. The move also improved her peripheral vision.

Katz smiled at her, turning his head also. "Four. Three men and one woman."

"American?"

"Not Oriental."

"Ah." Rikki nodded and looked forward again. "Then I suggest we walk faster."

Katz complied. "You have no way of alerting your people?"

Rikki bit her lip. "We have no communications gear on us. There are too many listening devices in this area. Perhaps they know."

The Israeli didn't think so. A cold chill spread down his spine. Reluctantly he released his hold on the young woman. They were nearly to the street now.

"Perhaps you should go on without me." Katz veered away from the crowd gathered at the mass-transit stop. He already knew about the attacks on Striker and the Phoenix Force members in South Korea. If there was violence, he didn't want any innocents harmed.

"Leave you?"

"I'll be along." Katz looked up and down Independence Avenue as if getting ready to cross. The glances afforded over his shoulder showed him that the two Chinese guards seemed troubled by the departure from their planned route.

"Ms. Hwan won't like that idea."

"Probably not," Katz agreed, "but it may be the best course of action."

A long black Mercedes limousine made the corner from First Street onto Independence Avenue, then cut expertly through the traffic toward Katz and the woman.

"There she is," Rikki said.

"Go." Katz gave her a gentle push to get her moving, then turned to the east, hoping to draw the four predators with him.

Instead, they gave him only a moment's notice and continued after Rikki as she walked toward the waiting limousine. The woman, a short brunette with a medium build, drew a Smith & Wesson .40 pistol from her purse, her movements steady and unhurried. The weapon came up in both hands, bracketing Rikki as she reached for the limousine's rear door.

Katz shouted a warning, realizing that he hadn't been the target at all. He flexed the muscles in his right arm. The limb below the elbow had been lost in the Six Day War, but he'd adopted a prosthetic that had interchangeable parts. He hadn't been as unarmed as his Chinese contact had believed. Housed in the artificial hand was a 4-shot .22 LR that he could fire through manipulation of his upper arm muscles.

One of the Chinese guards died as he turned around, catching a full load of double-aught buckshot from a cutdown shotgun wielded by one of the four killers. His corpse tumbled to the sidewalk as pandemonium erupted among the pedestrians.

Katz fired twice, and both .22 hollowpoint bullets scored on the woman's face as she moved the pistol toward him. She rocked backward and went down, the pistol flying from her hands.

The other Chinese guard succeeded in pulling his weapon and firing at the gunner closest to him. His bullet took the man in the leg and knocked him around. The other gunner moved smoothly, evading two girls who'd mistakenly run in his direction to get away from the more visible weapons, and shot the Chinese guard in the throat.

Katz was already in motion, streaking like a broken-field runner as the shotgunner shifted to take him out. The deep-throated roar of the 12-gauge shattered the crescendo of screams. A newspaper vending machine blew apart next to the Israeli. Metal slivers knifed into his legs and left side as paper exploded in a flurry of confetti.

Throwing up his arm while the shotgunner worked the pump action, the Israeli cupped his elbow in his left palm and fired his last two rounds from twenty feet away. Both hollowpoint bullets sailed through the man's dark glasses and fragmented inside the skull, ripping his brain to shreds. The dead man fell backward, and the shotgun clattered against the sidewalk.

The front door of the limousine jerked open, and a slightly built Chinese man in a dark suit stepped out with an Ingram MAC-10 on a shoulder sling. Firing the machine pistol with one hand, he ushered Rikki inside the waiting limousine with the other.

The surviving two assassins pulled back in a strategic retreat.

Before they could target him, Katz covered the half-dozen steps separating him from the dead woman. He scooped up the S&W pistol, then added to his cache when he found a full magazine clenched in her other hand.

"Come on!" Rikki yelled from the limousine.

One of the two assassins broke and ran. A hail of bullets from the MAC-10 caught him and drove him forward, off balance. He sprawled up against the base of the steps leading back up to the Capitol.

Federal guards sprinted out of the building, taking up positions in seconds. The surviving assassin seized a young woman and used her as a shield against the Capitol guards.

Shrill shrieks of rubber on concrete blasted over the sounds of the battle. Coming from the west end of Independence Avenue, a full-size Chevy van riding low on its tires barreled through the stalled traffic. The front bumper connected with a midget Toyota and shouldered it aside and over a fire hydrant. Immediately a plume of high-pressure water shot skyward.

The assassin saw the van and changed his course, heading toward it with his prisoner.

Knowing he would be taken into custody by the federal guards if he remained, Katz jogged toward the limousine. With his papers in order, he would have been sprung from lockup in a short time, but the opportunity to speak with Hwan might evaporate.

The van didn't stop for the assassin. Instead, it accelerated and raced straight for the limousine. The limousine driver realized his danger with enough time to put the luxury car in reverse and try to back away, the rear tires spilling out black smoke. But the effort was too little and too late, and the van rammed into the side of the limousine with weight and momentum behind it.

They came together like two metal leviathans. Glass and plastic from the grillwork and headlights exploded out of both vehicles. Rear tires screeching, the van's engine roared, and the limousine was pinned against the curb.

Katz was aware of two motorcycles slipping through the stalled traffic like a pair of sharks hunting up a blood trail. He changed his course, heading for the stopped commuter bus. Most of the passengers had already emptied from the metro carrier.

The Capitol guards reacted, closing ranks slowly and deliberately.

The lone assassin with his human shield had his attention divided between the federal cops and the van. He moved in crab fashion toward the van, holding the woman before him. The guy didn't see the Israeli until Katz was less than ten feet away and closing.

As the man's eyes registered on him, recognized the threat that was there, Katz raised the S&W and fired a single round between the assassin's eyes.

The woman screamed and covered her face with her hands. She struggled to remain standing while the dead man clung to her.

Still in motion, the Israeli rocketed his prosthetic arm forward, catching the corpse under its bloody chin and peeling it from the hysterical woman. Propelled by instinct, she ran toward two women who called out to her.

Autofire raked the street, interrupting the clang and bang of metal and the roar of the two straining vehicles deadlocked against the curb.

As Katz vaulted into the bus, he motioned the heavyset Puerto Rican driver out with the pistol. The man went without a word of protest. The Israeli dropped the S&W pistol on the seat, sat and reached around the steering column with his left hand. The diesel engines shuddered into life at once.

His move toward the bus hadn't escaped notice, though.

Two men bolted from the Chevy van and raced toward him. Beyond them, Katz spotted the motorcycles again. Both were riding double.

A bullet hammered off the side mirror in a shower of sparks and ringing noise. Slipping the transmission into reverse, Katz cut the wheel sharply and pinned the accelerator to the floor. He got a brief glimpse of the rear riders on the motorcycles as they dismounted. Both men carried short tubes.

The back end of the big metro transit bus quivered as it struck the Chevy van from the side. Metal screeched in protest and tore. The pair of gunners who'd exited the van stepped back, one of them forced up and over a car stalled in the street. Both of them fired at the front of the bus, chipping glass out of the windows behind Katz and starring the windshield.

Reluctantly the van gave ground, freeing the limousine.

Ducking the hail of glass that rattled inside the metal walls of the bus, Katz slipped the clutch and backed into the van a second time. The whole side of the vehicle crumpled, folding in on itself.

The limousine pulled around the bus, riding up over the curb and coming around on the right. With white smoke belching from under the crushed fender, the van backed away, ramming a pickup that had been abandoned by its owner.

One of the motorcycle passengers was in a kneeling position across the street in front of a copying shop. The tube extended in his hands, and a peep sight reared up.

Katz recognized the light antitank weapon at once and knew it was going to turn the bus into a long mass of carnage. He grabbed the pistol and leaped from his seat, going out the door toward the waiting limousine.

The limo's rear door was badly warped but evidently still

functioned. A petite Chinese woman sat inside and looked up at him.

"It has been a long time, Yakov," Chunae Hwan said, loud enough to be heard above the noise. She was looking as good as ever, dressed in a blue chiffon dress that didn't go with the mini-Uzi she held with practiced efficiency. Her black hair was cut to shoulder length, and she could have been anywhere from twenty to forty.

Katz knew for a fact that she was older than that. "Under similar circumstances, as I recall." The Israeli swung himself inside.

A phalanx of federal cops approached on the passenger side, shouting orders to stop or be fired upon.

"They've targeted the bus with a rocket launcher," Katz said. "I'd like to borrow that machine pistol."

Without a word, Hwan handed it over. "Drive," she ordered the chauffeur.

The federal cops were thirty feet away when Katz swung outside the limo and fired across its armored top. Aiming high, he emptied the Uzi in a solid roll of thunder, hooking himself onto the car with his prosthesis.

In response, the Feds went to ground.

An instant later, the warhead from the first LAW impacted against the bus, rupturing the side in a fiery gout as the limousine sidled over the curb and back into the stalled traffic across Independence Avenue.

Katz dropped back into the luxury car and tried to shut the door. It creaked closed but didn't catch.

Suddenly the driver swerved and yelled, "Hold on!"

There was enough time for Katz to register that the second LAW-wielder had somehow gotten around in front of them. He saw the puff of white smoke that signaled the weapon's discharge, then the explosion rocked the limousine.

CHAPTER EIGHT

Near Pepacton Reservation, New York

Carl Lyons sat in the passenger seat of the McDonnell Douglas MD-520 and cinched the Kevlar armor, getting ready for the drop. The mountainous terrain seen through the Plexiglas nose of the helicopter was still snowcapped in places, the fir and pine trees stark greens against the virgin white. Spring was slowly coming to the Catskills this year, and the ground was covered with shimmering streams carrying the melting snow away to the lower valley regions.

The pilot was young, tight-lipped and military to the marrow. He'd hardly said a dozen words as he worked the warbird toward the site.

Looking as if he'd been put together with railroad ties, Lyons was ex-military himself, and ex-LAPD. He understood and appreciated the younger man's mind-set. His blond hair was cut short, and his ice blue eyes were constantly scanning, reading information.

He was togged out in a counterterrorist suit overlaid with body armor in combat black. A Colt Government Model .45 rode on his right thigh in a drop holster. The .357 Magnum Colt Python rested in a strap on a holster across his upper left chest, clear of the other equipment he was outfitted with. He was going in heavy, loaded with extra magazines and speedloaders for the pistols, and extra 20-round drums for the Atchisson Assault 12 shotgun he'd chosen for his lead weapon. Other pockets held grenades, garrotes, handcuffs and a gas mask.

"You ready for this, kid?" Lyons growled as he spotted the targeted house over the next snowcapped rise.

"Yes, sir," the pilot replied. His face and voice were as empty of emotion as the mirrored aviator glasses he wore.

Lyons tapped the headset's transmit button. "Pol. Gadgets."

"Go, Ironman," Blancanales answered in his smooth voice.

"How about that heavy equipment?"

"Gadgets is hooking up the electronics now."

"I'm looking at the house." Lyons checked the notebook computer in front of him. They were tied into Stony Man Farm, getting their Intel straight from the Farm's computers.

"Should be getting a green light up there about now," Schwarz spoke up.

Lyons glanced over at the pilot. "You on?"

The guy checked the armament panel Schwarz had bolted in with an electric screwdriver less than twenty minutes ago. "Live, and five by five."

"Good enough."

The helicopter was a civilian aircraft that was in use by a number of police departments and businesses, but hadn't been outfitted with weapons when it set down in Newark International. They'd been in crates in the back, stripped-down systems that carried all the kick but none of the frills. Price had provided for a belly-mounted .50-caliber machine gun and one 12-tube rocket launcher. Lyons had buckled the machine gun into place through a removable plate on the floor while Blancanales mounted the rocket launcher and Schwarz tied the systems into the control panel.

"What about the targeting, sir?" the pilot asked.

"If that box shows you've got a lock," Lyons said, "bet on it. That guy back there running the wires, you don't find anybody better."

"This hasn't exactly presented him with optimum conditions, sir."

"Trust him," Lyons said. "I do."

"Yes, sir."

The Able Team commando pointed. "Put us down on the south side, then circle around and cover the north side."

"Yes, sir. When?"

"Now." Lyons pushed himself out of the seat and went back to join the other two members of Able Team.

Rosario Blancanales sat by the door dressed in armored black. His hair was salt and pepper, and his features were regally Hispanic. He was called the Politician because of his facility with human emotions, thinking and ability to bolster a friend or totally demoralize an enemy through psychological tactics. He carried an M-16/M-203 combo.

Hermann Schwarz, also known as "Gadgets" by those who knew about his affinity for booby traps and anything electronic, finished putting away the slim metal toolcase he usually carried, then reached for the M-21 Beretta sniper rifle at his side.

Lyons nodded at Blancanales.

Popping the lock, Blancanales shoved the door backward. Air rushed in, swirling through the small compartment.

Stepping into the doorway, Lyons held on and watched as the two-story ranch house rushed toward them. The natural wood finish made it blend in with the bare areas left by the melting snow. Three 4×4 vehicles, two Ford

Broncos and a Jeep Wrangler, were staggered along the east side of the house.

"First target's the computer system. Anything else we get is gravy," Lyons directed.

"Sir," the pilot called. The helicopter hesitated slightly in the air.

"Do it," Lyons ordered, "then get the hell around to your position."

"Yes, sir." The aircraft lost altitude rapidly.

Bracing himself against the sharp descent, Lyons slung the Atchisson, then gripped the rope in gloved hands. Once the chopper leveled off again, he went through the door and rappeled to the ground.

Bullets split the air as he descended, missing him by inches as he sped toward the ground.

"Gadgets," Lyons transmitted.

"Sniper," Schwarz replied. "Second floor on the balcony. You stay alive long enough for me to get there, I'll take him."

Shock ran through Lyons's legs when he hit the ground. He released the rope and pushed himself toward a fallen tree for cover. A bullet smashed into the Kevlar at his shoulder, momentarily numbing the area of impact. He unslung the Atchisson to provide covering fire while Blancanales smoked down the rappeling line. It wouldn't take the gunner long to realize the helicopter made a much easier target.

The house was more than fifty yards away. The spread of the double-aught buckshot wasn't going to hurt the guy even if it managed to hit him.

Lyons touched off two rounds anyway.

"Go," Schwarz said.

Without looking back, trusting his teammate implicitly, Lyons vaulted over the fallen tree and sprinted for the ranch

house, managing a zigzag route that took him behind trees
and large boulders. He concentrated on the front door to
the house, knowing that Blancanales would be circling
around to the west to cover the side exit that overlooked
the parked vehicles.

The gunner on the balcony stood amid a table and chairs,
partially covered by a wooden railing.

Bullets chopped bark, leaves and branches from the trees
around the Able Team leader. Ricochets whined and burned
close.

Then the sharp crack of Schwarz's M-21 blasted through
the 9 mm autofire.

Lyons was dimly aware of the balcony gunner being
driven over the side of the railing by the heavy 7.62 mm
round. Then the front door opened, and three men raced
out, armed with assault weapons.

A spray of rounds sizzled through melting snow clinging
to a pine-tree branch near Lyons's face. Reacting instantly,
coiling with the motion of a trained athlete, the Able Team
commando dived behind the shelter provided by the thick
bole of the tree.

More autofire clipped branches from the tree.

Lyons's headset crackled. "Sir?" the pilot called. "I've
got line of sight."

"Do it," Lyons snapped. He swiveled his head around
the tree and listened to the whoosh of the helicopter's
rocket launcher.

The warhead hit the ground almost at the feet of the three
men. Their bloody corpses twisted and flew, one of them
landing on the sloped roof jutting out from the second story.

"Way to fire," Lyons commented. He shoved himself
out away from the tree and streaked for the house.

Before he reached the house, a man fired at him from
the doorway.

Lyons loosed a double-aught blast from the Atchisson that cleared the door, but he wasn't sure if it put his target down. A plate-glass window overlooked the slope from beside the door. Knowing the people inside would expect him to cross the threshold, he fired three rounds into the window.

Glass imploded, fragmenting into deadly, spinning chunks. The lacy curtains jumped off their rods and twisted away like holey ghosts.

Lyons leaped from only a couple yards out, vaulting through the emptied window. Inside, he tucked and rolled, managing himself on his legs and one hand.

"Get the son of a bitch!" a man in a sheepskin jacket and handlebar mustache ordered. He leveled the Glock in his hand.

Coming up on one knee, Lyons triggered the 12-gauge and rode out the recoil one-handed. The double-aught buckshot impacted against the guy's chest and blew him back over a color television. Sparks jumped from the dead set, biting into the unfeeling corpse.

A machine pistol spit 9 mm rounds that chewed through the oak paneling above Lyons's head.

The Able Team commando fired again and cut the second man down. As he stood, he noticed a third dead man behind the front door. He jogged toward the dining room, glass crunching under his boots. Taking a position against the doorway, he tapped the transmit button on the headset. "Gadgets."

"Go," Schwarz called out.

"You see a satellite dish?" Lyons whirled around the corner, the Atchisson up and probing. The dining room had a hardwood floor and elegant candle sconces built into the wall. No one was inside.

Gunfire crashed from the side door.

"Second floor," Schwarz answered. "Got what looks like a bedroom in the southwest corner."

"Pol," Lyons called.

"Yeah?"

"Your location?"

"I'm inside, amigo."

"The stairs?" Lyons asked.

"No idea."

More gunfire ripped through the house. Lyons's cop instincts, picked up on L.A.'s meanest streets while he was still in uniform, warned him of the man who'd crept up behind him.

Whirling, Lyons knocked the big man's gun hand away with the Atchisson's barrel a heartbeat before the S&W .41 Magnum pistol thundered. He ripped a heavy-bladed combat knife from his combat harness as the big man roared and threw a meaty fist at his face.

Lyons slipped the blow and brought the combat knife around in a hard, vicious arc. The point went into the man's throat just below his Adam's apple, then grated along the spinal column for a second before burying in the wall behind him.

The light went out of the big man's eyes as he gurgled bloody froth.

Lyons pressed on. He found the stairwell in a narrow corridor between the dining room and kitchen. A moving shadow at the top of the stairs warned him that the second floor was still occupied.

He tapped the button on the headset. "Gadgets."

"Go." Schwarz had stayed outside the ranch house to act as backup and spotter.

"Can you give me a head count?"

"That's negative, Ironman. I see walking shadows, but

I haven't got a confirmation on a number. Second floor's not without weight."

"Roger." Lyons pulled a canister of CS gas from his grenade pouch. "Pol."

"Yeah?"

Lyons popped the CS canister, then tossed it up the stairs underhanded. White smoke started to spew at once. "I've got gas going in."

"Roger."

The Able Team leader, Lyons pulled out his gas mask and slipped it on. The CS gas had spread enough that it obscured visibility on the stairs.

At the top of the stairs, two men were doubled over, retching uncontrollably, but both struggled to bring their weapons up.

Stepping forward quickly, Lyons brought the heavy butt of the shotgun down on one man's neck hard enough to knock him unconscious. He spun on one foot, then delivered a roundhouse kick to the other man that flattened him up against the wall. Before the hardman could recover, the Able Team commando rolled him over, kicked his pistol out of reach and cuffed his hands behind his back. The retching went on, but Lyons knew it wasn't going to kill the guy.

By the time he was ready to go on, Blancanales had come up the stairs to join him, gas mask in place.

Lyons took the point while the other man backed him up. Three of the four bedrooms were empty. The last one held the computer they were looking for.

Evidently good money had been spent on the unit. The desk was full of hardware, and a tower sat on the floor nearby. A screen-saver image of a *Penthouse* Pet of the Month occupied the monitor.

"Hard drive's working overtime," Blancanales commented, glancing at the tower system.

"We'll let Aaron figure it out," Lyons answered. He slipped a cellular phone out of his chest pack and glanced at the CPU connections. With deft motions, he hooked up the cellular phone to the PCMCIA jack and punched in the number they were using for the transmission.

Akira Tokaido answered immediately. "Thrill me."

"Let's get on it, kid," Lyons said, then laid down the phone. He stepped to the west window to check the perimeters.

The helicopter hovered like a dragonfly to the north, the Plexiglas nose turned toward the ranch house.

"Gadgets?" Lyons transmitted.

"Go."

"Secure?"

"Battened down, buddy. You guys?"

"Working it." Lyons moved back from the window. He knew the operation was related to the one Striker and Phoenix were headlining in North Korea concerning the captured SEAL team.

Without warning, the screen saver disappeared from the monitor, replaced with numbers: 15...14...13...

"Pol," Lyons said.

"I see it." Blancanales was already in motion. "East side. There's a drift that might cushion the fall, and an incline that may offer some shelter."

11...10...

Lyons slammed out of the room, racing for the east window. Pol grabbed the handcuffed man and hustled him to his feet, aiming him for the window.

Fisting the unconscious man's shirt, Lyons dragged the guy to the window just as Blancanales shoved his prisoner through. Glass and woodwork exploded. Off balance, the prisoner fell onto the partially snow-covered roof and slid along the steep tiles, Blancanales almost on top of him.

"Gadgets," Blancanales radioed.

"Go."

"Pull back from the house." Repeating the orders for the pilot, Blancanales disappeared over the edge of the roof.

Lyons was close behind, slipping and skidding across the tricky surface. He kept his hand knotted in his prisoner's clothing. Lunging over the edge, he fell and crashed through a canopy of small trees. On his feet at once, he found his prisoner and dragged him along, down the steep incline, racing the clock, somewhere between a loping run and a controlled fall. He hoped the line of trees behind him would be enough to help blunt the concussion.

The house blew up in a roll of detonations. Fiery debris flailed through the sky and caught in the branches of the trees. Even though they were below the line of the blasts, Lyons was knocked from his feet by the force.

A couple minutes later, when it seemed the ground had quit shaking, Lyons pushed himself to his feet.

Not much remained of the house on top of the hill. Part of the foundation had been blown into the trees, and part of the remains were on fire.

"You figure the North Koreans?" Lyons asked.

Blancanales shook his head.

"Me, neither," the big ex-LAPD cop said, hoisting his prisoner over one shoulder. "Let's get a move on. Barb can let the state police have what's left over."

CHAPTER NINE

"Lock onto the transmission," Dixon Lynch ordered, leaning over the console.

"I'm trying," Gutter Razor replied. He sounded frustrated. His fingers massaged the keyboard.

Feeling the tightness in his chest, Lynch watched Razor's progress. He'd deliberately sacrificed the operation in New York. Though it had cost millions to set up, though that was offset by the profits it had turned in the past three years, the transmission site had a chance of providing him more information about the covert team he was hunting in the United States.

Their reaction time had been quicker than he'd expected, however. But the presence of the force at the ranch house had confirmed his thoughts that the covert team had a domestic arm, as well.

"They're into the computer," Razor stated.

Lynch glanced at the other monitors spread around the desk. "Kalico?"

"They're definitely not on the West Coast, love," the woman replied. "All the long-distance carriers there are clear of any signature the New York computer makes."

Lynch clamped down on the anger rising inside him. "These people are not intangible."

"I know, I know."

"Dammit, they're going to trip the self-destruct sequence." Unknown to the men who'd worked in the ranch house in the Catskills, Lynch had ordered the area mined in case he needed to destroy the evidence quickly.

"It's done, mate," Razor advised. "I've got a partial lock."

"Follow it," Lynch demanded. He watched the clock face float to the surface of Razor's monitor. The second hand swept toward zero, eleven seconds and counting down.

"Got it." Razor reached for the mouse and pulled down a menu. "I'm piggybacked on the transmission. Going for the short load. No time for anything else."

Lynch checked the clock. Eight seconds remained. Even the short load they'd prepared might not have time to make it. "Do it."

Razor flicked the cursor over a file reading "Clonetlk" and tagged the button. "It's done."

A ribbon opened up at the bottom of the screen: "Sending file: Clonetlk...20% complete...50% complete..." The numbers continued to fluctuate, gaining speed.

"The East Coast," Kalico called out. "South of the Mason-Dixon line."

Abruptly the second hand on the clock face overlaid the hour hand. "Transmission interrupt, drive error, reboot?" flared across Razor's monitor.

"Lost it," the Australian said.

"What kind of feed did you get?" Lynch asked.

"Ninety-three percent."

"Is it enough?"

Razor shrugged. "That's one of the most viable communications-capture programs I've ever written. It should be enough to secure contact if we can get on-line with them. We do, the rest of the program will feed automatically and restructure itself.''

''Good.'' Lynch smiled. He straightened and walked back to Kalico. ''Where's their base?''

''Somewhere in Virginia.'' The woman studied the graphs and charts that flicked across her screen. ''They were using a weather satellite over the East Coast for the transmission. When the house blew, they disappeared.''

Lynch took off his suit jacket and loosened his tie. ''That's fine. We'll find them. Check through government files starting with the Department of the Interior. Wherever they're at, they're on land that's been ceded to them.''

''Yes.'' Kalico accessed other areas open to her.

Lynch stepped back and took a deep breath. Things were progressing satisfactorily, even though it had taken longer to tag the covert team than he would have liked. He glanced at his watch. It was hours until the meeting in Seoul. A lot could happen.

''Dixon.'' Jon Cameron turned from his console. ''The general's package has arrived.''

Lynch nodded and summoned Eric Hardcastle, his chief security officer, from his position at the back of the building.

Hardcastle was a grizzly bear of a man, barrel-chested, and possessed a face squared off like a trenching tool. He moved with military precision he'd learned at officers' school in Berlin a quarter century before. His jumpsuit was black and armored, and held a multitude of deadly devices in the many pockets.

''We're going to take the trip with the general now,'' Lynch said, snugging his tie again. He slipped into his suit jacket and buttoned it.

''Yes, sir.'' Hardcastle's voice was heavy and carried a Germanic accent. He gave quick hand signals, and five of his men peeled away from the group of a dozen and flanked them.

Lynch strode toward the front of the building, stopping only long enough to pick up a notebook computer and a cellular phone. "General," he said, waving at the man, "are you prepared to accept delivery of your cargo?"

"Yes."

"Let's do it." Lynch led the way to the five-ton trucks under the cover of trees and camou netting. He took a seat in the first one while Hardcastle rode the running board on the other side of the door. One of the mercenary's men took the wheel.

General Sym clambered aboard his jeep. Without trying to be subtle, the man riding the rear deck uncloaked the mounted .50-caliber machine gun and took control of it.

"There's not a lot of trust here," Hardcastle observed with a grim smile.

"Do you want to trust them?" Lynch asked.

The big merc shook his head. "No."

Lynch settled back in the seat as the driver pulled them onto one of the two paths leading through the jungle away from the camp. "Neither do I."

"The general doesn't know it," Hardcastle said, "but he's sitting on enough C-4 to put him into orbit." He lifted a flap on his vest and revealed the remote control.

"Eric," Lynch said, "I've always admired your foresight."

A V22 OSPREY, ITS OUTSIZE tilt rotors pointing skyward, sat outside a hangar at the U.S. Army base near the center of Seoul. The USMC military markings had been removed, and the whole convertiplane had been repainted a flat black to blend in with the night.

The soldier left the chopper in a lithe jump while it hovered less than three feet above the pavement. Before he'd made half the distance to the Osprey, the rotors whined and beat a wash down at him that became a fierce wind.

Hawkins and Encizo lowered the door just behind the Osprey's nose.

"The gear?" Bolan asked as he climbed inside.

"Aboard and secure," Encizo replied, offering his hand.

Bolan took it for a brief moment. "I'd heard you had some trouble."

"Appears to be the night for it," Hawkins said.

"Have we got a target?" Bolan asked, moving toward the cabin.

"No." Encizo shook his head. "But we should have something soon. Stony Man's standing by for a com link as soon as we lift off."

"Let's do it." Bolan went forward.

Seated behind the controls, Jack Grimaldi, Stony Man's ace pilot, looked up. "Hey, Sarge, glad you could join us. Provisions are in the back. Got a couple thermal carafes of soup and some coffee." Expertly the pilot finished with the controls, got clearance from the base command and leaned into the engines.

The Osprey took to the air. Within seconds, the base was a twenty-acre patch in the middle of Seoul, and the convertiplane was streaking north, gaining speed. The city's night lights fanned out around it, flashing pools of neon rainbow.

"Has there been any other word on the hostages?" Bolan asked.

"Another confirmed casualty," Grimaldi replied. "They didn't say how. Could be from wounds, or the guy could have bought it back on the *Dragon's Gate* and they're just now telling us."

With Hawkins and Encizo seated almost comfortably behind him, Bolan brought the notebook computer out of his chest pack and set it up, plugging into one of the power supplies provided in the convertiplane.

"Going to be a little rough for just a minute," Grimaldi warned.

Bolan nodded, then glanced out his window as the pilot pulled back on the yoke and triggered the swivel action that moved the large propellers from helo action to their forward position. Once they were locked in and the ride became smooth again, Bolan turned his attention back to the computer. He added the cellular phone, dialed and waited.

The screen flickered, then offered instructions to allow for full video and audio.

Bolan input the commands, and a heartbeat later the monitor ghosted over, then showed the inside of the computer room. Barbara Price and Aaron Kurtzman looked at him.

"Hold on," Kurtzman said, "I'm patching Farmer Brown and the Man into the link, too."

The screen split, then images of Brognola and the President formed on the right.

"Phoenix Force is supposed to be in the loop, too," Price advised. "Phoenix One, can you confirm?"

"Here, Barb," a British accent said.

Bolan recognized David McCarter's voice immediately.

"Where are you?" Price asked.

"An hour, hour and a half away from Kimpo International Airport."

"Affirmative," the mission controller said.

"A week ago," Brognola said, looking at the monitor, "a covert team from Seal Team Six was put on alert regarding fissionable materials that were supposed to be smuggled into the North Korean military."

"Where did the fissionables come from?" Hawkins asked.

"Background Intel on the operation suggested China, or possibly Russia," the head Fed answered. "Neither has been confirmed. But with the state of affairs in both those countries at present, either is possible."

"Some of the guys who tried to whack Rafe and me were probably American," Hawkins said.

Price fielded the statement. "We're looking into that. Korean Intelligence is being very generous with their findings. As soon as they have something, we'll have it."

"The operation was called Knock-Knock," Brognola said. "The SEALs' orders were to find the fissionables and bring them back. Special-ops control had satellite lock on the group when the action went down. Then they were cut off."

"How were they cut off?" McCarter asked.

"I checked the satellite they were using," Kurtzman answered. "It was nuked, total meltdown."

"Do we know if the fissionable materials are in the hands of the North Korean military?" Bolan asked.

"At this point," the President replied, "I don't dare think any other way."

In terse sentences, Brognola told him about the threatening transmission Kurtzman had tracked back to the Catskill Mountains.

"Do the South Koreans know?" Bolan locked eyes with the President.

"At present, no," the Man said. "I feel that if they're made aware of the situation, it'll make your job all that much harder. If we have any chance of cleaning this up and getting those boys home, it's with a deliberate surgical strike."

Silently Bolan agreed. If the news broke, there would be

a lot of fingers in a very deadly pie. And there was no way to evacuate a country. "With this much high tech," the soldier said, "it doesn't sound like the North Korean military."

"No," Kurtzman replied. "And it gets better. You haven't seen the film that got sent to a number of international media shortly after contact was lost with the SEAL team."

Abruptly the monitor screen wrinkled in a colorful blitz and the SEAL attack footage was played.

"That can't be what happened," Encizo said quietly.

"We don't believe it is," Brognola said.

"When you put the footage in slo-mo," Kurtzman explained, "my friends tell me the motion on part of the fishermen seem to be a trifle too smooth. The SEALs jerk as they shift and change position. The fishermen flow from one position to the next. I looked at it, and maybe I saw what they're talking about, but I'm not sure. To cut it this fine, whoever spliced the real footage with the computer-generated enhancements would have to be a real pro."

"That doesn't sound like the North Korean military, either," Hawkins growled.

"No," Brognola said. "We think they've hired an outside party to manage the frame. Someone with a computer background and sources within the military. The picture they released of the last SEAL acknowledged as deceased looked like a photograph from home. The NIS checked into it and came up positive on that assumption. The picture that was given to the media had come from the SEAL's personal quarters at Coronado. The original was still there."

"No idea of who got it to these people?" Encizo asked.

"No. We're looking into it. Able took down a transfer point for a transmission that came into the Oval Office that plainly stated the North Koreans did have the fissionable materials.'' Brognola paused. ''There's no sanction on this mission, gentlemen, and no backup in case things go awry. You're on your own.''

''Is there any idea where the SEALs are being held?'' David McCarter asked.

''Nothing confirmed,'' the head Fed answered. ''But you can bet those boys didn't surrender to a handful of fishermen, or even a few North Korean troops. This was a total blackout mission, not even supposed to have a profile. They knew that.''

''What about Nampo?'' Bolan asked. ''It's on the coastline, giving it both sea and air routes, and only a short jump from the air bases in Pyongyang for a defensive posture.''

''It's where we're betting,'' Brognola told him. The monitor blinked and returned to the split screen showing Stony Man Farm and the Oval Office. ''Yakov had a meeting scheduled that he hoped would shed some light on the situation. Unfortunately we haven't heard from him yet, and from what we're getting from reporters on the scene at the Capitol building, there's been a disturbance involving the Chinese trade representatives.''

''Katz was meeting with them?'' Bolan asked.

''One of them anyway.'' The head Fed glanced to one side, and the soldier assumed Brognola was watching breaking news coverage. ''I'll let you know more when I can. Until then, good hunting.''

Bolan acknowledged and broke the computer connection. ''How long until we get to Nampo?'' he asked Grimaldi.

''About thirty-five more minutes,'' the pilot said. The broken terrain had given away to the flat, dark planes of the sea.

''Are they going to know we're coming?''

''Not if Aaron can spoof the satellites,'' Grimaldi answered. "We're making a tight loop up the coastline, then double back in from the sea. If everything goes right, we're going to be invisible to everything but radar." He tapped his flight book. "And Barb got me hard copy on most of those sites. We should be in good shape."

Bolan nodded and pushed himself up out of the seat. He wanted to get fresh clothes and take time to familiarize himself with the terrain around Nampo. A lot of lives were on the line, and he had the feeling a lot more were going to be in the balance.

CHAPTER TEN

Washington, D.C.

Boiling heat surged over the limousine. Inside, Yakov Katzenelenbogen fought for his breath and fed the remaining magazine into the S&W. His lungs felt as if they were searing.

Out of control, the bulletproof windshield a myriad of spiderwebbed cracks, the limousine rocked up over the curb and came to a halt. Fire clung to the wrecked front end of the luxury car, and the heat warped the Israeli's vision.

The driver had died in the initial blast, either from the glass chunks that had been blown free of the windshield or from the concussive force that had been unleashed.

"You are well?" Chunae Hwan asked as she pushed herself up in the seat. Her face was slightly ashen, and a dark bruise was already taking shape on her right cheek. She hefted the MAC-10 into position.

"Yes." Katz found the door latch and tried it. Surprisingly the door opened rather easily, creaking in protest. A hollow pop sounded, then the glass crystallized, occluding the view.

Rikki stirred, blood leaking down her forehead from contact with the glass partition separating the rear of the limousine from the front. Her eyes were already starting to deepen with black circles.

Knowing that at least a half-dozen guns were closing in on them, Katz shoved through the door and raised the .40-caliber pistol. His first pair of rounds smashed into the face of the man who'd fired the LAW, driving the corpse backward in a stumbling dance of death.

Sirens screamed around them, echoing over the confusion covering the street. From the sound of them, they were closing in fast. Behind them, the Chevy van struggled to get past the burning length of the bus. The flames had spread quickly, twisting through the interior of the vehicle.

A motorcyclist roared toward the Israeli, the black helmet and darkened face shield masking the biker's features.

"Get out of the car," Katz commanded. With the burst he'd fired at the federal cops to get them down and out of harm's way, he knew they were listed among the enemy. The diplomatic plates on the limousine wouldn't give them a moment's pause.

The van wrenched free of the burning bus, losing its bumper and most of the grille in the process.

Katz lifted the pistol, targeted the motorcycle's front tire and squeezed the trigger.

Immediately in response, the motorcycle tire deflated, one of the bullets shearing through the rim and warping it. The cyclist tumbled free and crashed against a stalled phone-repair truck.

"Yakov, over here!" The voice was familiar, and in Hebrew.

Katz glanced across the street and saw a Yellow Cab with its off-duty sign in place backing along the sidewalk toward the wrecked limousine. The driver was a gray-bearded man with a checked beret.

"This way, my friend." The cabbie waved enthusiastically, then brought out a full-size Uzi and hosed the front of the Chevy van. Already weakened by the collision with the bus, the van's windshield caved in under the fresh assault. The 9 mm parabellum rounds skated around the edges of the bulletproof glass and into the two men in the bucket seats.

Katz helped Rikki out of the limousine and urged her toward the cab.

"He is with you?" Hwan asked.

The Israeli gave her a grim nod. "You weren't the only one with a backup plan." He covered the two women's retreat toward the cab, then took the shotgun seat.

The cabbie jerked the transmission into gear and burned rubber leaving the scene. The second motorcyclist gave pursuit, riding double once more. The passenger worked with a LAW, popping it open to full extension.

Katz twisted in the seat and struggled to bring the pistol to bear. "Tobias."

"I see him, my friend." The driver cut across the street sharply, cutting in close behind a milk truck. Under his breath, he said an unending prayer but maintained a death grip on the steering wheel.

Unable to fire without fear of hitting innocents, Katz swore quietly. Behind the motorcycle, two prowl cars made their way through the hellground. With a surge of power, the bike closed the gap to twenty yards. It would be an almost point-blank shot with the LAW.

"Look out!" Rikki screamed from the backseat.

"I see them," Tobias said, then cut the wheel hard right, causing the tires to shriek with renewed intensity.

Three police cruisers slammed into position as a barricade that covered most of Independence Avenue where it intersected with Third Street. Police officers jumped out of the rocking cars and took up defensive positions on the other side.

Tobias didn't hesitate, his foot heavy on the accelerator. He aimed the taxi at the space between the third car and the street corner.

Katz braced himself, riding out the shock as the taxi grazed the police car's front bumper, then sped on. At least two bursts of shotgun pellets slammed against the side of the cab as it passed.

The motorcyclist wasn't so lucky. Evidently he'd seen the blockade late and made a futile effort to turn. The wheels lost traction, and man and machine went over the car in a confused tangle of flesh and metal. Triggered by the impact against the pavement, the LAW spit out its deadly warhead. White smoke trailed the charge until it slammed into the second story of a building on the corner and exploded.

Brick, glass and mortar showered on the street, thudding across the speeding taxi. Rubble under the tires made the vehicle slew out of control for a moment. Tobias clung steadfastly to the wheel and brought it once more under control. He accelerated again, streaking down Independence Avenue.

Katz turned in his seat and looked at Hwan. "I thought those people were after me. I was wrong."

"If they'd known who you were, they would have wanted you, as well." Hwan put the MAC-10 between her feet, then reached into her purse for a cigarette, paying no heed to the traffic fleeing from the taxi's approach. "Are we going to dump this car?"

"No." Katz lighted her cigarette, then fired up one of his own.

"The police will have a helicopter in the air," Hwan argued. "They can spot us at any moment."

"True, but they will be unable to stop us before we get where we're going."

"And where is that?"

"The Israeli embassy. Diplomatic immunity will be exercised for us."

Raising arched eyebrows, Hwan said, "They know about me? Who I am?"

"Yes."

"And they're going to let me enter?"

Katz nodded.

"How amusing."

"You won't, of course, be allowed free run of the building."

"Naturally."

Tobias handed back a handkerchief. "For the girl." He didn't take his eyes from the street.

Katz passed the cloth back to Rikki, who pressed it to her head to staunch the blood flow.

"There'll also be medical help on hand, Ms. Hwan," Tobias said, "should you want it."

"Am I and my associates guaranteed our freedom?" the woman asked.

Tobias looked into the rearview mirror. "Without question, Ms. Hwan."

"And you are?"

"Someone who can make that promise, I assure you."

She looked at Katz.

The Stony Man tactical adviser nodded. Tobias was very near the top of the Israeli Intelligence operation based in Washington.

"What do you want to know?" Hwan asked.

"The people I work with feel that the North Korean government has contracted a cybernetics specialist to manage some of the current crisis," Katz said.

"It's true."

"Do you know who?"

"No."

Katz studied the woman. He'd known her off and on for the past thirteen years. Chunae Hwan was notorious in intelligence circles, clever, inventive and never surrendering a morsel of information without getting something in exchange. She also lied extremely well, but without anything to go on, he couldn't challenge her. "What do you know about this person?"

"He's very good," she replied without hesitation. "And I understand he owns his own companies. He didn't necessarily take the job for the North Korean government for the money."

"Then why?"

"My people aren't certain."

Katz nodded, turning events around in his mind. Usually Hwan stayed in the field, playing her part near the heat of the action. For her to be in the United States meant that someone figured some of the important action was here, not in North Korea. He decided to play an ace. "My people discovered the base in the Catskill Mountains."

"Then you're moving very quickly on this."

"Is that what you're here for?" Katz asked. "The network this man has in place here?"

"To a degree."

Katz felt that was as honest as the answer was going to get. "Is this man an American?"

"We don't think so," the Chinese agent replied. "My sources indicate he's from somewhere in Southeast Asia."

"Japanese?"

"Possibly," Hwan admitted. "Given the computer angle, that seems like a natural assumption. But what Japanese would intentionally place so much destructive power into the hands of an enemy?''

For the moment, Katz let that line of questioning go. Other matters were pressing. By now Bolan, Hawkins and Encizo should have been in the air with Grimaldi, looking for their target.

"Do you know where the SEALs are being held?'' he asked.

"Perhaps. Do you have a map?''

From the inside pocket of his jacket, Katz took the one he'd brought with him.

Hwan unfolded it and studied it briefly. "There's a small town, part fishing village and part military base, called Nampo.''

"I'm familiar with it,'' Katz said. Price had already mentioned it as a possibility.

"They have a portable base there,'' Hwan said. "It went up only a few days ago. We managed to get pictures of it with one of our satellites after hearing rumors about its existence. Unfortunately the satellite soon after became dysfunctional, and we were unable to verify what it was or if it remained in place. A small ground team was sent in two days ago. They were never heard from again.''

"How did you know about the existence of the network in America?''

"We have spent some time developing other leads.''

"And no mention of the man responsible?''

"Not yet.''

For the moment, Katz chose to believe her. "You know what the SEAL team was there to discover?''

"Yes.''

Katz didn't ask her how she knew, whether it was from spies that had been watching American Intelligence circles, or from a more domestic angle. "Do the North Koreans have access to fissionable materials?"

"That," Hwan said, "I can't discuss with you."

Katz nodded, then looked at Tobias. The car was rocketing over the curving Buffalo Bridge at Q Street. A police helicopter was visible in the sky now, and at least two police cars were strung out in traffic behind them, struggling valiantly to close the distance. "Do you have a phone I can use?"

The driver gestured toward the mobile phone as he made the hard left onto Twenty-third Street.

Katz placed his call, using one of the cutout numbers he had for Stony Man Farm. He looked at Hwan. "I'll need exact coordinates on that portable base."

BARBARA PRICE STUDIED the wall at the other end of the computer room. News reports were still circulating about the captured SEALs and their possible fates. There wasn't much in the way of information, only sensationalism and the blood lust of media personalities seeking to improve their careers or ratings.

Personally the mission controller had never liked the limelight. She glanced at Kurtzman's desk. Bolan and his team were twenty minutes out from Nampo, circling in from Korea Bay. As yet, the North Koreans hadn't reacted with any hostile moves, though satellite scans revealed that the air base in Pyongyang was scrambling for possible launch.

Kurtzman was managing the computer spoofing of the North Korean satellites himself. Price could tell the big man was stressed by the operation by the set of his shoulders.

"Problems?" she asked, stepping closer.

"No. As far as the North Koreans know, they're looking at empty space out there." Kurtzman tapped the keyboard, bringing up other information on the trio of screens. "But I can't help wondering if the guy running the show over there is tied into other satellites I don't know about."

"It's a risk we have to take."

One of the phones on the desk rang and Price picked it up.

"I have coordinates," Yakov Katzenelenbogen said without preamble.

"Where?" Price asked, reaching down to activate the speakerphone.

The Israeli gave the location in degrees and minutes.

"Nampo," Kurtzman confirmed. "A little to the southwest, just off the coast." The area exploded into view on one of the computer monitors.

"How definite is this?" Price asked.

"My friend is with Chinese Intelligence. They've made discreet inquiries into the matter. They turned up a portable base in that area."

"Why didn't American Intelligence?"

"Perhaps," Katz said, "we weren't looking for the same things they were."

Price considered that. "Do they know if the North Koreans have the fissionable materials?"

"That can't be confirmed. One other thing," Katz continued. "There's a chance we can get a message in to the SEALs. Do you want to try?"

"Yes," Price said. "Can you do it in the next twenty minutes?"

Muffled conversation sounded for a moment, mixed in with the scream of police sirens, then the Israeli came back on the line. "I'm told that we can."

"Let's go for it," Price said. When Katz said goodbye, she broke the connection.

"The Chinese," Kurtzman said. "We receive word that

they've lost a shipment of nuclear material, but the diplomatic channels take a pass on coming clean about the matter. However, they've evidently fielded some kind of team into the area to recover or destroy them.''

"Raise Mack," the mission controller said, "and inform him. I'll call Hal."

Before she could make the call, Carmen Delahunt called for her attention. "I've tracked down the *Graceful Mu Lan*."

"What is it?" Price asked.

"A merchant mariner based in Singapore," Delahunt answered, referencing the information she had on her computer screen. "I broke into the maritime-records office in the capital city and found the man Hal noticed in the stills."

Price crossed over to Delahunt. "Show me."

"His name is Eliot Thompkins," Delahunt said as she tapped her keyboard. "He's forty-six years old. Once an American citizen, but he revoked that and became a citizen of Singapore in the late eighties. He was fleeing arrest in relation to a second-degree-murder investigation in Mobile, Alabama."

"What was the disposition of the case?"

Delahunt opened another window and quickly scanned the information. "A witness turned up twenty-one months later and gave a deposition that Thompkins acted only in self-defense."

"Who gave the testimony?" Price was intrigued, but she couldn't have said why, except that the way the matter was closed was too neat and bothered her on a subliminal plane.

"Another seaman. Brian Compton. Said he was on a long haul and didn't make it back to the States for months. The night the man was stabbed by Thompkins, the last he heard the man was going to make it. His story corroborates the evidence."

Price didn't want to let it go. "Is Compton somewhere in your records?"

After a few seconds of checking, Delahunt confirmed the man's employment. "He's listed as being part of the crew aboard the *Southern Star,* also owned by the Orang Laut Corporation."

"Orang Laut Corporation?" Hunt Wethers asked from across the room. "While looking for blueprints and building permits, I turned up that name in the list of holding companies on the piece of real estate in the Catskills. According to the documentation I've been able to trace, Orang Laut Corporation had the last clear title to the place. They were using it as a place of rest and recreation for corporate guests before selling it to Circus Hats."

Price followed the slender thread she'd been given. "Dig up whatever you can on Orang Laut Corporation. Primarily investors in the past five or ten years."

Wethers adjusted his pipe and nodded. "Are you thinking maybe the Catskills acquisition was pieced off on paper, but never really changed hands?"

"I'd like to know."

"I'm on it." Wethers turned back to his console.

Price glanced back up at Kurtzman. "Mack?"

The big cybernetics expert frowned. "Not yet. I'm having problems getting the com link on-line."

Checking her watch, Price found the window of opportunity to contact the team closing quickly now. She addressed Delahunt. "Run the rest of the pictures we have from the assassination teams who tried to take down Mack, T.J. and Rafael."

"I will." Delahunt turned to the task.

"Barb." The pitch in Akira Tokaido's voice was pure excitement. "Those files we swiped during Able Team's raid? I'm in." His hands darted over his keyboard.

"What have you got?" Price asked.

"Telemetry, linkups on-line, a piggyback I'm sure the guy who put that transmission together didn't know about and a back door into this system by someone who really knew what he or she was doing." On the screen, streams of data chains sped by.

"Is there anything useful?"

"As far as getting a copy of the transmission?" Tokaido asked, his attention squarely on the computer interface. "I'm not sure. I may be able to reconstruct part of it. But this may interest you a little more."

"Tell me."

"When that transmission was sent, someone was listening in. And I found him."

"Where?"

"Marine recruiting office down in San Juan, Puerto Rico." Tokaido glanced at her. "Interesting, no?"

"Yes," Price said. "Follow up on it. Get me an ID if you can, or at least narrow down the field."

"Can do."

Returning to Kurtzman's side, Price said, "You heard?"

The big man nodded. "Man, whoever this guy is that's pulling the strings for the North Korean government, he's tied in tight as a tick to the intelligence community. If he's covered his tracks well, he's going to be hard to find."

"I know. What about the call to Mack?"

"I think I've got the bugs worked out. Either they're experiencing some kind of electrical disturbance where they are, or someone's trying to jam us."

"Then play it close to the vest."

"I am."

"I'm sending Able into Puerto Rico to follow up on what Akira turned up. When you get the chance, we're going to need dossiers and covers for them. Something out of the

Justice Department regarding theft of federal property. Get Lyons an NIS cover, in case we have to go through military channels to get whoever's responsible.''

"No problem.''

Price put her call through to Brognola and the President, quickly bringing them up-to-date on everything they'd worked out, including the coordinates forwarded by Katz.

"Have you worked out the exfiltration?'' Brognola asked when she'd finished.

"If everything goes as planned and they're able to get the SEALs out damn quick,'' Price replied, "Jack will be standing by to pick them up. Any proof of the fissionables, Mack and Phoenix will decide whether they can stay in-country to pursue, then let us know.''

"What about McCarter and his group?''

"As soon as they touch down in Seoul, I'm routing them up to the Nampo region. They can assist in the search-and-destroy leg of the mission, or aid in the exfiltration if things get balled up.''

"Let me know.''

After agreeing, Price broke the connection, listening to Kurtzman tell her that he had Bolan on-line. "We have a possible target for you,'' she said. "Katz got some Intel we didn't have access to.'' She explained about the Chinese involvement, and the possibility that there was a unit on the ground in the vicinity.

"Sounds like we could have a conflict of interest,'' Bolan said. His words were broken up by static, making them hard to understand.

"Even so,'' Price replied, "our mission remains the same. We're working on getting a satellite connection in that area. Once we have it, we can patch more information to you, as well as keeping the communications link going between your team, Jack and Stony Base.''

Whatever comment Bolan might have made was lost in a sudden blast of static. Working frantically, Kurtzman tried to bring the frequency back.

Price checked her watch. The Osprey would be within striking distance within minutes. She watched the tracking beacon on one of the computer monitors as the convertiplane swooped back in toward the coastline, near to violating North Korean airspace.

It was nothing short of an act of war.

"I can't get them back," Kurtzman said, but he continued to try.

A cold feeling spread inside Price's stomach. The operation still revolved around the abilities of the men who'd been put into the play, but they hadn't counted on them being cut off from Intel support. She was deaf, dumb and blind to whatever they might be facing, with no way to help them.

"Wait," Kurtzman said, "I've got something coming from Mack's board."

A ripple passed through the central monitor, then the picture jumped. When it settled, iridescent green letters shaped out of tiny skulls scrambled into order and formed words across the ebony background: "They're about to become history."

"Dammit." Price turned her attention to the monitor carrying the Osprey's tracking beacon. Without warning, the signal faded from view, followed by the background.

"I'm cut out," Kurtzman said in a stunned voice. "They took the whole loop away."

CHAPTER ELEVEN

North Korean Airspace

"We're about a heartbeat away from a hell of a lot of trouble," Jack Grimaldi said. "Any farther and we become the start of another international incident. Do we go, or do we break it off?"

"We go," Mack Bolan answered, closing up the dead computer. Since the loss of communication with Stony Man Farm, there'd been no activity on the screen or the cellular phone line. "Whatever element of surprise we have left, that's what we'll go with." He stood up and shoved the notebook PC into his pack.

Hawkins and Encizo were already back by the Osprey's door, ready to deploy. Like Bolan, they were dressed in skintight nightsuits and had used black camou greasepaint to tiger-stripe their features. Black watchcaps covered their heads. They carried heavy armament, and a large bundle was between them, outfitted with a cargo parachute.

"Shift over to the local frequency we're going to use for ground operations," Bolan instructed. He slipped on his parachute. "For the moment, we've lost Stony Base. Jack?"

"Yeah?"

"You're on radio silence standing by."

"You got it." Grimaldi made an adjustment to the Osprey's heading.

Bolan felt the sudden lightness in the pit of his stomach that told him they were going down at a sharper descent. He nodded to Hawkins, then helped roll the door open. The wind blasted into the transport area. The Executioner pulled on a pair of bubble goggles to protect his eyes.

"Company," Grimaldi warned. "Radar's picking up two bogeys streaking toward us. I figure them to be MiG-29s from Pyongyang. We're gonna be cutting this close."

Bolan gazed out across the night sky, peering down into the jungle below. They were running out of water, putting Korea Bay behind them, the coastline closing fast, lined with trees and craggy rock. "When we make the jump, you turn and burn, get back to safe airspace as quick as you can."

A trio of F/A-18A Hornets from the USS *Thomas Paine* aircraft carrier anchored off the coast of Seoul had been deployed on a "routine" flyby at the same time the Osprey crossed over into North Korean territory. The Joint Chiefs of Staff had advised the President that they didn't believe the Communist forces would be ready to go on the offensive at the time.

Grimaldi dropped more altitude. "You guys are going in at five hundred feet. No time for any fancy moves. One minute coming up, and—mark."

Bolan grabbed one side of the bundle. With their cover blown, and no hope of a covert entry into the country, the gear might not make it into the hands of the men it was intended for, but the soldier couldn't pass up the chance.

"Automatic chute release is set for 350 feet," Hawkins said. "It'll come down hard, but it should be in one piece when it gets there."

"Thirty seconds," Grimaldi called out. "Fifteen. Ten. Go, go, go!"

Muscles straining, Bolan shoved the bundle out the door. It dropped immediately, seeming to fall through the black sky surrounding them. Encizo followed it, spreading into a starfish pattern immediately.

Bolan jumped next, not more than a heartbeat behind, with Hawkins in his wake. He smoothed back his sleeve to better see the altimeter on his wrist. Twisting in the air, he put the black planes of Korea Bay at his feet, then scanned the terrain coming up at him so rapidly. The wind numbed his face. He tapped the transmit button on his headset. "Rafe?"

"Yes."

"You've got the package. T.J. and I will establish perimeters once we're on the ground."

"Roger."

At 350 feet, the chute billowed up from the cargo bundle, spreading out a huge black mushroom topped by a smaller one that eclipsed a large part of the terrain.

Bolan glanced up at the Osprey, only to find Grimaldi still holding the same heading. He tapped the transmit button. "G-Force."

"I know what you're going to say, buddy," the pilot's grim voice came back. "But I can't zip out of here and leave you guys with your asses hanging out. Could be I'll just get the bum's rush out of here, no harm done. I do a little screaming about instrument malfunction, maybe they'll buy it."

"It's too late," Hawkins commented quietly. "Look northeast."

Bolan did, and saw the fiery contrails of the approaching MiG-29s scarring the sky. Operating at five times the speed of the Osprey, there was nowhere to run, and no time to do it in.

Set to warn of the three-hundred-foot ceiling on the jump, the altimeter on Bolan's wrist vibrated. He pulled the rip cord, and the trapped echo of the chute cracking open blotted out the noise of the jet engines shooting through the sound barrier.

Then there was no time to think about anything other than personal survival. Low-altitude, low-opening jumps were often hazardous, before the factors of night and thick jungle terrain were added in. The Executioner's landing was a flurry of whipping branches, painful thuds and the final slamming impact of hitting the uneven ground.

He keyed the headset. "Rafe, T.J."

"Standing," Hawkins called out.

"Bruised," Encizo said, "but intact."

"Get the gear stored," Bolan ordered. "T.J., you've got the north. I'll cover the east." He set out at an easy jog despite the heavy load of equipment he carried. In seconds a fine sheen of perspiration covered him under the armor and combat harness.

The staccato bangs of 23 mm cannon fire overhead told him that Grimaldi was being given no quarter. Slinging his AK-47, he climbed the largest tree he could find, working his boot soles deep into the bark to gain purchase. His gloves protected his hands.

Twenty feet up, he hunkered down beside the bole of the tree so it would camouflage his presence. Branches thrust up at different angles, but he had a field of view that showed the Osprey.

The MiG-29s easily outraced the Osprey, blowing by it in a crisscross of cannon fire that poked orange-white bursts of color against the black velvet sky. They were only warning shots, though. At that range, Bolan knew they'd missed on purpose.

"Jack," he said into the throat mike.

"Busy," Grimaldi called back. "You guys stay hard down there, get those boys home. Me, I got some business here that's not finished. Those MiGs are geared for a running prey, not me."

As Bolan watched, Grimaldi brought the Osprey around, as if heading for the coastline. More cannon fire blasted the air in front of him, cutting off his retreat. The Osprey pulled up sharply, climbing toward the thin sliver of moon.

For a moment, it looked as if Grimaldi were surrendering. However, when the plane reached the apex of its climb, the propellers rotated into helicopter position again, freezing it in place.

Overconfident, the MiGs flew in, but it was apparent that their need for speed to stay aloft wasn't going to permit them to remain with the Osprey. Without warning, Grimaldi opened up the convertiplane's M-61 A-1 Vulcan rotary-barrel 20 mm cannon. His aim was dead-on, and the explosive rounds slapped the closest MiG out of the air in a tangle of flaming metal. Armament aboard made two more explosions before the wreck hit the ground nearly five hundred yards from Bolan's position.

The second MiG had already committed to a flyby and couldn't heel around fast enough to target the stationary Osprey. The air-to-air heat-seekers carried by the North Korean fighter jet would prove almost useless if fired away from the Osprey. The missile's sensors were designed to pick up the heat from jet engines and vector in on them. The Osprey didn't give off enough of a heat signature to bring the missiles back around in a 180-degree turn.

Bolan knew that Grimaldi had banked on the MiG still being in range for a few seconds before it could renegotiate the attack. The Osprey came around, hardly losing any of its altitude as it hovered.

The MiG twisted in a vicious arc as the pilot realized the trouble he was in. Cannon fire from Grimaldi's 20 mm cannon chopped into the contrail behind it, then quickly closed the distance and hammered the fighter jet to fiery pieces.

"Son of a bitch," Hawkins said with quiet enthusiasm over the frequency. "That is one nervy, wily bastard."

Movement about thirty yards out alerted Bolan. The Executioner drew back into the tree to drape the shadows more tightly about him. He shrugged the AK-47 off his shoulder. With the incursion into North Korean territory, they'd chosen Communist weapons commonly used on that side of the DMZ, but they'd outfitted the rifles with flash-hiders and good-quality nightscopes that shouldn't be too closely questioned if found.

He stripped off the bubble goggles and peered through the AK's nightscope. Two seconds clicked by, and he was aware of Grimaldi's attempt to get back onto an escape course into Korea Bay.

The movement drew his eye, and he identified the North Korean soldier stealthily approaching the drop site. The warrior's finger tightened on the assault rifle's trigger.

Abruptly the night flared with renewed destruction that washed away the dark and stabbed down the nightscope, blinding the Executioner. He backed off, blinking, trying to restore his night vision.

Antiaircraft fire from at least three pieces of field artillery dotted the airspace around the Osprey in orange bursts

"They had us pegged from the git-go," Hawkins rasped. "We've got ground company on the move, too."

Gunfire broke out, sporadic at first, then quickly gathered intensity.

"Rafe," Bolan called over the headset.

"I'm done," Encizo said. "Gear's secured."

"Good. Let's see if we can get some distance in here." Lifting the AK-47, the Executioner looked through the scope while the thunder of the antiaircraft fire continued to rumble in a deadly drumbeat. He'd lost Grimaldi and didn't know if the pilot had made it out.

Dropping the crosshairs of the nightscope over his target, Bolan stroked the trigger twice. The heavy 7.62 mm rounds cored through the North Korean soldier's head and drove him down.

Before Bolan could lock onto the second soldier he'd spotted, a barrage of autofire ripped into the tree, severing branches and driving him back. As splinters ripped into his face, he knew his position had been compromised. He slung the rifle over his shoulder, barrel down, and leaped for a lower branch that looked thick enough to support the combined weight of his body and the equipment.

His gloves shredded the bark and almost slipped. Then he tightened his grip and got control over his fall. High-intensity lights raked the tree above him, illuminating the area he'd just left. Bullets ricocheted haphazardly around him. At least two of them thudded against his body armor.

A soldier with a flashlight taped to his assault rifle darted out of hiding at the foot of the tree and yelled a warning to the others, letting them know he was there. The flashlight beam arced across Bolan's eyes as he found temporary footing.

He slipped the 9 mm Makarov pistol from the counterterrorist drop holster on his right thigh and fired from the point. His first round took the man in the throat, knocking him off balance. Fired immediately afterward, taking the resulting rise into consideration, the second round blasted through the North Korean's skull just above his right eye.

The flashlight beam dropped into the foliage and formed an elongated bubble of light trapped in the brush.

A bullet struck the branch Bolan held, causing it to vibrate in his grip. He stepped off the branch and dropped the remaining eight feet, going to ground immediately. More autofire cut the grass over his head.

The Executioner moved, staying low. The operation had gone from rescue attempt to a fight for survival.

THE CAGE WAS primarily made out of aged bamboo that hadn't given under any amount of pushing, prying or pounding. Commander James Conrad had discovered that during his hours-long incarceration. It was further fortified by steel hardware that had been put together with no play.

Conrad sat because there wasn't room to stand. The cage topped out at five feet. His elbows rested on his knees, and his vision had been blurry for the past hour from fatigue and lack of sleep. When he saw the shadow slip to the side of the cage, at first he thought he was hallucinating.

Then Dwayne Sculnik twitched slightly, moving from sleep to a ready position in the space of a drawn breath. And Conrad knew he hadn't imagined the movement.

In the handful of hours since their capture and delivery to the campsite at Nampo, the SEAL commander had seen six different guards covering the bamboo prison. The North Koreans had been enthusiastic about ridiculing the Americans, going so far as to poke sharpened sticks between the bars and draw blood. That had ended, though, when Sculnik had taken a stick away from a soldier who'd gotten too brave, then rammed it into the guy's eye. It hadn't killed the soldier, but respect had been earned.

The North Korean general had appeared almost instantly, ordering his men not to fire, threatening the first man who did with his life. Conrad understood Korean a bit, but hadn't let on.

The shadow moved again, drawing nearer, staying close to the ground.

Conrad remained in his slumped position. Years of working with the men in his team and others like them let him know all of them except Thayler were alert. Seven men remained from his ten-man team. Two had died in the firefight, and Ensign Hamilton had been killed following an earlier attempt to escape. The North Koreans had overcome the SEALs by sheer numbers, losing men in the process, but had fought to keep them alive. Hamilton had been chosen for execution to break their spirit.

All it did was leave six very determined men behind in a bamboo cage. Thayler was out of it, in shock now with the loss of blood. Conrad didn't think he'd make it until dawn.

"One man," Sculnik said in a hoarse whisper that didn't carry outside the cage.

The shadow stopped moving ten feet out. "Americans," the accented voice said in English. "You are awake?"

"Chinese," Kennedy said. Part of his specialty was languages, and recognizing accents was an acquired talent.

Conrad's interest was piqued. He knew for a fact that Americans were working with the North Koreans, and one of the rumors his team had been told was that the fissionable materials had come from China.

He raised his head and whispered, "What do you want?"

"I carry a message," the shadow whispered back. "There will be a rescue attempt by your people tonight. Stay ready to move." Without another word, the man withdrew.

"Dwayne," Conrad said.

"Guy's history," Sculnik said in a normal tone. He sat

up and looked at Conrad. The rest of the team sat up, as well, except for Thayler, who was shaking from fever despite the fact Conrad and the others had covered him with their shirts to keep him warm. "So what do we do?"

Conrad looked around at the jungle.

"Could be a setup," Winters said in his Texas drawl. "Bastards seem to like teasing a man as much as a fan dancer working a convention of out-of-state Baptist preachers."

Suddenly the scream of jet engines rent the air overhead. Conrad barely scanned the afterburners on the MiGs before they were gone. He shifted, moving to get the circulation going again.

"We get ready," he said. "Then we see what happens."

It seemed like minutes, but only seconds passed before the first of the explosions pierced the night.

A quartet of North Korean soldiers sprinted out to cover the bamboo cage. One of the pock-faced corporals shone a flashlight through the bars and made a quick head count while the explosions continued.

"I notice they didn't send One-Eye out here to do the count," Sculnik said.

A look of pure hatred crossed the corporal's face, but he wisely stayed out of reach of the cage. "You expecting rescue, you can forget it. All the men who come for you, they die."

As Conrad scanned the sky, he saw one of the MiGs shatter into a thousand pieces. "Not without paying in blood," he replied.

The corporal backed his men off and spoke rapidly into his walkie-talkie.

"Confirming that we're still all here," Kennedy said.

Conrad nodded; he'd understood that much. He glanced

around. The team was awake and alert. They'd wait, then if an opportunity presented itself, they'd make the most of it.

CHAPTER TWELVE

Working the controls of the Osprey through a combined effort of instinct and skill, Jack Grimaldi knew when time had run out on his play. The convertiplane shuddered like someone stricken with palsy when the antiaircraft shell took it in the tail section.

Control went to hell in the same flash of light and thunder that shot up from the rear of the Osprey.

"Come on, baby," Grimaldi coaxed, working the yoke, "you may be dying, but you ain't dead yet. Not by a long shot."

The altimeter needle whirled as he lost altitude. The saving grace was that the drop took him out of range for the antiaircraft gunners. The downside, though, was the terrain that rushed up at him.

He wasn't long on options. Dropping into Korea Bay, supposing he survived the impact against the water and the subsequent undertow as the Osprey went down, was going to make him an easy target.

Working the controls as the convertiplane whirled like a dervish, he somehow managed to keep right side up. He cut the power to the twin props and hoped their continued gyrations would keep the fall from being too disastrous. In theory, with the props cut, they should have slowed his fall the same way the main rotor did on a helicopter.

But there were two of them not working well together, and the tail section had been shot to hell.

Instead of dropping straight down the way a helicopter did, the Osprey went sideways. The stubby right wing dipped into a wall of trees first. On impact, the prop shattered into deadly shards that pierced the convertiplane's body and Plexiglas windows.

Grimaldi felt an instant kiss of hot metal against his right temple, then the warm glow of blood spreading down the side of his face. Realizing there was absolutely no control left, he took shelter as best as he could. His seat-belt straps bit into him as the Osprey crashed through the trees and came to a sudden jerking stop.

For a moment, the pilot was stunned, the breath driven from his body. The odor of fuel flooded through the cabin and pushed the panic buttons on his survival instinct despite his dazed state.

When he tried to get out of the seat harness, he discovered the locks had been jammed. Reaching into his pocket, he unfolded a Leatherman Multi-Tool and raked the sharp knife blade across the straps, which parted easily.

Grimaldi stood uncertainly, pain throbbing across the side of his head. He put the tool away and drew the Colt .45 Government Model pistol from the military holster on his right hip. His armament hadn't been converted to Soviet standards. He hadn't been planning on getting shot down, but even if he had, there was no denying the Osprey as an American craft.

Deniability was still a factor, though. The mission couldn't be compromised.

Grimaldi stumbled toward the back of the convertiplane and found the side door had buckled from the impact and was ajar. The last quarter of the Osprey had been sheared away unevenly by antiaircraft fire.

Pushing himself through the door, he went down hard, landing on his face as a wave of dizziness and nausea swept over him, drowning his senses. He wasn't sure how long he lay there, but as soon as a semblance of consciousness returned to him, he shoved himself to his feet and managed a determined stagger. The jungle was only a few yards away, and he knew how to lose himself in it.

Twin shadows darted in front of him and spoke in what he assumed was Korean, since it was a foreign language and he was in that country. The words sounded commanding, coming from both shadows.

Grimaldi drew the .45 and leveled it before him. Before he could squeeze the trigger, though, something exploded at the back of his head, and his faltering senses faded entirely.

A BURST OF AUTOFIRE rattled the branches over Bolan's head and stripped bark from the trunk. He moved instantly, throwing himself in a headlong dive for cover behind a loose arrangement of boulders. Bullets whined off the flat planes of the rocks.

Hunkered down behind the boulders, Bolan knew he'd be overrun in seconds if he tried to hold the position. Plucking a rocket grenade from his combat harness, he shoved it into the BG-15 launcher clipped underneath the AK-47. The quadrant sights were on the side, and he brought them to bear as he pulled the assault rifle into his cheek.

Aiming at the cluster of gunners firing at him, he stroked the trigger.

The explosive struck the trees just above the North Korean soldiers' heads. Fragments from the antipersonnel grenade riddled the men, killing most of them instantly. Corpses flew outward from the blast site and remained unmoving.

Two other soldiers tried to pull back to safety.

Giving no quarter, the Executioner snugged the assault rifle's buttstock into his shoulder and fired a pair of rounds into each man. Both of them dropped.

In motion again, moving easily through the jungle despite the terrain, the Executioner tagged the headset. "T.J. Rafe."

"Here, Striker," Hawkins answered. The brief din of AK-47 fire echoed over the frequency.

"Go," Encizo said.

Bolan's feet crunched against the brush and dead branches that littered the ground. Evidently the noise was enough to alert a North Korean soldier taking cover behind a tree. The guy spun, trying to come up from the ground, raking his bayonet toward the Executioner's face.

Raising his assault rifle, Bolan blocked the thrust with his weapon, then lifted his foot and kicked the man back. He fired three times in quick succession, the heavy 7.62 mm rounds pinning the dead man to the ground.

"Go around to the east," Bolan called out over the frequency. Grimaldi had gone down almost a thousand yards away. "If they get us shoved over to the west of their position, they'll force us out into the water."

"Roger," Encizo responded.

"Copy," Hawkins said.

Bolan veered more to the right, running hard. Perspiration streaked him and soaked his clothing. The extra weight of his equipment and body armor was grueling, and if it had been daylight, he knew his pursuers could have trailed him by the depressions his boots made in the soft ground.

From the way the convertiplane had gone down, the soldier felt chances were good that Grimaldi was still alive. Keeping him that way would be another matter.

Gradually the terrain started a gentle incline, then became a hill. Bolan remembered it from the topographical maps he'd studied of the target area. At first he'd planned to stay away from the hill because it afforded a view over the coastal area. Any attempt at ascending it could have been spotted easily.

However, the ground pursuit was actively sweeping, not staying in one area.

To the left, someone touched off a flare. The crimson star flew into the night and hit its apex, then floated to the ground slowly on a small parachute.

Crouching, eluding the red streamers of light, the Executioner took a moment to scan the rest of the incline on the hill. Less than forty yards away, just below the crest of the ridge, three North Korean soldiers were finishing setting up a .50-caliber machine gun.

As the dying embers of the flare faded away, Bolan lifted the AK-47 and sighted his targets, working left to right. He squeezed the trigger rapidly, the sound of his shots setting off new patterns of autofire as the soldiers cut loose at shadows.

The first two soldiers in the machine-gun nest went down in rapid order. Diving behind the gun's tripod and the rocks acting as a barrier, the third man swept the .50-cal around, hammering rounds out across the foliage just down from the hill.

Coolly the Executioner waited, listening to the death song being woven around him, waiting for his shot. The machine gun protected the man's head and shoulders at the moment. Fifty-caliber rounds slammed into the tree trunk, sending long, ragged white splinters flying.

Bolan looked through the nightscope as the soldier's face came into view. He squeezed. As he rode out the assault rifle's recoil, he saw his target go down and backward, a dark flower blossoming between the dead man's eyes.

Only a few of the nearest soldiers had figured out what was going on. They fired at Bolan, charging up the hill.

Aware that he'd literally put himself between a hard place and a rock, the Executioner pushed free of the tree and sprinted for the machine-gun nest. Bullets dogged his heels, tearing chunks of earth and blasting rocks into fragments in his wake.

Diving into the protected area, Bolan yanked the corpses out of the way and reached for the machine gun. As he faced the oncoming wave of muzzle-flashes sprouting from dark silhouettes, he tagged the headset transmitter. "Take cover now!"

"Down!" Encizo called out, Hawkins echoing immediately.

Bolan unleashed the .50-caliber's full destructive power at the charging silhouettes, brass casings flying in gleaming trajectories all around him. He managed the ammunition belts with his free hand as they fed out of the metal ammo box.

The .50-caliber rounds chopped into the advancing wave of soldiers from right to left. Gray smoke from the old powder used in the ammunition curled in the still air at the hillside. The line broke, made only a brief attempt at reestablishing itself, then the soldiers dug themselves in.

Bolan managed to pick off two men who tried to fire at him. Bullets thudded into the hill over his head and against the rock in front of him. He ripped a pair of grenades from his combat harness and armed them, then tossed the bombs into knots of men he'd spotted. The grenades went off in quick succession, briefly quieting the gunfire yammering in response to his attack as dirt, foliage and bodies flew through the air.

Seventy yards away and closing rapidly, the twin headlights of a jeep knifed across the battlezone. The engine growled loudly, and the transmission whined as the four-wheel drive struggled with the loose terrain.

"Striker," Encizo called.

"I see it." Bolan reached for the machine gun and swung it around, bringing it to bear on the vehicle.

"Seems to me," Hawkins said, "we could use that jeep about now."

"Then get it done." Bolan aimed the machine gun deliberately, placing the sight blade into the center of the driver's chest. He squeezed off a single round with expertise.

Sixty yards out, the slug burst through the driver's chest and tore his lungs to pieces. He was dead before he could slump over the steering wheel. Out of control, the jeep pulled hard left and bumped into a thick spruce tree, then died. The two men aboard scrambled to take over the wheel.

A renewed assault came from the North Korean soldiers facing the hill. Evidently they'd made the mistake of believing Bolan had ran out of ammunition. With a long, sweeping burst that put at least four men down, the Executioner corrected that assumption.

Farther down the coastal plain, Encizo and Hawkins made short work of the two soldiers who'd remained with the jeep.

A warhead from a grenade launcher impacted the hillside only a few feet over Bolan's head. A small avalanche of dirt, grass, rock and brush rained over him, creating a cloud of dust that choked him.

A quick glance into the metal ammo box beside the machine gun told him he was down to less than a hundred rounds. He made the count, spacing them at targets. A brief fusillade of bullets clawed a soldier from a tree forty yards out, blasting the body free of the branches and dropping it into plain sight.

"Striker," Hawkins called.

"Go."

"Cavalry's coming. So are reinforcements for the North Koreans."

Bolan looked down the hill and spotted the jeep in motion. Hawkins manned the machine gun in back while Encizo took the wheel. "Don't approach the hill," the Executioner advised. "I'm just about to leave. Make for the Osprey and I'll see if I can catch up on a tangent over the hill."

"You sure?" Encizo asked.

It would be a hard hump, and Bolan knew it. But he also knew it was possible. "If I don't, we'll meet somewhere else. Find out what you can about Jack."

The jeep broke off the approach and took a circular route around the hill. Brief flare-ups occurred on either side of them, but Hawkins more than met the challenge with the deck-mounted machine gun.

Bolan fired through the last of the ammo belt in a solid roll of thunder. Scooping up his assault rifle, and mapping the terrain in his mind, he ran hard toward the probable intersection point he had in mind.

He saw the jeep's headlights only seconds before the grinding roar of the manual transmission reached his ears. At a glance, he confirmed that he was ahead of Encizo and Hawkins. His lungs burned from the sustained effort, but he held to the grueling pace. Without pause, he tagged the headset. "I'm coming in."

"Come on," Encizo replied.

"Right side."

Hawkins wielded the deck-mounted machine gun with grim efficiency, burning down a pair of snipers who'd climbed trees. The tracers hammered the bodies from the branches.

Stretching out his stride, Bolan came out into the clearing that probably passed as a road on most days. He leaned forward and grabbed the jeep's windshield, then hauled himself into the passenger seat.

"Keeping the jeep's not going to be an option," Bolan said as he readied the AK-47.

Encizo nodded. The vehicle was hard to handle, the wheels fighting every rut that had scarred the baked land.

"Company," Hawkins yelled. He threw out an arm to point out the jeep that was rapidly taking up a flanking action to their left.

Bolan slipped another rocket from his combat harness and thrust it into the BG-15. Machine-gun fire from the other vehicle ricocheted from the trees around them, and dug divots from the ground in the twin pools of the jeep's headlights.

Lining up his shot, waiting for a break in the treeline, Bolan compensated for the jeep's rough ride, then fired the rocket launcher. The warhead inscribed a slight arc that bent to gravity only a little, then detonated just behind the right front wheel.

The impact staggered the other vehicle, almost stopping it in its tracks. Fiery fingers clawed out from under the engine hood and quickly started licking at the windshield.

"They're out of it," Hawkins growled. "Engine's tanked whether they know it or not."

Wisps of gray smoke trailed the jeep as it fell farther and farther behind. Before it disappeared completely, Bolan saw two soldiers get out of it and start running alongside, passing it easily.

In less than a minute, the Stony Man team was at the Osprey's crash site. Encizo kept the headlights on full beam while Hawkins swept the mounted searchlight over the immediate vicinity. Spreading flames further lit up the area, consuming brush and foliage now, as well as fuel and combustibles from the convertiplane.

Bolan dismounted and moved ahead with the AK-47 at the ready. Blistering heat blew over him as the wind changed, warming the wet clothing pasted to him. The closest he could get to the Osprey's cabin was inches less than ten feet, but it was enough that he could confirm Grimaldi wasn't inside.

Knowing Grimaldi would have carried one of the radio headsets with him, the Executioner tried to buzz him over the open frequency. There was no response. Aware that pursuit was closing in, he returned to the jeep. Encizo and Hawkins got back into the vehicle, as well.

"Gone?" Hawkins asked.

"One way or the other," Bolan agreed. "Let's go, Rafe."

Encizo put the jeep into gear and drove back into the jungle, following a scarred trail that barely stood out against the heavy foliage. They went north, toward Nampo and the coordinates Stony Man Farm had given them for the portable base.

With less than two miles behind them and no encounters with ground troops, Hawkins pointed into the air. "Helo."

Three bright spots in the dark sky burned in a triangular pattern that defined the aircraft. Slowly it approached their heading.

"Stop the jeep," Bolan ordered. "We're on foot the rest of the way." He leaped out of the vehicle, took out his compass and found his bearings. Taking a straight course to Nampo wouldn't be advisable, so he plotted a trek that would bring them to the camp from the east, giving them plenty of room to maneuver if things didn't work out.

Hawkins lifted the hood on the jeep for a moment and worked industriously. Less than a minute later, he pulled back, then slammed down the hood. A grin twisted his lips. "C-4. A little surprise for the soldiers who don't want to walk anymore. Should confuse things for a while, too."

Bolan nodded and they moved out, grimly aware of how the odds had shifted against them. Shutting out the computer link from the Farm hadn't been an easy piece of work. Whoever was doing the counterintelligence work for the North Koreans was good, and had an impressive array of resources.

The Executioner couldn't help feeling that there was a hidden agenda in the works, as well. If the counterintelligence person had access to as much as was evident, there was no reason to work exclusively for the North Koreans.

At least, not on the surface. The real stakes in the deadly game weren't showing. Bolan was pretty convinced of that. A double-cross was in the works, and when it was discovered, all hell was going to break loose.

He and the two Phoenix Force commandos moved out at a distance-eating jog. Jack Grimaldi had joined the list of lives hanging in the balance, and the soldier was grimly aware the rescue effort was running on borrowed time against an unknown deadline.

CHAPTER THIRTEEN

San Juan, Puerto Rico

Seated in the copilot's seat in the North American Rockwell Sabreliner, Carl Lyons watched the designated runway at San Juan International Airport come rushing toward him.

Charlie Mott glided the jet to the ground, made a turn and headed back to the jet-debarkation area. He glanced out the window as he stripped off his headgear. "Looks like you're being picked up at the door, guy."

Lyons leaned across and looked out the window, as well. Standing near the gate entrance were two men in light-weight suits that wore the indistinguishable, impeccably creased stamp of career military. "Yeah. You got your cell phone?"

Mott unclipped the phone from his belt and showed it. "If I'm not with the plane, I'll be around the airport."

In the passenger cabin, Blancanales and Schwarz waited, peering through one of the triangular-shaped windows as Lyons opened the door and unfolded the stairs, then led the way off the jet. When he met up with the two men, he flashed the credentials Price had arranged that identified him as Naval Intelligence officer Captain Clark Lance.

Florid and balding, Major George Howland waved toward the airport. "Got a table inside at the Ionosphere Club. We can get out of the heat."

"Sure." Lyons followed the man into the building and the club. That early in the afternoon, the club didn't have much in the way of clientele. They took a table near the door. Lyons sat on one side with Schwarz while Blancanales went to arrange transportation. The Marines occupied the other side.

The waitress arrived in record time and took orders for two coffees and two iced teas.

"Your people didn't have much to say as to why we're supposed to provide you with these records," Howland said. Beside him, Gunnery Sergeant Mitch Kendall sat quiet and straight, his receding hairline touched by silver.

"No," Lyons said, "they didn't."

The major took out a pack of cigarettes and shook one out. "I'd like to know what's going on."

"I'm sure you would," Lyons replied, "but due to the sensitive nature of this operation, I'm not at liberty to tell you."

During the silent standoff, the waitress brought the drinks and departed.

Lyons tapped his watch. "Clock's ticking, Major. I'd hate like hell to report that I couldn't get the full cooperation of the Marines."

"Gunney," Howland growled, "give him the file."

Kendall did, but didn't look pleased about it.

Lyons flipped open the file, revealing it to Schwarz.

The top picture was in color, obviously from a Marine Corps graduation. The young soldier in the photograph was outfitted in Marine parade dress, his black skin contrasting sharply with the white hat. Soft brown eyes were set close together over a blade of a nose.

His name was Corporal Eddie Trask. He was twenty-six

years old, six foot two, 210 pounds and had been in the corps for five years, specializing in communications and computer programming. According to his file, he'd only gotten a high-school education, but was a genius when it came to computers. He'd been assigned to duty in San Juan since serving with the peace effort in Bosnia two years earlier.

Lyons closed the file and looked at Howland. "What can you tell me about him that this can't?"

"What exactly are you looking for?" the major countered.

"Conduct unbecoming a member of the corps would be a good start," Lyons answered.

For a moment, Howland remained tight-lipped, meeting Lyons's gaze full measure. Then he settled back in the booth. "Gunney."

"Yes, sir." Kendall laced his fingers together on the tabletop. "I've checked with Corporal Trask's immediate CO. There's been some concern over the corporal's involvement with the unsavory elements on this island."

"Such as?" Schwarz asked.

"We know he's been organizing some of the gambling that's gone on around the base."

"You want to give me a reason why he hasn't been suspended?" Lyons asked.

"We've been lacking proof," Kendall replied. "Five months ago, our investigators thought we had a witness willing to step forward and name Trask as part of an on-base bookmaking operation."

"Why didn't you?" Schwarz asked.

"The witness turned up dead," Kendall said, "and a private came forward and took the heat for the bookmaking operation."

"Was he the one who was organizing it?" Lyons asked.

"No," Kendall said. "However, he was involved."

"The witness?" Schwarz asked.

"Her killers were never found. The island PD has kept the case open, but I don't think we're going to discover anything."

Lyons didn't, either, but he remained silent. "With the sacrificial lamb offered, Trask stayed in place?"

"Exactly."

"Why didn't you ship Trask out?" Schwarz asked.

"The man's been in the military for five years," Howland growled. "There's certain options an officer has open to him. The corps isn't like it was back in my day, when a soldier was sent wherever he was sent whenever he was told."

Lyons nodded. "Trask worked it so he could hang on to this post."

"Yes."

"In more recent—discreet—inquiries," Kendall added, "we've discovered that Trask had a juvenile record back in Los Angeles. He was part of a gang that was related to the Bloods. When I talked to one of the detectives, I was told that Trask joined the corps after possibly killing two men in a rival gang during a turf war."

Lyons knew from personal experience that getting the juvie records hadn't been easy. "You must have carried some heavy weight at the PD."

"Actually," Kendall replied, "we found out through a contact in the sheriff's office."

"Once a man's been in the corps and given blood for it," Howland said reverently, "he never really walks away from it."

Lyons closed Trask's file. There was one other thing he needed to ask. "Where can I find the corporal?"

THE BAR WAS CALLED Piña Colada Blues and sat nestled in the bottom of the RedStone Motel, one of the recent additions in the series of renovations along the docks. The entrance to the motel was sedate, but the glittering sign above it announced the club's presence.

Lyons got out of the Chevy sedan Blancanales had driven from the airport. He clamped the panama on his head, then slid on a pair of dark shades from his shirt pocket.

"Any way you want to handle this, Ironman?" Blancanales asked as he got out on the driver's side.

"Sure," Lyons replied easily. "We go in and we place Trask's ass in custody. Get him somewhere we can ask questions."

"That's what I've always admired about you, Ironman," Schwarz said. "Your uncanny knack for finesse."

"You see any finesse available to you along the way," Lyons said, "feel free to trot it on out." He led the way into the motel.

The entrance to the bar was on the right, under a small green canopy festooned with bright parrots. Brass support rods were flanked by small palm trees in brass buckets that gleamed like molten gold.

A pair of bulky bouncers, one white and one black, lounged on either side of the doorway, wearing black T-shirts with the club's logo on them. Through the door, Lyons could see the familiar darkness gathered inside the bar, but the music was some kind of Spanish variation on rap.

The white guy peeled himself free and stopped in front of Lyons, one hand stretched out authoritatively. "There's a cover charge."

"Sure." Lyons reached for the folded twenties he'd

stuffed in his shirt pocket so he wouldn't have to go for his wallet and risk exposing the .45.

"Watch it, Earl," the other man said. "Son of a bitch has a gun."

"Gadgets," Lyons snarled.

"I'm on it." Schwarz stepped forward and slid his Beretta free, showing it to the black bouncer. His voice was cold and lifeless. "Don't."

The black bouncer stopped dead in his tracks.

However, the white bouncer had to have figured he had the edge. He reached for Lyons's shirtfront, obviously intending to manhandle him and take the weapon away.

Lyons let the guy step forward, then seized the offered hand, turned, twisted and converted the effort into a come-along grip. He kept the pressure just short of the breaking point, but he knew from experience that it was incredibly painful.

The bouncer struggled to bring his other arm into play.

"I don't think so, Binky," Lyons gritted. He applied more pressure, drawing a grunt of pain from the man. "Keep it up, and you won't be going to the gym for weeks, and you know what a few missed days can do to your schedule."

"All right. You're breaking my arm."

Quietly Blancanales entered the club and stood just inside the door, assuming a defensive position.

"I'm looking for a guy," Lyons said. "Eddie Trask. A jarhead. Do you know him?"

"Yeah."

"He inside?"

The bouncer nodded.

Holding the man with one hand, Lyons produced his ID with the other. "Captain Lance, Naval Intelligence. If I have any more trouble with you or your friend, you're going to be flexing in federal lockup. Okay?"

"Okay. Just let me go. You're killing my arm."

Keeping the Beretta hidden from hotel guests who'd noticed the activity at the bar's entrance, Schwarz stepped back from his prisoner, following Lyons into the club. The bar was long and polished, running out into the crowd on the other side of the room. Two bartenders worked the three sides, filling orders for the scantily clad waitresses, as well as keeping the curbside clientele serviced. Speakers located all around the room boomed out the hot Latino sound interlaced with screamed rap lyrics.

"Looks like the place has been furnished from disco hell," Blancanales shouted just loud enough to be heard over the noise.

"You seen Trask?" Lyons asked.

Blancanales pointed.

Squinting through the dark and the smoky haze, Lyons spotted their quarry to the left, hanging on to the edge of the low wall separating the tables from the sunken dance floor where a half-dozen couples gyrated wildly to the rap music. Trask looked to be holding court at the table. Four other men were with him, and none looked like regulation government issue.

"There's no way to do this quiet, Carl," Schwarz said as they started forward.

"Then let's get it done damn quick," Lyons said. He reached under his Hawaiian shirt and fisted the .45's butt, flicking off the safety. His finger rode the trigger guard with light pressure.

Trask spotted them when they were still fifteen feet away. He'd been laughing and joking with the other men, and he still continued. But Lyons had noted the dawning chill in his eyes as he swept his gaze over the approaching men. He excused himself and stood up from the table.

"Trask," Lyons called.

The response from the four men at the table was immediate and deadly. Weapons filled their hands in the blink of an eye.

Lyons whipped up the .45 and fired two rounds into the nearest man's chest as the guy pushed himself to his feet. The hollowpoint bullets threw the corpse back across the table while the thunder of the detonations drowned out the rap music.

Not wasting any time, Trask threw himself into full flight, catching Lyons slightly off guard. Even if Trask had recognized the big Able Team commando as some kind of federal officer, Lyons hadn't thought he would run so fast. The Marine corporal sprinted for the back of the club, bulling his way through patrons.

Lyons launched himself into immediate pursuit, cutting more deeply across the tables to gain a footstep or two on the younger man. Behind him he heard the hammer of weapons.

Still in full stride, Trask threw himself over the low wall separating the tables from the dance floor. When he landed, he knocked down two women and a man who'd been so involved in their own dancing that they hadn't seen him coming or heard the sharp barks of the gunshots. Trask ended up in a tangle of arms and legs.

Lyons jumped to the top of the low wall, losing the panama, then vaulted into the crowd, bringing Trask down just as he got to his feet.

"Ironman!" Schwarz yelled. "Look out!"

A moving shadow coming up at Lyons from the rear was all the warning the ex-LAPD cop received after the shout.

He had an impression of a big, burly man just as he rolled to the side, the breath knocked from his lungs.

The guy who'd attacked him was nearly seven feet tall, and built like a sumo wrestler.

"Kill that bastard, Maximo," Trask ordered, getting to his feet with effort.

Maximo's shaved head gleamed under the dance lights as he drew up a foot. He bayed like an animal scenting blood, stomping his foot at Lyons's face while the Stony Man commando lay on his back.

Letting go of the .45, Lyons grabbed the giant's foot in both hands. Muscles in his arms and chest burned with the effort of keeping the boot out of his face. He stopped it with less than an inch of breathing room.

The surprised expression on Maximo's face became one of distress.

"Bad move, Porky," Lyons growled. He twisted the foot as hard as he could.

Something snapped in the giant's leg and he fell away, remaining on his feet with effort.

Unable to find the .45 immediately, Lyons stood and set himself in a martial-arts ready stance, hands open and low at his sides.

Maximo threw himself at Lyons with no warning, lunging at the man like a flesh-and-blood avalanche.

Lyons shifted, then ducked beneath the giant's outstretched arms. He grabbed Maximo by the throat and the belt and lifted the giant off his feet. Managing the four hundred pounds of weight with brute strength, Lyons growled inarticulately, then brought the bigger man crashing down against the dance floor on his back.

The meaty smack of impact reverberated across the club, punctuating the rapid rap beat.

Lyons spotted his pistol less than a yard away and

snatched it up. He was breathing hard from the effort, and black comets sizzled across his vision.

Maximo struggled to get up.

Without a word, Lyons stepped forward and swung a boot into the giant's temple, rendering him unconscious. He turned and found Trask poised for flight. Lifting the .45, he said, "Your choice, guy. I'm too tired to chase you anymore, so you can give yourself up, or—" he eared the hammer back on the pistol "—I can shoot you in the ass when you try to run. I need you to talk, and I don't care if you can sit at the time."

Trask glared at him. "You're not here to kill me?"

"If I was," Lyons replied, "the deed would already be done."

"Maybe. And maybe you'd just like a quieter place to do it."

"I guess we could stop dicking around here," Lyons said, shifting his aim lower. "I'll just bust a cap in your ass here to show you I don't really mean you no harm."

"Who are you with?" Trask demanded.

"NIS."

"Bullshit."

"I need to know about that transmission that went down in New York earlier today," Lyons said.

"You *need* to know?" Trask looked more hopeful, and larceny glinted in his eyes.

"Yeah."

"Cut a deal?"

"If you've got the goods."

"How much trouble can you get me out of?" Trask asked. "Seems like maybe I'm caught here with my ass hanging out all over the place."

"That," Lyons said, "depends on you." He was aware

of Blancanales and Schwarz flanking him as San Juan cops flooded the club, giving orders in Spanish and English.

"Yeah, well, first thing we need to make sure of is that I don't end up in the local crime crib. The man I've been working for, he'll flat-ass take me out if he thinks I'm going to talk."

"Pol," Lyons said, "you want to handle the PD?"

"Sure." Blancanales moved off slowly, calling out to the uniformed officers in Spanish.

Lyons took a pair of handcuffs from his jeans pocket and shook them out.

"Hey, man," Trask objected, "I don't want to wear cuffs."

"No," Lyons said, "what you don't want to do is end up in the local jail." He twisted the Marine's arms behind his back and put the cuffs on. "Let's go while I'm still feeling generous."

DIXON LYNCH STOOD in the lead of the group of men on the long stone finger that pointed out into Korea Bay. General Sym was only a short distance away, looking irritable. His soldiers formed a solid line behind him beside the half-dozen jeeps they'd brought for the venture.

Wind whipped spray from the waves that crashed into the cay almost thirty feet below. Broken rock, worn smooth by the passage of time and tide, then cracked open again during storms, lined the brief stretch of beach area.

"We've about exhausted what little trust we had here," Eric Hardcastle said.

Lynch glanced at his watch but said nothing. With the night and the dark clouds roiling overhead, visibility was limited to a few score feet. To him, it was like looking at the black glass in a computer monitor. It didn't matter what appeared to be there or not there, only what he knew he could make happen. And this was simplicity, although the general and his people would believe it was magic.

"The guy knows there's no way a boat can land at that beach," Hardcastle continued. "Even on a good day. And there's no runway for a plane, even if it could make it across the bay."

"The North Korean government needs me," Lynch said. "No one else can get them what they want. But they have to be reminded of that."

His cell phone vibrated in his pocket, and he answered it. "It's me, love," Kalico said. With the satellite link managed by the computers at Nampo, the communication was static free.

"Yes," Lynch said.

"It appears that the insertion team has escaped the North Korean troops at the drop site."

"How?" Lynch pulled his trench coat a little tighter, trying to stave off the chill grip of the hungry wind.

"By killing a number of the general's troops," Kalico answered.

Lynch gazed across the distance separating him from Sym. The general had received several radio updates from his own troops but hadn't bothered to share any of them. "How many men?"

"Three."

"They're all free?"

"Yes. One bright note is that the team you had on hand managed to get the pilot from some of Sym's soldiers."

"I take it Sym lost a few more soldiers."

"You take it correctly, love. But things went smoothly. Sym's people think he was rescued by the Americans."

"So we have the pilot?"

"Indeed we do. Chances are, he'll be safely tucked away here by the time you arrive."

"Good." Lynch smiled in satisfaction. Events were coming together more quickly than he'd anticipated, but they were coming together right. "What about the program Razor insinuated into the covert team's computers?"

"We were unable to lock onto the frequency at the time of the transmissions," Kalico said. "So we settled for blacking out their communications and cutting them off."

"Was there a computer aboard the transport plane?"

"Yes, but it was purely navigational and weapons systems. The unit they were using to send and receive is still out there."

"Field as many teams as you can," Lynch ordered, "without getting the general's people suspicious."

"It's already been taken care of."

"Fine. Make sure they understand I want that PC located as soon as possible." Lynch turned over scenarios in his head. Finding the PC would make everything easier. Instead of trying to capture the signal from the covert agency later, his cybernetics team would be able to force the link and finish sending the program Razor had worked out. Whoever he was dealing with had to be under a great deal of stress at the moment, because they couldn't have ever been cut off from their computer systems as much as they were now.

"I've already taken care of that," Kalico said. "But we've discovered a problem we hadn't counted on."

Lynch waited, watching the dark swirl of clouds.

"When we sent the Realdeal file to the White House, one of the operatives we've been using down in Puerto Rico had evidently piggybacked in. Cameron found out about it shortly after you left."

"Has it been confirmed?" Lynch demanded.

"About ten minutes ago, a trio of Naval Intelligence men arrested Eddie Trask. Pictures I received from Cardoza match the descriptions of the men who attacked the Cat-skills site.''

"They found out about the piggyback and tracked it back to Trask."

"I'd think that was a safe guess."

"Dammit, I should have had Trask killed the first time I caught him fucking around with the Caribbean program-ming."

"You said it yourself, love—the man was too valuable to lose unless he stepped over the line."

"Well, the son of a bitch has stepped over it now." Far off in the distance, Lynch heard the drumming sound of helicopter rotors. "Can Cardoza take care of it?"

"He told me yes. According to his sources, the NIS peo-ple are taking Trask back to the mainland within the half hour."

"Let me know how it turns out. Trask knows enough to hurt us, perhaps, but not enough to let them stop us. We've come too far." Lynch punched the cell phone off.

Sym started to move forward, followed closely by his troops. They kept their weapons at the ready.

Lynch lifted the cell phone again, then punched in a two-digit speed-dial number. When the phone was answered on the other end, he said, "You're late."

"We ran into some bad weather, and the takeoff was rough."

"I don't want to listen to excuses. Can you get that chop-per down here?"

"Yes, sir."

"Then do it." Lynch put the cell phone back in his coat pocket.

The helicopter broke the cloud cover overhead and dropped toward the rocky outcrop. Rotor wash stirred up grit and small pellets, turning them into painful missiles.

With misleading ease, the Russian Mil Mi-17 Hip-H touched down on three wheels. Ten armed men in the advanced SIPE gear spilled from the cargo area, causing the North Korean soldiers to move back defensively. There were no lights; the helicopter crew had descended using infrared sensors and the landing lights Hardcastle's group had spaced around the site without being noticed.

All in all, Lynch thought the production was suitably awe inspiring. He walked toward the Hip-H and waved at the assault team in the SIPE armor.

In response, four of the men turned to the cargo bay, slung their weapons and reached inside. Lights came on a second later, revealing the packing crates on the pallet inside. Lynch had ordered them left in their original containers with the Chinese markings for effect.

The effect wasn't lost on Sym as he joined Lynch at the helicopter's side.

Lynch grinned broadly. "There you go, General. You've got enough nuclear materials to rearrange most of South Korea across the DMZ, take out Seoul and shut down any attempts by the Chinese or the Americans to stop you. Never say I don't deliver what I promise."

Sym gave him a grudging nod. "We'll see." He ordered his specialist on tactical nukes to the front.

In minutes the man had verified the delivery.

"But how did you get this here?" Sym asked. "Our Intelligence would have known if a helicopter had landed on our coast."

"Like they knew the Americans were coming?" Lynch reminded. Then he withdrew the comment before it had time to sting. "We're in my theater of operations, General. This is what I was hired for." He smiled. "But I don't plan on giving my secrets away. I'll see you back at the campsite."

Lynch walked back to his jeep, accompanied by Hardcastle and the personal bodyguard team the merc had assembled. There were still some problems to solve, Lynch knew, but mainly they were logistical ones. All the elements had been successfully put into the play.

The covert agency he'd targeted held some of the most dangerous men he'd ever gone up against. But he was a silent juggernaut rolling into their midst, and they hadn't a clue that he was among them.

CHAPTER FOURTEEN

Garbed in black, wearing a black rain duster over jeans and a sweatshirt, David McCarter sat atop the pedestrian overpass in downtown Seoul and watched his quarry through night glasses. A chill had settled over him, but he credited it to fatigue more than the weather.

"I don't know about you," Gary Manning said over the headset radio, "but I'm getting damn tired of pussyfooting around here while Mack, T.J. and Rafe are stranded somewhere with the North Korean army breathing down their necks."

"Patience, lad," the Briton urged. "As of this moment, they're still out of touch with Stony Base even more so than we." Phoenix Force's own computer had crashed earlier, but the telephone lines were still open through the cutout system. "If we go mucking about up there without knowing where to find them, it would be like looking for a needle in a haystack." He refocused the glasses as Isas Kirosawa moved around in his hotel room across the street. Barbara Price had made the ID after seeing the pictures Calvin James had sent in.

"If we make enough noise," Manning said, "they'd know where to find us."

"They also serve who stand and wait," McCarter reminded. They'd left the Japanese economic envoy at the

Hyatt Regency near Namsan Park. With the bodyguards in place there, the Briton didn't figure there would be any further problems.

"Standing would be better than sitting," the Canadian growled. "My ass feels like it died an hour ago."

In the motel suite, the Yakuza chief switched on the large TV and scanned the news channels, obviously interested in the events taking place in North Korea. McCarter didn't know if the interest was simply because the Yakuza appeared to be near the eye of the storm, or if the reasons ran deeper. The dossier Kurtzman had commandeered hadn't ruled out any possibilities. According to the info, Kirosawa was definitely a money mover for one of the largest Yakuza clans.

Cars continued in both directions two stories below the overpass, and occasional late-night carousers walked through the overpass itself. The rowdiest groups had been the media representatives, pushing the adrenaline levels to keep themselves alert for the stories breaking around them.

"Calvin," McCarter whispered.

"Yeah." The ex-SEAL shifted in the shadows behind the Phoenix Force leader.

"Ever think of running away and joining the circus, mate?"

"Not in a long time."

"Did the high-wire act ever catch your fancy?"

"I take it this means we're not going to be sitting on our butts much longer."

"No, I don't think so." McCarter put the night glasses in a pocket of his duster and snugged up the fingerless black gloves he wore. "I think we'll cross over and ask Mr. Kirosawa a few rather pointed questions."

"I'm down for that," James replied.

"Gary," McCarter said as he pushed himself up into a crouching position, "you'll keep a sharp eye about, eh?"

"Two of them," the Canadian said. "Kirosawa isn't known for taking chances."

"He appears to be alone in that hotel suite at the moment," McCarter stated, moving along the overpass with surefooted steps in spite of the heavy dew that had accumulated with the approach of morning.

"Yeah, but you can bet that little entourage he keeps around for the heavy work has got to be there somewhere."

"I'll keep it in mind."

The overpass butted into the hotel where Kirosawa was lodged. A small balcony outfitted with a wrought-iron table, four chairs and a furled umbrella stuck out from the sliding patio doors. The maroon curtains let out a slice of light that draped over the patio furniture.

Even stretching with James bracing him, McCarter couldn't reach the balcony. The brick wall ahead of him provided no purchase.

"Guess this is where we separate the men from the lads," the Briton whispered. He drew in a deep breath as he stepped back from the wall, then took two quick, running strides and hurled himself at the patio. He tried not to remember that two stories of empty space led to the unforgiving pavement below him.

One hand slid over the top of the balcony, and he managed an awkward grip. His right hand skated along the wet surface without securing purchase. Off balance, he twisted awkwardly, maintaining a fingertip hold on the balcony, then got his other hand over the balcony.

Breath burning in his lungs, he hauled himself lithely over the low wall. He nodded to James, then grabbed the ex-SEAL's jacket when he fell against the balcony's side.

McCarter felt the vibration shiver through the balcony, but didn't think it would have been noticed inside the suite.

In seconds James had joined him on the balcony.

"Door's locked," McCarter advised after trying it. "Think you can handle it quietly?"

James grinned and produced a set of lock picks. After a brief struggle with the mechanism's tumblers, the lock clicked open.

McCarter reached inside his jacket and took out his Browning Hi-Power pistol. Another pocket held a sound suppressor, and he threaded it into place while James did the same to a Beretta 92-S.

Carefully McCarter eased open the door, aware that a gust of wind could blow the curtains and alert Kirosawa that the room was being invaded, or simply drop the temperature with the same result. He went ahead without hesitation, following the pistol.

Price had okayed physical confrontation with Kirosawa if necessary. The man was high in crime echelons that had an international reach, which was enough to warrant Stony Man Farm's attention without all the variables that had suddenly been thrown into the economic-summit meeting. With Bolan, Grimaldi and two of his teammates missing, McCarter had decided to rattle a cage and see what popped out. Things definitely couldn't be any worse for the rescue operation.

The Phoenix Force commander went into the room quickly, and as quiet as a ghost. He held the Browning in a tight two-handed grip. He knew without looking that James was at his heels.

A sixth sense had to have warned Kirosawa, because McCarter knew he hadn't made a sound. The Yakuza leaned forward, his back to the approaching Phoenix Force commandos, and acted as if he were reaching for the cig-

arette pack in his shirt pocket. Then his hand flashed for
the stainless-steel Detonics .45 pistol resting near the lamp
base at his side.

Firing from the point, McCarter shifted targets and
squeezed the trigger.

The subsonic round smashed against the bulk of the Detonics and sent it spinning. Almost spent, the bullet buried
itself in the wall, leaving a thumb-sized hole because it had
flattened out.

Kirosawa shoved himself out of the chair, going after the
Detonics.

McCarter lunged after him, grabbed the back of his
jacket and manhandled him away from the pistol.

The Yakuza mobster spun, bringing up a martial-arts
kick that would have taken the Briton's head off if he'd
been standing there when it arrived. Instead, McCarter
dropped below it, then slammed the Browning's barrel into
Kirosawa's crotch.

A gasp of stunned pain leaked through Kirosawa's lips.
There wasn't even enough strength left to scream. He
dropped to his knees, then fell over on his side.

McCarter moved in without remorse. Kirosawa had a lot
of blood on his hands, and from his files, he hadn't paid
an honest price for any of it. The Briton grabbed a fistful
of the Yakuza's hair and forced his face into the carpet. He
screwed the muzzle of his weapon into the man's neck, at
the juncture of spine and skull.

"You do anything other than what I say, mate," Mc-
Carter gritted, "and I shoot your spinal cord through the
other side of your throat."

"Fuck you," the Yakuza said. He struggled to get his
hands under him.

Without hesitation, McCarter kicked him three times in
the side, hard enough to feel a couple ribs go. "Stop muck-

ing about. You move too much, you're going to send one of those broken ribs through a lung. Then we'll be forced to sit here until you drown in your own blood." He twisted Kirosawa's head until he could look the man in the eyes. "I must admit, though, that prospect isn't without certain allure."

"You're a dead man," Kirosawa said.

"I am, eh? Looks like I'll draw my last breath after you do."

James bent and secured Kirosawa's hands behind his back with a pair of plastic riot cuffs. Another pair was slipped around his ankles, and, with the electrical cord from one of the lamps in the room to join the sets of cuffs, there was no chance of the man's escaping.

"I'm just after some information," McCarter said. He took a chair from the dinette just inside the patio doors, turned it and sat so he could look down on his prisoner. "You cooperate, you get to live."

"And I should trust you on this?" Kirosawa snarled.

"It's the only deal on the table, mate," McCarter said in a cold voice.

"Who are you working for? Greco? Frost? Kandinsky? Or one of the other Yakuza clans wanting to break into our territory?"

McCarter smiled and mentally filed the names away. "You tell me."

"You'd better kill me," Kirosawa said, blood leaking down his mouth from his broken nose, "because if you don't, I'll kill you."

For a moment, McCarter was silent. Then he moved the pistol to within inches of the Yakuza's forehead. Sweat beaded out on the man's head and his eyes crossed as he unconsciously focused on the pistol.

"Bloody hell, mate, you've just convinced me. I can't

let you live." McCarter let the man see him take up the slight trigger slack. "Bang!"

In spite of his iron grip on his composure, the Yakuza flinched, blinked and turned slightly pallid.

"Tough guy," McCarter said to James.

"Probably eats nails for breakfast."

McCarter shifted the pistol. "Here's the deal. I ask you a question and you answer with the truth. If you don't answer, or if you tell me a lie, I shoot you through the right kneecap. You'll walk with a limp the rest of your life—if I let you live."

Kirosawa shook his head.

There was a knock at the door.

Just as the Yakuza opened his mouth to yell, McCarter shoved the pistol between his lips. Hacking noises followed. Easing up on the weapon, McCarter kept it in the man's mouth.

"See who it is," the Briton ordered. From his vantage point, he could clearly see the main door to the hallway.

James peered through the peephole. "It's a woman."

"Maid?"

"No. And she's a nice-looking woman. She's carrying an overnight bag."

"Accompanied?"

James leaned into the peephole. "Not by anyone I can see."

"Show her in." McCarter readied himself for action, already planning on a quick retreat down the side of the building by way of the patios if necessary.

Keeping the Beretta out of sight behind his body, James opened the door.

The woman didn't seem to notice James as she walked into the room. She was tall and brunette, certainly not out of her late twenties, McCarter thought. Arched brows and high cheekbones framed her light hazel eyes.

When she saw McCarter holding the gun in Kirosawa's mouth, a bewildered look spread across her features. Automatically she stepped back toward the door and spun, getting set to flee for her life.

"No," James said, moving in front of her and shutting the door. "Have a seat."

"You're American?" she asked in a French accent. She held the overnight bag protectively before her.

"Some of us," McCarter answered.

James took her by the arm and seated her on the couch.

"Are you going to kill him?" she asked, looking at Kirosawa.

McCarter thought the look held bloody few compassionate feelings. "We're thinking it over."

"And me?" She looked at him.

"That depends."

"I haven't done anything."

"Apparently you're associated with Kirosawa here."

"I've never seen him before in my life."

McCarter glanced at James. "Her purse."

James took the purse, dumped it onto the coffee table and rummaged through the contents.

James held documents and papers and quickly scanned them. "Her name's Blanche Delacroix. Says she's a French citizen, but her passport and visa show she's been living in Tokyo for the past five months."

Giving the woman a thin grin, McCarter said, "Fancy that. Kirosawa lives in Tokyo, too. Maybe it's all coming back to you now."

"Can I smoke?" the woman asked.

Sorting through the belongings on the table, James handed her a cigarette, then lit it.

She released twin streams of smoke through her nostrils. She looked at McCarter, some of the hard look gone, burned away by the fear that took its place. "I don't want to die."

McCarter nodded. "I can appreciate that."

Tears leaked from her eyes and ran down her face. Her hand shook as she took another puff on the cigarette. "So what do we do now?"

McCarter looked into her wet eyes. "What's your association with Kirosawa?"

Her reply was blunt. "He owns me."

McCarter remained silent.

"I'm a dancer," she explained. "I worked a lot of clubs in Paris. Exotic dancing. There was some trouble, and I had to get out of France for a while. A friend got me set up in Tokyo. After I was there a few weeks, Kirosawa came into the club and arranged for me to go with him. I tried to disagree with him, but I soon found out I didn't have a say in the matter. I don't think things could have been much worse if I'd stayed in Paris."

"What are you doing here now?" James asked.

"He told me to be here. Some of his men brought me on a commercial flight out of Tokyo." Her voice hardened as she gazed at the man. "I'm his property. He doesn't want to be seen in public with me, like I'm a real person."

"You know," McCarter said, "you sound like a woman who could use a fresh start somewhere else."

She looked deep into the Briton's eyes. "You think you can arrange that?"

McCarter nodded. "Yeah. Just as soon as we get some information from Kirosawa."

"He won't talk. He'd let you kill him first. It would be a lot easier than what his boss would do if he talked."

McCarter had come to the same conclusion. Getting information out of the Yakuza chief, if possible at all, would be a long, drawn-out and bloody affair. They didn't have time.

"What's he doing here?" McCarter asked.

"I don't know much, but I do know there's a deal in the air that his clan is very interested in."

"With the economic summit?"

"I'm not sure. But I know the SEALs getting captured by the North Koreans was no surprise to him. There were some phone calls yesterday that I overheard. He's been dead set against involvement with the Colombians and the Russians from the very beginning." Delacroix gazed at the Japanese man. "I've found that he's very prejudiced."

"What kind of business?"

The woman looked at McCarter. "Do you know anything about his clan?"

"They're heavy into politics and business, controlling labor, black marketing, and run a large chunk of the opium business."

"Yes. From what I gathered, the business he came here to discuss would affect all those areas. I've heard him say several times that he was afraid they would lose more than they would gain."

"Do you understand Japanese, Ms. Delacroix?" James asked.

The woman gave a sad smile and shook her head. "Understand some of it, yes. Am I able to speak it fluently? No. But being immersed in it as I've been these past few months, I've learned enough to know that what I'm telling you is the truth."

"Why was he interested in the SEAL team being captured?" McCarter asked.

"They were supposed to be evidence. The guy he's supposed to meet set it up to show everyone what he could do.''

McCarter nodded. Turning back to Kirosawa, he pulled the Browning from the man's mouth. ''Anything you'd care to add to that, mate?''

''She's dead, too,'' Kirosawa barked out through bloody lips.

''Kind of hits a note and hangs with it, doesn't he?'' James asked.

''Noticed that, as well.'' Before Kirosawa could move, McCarter swung the Browning against his temple and knocked him out. ''Let's get the lady out of here.''

James used an arm to rake all the woman's belongings back into her purse.

''Do you know any of the other people Kirosawa was meeting here?'' McCarter asked the woman.

She shook her head. ''All I know for sure is that they were all connected with crime families and organizations. I heard some names, but I never met any of those people.''

McCarter took her arm and guided her to the door. ''Let's work up a list of names, then, shall we?'' James fell into step behind him, bringing up the rear as they walked down the hall toward the elevators.

''He usually has guards with him,'' Delacroix said. ''They're next door.''

''Then let's go quietly and quickly,'' McCarter said. He kept the Browning out of sight in the folds of the rain duster. His free hand held the woman's elbow.

''You're really going to get me away from him?'' she asked.

''Yes.''

Unexpectedly she turned to him and kissed him on the cheek.

''Thank you,'' she said.

McCarter squeezed her arm reassuringly, wishing it was as easy to get Bolan and the others home safely. But the further they got into the mess stemming from North Korea, the more snarled it seemed to get. He had a chill premonition that the operation was going to cost more blood than the warriors had at first thought. He hoped he was wrong, but he knew better than to plan on it.

Near Nampo, North Korea

THE SECOND SLAP stung Jack Grimaldi into wakefulness. He'd been aware of the first one, but only in a detached way, though the pain from that was starting to penetrate his consciousness, as well.

He blinked, narrowing his eyes against the searing needles of pain that emanated from the harsh light beaming straight into his face. He was seated in an uncomfortable metal chair, his feet tied to the back legs and his hands cuffed behind him. Though he couldn't see much, he got the impression that he was in a small metal building.

"He's awake," a broad silhouette said, then stepped back out of the light.

"What's your name?" another voice asked, this one carrying a Southeast Asian lilt.

"Steve," Grimaldi said.

"Steve what?" The voice sounded patient, as if the speaker had all the time in the world.

"Steve Canyon. Maybe you've heard of me." Grimaldi concentrated. His vision was useless, but his other senses seemed to be working fine. Outside the building, he heard a steady stream of voices and noises.

"He's lying," the first voice grated. "'Steve Canyon' was a comic strip about a military pilot."

"You think you're funny?" the second voice asked.

Grimaldi worked his jaw and tasted bloody phlegm. He spit at the speakers.

The hand that came out of the light was so fast it didn't register until it was gone. His head snapped back, and he almost lost consciousness again. Fresh blood coated his lips.

"I know who you are," the second voice said. "You work for the covert agency based in Virginia."

Grimaldi worked hard not to display any reaction. A cold chill shot through his heart.

"We can do this the easy way or the hard way."

"I get a choice?" the pilot asked.

Silhouettes, barely discernible through the haze of bright light, shifted. "Drug him. Let's see what he has to say then."

A thin man with thick glasses stepped into the small circle of light, a hypodermic glinted in his hand.

Grimaldi struggled in the chair, fighting to get away. But it was no use. The needle slid painfully into his arm and searched out a vein. He felt its hot release burn into his bicep, then the drug snared his senses. As he started to fade out, he willed himself to forget everything he knew about Stony Man Farm.

"WE ACCESSED the security videos at Kimpo International through the CIA," Kurtzman said.

Barbara Price nodded, scanning the images in fast motion on the wall screen at the other end of the room. She felt bone tired and edgy at the same time, always a confusing state. There'd still been no word from Bolan and his team, and Kurtzman wasn't sure if they'd be able to put the communications satellites back on-line. McCarter had placed a phone call after the session with Kirosawa.

"Did you come up with anything?" Price asked. She

stepped back to the wall behind them and poured a fresh mug of coffee. She usually liked to stick with juices, but now she felt the need for the caffeine.

"Eight hits so far," Kurtzman said.

"Why the hell didn't we know about this?"

"We weren't looking for it," Kurtzman said. "We feed off information other agencies take in, without developing info of our own unless we've targeted an objective. Patterns like this one can be there, but unless we've been alerted to look for them, they slip right through."

"I know." Price reeled in her anger. It was more directed at herself than at Kurtzman or his people, but none of it was productive. Professionalism demanded as clear a mind as she could maintain. "Give me the rundown."

At the other end of the room, the images on the wall screen suddenly went into reverse. People filed back through the gate entrances at the airport in Seoul, returning hugs and kisses to greeters, and moving back to reboard flights.

"I've got it programmed to show you the highlights we've picked up so far," Kurtzman said.

Price sipped the coffee and watched. A glance at her watch and some quick mental gymnastics with time zones told her dawn was less than an hour away in North Korea. Bolan and Phoenix Force were about to lose even that defense.

"First up," Kurtzman said, tapping the keyboard, "Dario Rojas."

"From the cartels," Price said.

"Right."

The face at the other end of the room was aquiline, but cold and reserved. The man's black hair was swept back, but the left temple was marred by a line of silver hair that seemed to be the result of a knife-blade scar. He looked to be in his early thirties, but the biographical information on one of the computers on Kurtzman's desk gave his age as forty-eight.

"Came to his current position quickly," Kurtzman said, "and stepped on every corpse he had to along the way. Holds on to his little empire through a steady increase in the body count."

On the wall screen, Price watched the man arrive at Kimpo, flanked by a half-dozen bodyguards who looked the part.

"No one noticed him?" the mission controller asked.

Kurtzman shook his head. "With the economic summit going on, strangers arriving in Seoul is even more commonplace than before. Hell, a circus gets there every day. International economists, media, politicians. Phoenix did good when they spotted Kirosawa. It was just the tip of the iceberg."

Rojas continued on his walk, then the picture fuzzed over and footage of another arrival took his place. This man was blond and blue eyed. His haircut was vaguely military, but the horn-rimmed glasses lent him a softness that would have made most people never give him a second glance.

"Filya Sakharov," Kurtzman said. "Ex-KGB. Took to capitalism in a big way after the fall of Soviet communism. The CIA reports I've accessed suggest that he was already dabbling in the black market before leaving the spy business. He's a networker now, responsible for banding together several smaller groups who've been moving money and munitions through Eastern Europe. He's bringing bigger profits to the bottom line."

The scene shifted again, revealing a thin young man in an Italian-cut suit and what looked like a permanent five-o'clock shadow staining his prominent chin. He was lighting up a cigarette as he walked out of the boarding tunnel, brushing by the uniformed stewardesses.

"Johnny d'Arezzo," Price said. "This one I know from a mission package I've been putting together for McCarter and Phoenix. His father is actually the head of the Family in Sicily."

Kurtzman nodded.

"The d'Arezzos are involved with drug trafficking, too," the mission controller said. "Designer drugs and the heroin trade."

"Right," Kurtzman confirmed. "I didn't know it, but the DEA in New York and Boston had been keeping tabs on young d'Arezzo because he's been trying to make inroads into those cities. He and some of the Rastafarian posses have been having a running gun battle for the past sixteen weeks. You might want to have Able Team take a look into that when things cool back down."

"I will." Price stepped closer and watched the names and faces continue to fall as the computer program quickly sorted through hours of videotape.

They formed a who's who in an international rogues' gallery. Red haired and effeminate, Cornell Frost was there from a major Triad in Hong Kong. Tuan Dai, pushing sixty now and leaned out to a skeletal wreck of himself, was there from the Vietnamese Mafia scattered across the West Coast. Blas Greco, head of a Sicilian affiliate in Spain, joined the party, as did Nicolo "the Panther" Pansa from Las Vegas, who was obviously representing the interests of the old Family heads there, and also present was Seiji Watanabe of the Yamaguchi-Gama, the strongest Yakuza group currently operating in Japan.

"Dammit," Price said as she glanced over the faces. "Are they connected with the economic summit or to the incident in North Korea?"

"Hard to imagine these guys being interested in whether the North Korean government has tactical-nuke capabilities," Kurtzman replied. "Except for Sakharov. He'd have been glad to close the deal."

"But he didn't."

"Not according to the transmission that Hal and the Man received in the White House."

Price studied the moving images at the other end of the room. Watanabe walked down the carpeted corridor of the airport, four men flanking him, invisible to the rush of reporters swarming to get pictures of the arrival of the latest summit representative. "Get me patched through to McCarter."

Kurtzman slipped on a headset, then worked the keyboard.

Price flipped the various scenarios through her mind. None of them was pleasant. She truly doubted that the people she'd seen were there for the economic summit. Some of them would have a vested interest in what happened to the Asian economies involved, but for the most part, everything that was on the table to be worked out wouldn't affect their business. A flagging economy generally gave organized crime stronger footholds through corruption in political office and less resistance when government spending on law-enforcement agencies was cut back.

"I've got McCarter," the big cybernetics expert said a couple minutes later.

Price took up her own headset. "David, you turned up more than we could have expected."

"I didn't think we'd happened onto a new vacation spot for international thugs," the Briton said. "So what do we have?"

"I'm not sure, but I want you to stay with it for the time being."

"What about Striker, Jack, T.J. and Rafe?"

Price sensed the frustration in the Phoenix Force leader's voice. "We're working on it. So far, we've been unable to resecure a com link. Until we know where they are and what kind of shape they're in, we can't help much."

"And if it comes down to these blokes or our lads?" McCarter asked.

"The integrity of the mission into North Korea comes first," Price said. "You have my word on it."

"That's good enough for me. Now, what exactly do you want us to do with Kirosawa and company?"

"It's more than Kirosawa. We'll be sending you dossiers on others we've identified so far. There'll probably be more, and we'll send those along when we get them." Quickly Price brought McCarter up-to-date on Kurtzman's latest investigation.

"So for the moment, we're to keep an eye peeled?" McCarter asked when she'd finished.

"Yes. There's a connection to what's going on in North Korea, and we need to know what it is."

"How physical should we get with these chaps?"

"Keep your distance for now," Price advised. "When the time comes that we need to rock the boat, we can do it faster and harder if we know more about what's going on."

"Agreed. Keep me posted on the other developments."

"Of course. You do the same." Price broke the connection. She watched the footage at Kimpo International Airport start over.

"I've got Hunt working on identifying other possibles," Kurtzman said. "He's put together a multimedia sort program from CIA and Interpol files." He leaned back in the wheelchair and stretched.

"I've got a bad feeling about this," Price admitted.

"How so?"

"Checking the angles, it's not too hard to see that the North Koreans might have chosen this time to get a shipment of fissionable materials into the country and pose an even larger threat to the economic summit in Seoul."

"There was a lot going on in that corner of the country."

Price nodded. "They could have used all the additional security being focused on the economic summit as a smoke screen."

"It scans."

"Yeah, but what doesn't is how they were able to spoof our systems, much less even know how they were there." She looked at the cybernetics expert. "We're invisible, Aaron. To succeed, we have to be. But what are the chances that someone could stumble onto the frequencies we were using over there?"

"Slim, but it's possible."

She stared at the screen and shook her head. "I don't want to play it like that."

"The only other choice is to accept the fact that someone came looking for us. That's scary."

"What we could be looking at is a double smoke screen. Whoever's working with the North Koreans is following their own agenda."

"Yeah, but someone from outside North Korea is something we conjectured from the start. They definitely don't have the technology to alter the video footage on the *Dragon's Gate*. If it's more than just for the money, maybe the computer team took on the job as a means to get back at the American government."

"And where do the crime families we've been looking at come in?"

Kurtzman shrugged. "I'm playing devil's advocate here, Barb. I don't have all the answers."

"Neither do I. But I've got the feeling that we've played the part of the hunted more than we have the hunter."

CHAPTER FIFTEEN

Seated on the edge of the folding table to one side of the small prefab building where the American pilot was being held, Dixon Lynch watched the man as the drug took hold.

Perspiration filmed the man's brow, and despite the intense light shining on him, his pupils shrank even more. His head rolled groggily from side to side as he strained against his bonds.

"He's fighting it," Mendleson said. He was a medical doctor who'd worked for intelligence groups in South Africa a few years before—only he'd worked for both sides, getting wealthy in the process of hosting interrogation proceedings and mixing deadly little concoctions that were almost untraceable after being ingested or injected. Unfortunately, when it was discovered that he was working both sides of the street in the intelligence community, both sides had wanted to kill him. Lynch had saved him from that.

After a few minutes, the pilot's struggles ceased and his head lolled forward on his chest.

Lynch walked over to him, then squatted to look the pilot in the face. "Who are you?"

The eyes were unfocused, moving in spasmodic jerks. "Jack."

"Jack who?"

The pilot didn't answer.

Lynch repeated the question several times, then changed the pattern by asking who he worked for and what he was doing in North Korea.

The answers, when there were any, didn't make any sense or were obvious lies.

In fifteen minutes, Lynch had exhausted his patience. "Give him more truth serum," he instructed Mendleson.

The slight man shrugged. "I can, but you're taking a chance on cardiac arrest. I've given him about as much as I dare, considering his body weight and age."

"He's not answering the questions." Lynch got a grip on his anger. The man didn't pose a threat to his operation anymore. Neither did the three men out in the jungle.

"These drugs," the doctor said, "they are not foolproof. We're dealing with a strong mind here. Perhaps over a longer time period we could wear him down. Give me two days, and I could almost guarantee he'd answer any question you'd care to ask."

"I don't have two days here," Lynch said. "We're down to a matter of hours."

"This is the best I can do."

Lynch nodded. There were other things to attend to. He shifted his attention to Hardcastle, who stood in a corner of the room. "Get him to the general's people. Tell them our scouts found him out in the jungle."

"Sym will know that's a lie," the big merc replied.

"I don't think it'll matter," Lynch said. "He's happy with his nuclear materials." The phone in his pocket buzzed, and he answered it.

"We may have some trouble," Kalico said. "I just found out from our sources in Seoul that Kirosawa was captured and questioned regarding his presence in the city."

"By whom?"

"We're still trying to figure that out. I'm told one of

them sounded British while the other was probably a black American."

"They could be part of the group we're searching for," Lynch said. "Some of the descriptions we've managed to ferret out have indicated two men like that."

"I know. But you have to ask yourself how they got onto Kirosawa so fast."

Lynch smiled, relieved to a degree. "If they questioned Kirosawa, they don't have a clue about the big picture. It's possible the Yakuza was just noticed coming into the country and interrogated about the fissionable materials. His clan handles a fair amount of munitions. Besides, Kirosawa doesn't know my name yet. We have nothing to worry about." He started out of the building.

The camp was in the process of being moved. North Korean soldiers labored under orders yelled from commanding officers, scurrying like worker ants. Jeeps rolled back and forth, hooking up to trailers loaded down with equipment. The sky was turning pale gold and lavender in the east, fighting against wispy blue clouds.

"What about Trask in Puerto Rico?" Lynch asked.

"The agents who have him under wraps are getting ready to take him off the island. They've had to work everything through the red tape the military has thrown up."

"They definitely aren't with the military?"

"According to the information I've gotten, they are. But they're handling Trask themselves."

"Get a message to Cardoza," Lynch said. "Make sure he knows that I want those three agents dead, as well." He punched the End button and turned his steps toward the main building.

Engine roaring, a jeep came to a rocking stop in front of Lynch, cutting him off from the main building. General

Sym remained in the passenger seat. "I'm told you'll be leaving us."

Lynch nodded. He didn't glance over his shoulder; he knew that Hardcastle and his team would be there. Tensions between him and the North Korean general hadn't died away with the delivery of the nuclear materials. "My work here is done, and I think things will be less tense if I leave."

"So where will you go now?"

"To the next job."

Sym scratched his chin. "My superiors gave me explicit instructions that you were not to be bothered during your departure."

"I asked them if they would," Lynch said, "and pointed out they didn't have the launch codes to those Scuds yet." He smiled. "It wouldn't do them much good to blow them up here."

Sym nodded. "So I'd been told. However, I wanted to make something very clear to you—if by chance there is some betrayal you've committed that we have yet to discover, I will look for you myself."

Raising his right arm, Lynch snapped his fingers.

Immediately a trio of laser sights came into being on Sym's face. Two others flamed in the center of his chest. The general looked down at the ruby dots.

"I'll look forward to it, General," Lynch said. "Why don't you come looking anyway at some point?" Without another word, Lynch walked behind the jeep. The laser sights dotting the North Korean general disappeared an instant before he waved the driver into motion.

Lynch entered the main building and found Gutter Razor lounging against a wall just inside the entrance.

"That," Razor said, "is one tense bastard."

Lynch chuckled. "He hates being out of control of a

situation almost as much as I do. I can appreciate that. However, the only person going to call the tune around here is me. How are things progressing?''

The Australian waved a beefy arm at the command center. "Total meltdown. Won't be enough left here to work addition or subtraction."

Hundreds of thousands of dollars of equipment was being jettisoned on the operation. But there was no way to make the jump back to the *Shadow Scythe,* their submarine, with all of it. Lynch felt the losses were acceptable in view of what he stood to net on the operation. All the pertinent files had been sent on to his computers in Singapore, and to the *Shadow Scythe.* Information was the valuable commodity here, not the equipment.

"When do we pull out?" Razor asked.

"In minutes." Lynch spotted Kalico laboring industriously over a computer she'd pulled out of the main swath of destruction. He walked over to her. "What are you doing?"

"Getting Shatterstop on-line."

"Where are they?" Lynch leaned in and scanned the computer screen. Shatterstop was the code name he'd created for the eighteen-wheeler outfitted with a portable missile launcher in its trailer. Either way things went with the covert agency he'd targeted, Shatterstop was on hand to take the operation down.

"Rolling north out of Charlotte, North Carolina."

A map scrolled onto the screen and displayed the slow progression of an amber ellipse moving along a gridded area.

Lynch glanced at the legend in the lower corner of the map, then quickly estimated the distance to northern Virginia. "Even if our target is at its most extreme point," he said, "they're already within the four-hundred-mile radius the missile can reach."

"That's right, love." Smiling brightly, Kalico looked up at him. "I want to give them a few more miles and a defensible position. I'm thinking Roanoke." Her fingers flashed across the keyboard.

As the screen shifted, the view of the state enlarged, until it focused on the central area. "Roanoke," Lynch repeated. "Isn't that where the British colony disappeared during the settlement years?"

"Disappeared and were never heard from again," Kalico agreed. "You'll forgive me the drama of the poetic license, but I found it fitting. And the city is now the industrial, trade and transportation center of the southwestern portion of the state. Our truck should be able to blend in easily."

"How soon can they be there?"

Kalico consulted her watch. "Three, four hours probably. No more than six. I'm routing them around the major traffic areas so they'll make the best time."

"Fine. Do it." The estimate easily fit into the time frame Lynch had allowed for the operation, even with the pace picking up because the covert agency was tracking him sooner than he'd expected.

"It's done." Kalico stood up and waved to a man wearing protective clothing and carrying a tank of hydrochloric acid.

The man nodded and came over with the sprayer. With the first drenching of acid, the computer hissed and shot out a shower of blue-white electrical sparks. The keys melted in on themselves like falling soufflés.

"Let's go, love," Kalico said, taking Lynch by the arm. "It's getting positively beastly in here."

Lynch led the way out of the building, breathing shallowly because the smoke was burning the back of his throat.

The thunder of whirling helicopter rotors drummed into the cacophony of noise covering the camp. Overhead, the dark, unmarked silhouette of the helicopter dropped from the sky, ready to ferry Lynch and his team to the next phase of their operation.

"BOSS MAN!"

Bleary-eyed, Kurtzman glanced up from his computer screen and tried to focus on Akira Tokaido at the other end of the room. Above the young hacker, the wall screen showed footage presently being broadcast on CNN concerning the economic summit meeting in Seoul. Since no more news had been released in regard to the SEALs, the media had gone back to beating its original drum, adding the occasional accent by having various government officials asked if the capture of the special-ops team had something to do with the summit meeting.

Personally Kurtzman was growing to grudgingly embrace Price's theory that the summit meeting and the failed SEALs mission were all part of another, multifaceted danger. It was scary because the cybernetics expert didn't have a clue as to what the focus of such a Machiavellian enterprise might be.

"What?" he asked Tokaido.

"I think I've patched together a satellite com line we can use for Bolan and McCarter."

The satellite frequencies had been granted with some trepidation by the Chinese, through Yakov Katzenelenbogen's contact. Whatever programming had knocked out the American telephone satellites linking that part of the world with the United States had never released its hold. Kurtzman had proposed using the Chinese systems instead. Neither the President nor the Chinese premier had been happy about the situation, but the Man had waded into the fray with the information about the hijacking of Chinese fissionable materials that had gone unreported.

The result was that Stony Man personnel would have access to select Chinese satellites for a six-hour window to get their people out of North Korea. Kurtzman only hoped it would be enough.

"How compatible are we?" the cybernetics expert asked.

"Eighty-eight percent," Tokaido replied. "I've got some filter and merge programs running. I may be able to sift out another five to seven percent, but we're going to be pushing our window by then."

Kurtzman pulled up the program. "It'll have to do. You did a good job, kid."

"Thanks."

"What about our built-in safeties?" Kurtzman was cynical enough to realize that the Chinese might use the opportunity to put a virus into their own machines that could show up months after the fact.

"They're in place," Tokaido said. "Someone tries to hit us with a virus, we'll know."

"Okay, then," Kurtzman said, "let's see what we have." He brought the satellites on-line first, then opened a camera feed to his left monitor. Opening a window in the lower-left corner, he used the trackball to increase and aim the magnification.

In seconds, he was peering down at the hidden base near Nampo. The spy satellite only had infrared capabilities, and those weren't the caliber Kurtzman was used to dealing with. He strained to see what was on the screen as he picked up the phone and punched Price's extension number.

"Yes," she answered crisply.

"We've got video." Kurtzman moved the focus around slightly, finding it moved more jerkily and with a wider pitch than he was accustomed. It would take some getting used to.

"I'm on my way."

The heat radiation picked up by the spy camera was barely enough to distinguish the buildings from each other. An oblong blob skated west, away from the campsite.

"What am I looking at?" Price asked. She had come up at his side without a sound.

"A helicopter, I think." Kurtzman tracked the movement for a moment, then the arc swung too much and he lost it. He swore beneath his breath, cursing whoever had deprived him of his usual cybernetic arsenal.

"Who was on it?"

"No idea. We just picked up the video feed."

"I'll check with the Chinese."

"You can try that," Kurtzman said, "but with this equipment, I really doubt they're going to be able to tell you."

"Can you call Mack?"

"We can try." Kurtzman punched the cell phone's number in. "In theory, it should work. Akira's patched the Chinese long-distance carrier into the ones we usually use."

"Will the scrambler still work?"

Kurtzman nodded. "I added an extra kicker into the transmission and reception programs, as well. The Chinese won't be able to monitor or record our conversations in any way without setting off alarms and sucking up one of the nastiest little viruses Akira's ever cooked up. I put a warning in there to that effect that will trip if they start prowling around. Whatever they do after that point, we'll know, and they'll lose a whole hell of a lot of hardware."

The phone rang five times, then six, seven, eight and nine. Silently Kurtzman prayed that someone was alive to hear it.

IGNORING THE VIBRATION cell phone, Mack Bolan stepped out of the shadows and seized the North Korean sentry he'd targeted. He clapped a hand over the man's mouth, preventing an outcry, and drove the short, double-bladed fighting knife through the soldier's neck from the back, slicing deep into the spinal cord.

All motor coordination left the soldier, and he was a corpse by the time the Executioner hauled him back into the jungle. While he cleaned the knife on the dead man's clothes, Bolan slipped the cell phone from its pouch and said, "Go."

"Striker," Price said, "we're back on-line."

"Glad to have you." Bolan moved stealthily, circling the campsite. The recon he and Phoenix Force had been able to do had been sporadic and not overly informative. Time was working against them; full dawn was only minutes away and would strip whatever shadows still remained that would shelter them. They still hadn't found the SEALs or Grimaldi, but they'd witnessed the helicopter taking off only moments earlier. The only avenue left open to them had been penetration, leaving the odds against them. However, if Stony Man Farm was hardwired into the battlezone, those odds could be shaved. "How far back are you?"

"Equipment's not as good as it could be," Price admitted. "We had to get in through the back door with the Chinese. But we're in a position to offer full tactical support."

"Can you see the camp?"

"Yes."

"Give me a minute," Bolan said, "and let's wire you into the com link here."

"We'll be standing by."

Crouching under the branches of a broad pine tree, Bolan tapped the headset. "Phoenix Three."

"Go," Encizo called.

"Get the dish in place."

"Roger."

Encizo had been carrying the twelve-pound LST 5C satellite radio that could interact with the headsets and tie the whole band into the Stony Man frequency.

Bolan kept moving. The soldiers in the camp were moving at double-time, breaking camp and stowing gear, giving the Stony Man warriors their best opportunity to break into the site. Reaching down to his side, Bolan unleathered the Spetsnaz-styled Stechkin 9 mm automatic pistol from the counterterrorist drop holster. He carried the Makarov in shoulder rigging now.

The Stechkin was a deadly little piece of hardware, tooled solely for destruction and requiring the hands of a master to bring out the best in it.

"Do you know where the SEALs are?" Bolan asked.

"We believe they're northeast of your present position," Price answered. "We're showing eight men stationary, which makes them stand out among all the movement in the camp. It's the best guess we have."

"Okay." Bolan relayed the information to Phoenix Force, then stepped up his pace. From the recon, they'd figured as much, as well, but hadn't wanted to circle around that way until they'd exhausted the other possibilities. Going around that way put the camp between them and their escape route.

"I've got the point," Hawkins radioed back.

"On your heels," Bolan said. He stared through the foliage but couldn't make out the Phoenix Force commando. Staying low, he hurried to make up the distance, the Stechkin resting easily in his hand.

"We're green," Encizo called out.

Bolan gave the information to Price, then told his teammates to make the shift to the satellite channel.

"Stony Base to Stony teams," Price said. "Give me an affirmative."

"You've got Stony One," Bolan replied.

"Phoenix Three hears you," Encizo said.

"And Phoenix Five," Hawkins chimed in.

"Okay, gentlemen," the mission controller said, "the show is yours, but I'll be calling out additional Intel as we have it. Your current situation has the three of you up against at least forty or fifty of the enemy. We have no status reports on the SEALs' condition. However, we do know that three of them are dead, so it's possible that one of the figures we're reading could be a guard."

"Or G-Force," Bolan suggested. "We lost him during the initial scramble."

"What kind of shape is he in?" Price asked.

"I don't know." Bolan saw Hawkins for just a moment as the man went to ground to avoid being seen by a passing guard. "How are we fixed for exfiltration?"

"I'm running it down," the mission controller replied. "Best I can offer is a coastline pickup on a hit-and-git strike. And I still haven't confirmed that."

"Things here are going to go ragged," the Executioner said.

"I know. As soon as I put something together, you'll know." Price dropped out of the loop.

Bolan settled in behind a line of brush and scanned the campsite. A half-dozen soldiers were stripping camou canvas from stacks of fifty-five-gallon drums that he assumed were filled with fuel. Mentally filing away the location, he took out a pair of small field glasses and studied the campsite.

The bamboo cage was barely visible, and it took real effort to spot the human figures inside.

A five-ton truck ground its gears, then started away from the camp, following a trail through the jungle. A canvas tarp covered small artillery pieces. Besides the two men inside the cab, a third man rode shotgun on the passenger-side running board.

Bolan tagged the headset transmit button. "Phoenix Five?"

"Yeah," Hawkins responded.

"You see the heavy-five?"

"Affirmative."

"We could use it."

"I'm on my way." Hawkins dropped out of sight just as the truck disappeared around a bend in the trail.

"Phoenix Three," Bolan transmitted.

"Go."

"Ready some shaped charges. We're going to take advantage of that fuel dump."

"Which way do you want it headed?"

"Back toward the camp. I'm going to try for the cage."

"Roger."

Bolan shrugged out of his combat harness, but kept the Stechkin and three antipersonnel grenades. Then he circled through the brush, closing on one of the prefab structures that was close to the jungle. There was a sliding glass window in the wall at the rear.

Peering through the dusty glass, he saw a small room filled with bags of rice, beans and other foodstuffs. Evidently the operation had been set up to survive on its own for a couple weeks or more if it had to. Two soldiers were inside the room taking inventory. The front end of a jeep could be seen outside.

Bolan slipped the blade of his fighting knife under the window and yanked upward, snapping the frail lock. The ping of the metal giving way was covered by the roar of engines and whine of gearboxes. Throwing a leg over the narrow ledge, he followed it inside.

One of the men turned, working with the notepad. He saw Bolan and reached for his side arm.

The Executioner flipped up the Stechkin and fired a short, silenced burst that caught the North Korean soldier in the chest and drove him backward into wire racks holding packages and boxes of food.

The other man grabbed for the assault rifle leaning against the wall. Before he could get it, Bolan was on him. Wrapping his gun hand under the soldier's chin, the Executioner placed his other hand behind the guy's head and twisted viciously.

Bone crunched as vertebrae splintered.

Lowering the dead man to the floor, Bolan quickly stripped the jacket and matching uniform cap from him. He added the four extra magazines for the AK-47 the man carried, then scooped up the assault rifle, as well.

At the door, he pulled the cap low over his face, then stepped out into the campsite. The jacket and cap blended him in with the rest of the activity, and he kept in motion, not letting anyone get within fifteen feet of him. If the camp hadn't been so distracted, chances of being found out would have been even greater. But he'd figured the small disguise would have a good shot at being successful.

He skirted other soldiers, staying close to buildings. The bamboo cage was less than forty feet away, guarded by two men. The Executioner let the Stechkin drop into his hand and kept walking.

HAWKINS HAD ALREADY noted the way the trail switch-backed on itself after leaving the campsite. The first hundred yards was the hardest, running through soft ground and thick vegetation with all the gear strapped about his body. Vines and creepers pulled at him, tried to trip him, but he kept up the pace.

A glance to his right showed him the truck was just topping the rise about fifty yards out. Hawkins was already streaking along the downgrade. His lungs burned with the sustained effort, but he didn't break off the pace.

Twenty yards ahead of the laboring truck, he fell into position behind a tree at the side of the trail, masked by the jungle. He gripped the Stechkin, checking to make sure the sound suppressor was still screwed tightly into place.

As the vehicle passed, he threw himself into motion, pacing it at first, then dropping behind for an instant and racing around to the passenger side.

The guard riding shotgun on the outside was talking to the men inside the truck. He kept his assault rifle canted on his hip. His position also blocked the view from the outside mirror.

Hawkins redoubled his efforts, knowing the thud of his boots would be covered by the truck noises. When he was almost within arm's reach of the soldier on the running board, the man took out a cigarette, then turned back to light it in his cupped hands.

The North Korean's eyes went wide, and he dropped his cigarette and lighter as he tried to raise his assault rifle.

Lifting the Stechkin, Hawkins put a 3-round burst through the man's head. For a moment, the corpse clung stubbornly to the truck, then it tumbled free.

The Phoenix Force fighter had to vault the dead man and lost a step on the truck. He forced himself to go faster, not knowing if the men inside the truck knew what had happened. He leaped and landed on the running board, grabbing for the side mirror, seeing the faces of the two men inside the truck reflected, knowing they saw him, too. He brought the Stechkin around in his left hand, maintaining his hold on the mirror.

The truck jerked as the driver pinned the accelerator to the floor, while the soldier in the passenger seat flipped his cigarette at Hawkins's face.

Ignoring the cigarette, Hawkins brought the Stechkin to bear on the truck driver. He squeezed the trigger, firing through the passenger-side window.

The truck driver jerked with the half-dozen impacts that sprayed him, the 9 mm rounds coring into the door and leaving metal scars behind. Weaving dangerously, the truck went out of control, charging through the trees and brush like a behemoth gone berserk.

The remaining soldier shoved the door open, trying to knock Hawkins from the running board. But the Phoenix Force warrior held on with one hand even as the truck came to a sudden stop against a small copse of pine trees. The last guard was fumbling at his feet for his assault rifle, and Hawkins seized the chance to drop him with a head shot.

Pulling the two bodies out of the cab, Hawkins then hopped up behind the steering wheel. He started the vehicle and headed to the campsite. Tagging the headset's transmit button, he said, "This is Phoenix Five. Coming your way."

"Come on, Five," Bolan said. "Put the truck behind the fuel dump, on the southwest side as close as you can. You'll be drawing attention, but other things should be happening by then. Three."

"Go," Encizo responded.

"Get those charges in place."

"On my way."

The clearing came into sight. Dawn was a solid presence

now, catching the world in that instant of twilight just before everything became clear again. Tension knotted in Hawkins's stomach as he drove for the fuel dump.

When the first ragged burst of autofire sounded, he thought he'd been discovered. Then he realized the firing was coming from the area where they thought the prisoners were being held.

The North Korean soldiers acted confused for a lost moment, milling around until their commanders urged them into action.

Hawkins cursed fluidly and pressed harder on the accelerator. Whatever had screwed up in Bolan's play, he needed to be in position. When and if they managed the exfiltration out of the campsite, it was going to be a hell-for-leather ride.

CHAPTER SIXTEEN

Mack Bolan dodged to the right, away from the line of bullets tracking him. His cover had been blown when the officer trying to gun him down had called out orders to him and the Executioner hadn't responded.

He dropped to the ground and rolled, aware that three other North Korean soldiers were joining the fray. Bringing up the Stechkin, he zipped a half-dozen rounds across the officer's chest, knocking the man down and back.

Taking deliberate aim, the Executioner put a 9 mm sizzler into the center of the soldier's forehead. Dirt kicked into the warrior's eyes as the dead man's last rounds tore into the packed ruts in the earth only a couple feet in front of him.

As he got to his feet, he drew the Makarov with his other hand. Glancing at the bamboo cage holding the SEALs, he growled, "Get down!"

Immediately the special-ops team dropped.

Taking aim on the lock holding the door closed, Bolan spotted Grimaldi among them, looking worse for the wear but functional. The Executioner squeezed the Marakov's trigger, and the pistol jerked in his hand.

On the door, the lock jumped like a bass hitting the end of a shallow run. Another round cored into the lock and left it in pieces.

Turning his attention back to the North Korean soldiers, Bolan fired three rounds from the Makarov that blasted a gunner from the roof of the building adjacent to the bamboo cage.

Two rounds ripped through the North Korean uniform jacket Bolan wore and slammed against the body armor underneath. The SEALs flooded through the open door. Bolan recognized the lead figure as Commander James Conrad.

Conrad scooped up the AK-47 from the dead guard on the run, then turned and fired a blistering figure eight that took out two new arrivals. He glanced back at Bolan. "Have you got a plan, or are we just winging this?"

"A plan," Bolan replied. "Keep your group together and follow me."

"We've got dead in the building next door. I'm not leaving without them." Beneath the mud-stained blond hair, Conrad's face was bleached and hard.

Bolan nodded. The request was understandable, and he didn't intend to leave any dead behind, either. Bullets drove him into cover beside the small portable building across from Conrad and the SEALs. He pulled out a grenade. "Can your team handle them?"

Conrad nodded.

"Get it done."

The SEAL commander fired off a quick salute and pointed out members among his team to accompany him. Two of the SEALs had already scavenged other weapons from the fallen North Korean soldiers. One of them stayed with a man obviously too wounded to move under his own power.

Popping the pin on the grenade, Bolan lobbed the bomb toward the three gunners taking cover behind a trailer filled with boxes. The explosion overturned the trailer and blew the soldiers away.

"Sarge."

Bolan spun toward Grimaldi and tossed him the Makarov. Another burst from the Stechkin put down a North Korean soldier who'd had the pilot in his sights.

The two SEALs who'd remained to hold their positions continued to add to their firepower and provided a withering cover to Conrad and the two men who'd accompanied him to get the dead. Grimaldi added to the count with the Makarov, punching a bullet through the head of a man peering around a building farther down.

Conrad reappeared in the doorway of the building he'd charged into. He carried the corpse of an American serviceman over his shoulder.

"Stay here and hold this position," Bolan ordered. "We need wheels."

Conrad nodded. "For a while. I don't think they're going to give us much choice."

Bolan waved over Grimaldi, then jogged to the end of the next building. Beside an adjacent building, Bolan spotted a ten-wheeler with a canvas-covered back. The driver's-side door was open, revealing no one in the cabin.

Bolan tapped the headset transmitter. "Three."

"Go, Stony One."

"Your surprise package?"

"Ready."

"Five?" Bolan said.

"Go."

"Your truck?"

"Ready, Stony One. Should we attempt a rendezvous?"

"Negative, Five. Copy that, Three. We'll be headed your way in just a moment. Be prepared to take the heat off."

"Roger, Stony One."

Bolan set himself, fisting an extra magazine for the Stechkin. "Jack."

"I'm ready, Sarge, but that's a lot of open space."

Without another word, the Executioner broke cover and ran for the truck with everything he had. His boots thudded solidly against the packed, broken earth.

Halfway across the forty-yard distance, his peripheral vision picked up the jeep approaching on an interception course too fast for him to completely dodge. The soldier manning the .50-caliber machine gun mounted on the deck cut loose, overriding the other noises with fresh thunder.

A pair of bullets from Grimaldi's covering fire ripped into the passenger's face.

Guided by his instinct for survival, the Executioner leaped, skidding across the hood of the jeep. He impacted for one dizzying second against the windshield and cracked the glass on the driver's side. Then he was across, off balance, but figuring the moves.

He brought up the Stechkin as he rolled to his feet. The pistol jumped in his fist, and the subsonic rounds cycled through in coughing noises that were lost in the carnage. The blistering web of 9 mm manglers warped into the machine gunner and ripped him away from the big weapon as he tried to bring it to bear on Bolan.

The warrior turned and sprinted for the ten-wheeler again.

The jeep driver turned sharply, aiming for Bolan. Then his windshield starred again and his head came apart, letting the warrior know Grimaldi's marksmanship was holding up.

Bolan pulled himself into the ten-wheeler and searched for the starter with his foot, bullets ripping into the truck cab from the side. Ducking, hearing the engine turn over, Bolan slipped the transmission into gear and popped the clutch. The driving wheels churned and threw the ten-wheeler forward.

A pair of North Korean soldiers had sprinted into position at the front of the advancing truck in an attempt to stop it. Their bullets scattered across the grille, then they realized it was coming straight at them. They didn't have a chance to completely escape, and Bolan heard one of them splat against the truck's nose, then the wheels bounced along the right side as they ran over the man.

Bolan tagged the transmitter button on the headset. "Stony Base, this is Stony One."

"Go, Stony One, you have Stony Base."

"I've got dead and I've got wounded. How are you coming on that transport?" Handling the unassisted steering with brute strength, Bolan took the corner around the building near where Conrad and the SEAL team were waiting. A rampaging jeep with a three-man team was attempting to strafe them with the machine gun.

"It'll be there when you get to the coast, Stony One."

Bolan shifted gears, gaining speed, and put the accelerator down harder. The jeep driver was intent on the SEALs, not paying too much attention to what was in front of him. He didn't see the approaching truck until it was too late. Cutting the wheels hard, he tried in vain to avoid a collision.

Using the ten-wheeler's greater weight and momentum as a weapon, Bolan ran the jeep down. Even higher up and protected by the bigger vehicle, he was jarred into the steering wheel.

The ten-wheeler drove the jeep before it like a bulldozer, shoving it into the burning wreckage of the trailer that the warrior had grenaded earlier.

Bolan dropped from the truck cab as Conrad came hustling up with his men.

"We're aboard," Conrad called out, jogging forward.

Bolan nodded and slid in behind the steering wheel. The SEAL team leader jumped up on the running board and hung on. Grimaldi took up a position on the other side. As the Executioner took off, he handed Conrad the remaining two grenades. "Final party favors," the warrior said grimly. "Make the most of them."

Conrad grinned crookedly. "Always loved making an exit people talked about."

Since the wreck with the jeep, the ten-wheeler pulled slightly to the left, but Bolan noticed with satisfaction that none of the cooling system appeared to have suffered any damage. The headset crackled in his ear.

Price said, "Stony One, you're about to encounter an APC. Break off your course."

Bolan didn't have time to acknowledge before the tracked BMP-1 armored personnel carrier turned sharply around a portable building less than sixty yards away. Easily thirty years old, the Russian APC remained rugged and threatening. The right-side tracks tore up hunks of the earth as it maneuvered. The turret holding the 73 mm cannon rotated, coming to bear on the ten-wheeler.

"Shit," Grimaldi said.

A gunner on the APC deck fired a constant stream of 7.62 mm rounds that rattled against the front of the ten-wheeler and burst through the windshield on the passenger side.

"Hold on," Bolan said, cutting hard left. He double-clutched and powered toward the largest portable building at the site.

The 73 mm cannon roared, then a louder explosion sounded a heartbeat later, almost lost in the crash that sounded as the ten-wheeler smashed through the building's side. Two steel wall struts were torn out of their temporary moorings, and whole panels of metal siding were ripped free.

Knowing the APC would give pursuit, Bolan kept the accelerator down, gaining speed again as he raced for the other side. The windshield looked like a jigsaw puzzle with a few of the pieces gone. Vision was occluded by the criss-crossed cracks.

A brief impression of wrecked computer equipment strewed across the room was all Bolan got before the ten-wheeler smashed through the other side. He turned the wheels back to the right, catching sight of the portable building just as it collapsed.

The BMP-1 rolled after them, the tracks cutting deep into the earth and ripping the rest of the building to shreds.

Tapping the headset's transmit button, he said, "Stony Base, this is Stony One. Do you confirm the fissionable materials?"

"Affirmative, Stony One. But they're not at your location."

"Where are they?"

"Opposite direction. Headed for Pyongyang."

"How are they being transported? The helicopter we spotted earlier?" Autofire from the rear of the ten-wheeler let Bolan know the SEAL team wasn't content to get out of the battle without leaving its mark.

"No. It's a truck convoy that evidently left a little before the helicopter."

"Do they have radio communications with this camp?" Bolan steered around an overturned jeep and headed for the fuel dump. He spotted Encizo at the edge of the jungle, carrying the combat harness and gear he'd left behind.

"Yes," Price replied.

Hawkins was in a tree overhead. A grenade leaped from

his BG-15 and streaked past the ten-wheeler, exploding somewhere behind them.

"How far away are they?" Bolan asked. He glanced in the only surviving rearview mirror and saw the North Korean forces in a staggered line behind them. A handful of jeeps flanked the BMP-1.

"Five, maybe six miles," Price replied.

"Rafe," Bolan called out as the ten-wheeler passed the parked truck behind the fuel dump.

"I've got it," the Cuban answered.

"Can you get air transport for us, Stony Base?" Bolan asked.

"Negative, Stony One. There's an interception crew coming from Pyongyang now that will probably overtake your group before you reach the coast. Anything we put in the air, they'll be able to track on radar. It would only be a flying target in-country."

At their present rate of speed, Bolan knew the coast was maybe ten or twelve minutes away. He glanced in the rearview mirror and saw the APC and the jeeps come abreast of the fuel dump in a sweep to continue the pursuit.

"Now," Encizo growled.

The destruction caused by the shaped charges, the direction of their force aided by the truck parked behind them, was immediate. The series of explosions ruptured the fuel drums and set the contents on fire, unleashing not only the concussion and antipersonnel fragments, but a rolling wave of flames that stuck to their targets like napalm.

The BMP-1 rolled through the blast, but came out flaming. The soldier operating the 7.62 mm machine gun on deck turned into a fiery scarecrow that staggered, then dropped to the ground. The crews aboard the jeeps were wiped out at once, and the vehicles coasted to jerking stops on burning tires.

A cheer broke out among the SEALs in the back.

"That's something," Conrad yelled over the noise, "that I'm going to work on remembering."

Bolan slowed just for a moment so Encizo could swing aboard and Hawkins could drop out of the tree. His mind was racing, trying to figure the logistics necessary to secure the fissionable materials, as well. He wasn't going to settle for half a win, not when so much was at stake.

"What heading is the convoy taking?" Bolan pulled a compass from his pocket as the truck roared up over a ridge that allowed him to see the water of Korea Bay in the distance. He took a bearing, found a landmark he could focus on and put the accelerator down harder.

"North."

"Along the coastline?"

"Affirmative, Stony One. From maps we have of the area, that appears to be the best route to get to Pyongyang."

"The aircraft carrier has a Chinook transport chopper and a Marine hovercraft, doesn't it?" The play came together in Bolan's head as he wound along the trail.

"Yes." Price sounded thoughtful.

"How far out are they?"

"The *Thomas Paine* is fifteen miles out."

"Can they get the hovercraft ready to ship in the next few minutes?"

"I'll check and get back to you," the mission controller answered.

Bolan drove the big ten-wheeler to the extent of its capabilities and the surrounding terrain. Pursuit would be quick and relentless when it came.

"You're going after the fissionable materials," Conrad said.

Bolan glanced at the SEAL team commander. "Yeah."

"Seems to me, my team and I left a job undone. If you'll

take us, I don't think you'll find anyone who can walk who'll turn you down."

The Executioner nodded. Conrad wasn't asking for vengeance. That would have been unprofessional. He was just asking for a chance to finish what he'd started, and Bolan respected that.

Thirteen harried minutes later, the ten-wheeler arrived at the coastline, and Bolan spotted the tight trio of helicopters speeding toward the small harbor. Fishermen spread out around the water quickly retreated, pulling their boats into the safety of shore covered by trees and brush.

"Stony One, *Thomas Paine*'s Black Hawk Leader confirms visual," Price said.

"We see him." Bolan stepped out of the cab and glanced back down the trail.

Hawkins stood at the back of the ten-wheeler with a pair of field glasses. "They're there," he said grimly. "Going to be a hell of a horse race whether the choppers get here first, or the North Korean military."

Bolan took the AK-47 and the combat harness Encizo handed him and quickly strapped into it. "Then we're going to have to hold them, because they need time to make the pickup." He told Conrad to get his wounded and dead into cover away from the truck. The equipment crate they'd dropped a few hours ago from the Osprey had four RPG-7 rocket launchers, but it was too far from their present position to do any good.

The Executioner jogged toward a small rise on the left that would provide a defensible position. Throwing himself on the ground, he readied the assault rifle, spreading out his last three rockets and four spare magazines. Hawkins and Encizo found positions, as well.

"Stony One," Price called, "we're patching you in to

Black Hawk Leader. Also, the Chinook is en route with the hovercraft.''

"Good," Bolan said. "Have the Chinook standing outside the twelve-mile limit, under radar if it can."

"No problem, but what good is it going to do there?"

"When we find the truck convoy," Bolan said, adjusting the AK's scope for the three-hundred-yard distance he'd be working at, "it's going to be our way home."

"We're not going to be able to hold support for you for long," Price warned.

"There's no choice, Stony Base. Letting them get away with the fissionable materials will be like a knife at the throats of the South Koreans."

"I agree. Let me know if you need anything else." Price dropped out of the loop.

Two jeeps raced for the shoreline almost side by side, followed by another half-dozen vehicles. Machine-gun fire from the deck-mounted .50-caliber guns chopped into the canvas back of the ten-wheeler, shredding it.

"Stony One, this is Black Hawk Leader," a flat Boston voice said.

"Glad to have you, Black Hawk Leader. You're going to be making a partial pickup—three dead and one wounded." Bolan squeezed the BG-15's trigger.

The finned warhead jumped from the grenade launcher's mouth and streaked straight and true, slamming into the lead jeep's left front fender. The explosion rocked the jeep and turned it over, killing or seriously injuring the crew.

"Understood, Stony One. And we've got some firepower headed your way, too."

"A matched pair of Sikorsky H-76 Eagles," Grimaldi said as he fell in beside Bolan. He'd strapped into the gear he'd scavenged, as well as one of the spare headset units Hawkins had carried.

"Acknowledged, Black Hawk Leader, but we need at least two of those jeeps intact," Bolan said.

"Black Hawk reads you. We'll discourage them and leave a couple intact. Trust the hands that you're in, friend."

Bolan did. Peering through the AK's scope, he relayed the orders to the Phoenix Force warriors and Grimaldi. The crosshairs fell over the driver's heart in the second jeep. He fired a double tap, seeing the man's shirt jump as the bullets took him.

The jeep slewed out of control and flipped onto its side. Staying with the targets he'd chosen, Bolan fired methodically, hammering down the two men who'd survived the wreck. "That's one," he said.

The remaining six jeeps zipped around the remains of the first two. Abruptly the rearmost jeep pulled hard to the side and slammed into a tree. Only one of the men got up, but a single round from Hawkins's rifle knocked him to the ground.

"That's two," Hawkins said.

At the top of the hill behind the jeeps, the blackened form of the BMP-1 came into view and set itself.

Bolan estimated the range as being more than the four hundred yards accessible to either the AK-47 or the BG-15. Even if it wasn't, though, neither weapon would have penetrated the APC.

Glancing over his shoulder, Bolan saw the Sikorsky S-70/UH-60A Black Hawk thump down into the sandy rock of the harbor only a few yards from the SEALs, the rotors raking up dust clouds. The H-76 Eagles thundered overhead, heading for the line of jeeps.

The North Korean troops broke ranks as they realized the danger they were in. The Eagles never gave them a chance. A fusillade of 2.75-inch rockets erupted from the pods underneath the stubby wings, delivering hell on earth for the jeeps. Metal, dirt, rock and trees crashed back to ground as gravity usurped control from the concussive force.

At the top of the hill, the BMP-1 belched a 73 mm round that screamed through the air, then dropped into the waters of the bay, yards off its target. Water rained over the Black Hawk, drenching the beach.

A heartbeat later, a TOW missile dropped from the stubby wings of the lead H-76, then shot forward. When it hit and the smoke and pyrotechnics cleared, the burning corpse of the APC sat awkwardly atop the scarred crest of the hill.

Bolan pushed himself into motion at once, running for the jeeps that had survived the attack. Hawkins, Encizo and Grimaldi were at his heels, and the SEAL team only a short distance behind them.

"Black Hawk leader," Price called coolly over the frequency, "be advised that we are tracking six MiGs approaching your location at top speed. ETA is a minute and a half."

"We read you, Stony Base. Black Hawk Leader is pulling out. We've got the cargo."

Bolan slung his assault rifle when he reached the first jeep. A brief glance over his shoulder showed the three helicopters withdrawing from the battlezone. He put his hands on the jeep, joined by Grimaldi, and managed to flip it over after considerable effort. The vehicle landed roughly on its tires, but seemed to be holding together.

Hawkins and Encizo righted the other one.

Climbing behind the wheel, Bolan tried the ignition. The engine turned sluggishly, but it started. He engaged the transmission while the SEALs separated into two three-man teams. Grimaldi took the passenger seat, then kicked the warped folding windshield out of the way. Most of the glass was already missing.

Bolan turned to make sure Hawkins had gotten the other jeep started, spotting him just as the vehicle shot twin rooster tails of dirt and rock out. The warrior tapped the headset's transmit button. "Stony Base, this is Stony One." Pushing the accelerator down, he shifted through the gears, heading for the worn trail that knifed through the jungle.

"Go, Stony One, you have Stony Base."

"Do you still copy the truck convoy?"

"That's affirmative. They're nine miles from your present heading."

"Holding to the trail?"

"Roger. With the dawn, we have full visual telemetry."

Bolan pulled onto the trail out of the brush, mowing down low branches and small trees. "Do the MiGs copy the Chinook?"

"Not as far as we can tell, Stony One. But it's only a matter of time until they get a plane in the area with SLAR capabilities."

"Yeah, but SLAR requires a chopper or a fixed-wing aircraft, neither of which is going to be able to get here as quick as the MiGs."

"I'm counting on that, too," the mission controller responded. "A trio of F-18/A Hornets is going to stay just outside the coast in international airspace and on radar to run interference. The Chinook pilot's going to stick as long as he can."

In the rearview mirror, Bolan noticed the SEALs field-stripping and readying their captured Russian and Chinese-made weapons. Farther back, Hawkins followed in the other jeep. "Keep him matched up with the convoy, but far enough out that he's out of sight."

"Done. We'll be standing by."

Bolan kept both hands on the wheel, pushing himself and the vehicle to the limit.

Behind him, Conrad stuck a small flag of the United States of America to the spring-loaded whip at the rear of the jeep. Once it was secured, he popped it loose and it sailed into the sky, unfurling the familiar red, white and blue. "The colors are for us," Conrad said, sitting back and pulling his AK-47 across his knees. "Since they know who they're dealing with anyway."

Bolan understood. The warrior had fought numerous covert skirmishes and major battles in his war everlasting. In a land surrounded by enemies, with death at every turn, that rectangle of colors was more than a symbol: it was a reminder that other men had fought and shed blood to protect a way of life that was worth dying for.

However the present mission played out, the Executioner knew he was in good company.

Off the Coast of North Korea

THE GREENISH GLOW of the computer monitors and the radar screens bathed Dixon Lynch and his people as they sat in the small command module aboard the *Shadow Scythe*. Captain Rurik Persikov, late of the Russian navy, was at the helm of the submarine. A tall, lean man sporting a short-clipped dark beard going to silver, he spoke English for the benefit of his crew and Lynch.

"They got them out," Kalico said.

Lynch gazed at the satellite-fed monitor showing the carnage left by the covert force along the North Korean harbor. "I didn't expect anything less." He turned to Cameron. "You're getting this on tape?"

"Straight to CD," the man replied, manning his computer console with authority.

"I want copies," Lynch said. "Here, and back in Singapore."

Cameron nodded and punched keys. "You got it."

"How are they getting their communications relayed?" Kalico asked.

"Either the Russians or the Chinese," Lynch answered. The presence of the aircraft carrier and the carefully orchestrated assault to rescue the SEALs had let him know the covert force had tapped into another avenue for their transmissions. "Given the information we turned up, I'd bet on the Chinese."

"They're going to overtake Sym in a matter of minutes," Kalico warned.

"Yes." Lynch smiled, thinking about it.

"At this point, love, we do have the option of letting the North Korean military know there is a threat to the fissionable materials. They could intercept this covert team with jet fighters if they knew where to look."

"True," Lynch replied. "We could reduce the number of people we're up against, and severely hamstring the operation against the North Koreans. However—" he leaned in closer to the monitor "—the idea of Sym getting killed or losing the respect of his superiors is more entertaining."

"Yes, but these people—"

"These people," Lynch insisted, "are no problem. You take away their fancy gadgets and information-gathering systems, and you're left with an enforcement arm without direction." He turned back to gaze over the rest of the submarine. "They're not even aware of us."

"There is the problem of Eddie Trask."

"Trask is like the people in New York. They don't know anything about me. I worked their employment through other people, who can't be traced now. There's nothing but a trail of dead ends. And, quite frankly, the idea of the

North Koreans dropping a nuclear warhead into the middle of Seoul and the economic summit in retaliation is more stressful to me than these people are. I've got business down there in the next few hours. The covert agency can't touch me, but I don't intend to get blown up while cutting the biggest deal of my life.''

"You could be underestimating their abilities," Kalico cautioned.

Lynch looked at her. "No. I know these people. They haven't got a clue about me. They never will until it's too late. Shatterstop will be in place in a matter of hours, as well. If I need to, I can eliminate them in seconds." He smiled. "We've succeeded, fair lady, and it was even easier than I'd expected."

The woman nodded noncommittally.

Lynch removed his jacket because it was too warm in the *Shadow Scythe*. The sub represented five years of his attention, several million of his dollars and corporate espionage from deep inside the Skunk Works arm of Lockheed, the Navy and DARPA. The final bill came in at seventy-two percent under what he could have expected to pay if he'd worked from designs he'd developed himself.

She was powered by diesel-electric engines that could push her along at almost thirty knots, driven by the single-screw assembly. Given the circumstances, it was a reasonable enough speed. The boat was also of stealth design, capable of producing a radar and sonar cross section the size of a gull or a fish. Even if she was slower than many surface ships, first she had to be found.

From the beginning of his immersion in global criminal activities, Lynch had known he'd need an operations base that no one could find. For a time, he'd considered an island somewhere in the South China Sea. When he'd discovered the possibilities of a stealth submarine, he'd recognized the need for maneuverability. Once he started taking aggressive strides, his enemies would track him back eventually.

The *Shadow Scythe* made that all but impossible. She couldn't be found unless he wanted her found. And even so, she was armed with Mk48 torpedoes capable of wire-guided strikes as far out as fifty kilometers. The sub also had computers that were able to interface with the huge Crays Lynch had set up in Singapore.

The next phase of his campaign lay in Seoul, and he intended that nothing stand in his way.

"Captain," he said to Persikov.

"Mr. Lynch." The Russian turned to him, hands folded behind him at parade rest, spine stiff and straight.

"Your best guess at when I can expect to rendezvous with my party in Seoul."

There was no hesitation, and Persikov didn't glance at his watch or the clock at the conn. "Seven hours, at full speed."

Lynch nodded in satisfaction. He had a few phone calls to make to arrange the meeting. Once they were safely out of the net the Americans had set up around the Nampo coastline, he'd order a communications buoy released that could access his satellite channels and get everything lined out for the final pitch.

He surveyed the command center with pride. Though he didn't know that much about submarine protocol, he took pride in the fact that he controlled everything he saw, including the ex-Russian submarine captain who'd once been one of the most feared adversaries the U.S. Navy had faced.

"Razor," he called to the Australian.

"Yeah, mate?"

"Your program has been fed into their programming?"

Gutter Razor nodded. "The phone calls that we picked up in Seoul confirmed the complete feed. I ran a couple test patterns. We're in solid. They're ours the next time we make contact.''

Lynch turned to Kalico. "Give them their satellites back. Let's let them have a sense of some security before we strip it away entirely.''

CHAPTER SEVENTEEN

"Look, man, we either get off this island, or we all die."
In the backseat of the car, Eddie Trask flexed his arms
handcuffed behind his back.

Carl Lyons glanced at the red light holding him in check
at the intersection. They were in the Chevy rental, headed
for the nearest hotel out of the main drag of San Juan.
Blancanales sat beside him, turned to face their prisoner.

Schwarz was seated beside Trask. "Got a flair for the
dramatic, doesn't he?"

"Yeah," Blancanales said. "I noticed how quiet he was
while we were dealing with the *federales*. No sass then."

"I had to wait," Trask said. "I need to know how much
weight you guys can pull."

Lyons made his eyes hard in the mirror. "Enough weight
to drop you in the deep water somewhere with your shiny
new handcuffs and a big rock as your synchronized swimming partner—unless you have some answers for us."

"Shit," Trask said. "You're some kind of cop."

"Not anymore."

Schwarz turned toward the Marine, his eyes hidden behind mirror-lensed sunglasses. "Who are you working
for?"

"Don't I get a lawyer?" Trask asked.

"If you did," Schwarz said, "he'd be here now."

"You get a rock." Lyons made his voice cold and distant.

"Eddie," Blancanales said softly, "just talk to me. Maybe I can help you. Who were you working for?"

"Man." Trask let out a long breath. "You got a cigarette?"

Blancanales reached into his pocket and produced a pack. He shook out two and lit them, placing one of them between Trask's lips.

Trask let out a long, smoke-laced breath. "Thanks."

Blancanales waved it away, acting as if he were enjoying his own cigarette.

Lyons had seen the Politician buy the pack of cigarettes in the hotel lobby while all the jurisdictional questions were being sorted out with the local PD. They were the same brand as the ones that he'd taken from Trask while searching him. Well versed in psychological warfare, the flip side of Blancanales's talent lay in getting people to trust him.

"You're in a hell of a lot of trouble, Eddie," Blancanales said sympathetically.

"You don't know the half of it."

"Maybe. But I can get you out of some of it. Tell me who you're working with."

Trask took a deep breath. "You heard of a guy named Ramon DeSilva?" he asked.

"Sure. He's connected with the Colombian cartels."

"Is he the guy behind the New York transmissions?" Lyons asked.

"No, man. This is my story. Let me tell it."

"Go ahead, Eddie," Blancanales said calmly.

"I'm putting my head in a noose here," Trask said belligerently, "and I don't think your partner appreciates what I'm having to do."

"It's okay."

Lyons kept the car in motion, figuring if he stopped at the hotel any time soon, Trask would shut up. Still, he kept his eyes roving, working the streets in practiced sweeps that would let him know if he was being tailed. Acting as if he didn't believe Trask was one thing; ignoring the warning in light of everything else was stupid.

"I got hooked up with DeSilva while I've been at San Juan," Trask said. "He manages a lot of shipments into Florida and needed someone who could figure out where the DEA and Coast Guard was going to be, when the best time was to try to get a shipment in. Then I started putting together some small buys, rolled the money over and re-invested it, found some guys willing to take a plane into Florida and got some heavier action going on."

"You must have been living lucky," the Politician said, "if DeSilva didn't step on you for invading his territory."

"Hey, fuck you. I know what I'm doing. DeSilva, he was putting through maybe seventy percent of his shipments. You know what my average was?"

"You know computers," Blancanales commented. "You had an edge on him."

"Damn straight." Trask leaned back in the seat and tried to appear comfortable. "I'm strictly twenty-first century, man, and DeSilva comes on like some feudal warlord. If something gets in his way, his first impulse is to knock the shit out of it."

"So what was your average?" Lyons asked. He made a lane change and checked the rearview mirror. Behind him, a Chevy Suburban cut off a station wagon to follow the lane change. Lyons's cop radar clicked on softly and locked onto the Suburban. Mentally he prepared his next moves, taking advantage of the traffic, buying time and looping back down into the heart of the city. He glanced in the rearview mirror and caught Schwarz's gaze, then deliberately tugged on his earlobe.

Schwarz nodded imperceptibly but didn't look back.

"Every shipment I sent," Trask said, "got through and made money. DeSilva had a guy watching me. He knew it. Took him three months to come offer me a job."

"And you took it?" Blancanales asked.

"For more money than I was making on my own hook, better protection and enough weight that most of the locals stayed away from me? In a heartbeat. He took his shipment completion from seventy percent to ninety-two percent in six weeks. I put him in contact with new clientele, too. Man, I'm a god to DeSilva."

"So who are you afraid of?" Lyons asked.

Trask was quiet for a moment. Lyons watched the guy lock eyes with Blancanales, who fired up a fresh cigarette for him. "I don't know," Trask said.

Behind the rental car, the Suburban cut the distance slightly. Lyons put his foot on the accelerator and beat out a yellow light, leaving the big truck stranded behind a flatbed hauling produce. He didn't intend to lose the tail, but he'd gain some time.

"DeSilva comes to me maybe a month ago," Trask went on, "and tells me about this guy who's making him an offer to work out arrangements between himself and the Sicilians and the Triads. Guy's thinking maybe DeSilva would like to branch out, ship a little cocaine into Europe and Asia and get some heroin to spice up what he had to offer to Americans."

"That would make trouble with the Sicilian Mafia on the East Coast and the Triads on the West Coast," Schwarz said.

"No, man." Trask shook his head. "He was going to act as go-between, iron out all the details and bring it together. He kept talking about maximizing profit. I could tell because DeSilva suddenly had those words in his vocabulary. Maximizing profit. DeSilva liked that.''

"So how did you get connected to him?"

"Part of the deal this guy was offering," Trask said, "was that he was going to launder the money, too. All those extra bucks, man, they had to be put back on the books somewhere if the interested parties were going to really maximize the profits."

"This guy was going to arrange that, too?" Blancanales asked.

"You got it."

"Where?"

"Russia."

Lyons eyed the Suburban in the rearview mirror. The driver had come on slightly too fast, but had slowed, blending in with the traffic a hundred yards back, pacing.

"They're doing a lot of business in Russia these days," Blancanales commented.

"No shit, Sherlock. Got a guy down here in the islands, on Aruba, by the name of Kandinsky who moves the drug money around. This guy, he's supposed to fix DeSilva up with Kandinsky as part of the deal."

"Can he?" Schwarz asked.

Lyons noticed that Gadgets had shifted in his seat, readying the H&K MP-5 SD-3 between his feet. Trask was oblivious to the move.

"That's what DeSilva wanted me to find out," Trask said. "He knew I'm damn good with computers, and this guy had broken into his computer network—the one off the books—in Medellín and left the message. I monitored some of the transmissions, developed a capture program and dug into this guy. But hot damn, he's good! Closest I got was somewhere in Singapore."

Lyons filed the information away. The update Price and Kurtzman had sent along had mentioned the Singapore connection.

"You don't know who this guy is?" Blancanales asked.

"No. Like I said, he's one of the best I've ever seen."

"But you found out about the transmission from New York," Lyons inserted.

"Yeah, but it truly took some digging, brother. Weeks full of long hours. I piggybacked in when he zoned the White House."

"Did you copy it?"

"Couldn't. He had it geeked so that wasn't possible."

"What else can you tell us?" Blancanales asked.

"We cutting a deal?"

"Yeah," Lyons replied. "If your info's good, you lose the stripes and the military pension, but you get to walk."

"Where?"

"Back to the States."

"No way." Trask shook his head. "Leave me here. I'll take care of my own self."

The Suburban came closer, purring along like a big cat ready to pounce.

"Done," Lyons said. "Tell us what you have."

Trask smiled. "I can tell you one thing—this guy's all over this North Korea thing with the SEALs like stink on a damn skunk. Also, he's got a clandestine little ops around in Virginia code-named Shatterstop. He's been playing games with the telecommunications systems, but I tracked him today and yesterday. A few hours ago, Shatterstop went mobile. I tracked it through cell phone relays. It's some kind of vehicle, but I don't know anything more than that."

"This guy tagged you for the New York deal?" Lyons asked.

Trask nodded. "I think so. I wanted to get off the island, but being in the Marine Corps, that would have put me AWOL and maybe made DeSilva suspicious enough to send somebody to whack me. So I decided to keep my head low and hope he missed me."

"You got anything on Shatterstop?" Lyons asked.

"Sure. Disk back at my crib. Kind of lean, but it's there."

"And no idea who this guy is?"

"No."

"Or where?"

"Where he's from originally, no. But I'd guess that son of a bitch is somewhere in North Korea right now. I saw the tapes they been playing on TV. I can't prove it, but I don't think we're looking at the real thing there. To have that kind of equipment on hand and get that kind of quality, he'd have to be there." Trask leaned forward and let Blancanales take the cigarette butt from his mouth. "If this guy's a phreak like I think he is, he likes to work the gig and see the results for himself. Proximity has got to be a turn-on, and so is being in control."

Lyons had it figured the same way.

"So where's DeSilva?" Schwarz asked.

"Seoul," Trask answered.

"What's he doing there?" Blancanales asked.

"This guy, he's in town for his first big meeting between the people interested in doing business with him," Trask said.

"Where?"

"Don't have a clue, man. I figure he's using the economic summit as a smoke screen, but he's evidently wired the North Koreans as a support group for him. Things get kind of hot for him in Seoul, he makes the jump back across the DMZ and he's home free for a while. Then he fades back into whatever secret place he's made for himself.''

Lyons made an abrupt left-hand turn and roared north down a side street. The Suburban's driver, closing fast, suddenly realized he'd been made and was in danger of losing his prey.

Skidding, the Suburban fishtailed out of control for a moment. Its bumper kissed a parked Toyota and smashed the little car's whole left side. Horns blared as the Suburban freed itself amid a flurry of metallic shrieks and cut across the oncoming traffic from both directions, smashing through a stalled panel truck and muscling an older Lincoln out of its way.

"Take the wheel," Lyons told Blancanales.

The Politician reached across and seized the steering wheel just as Lyons abandoned it.

"And the brake," Lyons said. "Hard left into the alley and I'm going to drop out. You go halfway down and stop. While they're deploying to come down on you, I'll surround them."

"You're going to surround them?" Blancanales echoed.

"Sure. Me, myself and I." Lyons slipped the Mossberg 500 pump shotgun from under the seat and glanced at Schwarz. "Bursts, pal, and mind where I'm at."

Schwarz gave him a tight nod.

Glancing over his shoulder, Lyons saw the Suburban speeding after them, cutting their lead. The big ex-LAPD cop turned the wheel hard, guiding the rental car into a narrow alley. A handful of pedestrian shoppers scattered.

"Keep going," Lyons said, then opened his door and leaped out. His momentum almost pushed him from his feet, but he kept his balance and brought himself to a sudden stop against the brick wall beside an overflowing garbage container. Shoving stacks of empty cardboard boxes out of his way, he took up a position and heard the shrill of tortured rubber cover the other street sounds coming from beyond the alley's mouth.

The Able Team warrior brought up the Mossberg shotgun as Blancanales braked the rental to a halt, effectively bottling the alley. The reverse lights flared white as the Politician shifted gears, further warning their pursuers they weren't going anywhere.

The Suburban came around the corner shredding rubber. A glimpse over the top of the garbage container showed Lyons at least six heads inside the vehicle. Skidding, it briefly slammed into the side of the alley, but lost only a little speed. Paint flakes and brick dust swirled in its wake. It passed Lyons's position and he could hear the men aboard screaming out warnings about the car ahead of them.

Even as the Suburban's brake lights flared, Lyons launched himself into action. Holding the Mossberg across his chest, he raced for the big truck's rear bumper. Two faces in the rear windows looked surprised. The men spun around in the seats, bringing up assault weapons and leaving no doubt about their intent. Lyons brought up the shotgun and loosed a charge of double-aught buckshot that crashed through the glass, blowing them back.

Without pause, locked onto the slewing back end of the Suburban, Lyons grabbed on to the spare tire mounted on the back hatch, then vaulted up onto the rear bumper. The vehicle swayed under his weight. Still scrambling, he climbed the back of the Suburban, putting a foot on the spare tire and pushing himself to the top.

Ahead of the truck, Schwarz slid out of the rental car with the H&K MP-5 and raked staggered bursts across the front of the vehicle. One of the shooters got out on the passenger side and tried to take up a position.

Lyons pumped the shotgun, bringing it to bear on the guy as he spun, and loosed a blast that took him squarely in the chest and knocked him to the pavement. Still on the move, aware that he was in a potentially vulnerable position, the big Able Team warrior racked the slide and aimed at the roof slightly ahead of him where he figured the middle seats would be. He pulled the trigger, and a series of gaping holes appeared in the sheet metal, followed by men's screams.

A man bolted out of the rear door behind the driver, but a burst from Schwarz stretched out his corpse.

With a snare-drum roll, a line of bullets punched holes through the Suburban's rooftop, searching for Lyons. Moving swiftly, Lyons fired four more times, racking the slide and squeezing off the rounds as quickly as possible. The Suburban lurched into motion as the driver rediscovered reverse. Lyons saved the final two rounds for the driver's side, firing them through one after the other.

A second before the Suburban slammed to a jarring stop against the alley wall, Lyons leaped to the ground, well away from the front bumper. Holding the shotgun in one hand, he drew the Colt Government Model .45 from the paddle holster at his belt with the other.

Schwarz and Blancanales closed in with their weapons at the ready. No one remained alive inside the van. Five out of the seven were of Asian lineage, and the other two were European or American, judging from the tattoos on both of them, which were nautical in nature but not necessarily military.

Lyons yanked the corpse behind the steering wheel out onto the ground with one big fist, then knelt to go through the clothing. "May be a waste of time, but let's search them anyway. Could be a chance that if they were using faked

ID, Barb or the Bear could trace them back and vector in a search pattern for these people.''

Schwarz took out a small camera and quickly snapped off a roll of film.

They were finished in minutes. The only find of significance was a 35 mm picture of a young, lissome woman standing by the railing of what appeared to be a good-sized yacht. The coastline of a large city was spread out behind them, partially blocked by a passing oil tanker. Blancanales had found the picture tucked inside a new wallet beside crisp American dollars. In the picture, the dead man he'd retrieved it from had his arm around the woman.

Blancanales flicked the picture with a thumb as they headed back to the rental, leaving the dead strewed behind them. "Anyone want to bet this is a new love interest?" he asked.

"Could be somebody he was holding the torch for," Schwarz commented as they got into the car.

Lyons guided the car out onto the street, turning sideways for a moment, and shot through the gap in the traffic. Taking a right on red at the next corner, he got his bearings and kept moving.

He kept constant check on all the mirrors, but couldn't spot anyone following them.

Using the cell phone, he called Mott and told the pilot to be ready for instant takeoff when they arrived. When he punched the End button, he knew things were falling into place. Too much information was coming their way, and his cop's sense told him that.

The problem was, he didn't know for sure what kind of deadline the Stony Man teams were up against. Or what kind of shape they were in.

BARBARA PRICE STOOD watching the images on the wall screen at the far end of the room. The view was from a geosynchronous satellite twenty-three thousand miles out in space, and showed Bolan and the Phoenix Force warriors in pursuit of the North Korean convoy carrying the fissionable materials. The last contact with Bolan had been more than eight minutes earlier. She'd logged the time mentally, then kept an eye on the sweep of the second hand.

The convoy resembled a convoluted earthworm twisting and turning along the coastal road. The jeeps Bolan, Phoenix Force and the SEALs occupied were only minutes away from overtaking the trucks.

One of the monitors on Kurtzman's desk showed the placement of the U.S. forces out in Korea Bay. The MiGs had backed off from the helicopters carrying the wounded and the dead back to the aircraft carrier as soon as the American fighters had fired a couple of warning missiles. So far, none of the North Koreans seemed to know there was a threat to the convoy.

The brief phone call from Lyons had brought Price up-to-date on the events in San Juan, and she'd quickly relayed it to McCarter and his group in Seoul. The Phoenix Force leader had suggested that they discreetly interrogate one of the probable attendees to the meeting that was taking place in addition to the economic summit. Price had agreed.

She glanced back at the wall screen and saw that the MiG patrols had widened, almost overlapping the convoy. If the North Korean pilots spotted the Chinook carrying the hovercraft in, the mission controller had no doubts about what would happen. Tension filled her, but she made herself breathe through it.

"Barb."

Price glanced at Kurtzman.

The cybernetics expert tapped his keyboard and considered one of his monitors with grim regard. "Our telecommunications into North Korea is back on-line."

"How?"

Kurtzman shrugged his big shoulders. "Beats me. It wasn't anything new that we've done." He looked at her. "Do you want to switch over to our systems?"

"Can you?"

"Yeah."

"Without losing anything that's going on now?"

"I'm pretty sure."

Price considered the option, turning over the pros and cons. "Do you feel safe about using our systems over there?"

"No," Kurtzman answered at once. "Personally I don't want to use anything we've got open to us over there until I've had a chance to run diagnostics and check the integrity on them."

"Then don't," Price replied. "We've got what we need here. Let's go with this. Check out those systems, and let's see what you come up with."

Kurtzman nodded and turned his full attention to his board.

Price continued to watch the scene unfolding on the wall screen. The confrontation was only minutes away, counting down. Despite Striker's report that what appeared to have been the computer command center at the base had been destroyed, more than anything else she wanted to know what had happened to the team that had manned it. As long as they were loose, she didn't feel the operation was anywhere near safe. Or close to being completed.

"OKAY, MATES," David McCarter said, "let's paint this one by the numbers, shall we?" He sat in the driver's seat of a Nissan compact car, drumming his fingers impatiently on the steering wheel. The downtown streets of Seoul were already heavy with morning traffic. He was parked in an alley beside the Lotte Department Store, Seoul's largest shopping center.

"We're making the turn and coming at you now," Gary Manning said.

McCarter shoved the gearshift into first, kept the clutch in and built up the rpm. The play Phoenix Force had set into motion was tricky, much more than the "discreet" interrogation he'd told Price they'd be attempting. But the Briton felt confident the team could pull it off.

After reviewing the crime connections Kurtzman and his team had turned up from the Kimpo International videotapes, their selection of victims had been simple. Nicky Steranko was heir to the Steranko Family empire in Philadelphia. Leo Turrin had provided other pertinent facts that had influenced McCarter's choice.

At thirty-four, constantly protected by his father, Steranko had never had to scuffle for position or power among the American Mafia. He was egotistical and cruel, and dallied in rough sex to such a degree that Papa Steranko had a whole new crop of problems during the past few months. From what Turrin had turned up, Nicky Steranko had killed three working girls in Philly's red-light district and the bodies had surfaced with evidence linking Nicky to the murders in spite of his father's best efforts to bury them.

A homicide cop had made the connection solid enough through a history of past indiscretions to drop weight on Nicky. On the surface, Papa Steranko was boasting how Nicky had gone to make "the big deal," that everyone had been waiting on. According to Turrin, Nicky was actually hustled out of town one step ahead of a federal arrest warrant.

Once they had the Intel, McCarter had managed the interception they were playing out in short order. A few bribes at the hotel where Steranko was staying had provided a loose itinerary. Brutally simple and direct, it was the kind of plan the Briton favored.

"Has he made you, Gary?" McCarter asked.

"The guy's more interested in the girl his people picked up a few minutes ago."

"What girl?" McCarter asked.

"Looks like an escort service," Manning said. "You had to watch close, but money changed hands, and the guy who'd been standing with the woman said his goodbyes and went back into the motel."

"Papa Steranko's going to be pissed when he finds out," Calvin James said. His voice was light and enthusiastic. "I bet Nicky wasn't allowed any playmates."

"Look alive," Manning said. "The Mercedes just passed the Midopa Department Store."

McCarter knew that put their target through the last intersection before they reached his position. "Calvin, you have the go."

"Affirmative. Ready, set...hit it!"

Pinning the accelerator to the floor, McCarter streaked out of the alley, pulling slightly to the left to avoid a flock of shoppers. He scanned the street scene ahead of him. The dark blue Mercedes with Nicky Steranko and his entourage had only a second's notice before McCarter drove the Nissan into the right front fender.

The collision was loud and violent, pulling the Briton hard against the seat belts even though he'd been prepared for the impact. A heartbeat later, James cut across oncoming traffic and smashed into the Mercedes on the other side, trapping it and snarling passage along the street.

McCarter shoved the door open with difficulty even though he'd left it unlatched to prevent getting trapped inside. The creak of warped metal crunched through the flood of surprised and alarmed voices around them.

Getting out, McCarter drew his Browning Hi-Power from shoulder leather and slid on a pair of yellow-tinted aviator sunglasses. The hard guy on the passenger side of the Mercedes tried to bring up a mini-Uzi and shove it through the broken glass of the window.

Firing from the point, McCarter placed a 9 mm round through the middle of the man's forehead. James was on the other side, yanking the door open and spilling the unconscious driver to the ground.

At the sight of gunplay, the bystanders drew back instantly, taking shelter in doorways and recesses along the buildings.

McCarter grabbed the rear door handle and yanked it open. Nicky Steranko occupied the seat with another man and a nicely dressed young woman who was screaming hysterically, adding bits and pieces of Dutch profanity. Steranko recoiled from McCarter, pressing a hand to a scalp wound he'd somehow acquired.

"Who the hell are you?" Steranko demanded.

McCarter motioned with the Browning. "Out. Now."

"Do you know who my father is?" Steranko demanded. "You're a dead man. Do you hear me? I'll piss on your grave."

Knowing time was already working against them, McCarter reached in and grabbed the man's expensive suit jacket. Using weight and leverage, he yanked Steranko out of the car and manhandled him over the trunk. James had the other man covered and was relieving him of his pistol.

"You're okay, miss," McCarter told the young woman. "You're not part of this."

The fear was still deep inside her, and though she'd stopped screaming, she wasn't moving, either.

"You'd better get on with yourself," McCarter advised, "unless you intend to be part of the investigation later. The police, I'm afraid, won't be in any way considerate."

"You bastard," Steranko snarled, sending bloody spittle flying. "I don't know who you think you are, but—"

Placing a hand behind the mafioso's head, McCarter shoved Steranko's face into the car's trunk. Holding Steranko down, the Briton shoved the Browning's muzzle into the man's mouth. "Another bleeding threat, mate, and I forget I need you alive. You understand?"

Steranko nodded, visibly shaken by the presence of the gun in his mouth. His eyes were magnetically drawn to the cocked hammer.

"All right, let's go." Holding his prisoner's arm behind him in a come-along grip, McCarter hustled him toward Manning's waiting gray Dodge Caravan. He shoved Steranko through the open side door as James entered through the passenger side. Manning got under way immediately, cutting a sharp U-turn that put them in the empty right lane that had been blocked by the car James had abandoned.

Driving fast, the Canadian put distance between themselves and the scene.

"Now," McCarter said coldly, "we're going to talk."

"I'm not telling you a fucking thing," Steranko said belligerently.

"Oh, yes, you are," McCarter said. "Because being able to talk and telling me what I want to know is the only thing that's going to keep you alive." He raised the Browning and pointed it at the man's ample stomach. "I don't have any problems at all about putting you down for the deaths of those women in Philadelphia. In fact, I'm rather against the idea of letting you walk at all. I think you're a bloody pestilence that needed eliminating."

Steranko's bloody lower lip trembled.

"Do you know how long it can take to die from getting gut-shot, mate?" McCarter asked calmly. "I mean, by someone who knows what they're about?"

"What do you want to know?" Steranko asked.

McCarter showed him a cruel smile that would have shamed a shark. "When and where is that meeting you're supposed to attend this afternoon? We'll start with that. Then I'll want to know something of the guest list."

Steranko only had a little difficulty talking, but once he started, it all came out.

CHAPTER EIGHTEEN

Korea Bay Coastline, North Korea

"Stony One, this is Stony Base."

"Go, Base," Mack Bolan said into the headset's mouth-piece. "One reads you." He downshifted the jeep, lugging into the incline, feeling gravity heavy on him now.

"When you crest the hill you're presently on," Price said, "you should have a visual on your target. Chances are they'll see you, too."

"Affirmative, Base. The Chinook?"

"With you. A team's ready to hit the water with the hovercraft."

"When we engage the convoy," Bolan said, "have them do that."

Price dropped out of the loop.

Gunning the engine, Bolan followed the crooked trail to the top of the hill. Vegetation was sparse on top, and he knew they wouldn't have adequate cover. "Phoenix Five, did you copy?"

"That's affirmative, Stony One. Let's lock and load."

With no chance at cover, the Executioner opted for surprise. Keeping down the hammer, he guided the jeep over the hill. Sunlight lit up the expanse of ocean to his left, less than a mile away. The convoy consisted of four vehicles, a jeep followed by a two-and-a-half-ton truck and two more jeeps. They were less than a quarter mile away, down in the bottom of a V-shaped valley.

"Commander," Bolan called to Conrad as the jeep started slithering along the downgrade.

"Sir," the SEAL leader responded.

"Are you familiar with the BG-15?" Through the haze of dust left by the North Korean military vehicles, Bolan spotted the two rearmost jeeps dropping back on an interception course. He knew they'd be calling in for aerial support at the same time. The last deadly numbers were trickling away on the play.

"Russian grenade launcher," Conrad answered.

"Can you hit anything with it?"

"From a moving vehicle?" Conrad grinned. "Hell, if it's going to be a sporting event, how about we get something down on it?"

Bolan passed back the AK-47, then the bandolier of rockets. "You take out that forward jeep before it can reach the top of the hill, lunch is on me."

"I'm on it." Conrad fed a rocket into the tube and tried to manage a kneeling position on the jeep's back deck.

Machine-gun fire rattled along the trail, marching in ragged and dusty footsteps toward Bolan's jeep. The warrior tagged the headset's transmit button. "Phoenix Three."

"Go."

"You're our cover. I'm going left. You go right."

"You got it."

Bolan scanned the terrain as the North Korean machine gunners tried to find the range. The lead jeep and the truck didn't slow. "Commander."

"Sir."

"I'm going to find you a level spot. You get the one shot."

"Tell me when."

Bolan nodded. Halfway down the valley wall, he tapped the brake and held the wheel steady. The terrain was as even as it was going to get. "Fire!"

The rocket whooshed overhead, spreading out a fan of heat in its wake. "It's away!" Conrad yelled.

Bolan shifted gears and accelerated, driving into a cloud of dust that he could use as camouflage for a few precious seconds. He heard the yammer of the big .50-caliber in Hawkins's vehicle and knew Encizo was at work.

The BG-15's HE round caught the jeep in dead center, delivering a solid punch of instant carnage. Bodies were blown from the vehicle, and it jumped like a scalded cat, losing purchase on the incline. Still, momentum managed to shove it a few feet farther before gravity reclaimed it. Spinning sideways, the flaming jeep suddenly went end over end, crashing back down on top of the truck. Hammered by the jeep's weight, the big truck shivered, struggled for a moment to push the extra tonnage, then gave up the fight.

"Great shot," Bolan told Conrad.

"It wasn't all skill," the SEAL team leader confided.

"Enough of it was," the warrior replied. "If the skill wasn't there, the breaks wouldn't come." He shifted, again gaining speed. He heard the hot brass hitting the rear deck behind him as one of the SEALs aired out his own machine gun.

A ragged line of bullet holes appeared in the side of the jeep ahead of them. Some of the rounds had to have been tracers, because when the jerrican mounted on the rear was hit, it exploded in flames, bathing the jeep crew in fire.

Bolan worked the gearshift and the steering wheel and blew by the sudden inferno.

Encizo's marksmanship accounted for the last jeep, cutting its wheels out from under it and sending it skidding out of control. Before the crew could recover from the sudden impact against a tall tree, the .50-caliber machine gun roared out a death song, knocking the bodies from the jeep.

Men were already starting to fan out around the stalled truck, taking up holding positions behind rocks and clumps of brush. Return fire picked up intensity, slamming into the jeep.

A trio of rounds struck Bolan at different points across his chest, glancing off the body armor. "We're leaving the jeep," he told Conrad.

The SEAL leader nodded and loosed a couple rounds from the AK-47 that took down a North Korean soldier sprinting to another position.

Applying the brake, Bolan swerved sharply and brought the jeep to a halt behind a copse of trees off the trail. He leaped from the rocking vehicle as Grimaldi and the SEALs deployed behind him. Drawing the Stechkin, he raced forward, moving the line of engagement to the enemy. A quick burst rattled a soldier from the trees and dropped his body less than ten feet away.

Bolan took cover behind the tree and grabbed the soldier's corpse. As bullets chewed bark around him, he hauled the body toward him and hit the transmit button on the headset. "Stony Base, this is Stony One."

"Go, One."

"Do you have a fix on us?"

"Affirmative, One. The hovercraft has been deployed and is on its way to you."

Glancing to the west, Bolan saw the finger lake that spilled in from the coast, glinting between the trees and accumulated water foliage. "There's a waterway most of the distance."

"Yes," Price said. "Base has confirmed it and advised Skate Leader."

Bolan stripped two grenades from the dead man, then flipped them toward the ragged line of North Korean troops. The explosions killed at least five more men and wounded others.

Around him, following the spearhead he'd launched, Grimaldi and the SEALs spread out and fired at will. He tapped the headset. "Phoenix Three."

"Go, Stony One."

"You've got the camera, and we're going to need shots of this for proof that the North Koreans had the fissionables."

"I've already got some footage on tape. We get a look inside that deuce-and-a-half, we'll have it locked."

Bolan picked up the soldier's rifle. Expecting to find an AK-47, he was pleasantly surprised when he discovered the rifle was a Dragunov SVD sniper rifle. When he checked, the magazine had only two rounds expended from its box of ten. The soldier's pockets yielded three more magazines.

"Sarge!" Grimaldi called out in warning.

Bolan had already heard the footsteps approaching his position. He wheeled around the tree with the Stechkin in his fist and unleashed a long burst at the two soldiers less than twenty feet away. The 9 mm rounds caught them and knocked them back.

Sheathing the Stechkin, the Executioner shouldered the Dragunov and stepped into position beside the tree. Both eyes open as he breathed out a half breath, he marked his targets mentally, then peered through the PSO-1×4 scope. Laying the crosshairs on the head of his first target, he took up trigger slack, then squeezed.

The heavy 7.62 mm round snapped back the soldier's head and sent his corpse sprawling. Rolling with the recoil, moving on to his next target, the Executioner laid down a withering barrage of single-shot destruction. His second shot cored through the next man's chest, picking him off from behind a tree, while the third knocked him down. Shots four and five hit two more gunners, but he was sure of the kill only on one. Six crashed through the temple of a soldier who'd fired a grenade launcher at the SEALs, sending Conrad and one of his people to ground as dirt and rock spewed over them. The final round finished off the man the warrior had figured he'd only injured earlier.

Dropping the empty magazine, Bolan shoved another home. He paced his shots, but only managed to secure three more casualty hits with the next ten rounds. The pace of the firing was important even if it wasn't telling, part of the warrior's psychological arsenal.

When the LCAC Hovercraft sped into the valley over the surface of the finger lake, its blowers sounding like a pack of sulfur-breathing beasts from hell, the North Korean soldiers broke ranks and stood their ground uncertainly. The hovercraft didn't hesitate as it crossed from the water onto land. Four sailors manned it, two of them standing beside the 40 mm deck-mounted machine cannon.

Bolan fed the Dragunov a fresh magazine, then tapped the headset. "Skate Leader, this is Stony One."

"Go, Stony One, you have Skate Leader."

"I've got some targeting coordinates for you."

"Let's have them. Things look a bit unsettled down there for us to start in on the fly." The hovercraft came to a smooth, even stop in spite of the broken terrain visible under the skirting.

Bolan called out the coordinates with a marksman's eye and stood ready to correct if he needed to.

The 40 mm machine cannon drummed death with a blistering series of throaty coughs. The high-explosive and antipersonnel rounds dropped into the ranks of the North Korean soldiers with an accuracy that was deadly and demoralizing. In seconds the North Koreans gave up trying to defend their prize and fled.

"Move in," Bolan called out to the Phoenix Force warriors and the hovercraft crew. The SEALs followed their lead. He shoved a new magazine into the Stechkin and slung the Dragunov as he double-timed it to the wrecked truck.

At the truck, he and Hawkins held the others back, then went forward to make sure the cargo hadn't been booby-trapped. If the North Korean commanding officer had been thinking, an international incident could still be arranged that would further incriminate the United States. Detonation of the fissionable materials, if possible, could be blamed on the invading American forces.

A quick survey turned up nothing. The crates were a jumbled mess in the back of the truck. Broken boards showed white, but the shielded containers holding the radioactive materials appeared to be intact. One of the hovercraft crew handed in a Radiac Set and Hawkins moved the wand around, scanning the dials.

"Clean," he announced, passing the set back to the sailor.

"Rafe?" Bolan asked, turning to look for the Cuban.

"Got it," Encizo said. He held the minicamcorder from his pack on his shoulder, playing it over the truck's contents. "I'll get some more footage as we get the crates and cargo out."

Bolan grabbed the nearest one with Hawkins's help, and they passed it out to the waiting SEALs and sailors. The Chinese writing on two sides was clearly visible, painted on in a virulent crimson. The canisters were heavy and awkward, but in less than two minutes, they'd cleared the truck.

Out in the morning sun again, Bolan found himself drenched with perspiration, aching deep in the large muscles of his body where the lactic acid build-up had reached painful concentrations. His body needed downtime, but he knew the mission wasn't over yet.

The headset buzzed for his attention. "Stony One, this is Stony Base."

"Go, Base," Bolan said, helping Hawkins move one of the canisters to the waiting hovercraft.

"You've been picked up. We scan two MiGs racing toward your position. ETA is a minute and a half."

"Affirmative," Bolan replied. He glanced up at Skate Leader.

"I copy," the hovercraft captain replied, then turned to his crew and urged them onto the hovercraft.

Ordering a brigade line set up with the Phoenix Force commandos and the SEALs, Bolan and Hawkins handed up the canisters. Some of the team put them on the hovercraft's deck while others belayed them with cargo netting that had already been secured on one side.

Twin contrails appeared in the sky, coming at a dead run from the south.

"Stony One," Price called.

"I see them," Bolan said as he and Hawkins scrambled aboard. The deck crew set up on the 40 mm machine cannon while the pilot powered up the hovercraft and sent it skidding back out into Korea Bay.

"You know how to use one of these?" the hovercraft skipper asked.

Bolan glanced at the Stinger missile launcher with the warhead already in place. The power cords were wired into the hovercraft's power supply. "Oh, yeah."

"The admiral mentioned there might be some problems with aerial reinforcements. I figured we might as well have a couple equalizers on hand if it came to it." He lifted the second Stinger from a metal equipment box welded to the hovercraft's deck.

"Not exactly the typical kind of stores you'd find on-board an aircraft carrier," Hawkins commented.

"Maybe you're not supposed to, but you'd be surprised at what's in our inventory these days."

Bolan settled the Stinger over his shoulder and readied the launcher. He shrugged out of the Dragunov and managed a somewhat steady stance as the hovercraft deck vibrated beneath him.

The MiGs thundered through the air, then the on-board cannon started blowing holes along the hillsides and valley. Their initial run scattered rock, earth and water over the crew and passengers of the hovercraft. The 40 mm machine cannon from the hovercraft punched holes in the morning sky but couldn't get close enough to their targets.

Bolan doubted they'd survive another pass.

"I'm locked on," the hovercraft skipper shouted over the roar of the huge fans.

"Fire away," Bolan ordered.

With an explosive whoosh, the Stinger missile took flight. Five feet long and packed with a smooth-case fragmentation warhead, the deadly arrow screamed into the sky, tracking its prey by homing in on the jet's exhaust plume. Evidently the North Korean pilot never knew death was coming for him, because he never took evasive action. The missile caught up with him while he was making the wide turn that would bring him back around. The explosion ripped the jet from stern to nose, leaving only a tangled mass of fiery debris to rain over the countryside.

The Executioner immediately fired his second missile.

The other jet was on the approach now, either ignoring what had happened to his partner or not aware of it. Cannon fire hammered into the earth, leaving craters behind as it tracked toward the hovercraft.

The Stinger flew straight for the MiG. Bolan and the others took cover on the hovercraft as the cannon fire closed to within yards. Then the missile struck the jet and blew it out of the air.

Bolan handed the launcher back to the hovercraft skipper. "We're done. Let's get out of here."

A few twists and turns along the waterway, and they were out to sea. Black smoke coiled into the air from the wrecks of the North Korean land transport and downed jets.

Bolan stood at the railing and scanned the sky. The salt air and the spray felt good, though he was nowhere near relaxed.

"I never did get your name."

The Executioner turned and saw Conrad standing behind him. "You weren't supposed to."

Conrad grinned. "Yeah, I kind of got that impression along the way. Still, I'd like to shake your hand and thank you for getting my team back home."

Bolan took his hand. "You're not home yet, sailor, but you will be."

"Yes, sir. That's good enough for me."

The headset crackled, and Bolan adjusted the pencil-thin mouthpiece. "Go, Stony Base. You have Stony One."

"We've got a tentative ID on the computer team that set the North Koreans up on this play," Price said. "When you get aboard the *Thomas Paine*, we're going to debrief you."

"Where is he?" Bolan asked.

"We're still working on that. We believe we know

where he's headed. Once you get aboard the carrier, we'll get you the whole story. As much of it as we know."

Bolan dropped out of the loop and reviewed what he knew of the mission, wondering what dangers the escaped computer team posed.

"What's up?" Grimaldi asked, coming up beside him with the Phoenix Force.

"I'm skulling it out," Bolan said, "and it doesn't look good."

"We heard the transmission from Barb," Encizo said. "She didn't sound happy."

Bolan looked at the SEAL team resting against the opposite side of the hovercraft. Rations were being passed out, and they ate and drank ravenously. "The computer team wasn't at the site when we rescued the SEALs," the hellfire warrior said. "They knew we were coming."

"Stands to reason," Hawkins agreed.

"And from the message Hal and the President received at the White House, it was these people who stole the fissionable materials from the Chinese," Bolan said. "But I have to ask myself why."

"The money," Grimaldi said.

"Always an option," Bolan replied. "Was it enough to risk blowing their cover like they did? Evidently they've had a solid operation in place for some time. Why not negotiate the delivery through a third party, never become involved at all?"

"The only answer is that they wanted something for themselves," Encizo replied.

Bolan nodded in agreement. It was the way he read it, too, but he didn't know what the answer was. Any way it went, he knew there was a hell of a butcher's bill waiting somewhere, and he was sure the unknown player in international politics was standing by to collect. The Executioner intended to see that debt settled.

CHAPTER NINETEEN

Aboard the Shadow Scythe

Dixon Lynch sat in the small office that he'd ordered built on board the submarine. He didn't really like it. The room was small instead of spacious, orderly instead of ornate. He gazed at the monitor ahead of him as the satellite relayed pictures of the hovercraft streaming out to sea in Korea Bay under the protection of American fighter jets.

Kalico lounged in the red leather chair in front of the desk.

"I see the North Korean military has lost their little toys," the woman said.

Lynch leaned back in the chair, allowing himself to relax only slightly. He'd always maintained that edge of readiness that he felt put him one step ahead of any competition that might have stood against him. The American covert force was no different. "The Americans think they've won," he said. "The North Koreans feel they've lost. As far as any of them are concerned, it's game over."

"Are you so sure?"

He looked at the woman, and a slow grin spread across his face. "Yes."

"They know about the upcoming meeting in Seoul," Kalico stated.

"What makes you say that?"

"Nicky Steranko was abducted only minutes ago."

"By whom?"

The woman shrugged. "Lambert wasn't sure, but Steranko didn't turn up on any Seoul police reports. He's thinking they could be part of this covert force you've been chasing. There were only three of them, and they moved very fast and were very sure of themselves."

Lambert was the go-between for the meeting in Seoul.

"Steranko is a bottom feeder," Lynch said. "If I'd felt certain his father would have gone for the arrangement I've invested in without him here, Nicky wouldn't have been present at all.

"There was trouble in Philadelphia. Maybe it just caught up with him."

"And maybe it didn't."

Lynch felt the slow burn of anger. He didn't like to be questioned. "So what do you suggest?"

"We lay low," Kalico said. "Wait and see what happens."

"No."

"You're doing very nicely for yourself, love, without all this added grief," Kalico argued.

Lynch chuckled, but it was dry and without mirth. "Of all people, you should understand me most."

"I do," Kalico said. "That's why I'm trying to make you see what's going on. These people are bloody damn good at what they do, Dixon, and they're breathing down your neck at this very moment. But you don't seem to be aware that they're even there."

"Wrong," Lynch argued. "I've got them exactly where I want them. You're forgetting Shatterstop."

"You're forgetting the hole Eddie Trask has put in your systems. You don't know what has leaked out."

Lynch shook his head. "These people can't touch me. One move on their part, and I blow up that little hidden base of theirs." He lifted a hand and closed it into a fist. "We have them now. We've got a virus inside their programming that will survive whether they do or not, and they exist only at this moment because I haven't chosen to destroy them already."

"Then destroy them," Kalico said, "and schedule this meeting at some other time. These people will still want to deal a few months from now."

Lynch placed his elbows on the arms of the chair and laced his fingers together in front of his face. "No."

"Why?"

"Not until Razor has found out how much access we have to their systems."

"Eighty percent or a hundred," Kalico asked, "is it really going to matter?"

"It does to me," Lynch answered. "I don't like settling for anything but the best. If I quit before I've gone the distance, I don't get a full measure of what I can do. I'll break them and come out on top. Count on it."

USS Thomas Paine

MACK BOLAN HELD a cup of coffee cupped in his palms and focused on the computer screen that had been set up in the aircraft carrier's combat-information center. The *Thomas Paine* was holding its present position and keeping an eye on developments along the North Korean coastline. So far, there'd been no attempts at retaliation.

The mood in the CIC was somber, and the big warrior could feel it. The SEALS were safely back among their own, and the fissionable materials were out of enemy hands, but unfinished business hung on the horizon.

"His name is Dixon Lynch," Barbara Price said. "We turned him from leads we've picked up that pointed to Singapore." On the screen, the mission controller stood beside Hal Brognola and Kurtzman in the computer room. "Hal spotted a tattoo on one of the men who attacked Mack near Seoul, and it traced back to a ship registered in Singapore that's owned by a holding company Lynch has a major investment in. And Able turned up a photograph in San Juan that we matched to Singapore. It was shot from a yacht. Aaron was able to get the yacht's name from a reflection in the water. She was the *Golden Fleece*, and she's owned by Dixon Lynch."

"The property in the Catskills that Able Team invaded also led back to a holding company in Singapore that belongs to Lynch," Kurtzman said. "Eventually. Make no mistake, this guy is good at what he does."

The computer monitor blinked, then a color still of a black man in an expensive suit addressing a group of businessmen filled the screen.

"This is Lynch?" David McCarter asked. Like Able, he was tied into the transmission via satellite. While Phoenix Force had holed up in Seoul, Able Team was in the air, winging toward Virginia.

"Yeah," Brognola said. "There's not many pictures of the guy. He's definitely reclusive."

"He was at the base camp in Nampo," Grimaldi said.

Bolan studied the face, knowing it belonged to the man who'd boarded the helicopter before the Stony Man team had gone in after the SEALs.

Grimaldi, Hawkins and Encizo sat around the oblong table in the CIC and ate from the sandwich tray sent up by the galley. Showers and fresh clothing were still in the future.

"Dixon Lynch," Barbara Price said, "is a self-made man."

A new picture took shape on the computer monitor, showing a multistory downtown building made up of light gray stone and black glass and detailed in chrome. As the monitor zoomed in for a closer look, Bolan saw the name SmarTech emblazoned in orange across the second-story face where it could clearly be seen from the street.

"This is his primary headquarters," Price went on. "No one in the intelligence community has much on him. Vague references, footnotes and a few questions."

"He hasn't been a big player in international crime?" Bolan asked.

"On the surface," Price said, "it doesn't seem so. After looking at his portfolio, what we could find of it, I'd say he's been more than active, but he's really been careful about it."

"Then why this operation in North Korea?" Grimaldi asked. "Guy had to have known he was going to be blown. Hell, he didn't bother trying to disguise himself when he questioned me."

"Because he didn't think he had anything to worry about from you," Gary Manning said.

"He knew I wasn't regular Army," the pilot stated. "He kept asking me about the group I was with. He knew there was a covert organization in the works."

Bolan looked at the screen. "He knows about Stony Man Farm. Maybe not the name or the location, but he knows about it. How closely was he tied with the intelligence community?"

"Lynch is a prime developer in communications programming," Price said. "For the past five years, his company has pioneered work in the field that's getting adopted around the world. And he's developed systems for a number of businesses that were actually fronts for espionage agencies.''

''Gives him access to a number of agencies if he's careful about putting his own programs into the software,'' Blancanales declared. ''What about it, Aaron? Can the guy have gotten away with it?''

''Sure,'' Kurtzman responded. ''No matter how many antivirus programs are developed, there's always a hacker out there working on something with a new spin.''

''The Stony Man systems are on-line with a number of agencies without anyone being aware of it, right?''

''Yeah.''

Carl Lyons broke into the conversation. ''Was Lynch operating in the black?''

''Yes,'' Price answered. ''His company has been showing growth every quarter for the past nine years.''

''Then he didn't need the money the North Koreans were paying him,'' Lyons said.

''The fissionable materials and charade pulled on the U.S. government had to have brought in a huge chunk of money,'' Calvin James stated. ''Cash can't be overlooked.''

''What's this guy worth?'' Schwarz asked.

A parade of stock quotes, business-magazine articles and legal papers flowed across the screen.

''Conservatively,'' Price replied, ''our guess is somewhere in the neighborhood of two billion dollars. Of course, a lot of that is tied up in properties and investments.''

''Any cash-flow problems that you've been able to discover?'' Hawkins asked.

''No.''

''His getting involved with the North Koreans doesn't make any bloody sense, then,'' McCarter said.

Bolan got up from the table and refilled his coffee cup.

He remained standing and looked at the computer monitor. "Pol?"

"Yeah?" Blancanales said.

"Give me a surface judgment of this guy."

"Probably do better if I had a chance to study him more."

"Yeah, but you've seen the building, and you've seen the business reports. Lynch doesn't have any partners."

"Nobody that can unseat his control," Blancanales said. "I noticed that. And that damn building is strictly for show. If he's doing business worldwide, and his systems are good enough to constantly bring in profit after profit during a time when the computer industry is constantly changing, he didn't need that building."

"Could have been a tax write-off," Hawkins said.

"No," Blancanales said more confidently. "Lynch does things for effect. He's big on ego. The incident with the *Dragon's Gate* and the SEALs shows that. Since the fissionables weren't aboard the trawler, it would have been easy to simply let the SEALs go away empty-handed. Instead, he filmed it, and if Aaron is right, enhanced the images at considerable cost to falsify what really took place. He's a control freak."

"But he's deep into money," Bolan stated.

"Yeah."

"What about the leads we turned up in San Juan?" Lyons asked. "Trask definitely pointed the finger at someone who was trying to network the cartels, Yakuza, Triads and the Mafia from America, Sicily and Russia. That sounds like our boy, Lynch."

"But why would those people let him have a piece of the pie?" McCarter asked. "He'd have to bring something to the table."

In Bolan's mind, some of the possible connections began

to surface. "Lynch could offer information that can't be gotten anywhere else."

"You're thinking Lynch has been siphoning off information through the systems he's sold," Blancanales said. "Worked just right, maybe he could clean up with those people."

"And that would make the North Korean gambit just a trial run," Price said. "A showcase for the people he's assembled in Seoul."

"I think it was more than that," Bolan said. "The events in North Korea weren't just a trial run. He was after something."

"What?" Brognola asked.

"Us," Bolan stated.

"Damn," Kurtzman swore.

"He knew about you and Phoenix," Price said. "I could understand that, because security's hard to keep intact when you're operating on the fly and through other agencies. But if he was tapped into our network the whole time..." She left the rest unsaid.

"The Catskills site was an acceptable loss, too," Kurtzman said. "The people Able turned up there didn't know anything that could hurt Lynch. Hell, they didn't even know who they were really working for. And I tried to capture the video being transmitted into the White House."

"Bait," Bolan said. "While you were reaching for him, he could have been reaching for you."

"Our communications were taken off-line when you people penetrated the Nampo site," Price said. Her voice let everyone know she didn't like the way things were coming together. "If Katz hadn't been able to buy us time with the Chinese Intelligence systems, we wouldn't have been able to coordinate the rescue effort."

"It scans," Bolan said. "Lynch didn't take on the North

Korean job merely out of ego or even to show these people he's trying to do business with what he can do. Given that he knew about Stony Man Farm, he escalated the pot regarding the fissionable materials and the captured SEALs to the point that he knew we'd have to buy in. Think about it—Stony Man Farm's computers are tied in covertly to most of the systems in the world."

"There's no one that has more access than we do," Kurtzman stated.

"Our intelligence network is a double-edged sword," Price said. "It's our country's greatest asset, but if it was used against us, there's no telling how much devastation could be wreaked before we had a chance to stop it. Even revealing our insertion into other intelligence agencies could severely hamper international relations for a long time."

"Even though those countries spy on us," Lyons growled.

"It's not a matter of who does it," Brognola argued. "It just matters who gets caught at it." He paused. "Have we got a handle on this guy?"

"So far," the mission controller said, "we have the address McCarter and his team turned up. And we're tracking something called Shatterstop through Virginia. It appears to be headed for Roanoke."

Kurtzman was busy at the computer keyboard. "I have some other bad news. Our negotiated time through the Chinese interfaces is about up. Ten more minutes, and we have to clear this frequency. It'll mean either a communications blackout from the Farm, or chancing the computer systems here."

"The risk is too high," Brognola growled. "If Lynch and his people have gotten to us, they're going to know every move the Stony Man teams make." He popped a couple antacid tablets into his mouth and chewed. "We'll be off-line until we can scare up something else."

"I agree," Bolan said. "But a point to keep in mind is that Lynch might not need the Farm intact if he's already into the cybernetics systems."

"Shatterstop?" Schwarz asked.

"That's what I'm thinking," the warrior said. "Could be a fitting name."

CHAPTER TWENTY

The suite of rooms Lynch had rented for the meeting was at the top of the Koreana Hotel. The establishment had been recommended to him by a number of his company's Japanese customers, and a visit there the week before had assured him it was more than satisfactory.

He waited in an opulent office he'd arranged at the other end of the floor, staring out over the Seoul skyline until he was fashionably late. Across the street was Toksukung Palace. Only the palace's main gate and audience hall still stood. From his readings, Lynch knew the king's courtiers and ministers had once waited in ranks to greet the king, offer advice and ask the royal favor in the attendant gate and flagstone courtyard.

It suited Lynch's sense of style to be so close to a place of power while he was assembling his own empire. He ran a hand down the expensive lines of his Italian-made suit and briefly considered his image in the window. There'd never been a time when he felt more ready to take on business negotiations.

The door behind him opened.

He turned and found Kalico standing there, dressed in a short business skirt and jacket that still came off as sexy. ''The mob grows restless, love,'' she said. ''They're anxious to see the master of ceremonies. Some of them are threatening to leave.''

''But none of them have?'' Lynch asked.

''No.''

''And none of them are threatening too loudly?''

''No.''

''Then it sounds like the perfect time to make my entrance.'' Lynch glanced briefly at the security monitors built into the desktop. The pictures were all black-and-white, but the cameras were spread about enough to give good cross sections of the suite. More than seventy people were inside the room, divided into their individual groups.

Lynch pressed a button, and the monitors recessed again into the desktop, hardly leaving a seam at all. He hadn't been surprised that the hotel management had such devices available. For the right price.

''How do I look?'' he asked his companion.

''Dynamic,'' she replied. ''The epitome of a rogue male.''

''The hell with that.'' Lynch shot his cuffs as he headed for the door. ''Do I look like a guy who can deliver?''

''Yes.''

''Good. You walk into a room with the deal in your pocket, not like it's laying on the table.'' Lynch stepped through the door and saw Eric Hardcastle waiting for him with five of his handpicked mercs. All of them were dressed for a social event. Lynch had picked up the tab for the suits, getting the very best money could buy, also ensuring that the suits could hide the weapons Hardcastle and his team would be carrying. ''Ready?''

Hardcastle nodded.

''Then let's do it.'' Lynch walked toward the suite.

Two of the mercs walked slightly ahead of him, with Hardcastle and another man flanking him, and two men brought up the rear. More of the mercs had already joined the crowd waiting in the suite, blending with the crowd and ready to step in if it became necessary. Still more were secreted away in other rooms on the floor.

Lynch didn't hesitate at the double doors leading into the suite. He pushed them open and walked across the red carpet leading to center stage.

Every head in the room turned to look at him. He recognized most of them only from research he'd done getting ready for the deal, and Kalico was there to help him remember anyone he wasn't sure about.

Round tables were scattered around the large space, with plenty of room between them. Seating charts had been made, and Lynch's people were seeing to the catering. Potential enemies and competitors had been kept separate, and notice had been given that personal differences were to be kept shelved during the meeting. Three long buffet tables made a loose triangle that further divided some of the guests. The center of the room had been left open, giving Lynch the stage area that he wanted.

"Ladies and gentlemen," he said in English, knowing that all of the guests spoke that language or had translators present, "forgive me for being late, but there were some last-minute details to attend. As you've seen from the morning news, I've had rather a full schedule."

Three men rolled a podium with a small attached dais into the center of the room. They locked the wheels down, and Lynch stepped onto it. He tapped the wireless microphones and heard the deep thumping echo back to him from the speaker system around the room. Huge monitors mounted in the upper corners of the room came on, filling with his image. The effect, he felt, was everything he'd wanted it to be.

"The North Koreans lost the materials you'd procured for them."

Lynch looked for the speaker and found her. Her name was Lyao Sin Fong, and she was a major mover in flesh and opium in Hong Kong these days. Sleek and deadly in a pale blue, formfitting dress, she idly smoked her cigarette in a long-stemmed holder, her black hair cut off at the shoulder.

"Yes, they did," Lynch answered. "I was paid to deliver, and it was done. After that, they were on their own. Evidently they weren't prepared for success."

"Or perhaps they were, in the end, betrayed." Her voice was flat and unaccusing but quietly curious.

"No."

"Kirosawa was attacked in his apartment," Oleg Dresdov said. He was one of the prime forces behind the straw banks that had cropped up in Russia after the fall of communism, and had bilked speculators on both sides of what had been the Iron Curtain to make his fortune. Reports indicated that he was now worth millions of dollars, and had any number of legitimate investors waiting to find him and either take him to court or have him assassinated. "And no one has seen Nicky Steranko since this morning. We've heard reports that he was kidnapped by police agents."

Lynch made his tone inflexible. "At the outset, I told you there was considerable risk in joining me here. Just as I told you there was considerable profit for those who did."

"Maybe we should get to the profit part," Ethan Goldstein said. Tall and built like a hungry wolf, the Israeli cocaine trafficker had begun by working with the Colombians, but had lately started branching out, joining up with the Russians in Eastern Europe.

"Sure." Lynch looked through the audience and found Kirosawa sitting with a group of Asian crime lords. "Mr.

Kirosawa, do you know who invaded your rooms last night?"

"No," the Yakuza chieftain replied. His face looked pale and bruised. A white bandage covered his temple.

"Were they Seoul policemen?"

"No."

"American agents?"

"One, perhaps."

"The other?"

"British, I think."

"You'd never seen either of them?"

"No."

"Never had business with them?"

"No."

"But they definitely knew you, right?"

Kirosawa nodded.

Lynch addressed the whole audience. "You've all heard about the American covert team who rescued the SEALs the North Koreans had captured. Let me show you them in action." He waved at the monitors on the walls.

A montage of shots, specially engineered by Kalico, filled the screens. All of them centered around the men who'd invaded the Nampo site. The violence was bloody and swift, somehow more threatening without the sound. Some of the footage was in infrared, and the figures moved like vicious green ghosts across the screens. When it ended, the audience was quiet.

Lynch softened his voice deliberately, working to get the attention of every man and woman present. "There is a force out there," he said, "that's above the DEA, the Coast Guard, any police department you could name, above Interpol and above the CIA. They have military backing, training in a dozen or more different arts of killing, and information on every one of you. At any time, one of you could become their target. Make no mistake, these people have declared war on crime, on your businesses. They'll take you down if they're pointed your way, and you'll never see a day in court."

The conversations were out of control for a moment. More than a few of the people stood up and paced angrily.

"Mr. Lynch," Carmine Vecchione of the Naples Camorra shouted above the others, "we are not children to be frightened away by your stories. Or your films." He was a leonine figure, well into his forties, with his dark hair swept back. "We've all seen the fantasies you can work with your computer graphics."

"Yes, Mr. Vecchione, you have." Lynch smiled disarmingly. "However, what I'm telling you is the truth."

"And you can somehow protect us from these people?" Lyao Sin Fong demanded. "For a price? Have you gotten us here to bribe us or blackmail us into paying you to protect us from some imaginary agency?"

"It's not imaginary," Lynch countered. "Many of you have already been talking among yourselves about these people. You've had operations that have touched on some of their work." He searched the audience. "Ramon DeSilva."

The cartel leader looked up.

"Maybe you'd like to tell this group about what happened to your predecessor, Luis Costanza, a few years ago."

"He was assassinated," DeSilva answered. The man didn't bat an eye.

"By whom?"

"There was a lot of talk about an American military team that was sent after Costanza."

"Was there any truth to these stories?"

"Yes. The cartels had people who told us Benito Franco,

before he was killed, was deeply involved with a group of American soldiers.''

"Right.'' Lynch looked around the room, listening to the quiet settle down around him as he recaptured their attention. "At that time, Costanza was building a supercartel, one capable of taking on the American police forces. Some cartel leaders joined him, others he blackmailed or killed.''

"It is true.''

Lynch knew he'd regained control. He felt the deal closing around him, the magic of the moment. He abandoned the podium, walking in DeSilva's direction, making them listen to hear him. "Costanza was a threat that couldn't be reached through normal, legal means. He was marked for death by the covert agency I'm telling you about.''

"If you're not offering protection from the people,'' Goldstein said, "what are you offering?''

Lynch held his hands out at shoulder width, a move further designed to pull their attention squarely on him. "These people have an information network beyond anything you've ever seen. I've studied it. In order to be effective, in order to remain a secret, they've managed to tie themselves into every major law-enforcement agency and espionage department in the world.''

"Who are these people?'' Kirosawa demanded.

Lynch shook his head. "I don't know their names.''

"Then how do you propose to kill them?''

"Killing them is only one option that can be acted on,'' Lynch said. "That's not even a profitable one. If you kill these people, more will simply take their places. All you can do that way is slow them for a while.''

"Then what do you propose?'' Goldstein asked.

"What if your organizations could be tied into an international source of information detailing what most of the police agencies in the world are doing while you're moving your product around? What if you could ferret out under-cover officers within your ranks? What if you could take a look at the evidence a prosecuting body had against your operation and have your lawyers prepare a better defense? What if you could research officials who could be bribed or blackmailed?''

"What are you talking about?" Kirosawa asked.

"Their computer systems," Lynch replied. "I've pene-trated them. Everything they know, I know. Everything they can access, I can access." He paused. "And for a price, so can you."

"Can you prove this?" Lyao Sin Fong asked.

"Sure," Lynch replied. He waved to the technicians in the corner. "I'd be glad to."

"STONY ONE TO STONY BASE," Mack Bolan transmitted. "We're in position and waiting for the green." He stood in the cargo area of a Bell Model 412SP helicopter. Jack Grimaldi sat in the pilot's seat, handling the yoke with au-thority as he flew the craft toward the Koreana Hotel.

"You've got your green, Stony One," Hal Brognola re-plied. "The Man wants Lynch and his operation taken out ASAP. Base will be standing by."

"Affirmative." Bolan dropped out of the loop and glanced at Grimaldi. "Take her in, Jack."

The pilot gave him a thumbs-up and started to lose al-titude. The streets and shopping areas of downtown Seoul grew closer, the taller buildings a threat to the helicopter. Still, Grimaldi navigated between them easily.

"Pop the door, David," Bolan said.

The Phoenix Force leader nodded and slid the cargo door open. Wind rushed in, filled with the smells and noxious fumes of the city. Despite the hard afternoon sun, shadows lingered at the foundations of the tall buildings.

Clad in the combat blacksuit, Mack Bolan was a dreadnought of carnage waiting to be unleashed. He carried the big .44 Magnum Desert Eagle on his hip, and the 9 mm Beretta 93-R rode in shoulder leather. His body armor was laden with extra magazines, incendiaries and other tools of his violent trade. A Neostead combat shotgun was holstered over his back on his right shoulder.

The five members of Phoenix Force were similarly clad and armed to the teeth.

The penetration of the hotel suite was going to be strictly a hit-and-git mission. From what Stony Man Farm had learned, there were no innocents on the top floor. All of Lynch's guests were criminals, whether they were wanted in their home countries or not. The flip side of the coin was that the Stony Man warriors were decidedly outnumbered.

"Get ready," Grimaldi advised.

Bolan stripped off his headset for a moment, then pulled on the Nomex balaclava that covered everything but his eyes. He reseated the headset, then pulled the mouthpiece forward. "Count off," he instructed the other warriors.

They did, assuring radio communications were solid.

Hawkins and James readied the rappeling lines, holding the coils of rope in their arms as they knelt by the cargo door.

Bolan glanced at the approaching rooftop. The streets below looked a long way down.

Abruptly the rooftop was under them, and Grimaldi was pulling up the chopper's nose. "Go!" the pilot ordered. Under his competent hand, the aircraft hovered scarcely twenty feet above the rooftop, maintaining a vantage point that could oversee the whole rooftop while providing a proximity position.

Hawkins and James flipped out the door, holding tight to the rappeling lines as they slid rapidly down them. They landed on their feet and held the lines taut for the others to follow. Manning and Encizo went next.

"Company, mate," McCarter said, pointing toward the small group of men hovering around the HVAC units less than forty yards away. "If they get off a round, we're going to lose something of our little surprise."

Without a word, the Executioner drew the silenced Beretta 93-R. It was chugging in his fist, spitting death, even as he was aware the Briton was doing the same with a Hi-Power. The five guards didn't get a chance to loose a single shot as the 9 mm rounds knocked them down. The Stony Man warriors reloaded automatically when their weapons blew back empty.

Still holding the pistol in his fist, Bolan seized the rappeling line and went down. The rope burned along his glove and boots. McCarter was only a heartbeat behind him.

"Gary," Bolan said, "you're with me."

"On your heels," the Canadian said, settling the satchel pack he'd prepped earlier over his shoulder.

Bolan sprinted across the rooftop to the HVAC. Kurtzman's research had revealed that the top-floor suites had their own duct system and independent air-conditioning units. If the rest of the building lost power, the top suites would still be comfortable. When reviewing the hotel's stats, the Executioner had decided to make use of those systems.

He slipped a pair of bolt cutters from one of the armor's modular pockets, located the duct work he wanted and snipped the locks. A couple seconds later, the grate was off. The straining motor was audible, sucking in air to be cooled and pumped inside the building.

Manning shoved the satchel inside, lodging it in place.

"We're go." He slipped the H&K MP-5 SD-3 from his shoulder.

"David?" Bolan transmitted.

"Another few seconds," the Briton replied.

Bolan scanned the rooftop as he and Manning jogged over to the side of the building where the suite's banquet room overlooked the Gate of Transformation by Light. A glance skyward showed him that Grimaldi had taken the helicopter back up. It looked like a red-and-white shark cruising against the blue sky. The rappeling lines still hung from it.

"Stony One, this is Stony Base," Kurtzman called over the headset.

"Go, Stony Base, you have One."

"Lynch is trying to access the computer," the cybernetics expert said.

For the time being, Stony Man Farm had remained offline from its own systems. Kurtzman and Tokaido had discovered contamination among their files and programs, but they hadn't had time to do anything about getting rid of it. That would take days, perhaps weeks, to do properly. If tampered with too much, Lynch would have known he'd been found out.

Yakov Katzenelenbogen had arranged for alternate systems to be used through known Mossad channels. The resulting network had been almost as good as what was normally possible through Stony Man Farm, but everyone knew they were going into battle with less than what they could have had.

"How much time can you buy us?" Bolan shook out his nylon cord and collapsible grappling hook while Manning did the same.

"A few seconds. Anything more and he's going to know something's wrong."

"David?" Bolan asked. He stepped over the edge, set himself and let the cord take his weight. It wouldn't be long before people below noticed them and called the police department.

"It'll do, mate."

Bolan and Manning dropped down on either side of the large plate-glass windows. Diaphanous curtains covered the glass on the inside, and heavy tinting kept anyone from easily seeing into the suite.

"He's rebooting," Kurtzman said, "trying to make the connection again."

Manning reached into his munitions pack and spread out fingers of C-4 across the glass, no more than three or four inches long. The curtain's valance hid the action from anyone inside the suite who might have been looking in that direction. The Canadian shoved preset timers into the gray white worms of explosive. "Going to set up alternating vibrations when it goes," he said. "It'll cause an implosion and drop the glass almost straight down. Won't be much left to slow us down."

Bolan nodded and drew the Neostead from over his shoulder, resting his weight easily on his feet. The South African combat shotgun was a study in the true meaning of lethal. Twin tubes ran on top of the barrel, carrying six rounds of double-aught buckshot apiece and feeding directly down into the breech. The laser sight was a further demoralizer.

"That's it," Kurtzman said. "I've got to let him in."

"Do it, mate," McCarter said. "We're inside."

Bolan listened to the whisper of the doomsday numbers counting down on the play. Stony Man Farm had been able to trace Shatterstop as far as Roanoke, and thought they'd moved Able Team to somewhere within a nine-mile radius. But without a chance to tag a communications transmission from Lynch, they couldn't locate the domestic arm of SmarTech's operation.

"Sarge," Grimaldi transmitted, "we've got trouble. Evidently a relief crew just came up for the guys on the rooftop. They know their security's bleeding."

"Pull back, Jack," Bolan said. "Don't give them an easy target."

"Shit," the pilot responded. "They've spotted your line and Manning's. They're coming over."

Bolan glanced at the edge of the rooftop. One slash across the nylon cord, and there'd be only the street and certain death waiting for them below. Time was running out.

Roanoke, Virginia

CARL LYONS HAD NEVER liked feeling helpless. It had happened with increasing frequency during his days on the LAPD as criminals and well-schooled lawyers learned how to use the very legal system against him that he fought to uphold. When he'd been offered the chance to join the Stony Man team, there'd been no hesitation. Once, the law had offered a demarcation between right and wrong, but that line was blurred. Stony Man Farm had bypassed the courtrooms and their tangles, moved the action right back onto the playing field of good versus evil, and he stood firmly entrenched on the side he'd always chosen.

The times of feeling helpless and frustrated were fewer now, but he still didn't like them.

He particularly hated this one.

Night had fallen over Roanoke hours earlier, and his watch told him it was only a few minutes away from midnight. Parked at a scenic overview in the foothills of the Blue Ridge Mountains, he was almost on home ground.

The thought wasn't as comforting as it normally would have been.

Stony Man Farm was only a couple hundred or so miles away, near the Shenandoah National Park. The realization that the Farm was well within striking distance of a number of ground-launched missiles left a cold stone in his stomach.

And that was what they'd all agreed they were looking for. From Trask's files on Shatterstop, the operation could be nothing else. If Dixon Lynch hadn't been able to quietly corrupt the Stony Man cybernetics systems, he'd meant to see them destroyed. At some point during the North Korean operation, Lynch had managed to target the counterterrorist hardsite.

Lyons didn't like the idea of the Stony Man support team remaining on-site, but they'd had no choice if they were going to help target Lynch for Phoenix Force and Bolan. And there was no way to quickly transfer all the systems somewhere else even as a backup Intel site. However, the "farm hands" had been cut back to a skeletal crew that was strictly voluntary.

He stood to one side of the Dodge Ram 1500 4×4 pickup and raked the surrounding terrain with night glasses. Somewhere out there, death lay in wait.

The headset crackled in his ear, then Price said, "Able Team, stand ready."

"We're here, Barb," Lyons answered.

Blancanales and Schwarz replied as well.

Even after Bolan and Phoenix Force engaged Lynch at the hotel in Seoul, Lyons knew, it could take time for Kurtzman and his team to track down a transmission. Too damn much time. And that was if Lynch made a call. There was every possibility that the attack was to take place if a call *wasn't* made.

Lyons continued to rake the terrain with the night glasses. His eyes felt grainy and tired, and the moonlight played tricks on his vision. He was outfitted in boots, jeans and a flannel shirt, with a windbreaker covering the Colt .45 Government Model pistol on his hip and the .357 Magnum Python revolver in shoulder leather. Inside the cab of the Dodge was a CAR-15. Extra magazines filled his pockets.

As he watched, an orange 1966 Ford Mustang with four women inside pulled off the main highway running from Roanoke to Salem into the rest stop less than a thousand yards from his position. An idea came to him as he watched the women get out and approach the various trucks parked there, avoiding the passenger cars and family vans. It was strictly from the cop days on the streets, but he thought it might work.

Getting back into the pickup, he cranked the engine, turned and headed back to the rest stop. He tagged the headset's transmit button. "Pol. Gadgets."

"Go," Blancanales responded, followed a heartbeat later by Schwarz.

"Got an idea I've got to play out," Lyons said as he cut into the rest area. "Saw a carload of lot lizards arrive to work on the night trade at a rest stop here. Got me to wondering how many other places they might have stopped at, and who they might have seen."

"Want some backup?" Schwarz asked.

"Negative." Lyons pulled the big 4×4 pickup to a halt behind the Mustang, blocking it in and instantly getting the attention of the four women. "If something comes of it, I'll let you know."

"Stay hard, Ironman," Blancanales advised.

A peroxide blonde in a black leather miniskirt, silver-studded black leather vest and pumps walked toward him.

She was in her early thirties, Lyons guessed as he stepped out of the truck, and hard enough to push back when leaned on.

"Hey," she said, "that's my car you're blocking in there, asshole."

"Yeah," Lyons said, "I kind of figured that."

The way her hand drifted to her back as she continued walking toward him let the big Able Team warrior know she'd reached for some kind of weapon. Her cheeks were rouged and her lips were deep red, not blunting the hard features in the slightest. "Maybe you want to move it away before you get hurt." She stopped six feet from him.

"I don't think I'm going to get hurt," Lyons said, taking out his wallet and letting her see the pistol in shoulder leather. "I'm a real live do-gooder. Got my shield to prove it. Bullets bounce right off." He showed her the badge Price had set up for his cover.

"You're not local," the woman said, not relaxing.

"Fed," Lyons told her, putting the badge away.

"Federal vice?" Her look was complete disbelief.

Lyons shook his head. "I'm looking for somebody. Thought maybe you might have seen them."

"I'm not too good at faces," the woman said. "Working in the dark all the time, you know how it is."

"Where have you girls hit tonight?"

Glenda smiled and pulled a cigarette from her purse. "Don't I have a Fifth Amendment or something around here?"

"The guys I'm looking for are bad news," Lyons said. "You'd probably remember them. They wouldn't want attention."

"That fits a lot of drivers. Guys out here are sometimes dodging the IRS, ex-wives and their lawyers, and parole officers."

"Figure three or four guys in the same truck," Lyons said. If it was a missile, the Shatterstop team would need that many men to launch.

Her brow wrinkled. "Clean-cut guys?" She dragged her fingers along her chin. "Military haircuts and hard-ass attitudes?"

"I don't know," Lyons replied honestly. "I haven't seen them."

"There was a truck Gina ran into at the rest stop a couple miles back, like they were headed into Roanoke. We were working the lot until a state police cruiser moved us on." She took another hit on the cigarette. "When I saw you, I figured tonight just wasn't our night."

"What about the truck?" Lyons said.

"Gina said she saw these two guys get out of a cab with Chinese takeout. She thought that was strange to begin with, but figured what the hell, if they could afford a cab back into town and Chinese takeout, they could definitely afford a couple of us. She followed them back to the truck, but didn't see any dollars under the windshield wiper, which is how we usually know a driver's looking for some companionship. Still, she thought she'd give it a try, you know? All they can do is turn you down, right? They can't kill you."

Lyons knew differently, but he didn't say anything. A prostitute was a serial killer's prime target.

"Gina knocks on the door, right? Guy opens it, asks her what the hell she wants. He tells Gina she should take it on somewhere else. Rude, you know. Guys don't always have to be so damn rude about it. A girl's got a right to make a living."

"How many were in the truck?"

"Four. For sure. She didn't have much of a chance to look around. The guy she was talking to, he shoved a gun in her face, told her she'd better leave or he was going to scatter her brains in about one second flat. She left.''

"What was the name on the truck?" Lyons asked.

The blonde hit the cigarette again and coolly blew smoke. "I don't know that I remember. My mind gets kind of fuzzy on me sometimes.''

Lyons got a couple hundreds from his jeans pocket and handed them over. "Give me a name.''

"Longarm Transit,'' Glenda replied. "Fancy Peterbilt rig with a custom paint job. Trailer's got a painting of a giraffe that looks like it's all legs. You can't miss it.''

Lyons said thanks and climbed back into the Dodge Ram. By the time he'd cleared the rest area, he'd already radioed the information to Blancanales, Schwarz and Stony Man Farm.

He stared through the windshield as he pressed his foot harder on the accelerator. It might be a false lead, but he didn't think so. It felt right. The net was tightening, but it remained to be seen who was trapping whom.

CHAPTER TWENTY-ONE

Dixon Lynch didn't worry about the first two failed attempts to get into the covert agency's computer system. As far as he knew, they hadn't gone back on-line since they'd shifted over to the Chinese systems. It was possible that with the pickup of the insertion team by the aircraft carrier near Nampo, they'd shut down so they wouldn't be overheard by military-intelligence communications going through that sphere of influence.

He worked the keyboard confidently, every eye in the room on him, using the pass codes Gutter Razor had engineered for him. The screen flared to life, reflected on the monitors depending on the walls.

"Where do you want to go?" Lynch asked. "What do you want to see?" He typed, already having an agenda in mind. Accessing the Japanese National Police files, he reached in for the information on the Yakuza. "How about you, Mr. Kirosawa? Wouldn't you like to know if there are any undercover officers planted in your organization?"

There was no answer, but the rumble of conversations grew steadily louder as the screen changed, showing files in Japanese.

"You can't speak the language?" Lynch said with a smile. He activated one of the pull-down menus. "No problem. The programming allows for multilingual capabilities." He tapped the mouse buttons. The screen wavered, then the Japanese characters vanished, replaced by Russian, German, French and finally English.

An hour aboard the *Shadow Scythe,* working the systems Razor had freed up to his plundering so far, had given Lynch enough experience to freely cruise the files. Abruptly two faces appeared on the screens in full-frontal and profile shots.

"Do you recognize them, Mr. Kirosawa?" Lynch asked.

"Yes," the Yakuza chieftain said. "They are men within my organization."

Lynch entered new commands. The full-frontal pictures of the two men remained, shunted over to the right, then more pictures appeared on the other side. Both men were shown in Japanese National Police uniforms, looking considerably more clean-cut. "I can get you names, induction dates and training sites they attended." Lynch looked at Kirosawa. "How much would you be willing to pay for such information?" He didn't wait for an answer. "And today you get it free. But you have to ask yourself, how many more are there like that?"

The conversations grew, and Lynch knew they were beginning to see the potential.

"This agency is real, ladies and gentlemen," he said. "Only now, instead of working against you, they can work for you, too." He paused. "And I can give it to you. Many of you have already started working together, forging a crime industry that moves at least a half-trillion dollars a year. I know. I've done the research. And you're getting more savvy in what to do with those profits. At least a quarter trillion per year is going back into legitimate businesses, providing further growth and a varied portfolio."

"What do you want out of this?" Oleg Dresdov asked.

Lynch turned, flexing his hand at his side so the cam-

eraman he'd stationed for the meeting would switch back
to him, then signaled for a close-up. He gave the assembled
group of thieves, murderers and robber barons his best win-
ner's smile. "That's easy," he said, "I just want a piece
of the action."

"DAMN, THIS GUY IS SCARY," Aaron Kurtzman said. His
attention was focused on the wall screen at the end of the
room. The video feed was coming from the computer
Dixon Lynch was using in the suite at the Koreana Hotel.
Barbara Price didn't know how the cybernetics expert had
managed it, but somehow he and Tokaido had tied in the
corrupted programming linked to Lynch's CPU to pick up
the video and audio feeds and bring them through the borrowed Mossad channels. It was purely passive, though, and
any action on their part to interact or interfere with Lynch
would have brought the corruption and viruses into the Israeli systems—and alerted Lynch.

She finished her emergency phone call to Tokyo and
hung up. She had a contact in the American Embassy there
who could get in touch with the Japanese National Police
and get the two blown undercover officers out of danger
before Kirosawa had a chance to call in and expose them.

"Yeah," Brognola said, "but there's been some good
come out of this, too. Without Lynch, we wouldn't have
known about Aleksei Kandinsky's organization down in the
Caribbean."

Silently Price agreed. Kandinsky's activities had been
noticed, and patterns had been developing in that part of
the world regarding Yakuza activity, the cartels and the
Russian Mafia, but investigating Lynch and DeSilva had
unveiled more of the stranglehold Kandinsky had on Aruba
and other Caribbean areas. The mission controller was al-

ready taking notes, assembling files and planning an exploratory probe into the area in the near future.

"They *are* organizing out there," Brognola went on. He unwrapped a cigar and thrust it unlighted into the corner of his mouth. "They're getting harder and smarter, and it's up to us to cut them down to something regular police agencies can handle."

No one said that all hinged on whether any of them was still there. Shatterstop was still a loose cannon, perhaps literally. Price shook the thought from her mind. Able Team was riding a bet, and she'd always been willing to back Lyons's hunches.

But the clock was moving.

"Geez," Kurtzman said, glancing back at one of the monitors on his desk.

Price leaned in for a closer look. The satellite provided through the Mossad Intelligence network was good enough to show the small group of men who'd walked out onto the rooftop of the Koreana Hotel.

"It's about to hit the fan," Brognola commented. "Where's David and his team?"

"Inside," Price replied.

Lynch's security group jogged into motion, heading for the side of the building where Manning and Bolan had started their descent.

"Tell him to open the ball," Brognola growled. "It's all-or-nothing now, and we're going out down and dirty."

Price reached for the radio.

MCCARTER PEERED around the corner into the hallway. There were two rooftop entrances, and his team had come through the narrower maintenance one instead of the elevator-assisted delivery entrance.

The stairs allowed only one man to pass at a time. Phoenix Force went in single file, led by McCarter.

At the end of the hall, two men stood guard with automatic weapons. They were professional in their dress and attitude, but weren't expecting any trouble.

McCarter lifted the silenced Browning and put two rounds into the back of the head of the man on the left. As his corpse stretched out forward, the second man turned and tried to back away to cover at the same time.

The Briton raced forward, the Hi-Power level before him. He stroked the trigger again, coring a round through the center of the man's heart, then once more, making a scarlet ruin of his target's throat before he could loose a dying scream.

Grabbing one of the bodies, McCarter pulled it back into concealment while James did the same with the other. The double doors the guards had been assigned to opened out into the main hallway. Some of the details were different than the blueprints Kurtzman had snatched from the hotel files, but that was to be expected since the modular walls allowed for reshaping of the rooms.

Hawkins and Encizo quickly mined the doorway. If they had to use it in their retreat, the explosions could kill gunners who were hot on their heels. And if they went out another way, the explosions could provide further distraction.

The headset beeped in his ear. "Stony Base to Phoenix One."

"Go, Stony Base," McCarter replied. "You have Phoenix One."

"Striker and Phoenix Two are about to receive company," the mission controller said. "They're going to need some support."

"We're on our way," McCarter said grimly. He filled

his empty hand with his other Browning, glancing around at his team and making sure they'd copied the transmission.

"Let's go for it," Hawkins growled.

"I got the point," James said. He handled his H&K MP-5 SD-3 with both hands and went forward.

"Double-time, lads," McCarter urged, then followed the ex-SEAL into the corridor. Hawkins trailed him, with Encizo bringing up the rear.

A cluster of bodyguards from different crime lords and mercenaries in Lynch's employ stood in front of the double doors. Guns filled their hands as soon as they spotted the black-clad Stony Man warriors.

McCarter and Phoenix Force gave them no quarter. Bringing up his Brownings, the Briton started triggering rounds as quickly as he could, burning through both magazines. Brass leaped and glinted, spilling to the carpeted floor. Bullets tore through the expensive door, chipping away the hand-tooled wooden exterior.

Return fire from the guards ripped fluorescent lighting fixtures from the ceiling and spilled them in a chemical haze and burst of sparks to the floor. Divots from the plush carpet were ripped loose and sent spinning.

"Split off!" McCarter commanded, waving Hawkins and Encizo to the left.

The two Phoenix Force warriors pounded down the hallway.

McCarter took one side of the double doors while James took the other. Holstering the Brownings, the Briton pulled the H&K MP-5 SD-3 from his back. He tagged the headset's transmit button. "Stony One, this is Phoenix One. If you needed a diversion, mate, this is as good as it gets."

There was no answer.

Unable to wait, McCarter kicked open the double doors and met a hail of bullets coming in his direction.

SHOULDERING THE NEOSTEAD, Bolan waited for the first of the rooftop security guards to look over the side as he heard McCarter's words die away. When the guy did, the Executioner squeezed the shotgun's trigger and rode out the recoil.

Caught dead center by the hot charge of double-aught buckshot, the guard's head went to pieces.

"Go," Bolan said to Manning. The men up top could cut the nylon cords without ever exposing themselves.

"Fire in the hole!" the Canadian yelled, turning away from the big window.

Bolan shielded his face with an arm, keeping the Neostead at the ready. Through his fingers, he saw the plate-glass window fragment into a thousand gleaming shards, then drop almost straight down. "Jump," he told Manning, flexing his legs and propelling himself from the side of the building. His free hand caught the line, ready to pay it out from his harness when he needed to.

He flew away from the building in a short, tight arc, mirrored by Manning on the other side, then he was twisting, navigating his way through the gaping maw of the destroyed window.

Without warning, he felt gravity grab a more fierce hold on him, and he knew the nylon cord had been severed. His swing turned into a fall.

DIXON LYNCH STOOD frozen for a moment, not knowing which way to move. He saw the black-clad gunmen invade the suite despite the firestorm that met them. The bodyguards and security people were the first to react, knocking down their employers and taking up defensive postures behind whatever cover they could find.

Then the main window overlooking the street exploded and rained to the carpet just inside the frame. Screams and yells punctuated the noise, but were almost lost amid the bursts of autofire.

Then, incredibly, two more black-clad commandos swung in through the emptied window, hanging from thin black cords. One of them landed off balance, trailing a slashed length of the cord after him. Three of the Yakuza fired at him as he rolled and came up on his feet. The shotgun roared in his hands, kicking out smoking shells. The Yakuza went down like tenpins.

"No," Lynch said in a hoarse voice. He couldn't believe they'd actually gone up against him with so much to lose. And to walk into this suite, knowing it would be filled with nothing but enemies easily outnumbering them, it was lunacy.

He raked the Glock 23 from under his left arm and fired at the black figure with the shotgun, ignoring the guns blasting around him. He was sure he'd hit the man at least twice.

"Get down, Dix," Eric Hardcastle growled in his ear. The big mercenary dropped a heavy hand over him and pulled him away. "We've got to get you out of here. Relax and let me do my job."

Lynch went with him, digging for the cell phone in the holster at his waist. The people who'd orchestrated the strike were dead, history, whether they knew it or not. He punched in the numbers for Shatterstop.

Hardcastle became an elemental force of elbows and knees playing a sonata of bone-crunching violence. His pistol boomed repeatedly as he marched Lynch and himself to the exit in the rear of the suite.

"You double-crossing son of a bitch!" one of the American Mafia representatives yelled as he pointed a pistol at Lynch.

Hardcastle dropped him with two shots through the face and kept Lynch moving over the spasming corpse.

Lynch's conversation with Shatterstop was brief. As he punched the End button on the cell phone, a rolling voice that sounded straight out of a winter graveyard called out to him.

"Dixon Lynch!"

Although unwilling, Lynch turned to face the speaker.

The black-clad warrior with the shotgun stood framed by the empty window behind him, the hard light of early afternoon spilling in after him. He had the shotgun in his off hand now, and he aimed a big pistol at Lynch from less than forty feet away.

Suddenly Kalico was there, leaping at the man in black with a knife in her fist and screaming like a banshee. She wrapped an arm around his throat from behind and raked at his hooded face with the blade.

The big pistol fired just as Hardcastle slammed into Lynch and knocked him through the exit. "Move!" the mercenary yelled.

The cell phone fell from Lynch's fingers and dropped to the carpet. He didn't care. All that mattered was that he could get away. Hardcastle was already ordering the helicopter they had standing by to meet them out in the street in front of the hotel. A flying wedge of mercenaries bristling with guns surrounded Lynch and herded him down the hall to the private elevator he'd arranged.

They hadn't beaten him. There was still a lot he could accomplish before they shut him out of their cybernetics systems.

There was a short wait on the elevators. The constant din of gunfire filled the hallway with noise. He got himself together, taking a new grip on the Glock in his fist. They'd set him back, but they hadn't stopped him. He was hurt, but he wasn't finished.

The elevator arrived, and he allowed Hardcastle to put

him on it. He had a lot to do once he reached the *Shadow Scythe.*

"DID YOU GET IT?" Brognola asked.

Kurtzman shook his head, studying the computer monitors spread across his desk. "The call went through too quick. I couldn't lock on securely enough." He swore with feeling. They'd known Lynch would place his call through a conventional phone line or a cellular handset, and he'd set capture programming in the communications systems to snare any calls made to Roanoke, Virginia. "It was made to a cell phone. I couldn't get the triangulation set up in time once it bounced off the cell tower in Virginia."

He glanced up at Hunt Wethers's station, where radar watch was being kept in a two-hundred-mile radius around the Farm. So far, nothing had appeared on the event horizon.

Brognola dropped a friendly hand on his shoulder. "You did what you could, Aaron."

In the background, Price was relaying the information to Bolan, Phoenix Force and Able Team. Kurtzman watched the monitors with keen anticipation. He'd done what he could, but he knew it wasn't enough. Not by a long shot.

THE NOMEX HOOD Bolan wore had a Kevlar lining on it that left only his eyes, nose and mouth unprotected in the form of a keyhole. Blunt trauma would generally knock a man out, but it might not kill him.

The woman's blade scratched over the Executioner's right cheekbone as she stabbed at him, but never reached his flesh. She remained locked onto his back, however, and drew back her arm to make another attempt. Lynch and the mercenary Price had identified as a German named Eric

Hardcastle had disappeared through a door at the rear of the room.

An Italian-looking man with a chrome pistol fired at Bolan before he could move.

He was caught flat-footed, and the bullets hammered against the Executioner's armor, bruising the flesh beneath. Raising the Desert Eagle, Bolan loosed a pair of 240-grain skull-busters that erased the man's features and threw his corpse backward.

He twisted as the woman stabbed at him again, deflecting her aim and causing the point of the knife to dig into the Kevlar atop his shoulder. Before she could recover, he leathered the big .44 and grabbed her striking elbow. With one lithe move, he flipped her over his shoulder.

Bullets meant for the Executioner caught her in the chest. Shock filled her face as she put a hand to her breast and it came away bloody.

Bolan drew the Desert Eagle in one smooth motion and fired a steady roll of thunder blasting the life out of the killers, then grabbed the woman's blouse and tugged her to the brief safety of an overturned table. One look at her wounds told him there was nothing he could do.

"You know," she said in a ragged voice as a thread of crimson trickled from the corner of her mouth, "I really loved him. And he didn't care for me at all." Abruptly light left her eyes, and her head lolled to the side.

Bolan didn't know who the woman was. Maybe he'd never know. It depended on how things worked out on the Seoul end of the operation. He sat on his heels beside her and thumbed fresh rounds into the Neostead. Lynch couldn't be allowed to escape. They just needed him running.

He tagged the transmitter. "Phoenix Two."

"Go," Manning responded.

"It's time."

"Affirmative." A heartbeat later, a huge explosion of noise echoed through the room. Immediately afterward, roiling black clouds of smoke blew from the ductwork and invaded the suite.

Bolan reached into one of the pockets of the modular armor and pulled out a gas mask with night-vision goggles attached. He pulled it on, threading the pencil-thin mike through the mask. A pair of gunners looking for cover came around the table. Lifting the shotgun, he cleared them out of the way with two blasts. "Phoenix One."

"Go, mate."

"The pigeon flew through the back."

"I saw him. If you and Two would like to take a run at him, we'll cover before we pull back."

"See you out front."

"You can bloody well count on it."

Bolan pushed himself to his feet, blasting away with the 12-gauge three more times, putting down two more targets. The confusion inside the suite was nearly complete. With the advent of the CS-laced smoke from the munitions satchel Manning had stashed in the return-air system, more of Lynch's guests were losing their stomach for the fight.

"Two," Bolan growled.

"You look over your shoulder," the Canadian said, "that'll be me."

The headset chirped for his attention.

"Go," he said, pausing at the rear door. Black smoke was pouring out into the corridor, and he got a glimpse of the private elevator's doors closing.

"If you can find Lynch," Price said, "see if you can get the number he called in Roanoke. We missed the connection."

Glancing back at the floor, Bolan spotted the cell phone

he'd seen Lynch drop. He stooped and picked it up, then punched the Send and Redial buttons. "Try it now," he said. Out in the hallway, he dropped the phone gently onto the carpet. Someone on the other end of the line said hello.

"The elevator?" Manning asked, joining him.

"Yeah." Bolan paused at the doors and leathered the shotgun across his back. "We've got to keep the pressure on, keep Lynch running and in our sights." He stuck his fingers through the double doors and pushed them open.

Down in the elevator shaft, the cage was two floors below and continuing to drop rapidly.

"I can do that," Manning promised. "Provided we can get onto that cage quietly."

"Let's go." Stripping off the Kevlar-lined Nomex hood, Bolan replaced the gas mask and NVGs. Leaning out into the shaft, he wrapped the Nomex hood around the steel cable, then locked his boots around it, as well, and started to slide after the descending cage. He started gaining on it, but the Nomex hood was heating up fast. He kept count of the floors as the cage descended.

"It's affirmative," Price said as his boots touched the top of the cage. "We've got lock and triangulation. Able Team is closing in on Shatterstop now."

"Shut them down," Bolan said. He stepped off onto the cage, causing as little disturbance as he could. Manning joined him a second later.

Without a word, the Canadian set to work preparing a shaped charge atop the elevator cage. "We're going to need some room when this goes."

Bolan nodded.

"How far are we from the first floor?" Manning stood up, finished. A remote detonator was in his hand and a tight grin was on his face.

"Six more stories."

"We need two of them for a safety zone."

"Go," Bolan said, and reached for one of the passing struts. The cage was going fast enough that the sudden stop strained his muscles and joints when he stepped off onto one of the support struts. Perspiration covered his face and gleamed along the exposed skin of his wrists.

The cage stopped on the first floor, and the ding of the doors opening echoed through the shaft.

Clinging to the side of the elevator shaft, Bolan tapped the headset's transmit button. "Phoenix One, this is Stony One."

"Go, Stony One." The Briton's tone was clipped but unhurried.

"Your situation?"

"We're going topside, mate. Meeting up with G-Force. We'll be ready to pick you up in seconds. It seems we weren't the only ones with a helo standing by."

Manning touched off the detonator at Bolan's nod. Enough time had elapsed that the warrior felt certain Lynch had had time to leave the cage.

The explosion was loud and echoing, trapped as it was inside the shaft. The heat billowed up but quickly dissipated.

When Bolan looked back at the bottom, he saw the cage was a jumbled wreckage. He started down, working his way through the support lattice. When he reached the cage, he drew the Desert Eagle and peered through the crawl space left above the warped elevator doors. He caught a glimpse of Lynch, Hardcastle and the mercenaries disappearing through the main doors leading onto the street.

Rolling through the gap, he landed on his feet and gave pursuit. In order to completely put Lynch's threat behind them, his main computers had to be taken out. Price, Brognola and Kurtzman had all agreed that the man had undoubtedly backed up a lot of what he'd discovered on those units.

Kurtzman's team had turned up the probable existence of a submersible in the files they'd accessed through the Mossad Intelligence network. Finding out where it was berthed at the present was another matter.

Bolan made the main lobby doors with no resistance. A housekeeper pushing a cart of cleaning supplies backed away from him, and a guy running a floor waxer switched off his machine and abandoned it.

Out on the street, Hardcastle and his team blocked off a section with smoking emergency flares. The crimson-and-yellow fog drifted upward at first, then was beat back down by the descending Mil Mi-8 Salon helicopter. The chopper didn't touch the ground, hovering only a few feet above it. Lynch and his people scrambled aboard, then it quickly rose into the sky, threading between buildings. Traffic came to a stop in the streets, and a few collisions by surprised motorists further confused things.

Keeping the Desert Eagle up and at the ready, Bolan tapped the headset transmit button. "Stony One to Stony Base."

"Go, Stony One," Price replied.

"Have you got your target?"

"We're tracking now."

Bolan jogged out onto the street as the helicopter disappeared in the distance. "G-Force?"

"On my way, guy."

Glancing up, the Executioner watched the Bell Model 412SP drop quickly. The cargo door was open, and the four other Phoenix Force commandos could be seen inside. James kicked at a rolled bundle in front of him. Spinning out like a dropping spider, a rope ladder trailed out of the aircraft.

"On the fly, mate," McCarter said over the radio. "The local constabulary has a bird in the air, as well. We don't have time to tarry."

"What, no curb service?" Manning groused.

Bolan broke into a run, plotting an interception course in his mind as he made his body accept the demands he was putting on it. Manning raced along beside him.

Without warning, a group of Japanese burst from the hotel directly in their path and started brandishing guns, forming a protective barrier around an old man in their midst.

"Go," Bolan ordered Manning, drawing the Desert Eagle and slowing. He took a two-handed grip, aware that the Canadian had made the rope ladder and was now clinging to it.

The Japanese gunners opened fire, aiming at the swinging target and Bolan.

Concentrating on his field of fire, the Executioner emptied the clip rapidly as bullets sliced the air around him. Eight rounds, carefully placed and dead on target, punched five of the Japanese shooters backward, tangling everyone else.

Behind, sprinting now, Bolan raced for the swaying rope ladder. Grimaldi was still in forward motion, unable to come to a complete stop without becoming an even easier target for the gunners firing from the upper floors. Bullets had already spiderwebbed the Plexiglas nose.

A row of cars parked at the curb blocked Bolan's path as a pair of Seoul police cars came shrieking around the end of the block ahead of him. Their whirling blue cherries flickered inside their plastic cases.

Bolan knew he'd only have one chance at the brass ring. Leathering the Desert Eagle, he pushed himself, his breath like liquid fire spilling through his lungs. He raced up the rear of a Volkswagen bug, losing his balance for just a moment as the small car shifted on its springs and shocks under him. Then he vaulted to the top of a Mercedes in front of the Volkswagen. The ladder remained just out of reach.

Marshaling his remaining speed and strength, he threw himself from the top of the Mercedes toward the rope ladder. His fingers grazed one of the rungs, then slid down to the next as he started to fall. He closed his hand around it. His shoulder burned from the sudden exertion, then he found a foothold and made it bearable.

"He's on," McCarter said. "Haul him in."

Working carefully as the helicopter rapidly gained altitude, Bolan scaled the rope ladder while Phoenix Force reeled him in. They had Shatterstop located and Lynch on the run. All that remained was to see if the Stony Man teams could pull it all together.

CHAPTER TWENTY-TWO

More than two dozen eighteen-wheelers were parked at the Roanoke rest stop. The camper trailers, vans and motor homes easily more than doubled that number, which amounted to a confusing collection of vehicles.

Carl Lyons made the turn into the rest stop's access road, eyes straining to find the Longarm Transit truck. He braked for a couple weary parents carrying an ice chest and herding three young children toward the picnic area.

"I've got him, Ironman," Blancanales said calmly. "He's dead ahead of you, already pulling out."

Peering farther down the road, Lyons spotted the Longarm Transit truck speeding up the incline leading back to the highway. The Able Team warrior shoved his foot down on the accelerator and scooted around a station wagon pulling a camper trailer and negotiating a parking spot.

Coming out around the station wagon, Lyons was caught flat-footed by the second truck charging at him, pinned in the sudden glare of its headlights. He tried to swerve and speed up, but the effort was too little too late. The second truck caught him like an avalanche of steel, taking the 4×4 pickup broadside.

The seat belt seized up around Lyons, and he lifted an arm to keep the chunks of safety glass from the shattered windshield out of his face. He got a brief glimpse of the line of parked cars coming up fast from the left, then he was smashed into them. He hit the side of the truck hard, almost slipping into unconsciousness.

"Ironman!" Schwarz called.

"Here, dammit!" Lyons answered. Blood trickled warmly down the side of his face as he turned and stared at the huge grillwork of the Peterbilt plastered across the passenger side of the Dodge Ram. Ahead of him, the Longarm Transit truck was pulling onto the highway, streamers of gray smoke pouring from the double stacks. "Pol, stay with that bastard!"

"I am, amigo."

A second later, Blancanales whipped by on the highway in his bronze Suburban.

"Hang on," Schwarz called. "I'm on my way."

"You and Dick Tracy," Lyons growled as he filled his fist with the .357 Python and struggled to get free of the seat belts.

The Peterbilt pulled away, metal screeching as it tried to stay locked to the Dodge. The lights on the left side had been smashed and left empty sockets in their place. Moving quickly, a pair of shadows came around the right side of the vehicle, facing Lyons with machine pistols.

Without hesitation, the Able Team leader raised his weapon and started to fire, emptying the pistol rapidly. Both shadows stumbled back and went down. The throaty roar of the Peterbilt escalated as it stopped fifteen feet away. Shuddering, the big rig surged forward again, rushing at the pinned pickup.

Leathering the empty Python, Lyons scrambled through the Dodge's window after trying the door and finding it stuck. He climbed and fell out of the window, landing on the warped trunk of a sedan. Pushing himself to his feet, he ran along the length of the car as the Peterbilt rammed into the pickup again.

Shaken by the collision, the car rocking under him, Lyons lost his footing and went down, managing at the last moment to get a boot on the front of the sedan and push himself toward the open space in front of the car. He rolled and got to his feet just as the Peterbilt shoved the pickup and sedan forward, trying to run the Able Team warrior down.

Lyons drew the Colt .45 Government Model and lifted it toward the Peterbilt's windshield. The wrecked tonnage came at him, fast enough that he had to keep moving quickly to avoid it. Trees went down under the tangle of vehicles. Antitheft alarms on two cars on either side of the truck went off, adding to the din.

He aimed at the driver's side of the truck and put all eight rounds through the windshield in an area that could have been covered by a dinner plate.

Abruptly the truck jerked to a stop, shivered and died.

"Ironman!"

Lyons glanced up and saw Schwarz coming toward him in the blue Jeep Renegade he'd been using to scout the highway in their search for Shatterstop. "Go around. Meet me on the other side and let's make sure this one's down."

The Jeep's wheels tore chunks from the earth and sent them spinning as Schwarz powered for the rear of the huge tractor trailer.

Dumping the empty magazine from the .45, Lyons recharged the weapon while sprinting around the front of the Peterbilt. A speedloader dropped six more rounds into the .357. Keeping the gun in his left hand, he leathered the .45 and raced to the truck's side.

Grabbing the handle, he yanked the door open and let

the .357 Magnum pistol lead him in. A dead man sat behind the steering wheel, most of his face blown away.

Lyons dropped back to the ground and swiveled to cover the side of the trailer as he advanced to the rear. His breath was hot and ragged, and he took a two-fisted grip on the pistol. "Pol?"

"Go."

"Your quarry?"

"Still on him."

"Heading?"

"Sticking with the highway, Ironman. But I had a particularly nasty thought. If Lynch is really good with communications programming, he ought to be hell on wheels with targeting systems."

"Stay with him," Lyons advised. "Me and Gadgets will have your back door in a minute."

Schwarz had left the Jeep running at the rear of the trailer. People were already starting to gather, demanding answers and cursing.

"Empty," Schwarz said as he clambered down from the trailer, a high-intensity flashlight in his hand.

"Running blocker for the main unit," Lyons said.

"That's the way I figure it." Schwarz climbed behind the Jeep's wheel.

Sliding into the passenger seat, Lyons reached into the back and took up Schwarz's CAR-15. "You copy Pol's transmission?"

"Yeah."

"Let's roll."

Getting out of the rest stop took just a moment. Some of the truckers didn't want to give ground, demanding to see badges and wanting to know what had happened. Lyons thrust the assault rifle through the door and loosed a burst into the air. In the silence that followed the rolling thunder of the CAR-15, he shouted, "Federal marshals! Stay the hell out of the way!"

The crowd peeled back, and Schwarz raced through them. The road was blocked by rigs that were trying to get out of the area. Using the 4WD shift-on-the-fly function allowed by the Jeep, Schwarz headed off-road and cut across the grass and through the trees to reach the highway.

Lyons held on tight, bounced around unmercifully by the rough ride.

Once on the highway, Schwarz pinned the accelerator to the floor and went through the gears by the numbers. The speedometer needle rose fast.

Tagging the headset's transmit button and peering through the Jeep's streaked windshield, Lyons said, "Pol?"

"I'm here, guy."

"The truck?"

"Holding steady at around a hundred and ten."

"What about the mile marker?" Lyons asked, catching sight of the marker Schwarz pointed out while racing around a Winnebago.

Blancanales relayed it to him.

Doing the quick arithmetic, Lyons figured the Peterbilt was only three miles ahead of them. He glanced at the speedometer again. The Jeep was hitting one-forty. None of the vehicles Able Team had requisitioned for the mission was running stock. "Can you shoot the tires out?"

"I tried," Blancanales said. "They're run-flats. And while I was up there, the driver pulled the rig around and had the trailer kiss the front end of my car. If I get into an ass-kicking contest with him, I lose."

"We'll be right there."

Schwarz had to go off the shoulder to pass two cars running abreast. The Jeep vibrated as if it were trying to

come apart, left a cloud of dust behind, then roared back
onto the highway.

"Shit," Blancanales said. "They just blew the trailer
cover off. There's a Scud set up in a mobile launcher in
back."

"They'll have to stop before they can launch," Lyons
said.

"Maybe you'd better tell them that," Blancanales said
grimly. "They've got a team back there setting up now."

Lyons glanced at Schwarz.

The other man shook his head and pointed to the accelerator pinned to the floorboard. "I'm flat out."

Lyons nodded, then prayed they'd be in time. Everyone
holding the fort at Stony Man Farm was depending on
them. Ground zero would wipe them all out.

They crested a hill and started down a long grade, narrowly avoiding the tangled wreckage of sheet metal that
had been the trailer. At the bottom of the hill, Lyons spotted
the Suburban following behind the eighteen-wheeler. Autofire flashed along the back of the flatbed trailer behind the
big tractor rig, and sparks flared from the front of Blancanales's Suburban in counterpoint.

"Get alongside," Lyons directed. He looked farther
down the highway. The grade curved and remained uneven
for another mile or two, then a flat run stretched out for a
distance. He knew there'd be plenty of time to launch the
Scud and get it off once the truck reached that part of the
highway. "Right side."

Schwarz nodded.

"Pol." Lyons dropped the canvas top on the Jeep, letting
the wind take it and blow it back. He stood in the passenger
seat, then went into the back, holding on to the roll bar.
The CAR-15 was slung over his back.

"Go," Blancanales said.

"We need a distraction."

"Say when."

Lyons stared at the truck as Schwarz cut the distance to fifty yards. Two of the three men on the flatbed were engaged in shooting at the approaching Able Team vehicles. The third man was laboring over a launch-command setup mounted near the tractor rig.

As Lyons watched, his eyes tearing from the rushing wind hitting him in the face, the Scud missile suddenly elevated, its nose rising up to a level just below the air foil mounted on the truck cab. When the propellant was ignited, it would leap into the air and streak toward its target.

Bullets crashed into the front of the Jeep and took out most of the windshield.

Alongside the trailer, Blancanales opened fire, using the assault rifle one-handed as he fired through the passenger window. The autofire sent the men on the flatbed scrambling for cover. Without warning, the Peterbilt swept over to the left, trying to take out the Suburban with its greater size and weight.

The flatbed connected and knocked the Suburban into a skid. But Schwarz moved in for the kill, cutting the distance to nothing. Just as he drew even, though, the flatbed came back across, trying for the Jeep.

"Hold it," Lyons said, leaning out away from the 4×4 to reach for the trailer. "Just a little more."

The flatbed was level with his waist. The pavement between the vehicles was passing at more than a hundred miles per hour. The engines worked hard and loud, making conversation even by the headsets almost impossible.

With only inches separating the truck from the Jeep, Lyons jumped with everything he had. There was a brief feeling of near weightlessness, then he slammed down on the metal floor of the flatbed. Bullets inscribed fresh scars against the steel surface.

Wind whipping against him, Lyons rolled toward the Scud, coming up underneath the tail section of the missile. He pushed himself to his knees, feeling the vibration of the truck tires beneath him. Unslinging the CAR-15, Lyons stood and whirled around the Scud, alerted by the pounding of running feet.

He caught the approaching gunman almost point-blank. The guy's rifle went off and unleashed a spray of bullets that rattled across Lyons's rib cage, deflected by the body armor he wore. The sudden pain robbed the big Able Team warrior of his breath, but he remained locked on his target. Caressing the trigger, he fired a triburst into the man's face.

Staggered, the corpse lost coordination and was propelled forward by the motion of the Peterbilt and the wall of wind from behind.

Lyons slapped the dead man aside with the CAR-15's barrel. Flailing, the corpse tumbled from the trailer, then vanished under the wheels of Schwarz's Jeep.

The Scud shifted slightly in its cradle, letting Lyons know it was ready for ignition. The flat section of the highway was less than two hundred yards away and closing fast.

He went forward, the assault rifle canted across his chest, held in both hands. Movement on the right alerted him, then he saw Schwarz bring the Jeep in close.

"Ironman!" Schwarz called out. He managed to reach out a hand and hold the Jeep steady. "You may need some help shutting down that launch system."

Kneeling, Lyons reached for his teammate, but the distance was too great.

"Look out!" Blancanales yelled. He had the Suburban behind the trailer now, within only feet, staying in a position where he could see most of the flatbed. "Guy coming up behind you!"

Before Lyons could turn, he felt a bullet graze the inside of his left thigh, spreading burning fire in its wake. Ignoring the pain, he drew the .357 from shoulder leather and fired three rounds into the man's forehead as fast as he could squeeze the trigger.

The gunner fell, rolled, then vanished over the side of the trailer.

Turning back to Schwarz, Lyons stretched out his hand and caught his teammate's arm as the eighteen-wheeler slammed against the Jeep and sent it spinning out of control. For a moment, Schwarz hung from Lyons's hand, feet only inches above the highway. The Jeep rolled over and over from the impact, going to pieces in seconds.

"Grab something," Lyons urged, feeling as if his arm were about to be pulled from its socket.

Instead, Schwarz raked his Beretta 92-S from his hip and pointed almost at Lyons's head. Brass nearly jumped into the big ex-cop's face as Schwarz squeezed the trigger, and his grip slipped.

The third man aboard the flatbed crashed down only inches from Lyons as Schwarz holstered his pistol and reached for the lip of the trailer bed. In seconds he was aboard.

Lyons raced with Schwarz to the fire controls bolted into the floor of the trailer. The truck swerved suddenly, and a line of cars got past on the right, so close that an immediate series of honks started.

Glancing at the series of dials and lights, Lyons couldn't make heads or tails out of the firing station. Schwarz moved immediately, punching different buttons and flipping different toggles. His finger dropped to a round keyhole.

"Son of a bitch," Schwarz said. "The missile's on automatic, and it's been locked. We need the key to shut it down.''

"Check the dead guy over there," Lyons said. "I'll get the driver."

Schwarz nodded and moved off.

The Scud whined and whirred as it made more adjustments.

Stepping forward from the trailer, Lyons crossed to the tractor, negotiating the distance with difficulty on his wounded leg. He saw the driver reflected in the side mirror, a thick man with curly brown hair and a gunslinger's mustache.

Without warning, the driver shoved a Smith & Wesson .40-caliber pistol through the window and tried to fire backward at Lyons. Lashing out instantly, the Able Team leader slammed the .357's barrel across the man's wrist, breaking it with a harsh snap.

The tractor veered sharply out of control for a moment before the driver straightened it. By then, Lyons was on the running board. He screwed the pistol barrel into the man's neck.

"I want the key to the firing center," Lyons ordered.

"I don't have it, man," the driver said, nursing his broken wrist.

"Ironman," Schwarz called over the headset, "the guy back here doesn't have it. What about the driver?"

"He says no." Lyons held on while the driver navigated around a four-car convoy. "Who has the key?"

"Craft," the driver responded.

"Describe him."

The description fit the second man Lyons had shot. He knew there wasn't enough time to attempt to retrieve the key from the body lying somewhere back along the highway. "Pol."

"Go."

"Pull up alongside. We're getting off."

"On my way."

"Ironman," Schwarz said.

"Go."

"According to the counter back here, we've got forty-two seconds to ignition."

"We're getting off," Lyons said. "Come take this clown."

Blancanales pulled up beside the eighteen-wheeler and held steady as Schwarz came forward and Lyons opened the tractor's door.

"Out," Lyons commanded the driver, taking the wheel himself and making sure the cruise control was locked on.

Schwarz made the leap onto the Suburban's roof first, then hooked a foot under the luggage rack and reached for their prisoner. The guy went, held in check by Schwarz's Beretta.

Lyons had been keeping a mental countdown going. If he was right, he had only eighteen seconds left. Checking to his left, he made sure Schwarz and the driver were secure. He left the cruise control on. "Pol?"

"Yeah."

"I'm going right—hard. If I'm going to make it off here in one piece, you're going to have to be right there."

"You can count on me."

"I am."

To the right, blurred by the cracked glass in the passenger window, the roadside dropped in a sharp ditch. Evidently the highway had been built up at this point to help with flooding.

Both hands on the wheel, seeing a knot of ruby taillights only a short distance away and spread out before him, Lyons said, "Now!" He pulled on the wheel, keeping the door open with his foot.

The tractor's tires shrieked in protest, but held to the road, taking the sudden sharp right turn.

Satisfied that the truck was on course, knowing his safety margin before ignition had dropped to eleven seconds, Lyons threw himself out the door for the Suburban's roof. He landed hard, off balance, knowing how a bug had to feel when it found an unexpected windshield. Then he was slipping, sliding for the end of the Suburban and the highway rushing past at a hundred-plus miles per hour.

"I've got you, Ironman," Schwarz said.

Lyons felt a hand close around his wrist and stop him. Finding the luggage rack, he managed to roll over and look for the eighteen-wheeler.

For a moment, it looked like the truck was going to hold steady past the point of ignition. Lyons felt a cold chill pass through him, then sudden exultation as the tractor's wheels went off the highway and caught in the overflow ditch.

The rig turned sharply, jackknifing the trailer. Propelled by the momentum and weight, the trailer went crashing through the tractor, smashing it to pieces. The Scud didn't fare any better, falling from the cradle and spilling across the ground.

Trailer, tractor and missile left gouges scarring the ground, took out several yards of barbed-wire fence and came to a stop in a field. And remained there.

Blancanales brought the Suburban to a stop at the side of the road. Schwarz got their prisoner from the roof and handcuffed him, then unceremoniously stuffed the guy into the rear of the Suburban. Cars on both sides of the freeway stopped, and drivers got out with cellular phones, asking if anyone needed help.

Lyons waved them back and told them to call the state police, enforcing his words with the badge and his authority. When he rejoined his teammates, they were looking at the destruction.

There wasn't much left of the eighteen-wheeler.

"Looks to me like someone's going to need a new Peterbilt," Blancanales said with a tired smile, then turned to Lyons. "How about you, Ironman?"

Glancing down at the blood staining his pant leg from the wound along his inner thigh, Lyons said, "Nope. But it was a near thing."

CHAPTER TWENTY-THREE

Inchon, South Korea

"Able Team just took out Shatterstop," Hal Brognola said.

"How are they?" Mack Bolan finished shrugging into his aqualung as he stood behind Jack Grimaldi and peered through the Bell Model 412SP's Plexiglas windows. The helicopter carrying Dixon Lynch and his inner core of bodyguards was streaking westward over the city, toward the coastline.

"Standing," the head Fed replied.

"Couldn't ask for anything more," the warrior said. At their present speed, the choppers would reach the coastline in under six minutes. He guessed that if Lynch had a two-minute lead on them, he'd be able to vanish into the open sea. The satellite tracking systems, including the SOSUS array that had been set up by the U.S. Navy during the past few hours, hadn't been able to find the stealth sub that Kurtzman and his team had turned up on their search through Lynch's records.

The helicopter that carried Lynch, however, was a different matter. Stony Man Farm had locked on through the satellite systems, and two SLAR-equipped Navy choppers moved through the area as backup in case the satellites crashed.

"Just wanted you to know the pressure's off here," Brognola said. "That way you can stay focused on your end of the mission."

"Affirmative," Bolan said.

"You people stay frosty up there," the head Fed told them.

If Lynch was allowed to escape, havoc could be wreaked that would have far-reaching consequences. It was possible Lynch's computers were downloading files from across the world that would create problems for law-enforcement agencies, as well as government bodies. To say nothing of the political backlash that would strike if Stony Man's presence became known.

Still clad in the combat nightsuit, Bolan had added the aqualung and scuba mask with a built in UTEL-system, and a compressed-gas speargun. He'd strapped a Randall combat knife to his right calf, and a quiver of bolts for the speargun hung down his left hip.

"They're going down," Jack Grimaldi called.

Bolan had already noticed the descent. His gear was strapped down, and he was ready.

Lynch's helicopter was well out from the coastline, skimming low over the Yellow Sea, skirting southwest under Inchon. The city was a thriving harbor and heavily industrial. Yachts dotted the water, some farther out and some still tied up at the docks. Sailboats, gaily colored and looking frail against the immensity of the sea, sprinkled the water. The tide was out, leaving yards of mud flats exposed. Children were running below, playing under the protective eyes of their parents.

Lynch's aircraft pulled up short, coming around broadside in its effort to slow rapidly. A freighter was directly below the helicopter. Men were scrambling across the deck, clearing a space for the helicopter to land.

"Stony One to Stony Base," Bolan transmitted.

"Go, Stony One. You have Stony Base," Price replied.

"Can you get a reading on the sub?"

"Negative, Stony One. If it's down there, it's hidden from everything we have access to."

"Affirmative."

"That's got to be it, mate," David McCarter said. "Lynch knows the U.S. Navy owns this part of the ocean. There's nowhere for him to go but under."

Bolan nodded in agreement. He took up a pair of binoculars from the storage compartment beside Grimaldi and trained them on the freighter. She was the *Leaping Jack,* and was flying Malaysian flags.

Grimaldi was closing the distance, imitating the helicopter's approach and going in low.

Suddenly water roiled up at the leeward side of the freighter. All hands on deck moved in that direction, and Bolan could tell from the way they acted that they were amazed first by the appearance of the chopper, and even more so by the submarine surfacing. It looked like a black wedge, pyramid shaped, and covered with triangular facets, designed to elude radar and sonar.

"There!" McCarter said.

Bolan nodded. "Take us in, Jack." He pulled the scuba mask over his face and clicked the UTEL earpiece into place. Going back to the cargo area, he joined Phoenix Force at the sliding door and strapped on his fins. "Gary, Calvin, you're with me."

Both men nodded. James's experience with the SEALs would help Manning with the placement of the shaped charges. If the sub got below sixty feet, the Stony Man warriors would have to give up the chase. McCarter's team was assigned to affix a satellite transponder during that time, in the event that the sub did get away.

Leaning away from the helicopter into the wind, Bolan saw the activity on the deck of the freighter as Lynch and his party raced for the sub. A ladder was thrown down and attached to the sub's conning tower. Lynch was the first man on, scrambling quickly for the hatch.

Abruptly bullets struck the sides of the Bell Model 412SP, coring through the sheet metal. Grimaldi stubbornly held the craft on target.

Bolan stood poised in the cargo door. The sea was a bright sheen less than six feet below him.

"Go!" Grimaldi said as bullets scarred the Plexiglas windows of the helicopter's nose.

Leaping from the aircraft, Bolan dropped into the Yellow Sea. He went down at once, holding the speargun in one hand, a bolt already in place. Waving with his free hand, he turned toward the sub, getting himself oriented.

The sub hadn't moved, lounging under the water by the freighter like a huge steel shark.

Manning and James knifed through the water not far from his position, and wasted no time in getting turned around, as well. The rest of Phoenix Force made their entrances only a little farther on.

Bolan swam hard, kicking his fins with everything he had. Even with the unique design, it was easy to spot the diving planes at the rear of the boat. He closed on them, wrapped a hand around the nearest structure and slung the speargun over his shoulder. Taking the demolitions he'd brought from his backpack, he started affixing them to the diving planes.

"Mack, look out!" Encizo called.

Looking to his left, Bolan was already in motion, moving out of line with the diving planes. A frogman in deep blue and orange swam toward him, flanked by three other men, trailing bubbles behind them.

A silvery explosion of more bubbles signaled the release of the spear the lead man fired. The spear ripped by the Executioner with only inches to spare, leaving a swirling wake of bubbles.

Slowed by the water, Bolan slipped his own speargun free and fired from thirty feet out. His bolt knifed through the water and took the lead swimmer in the face.

The man's body suddenly went slack as his arms made a futile grab for the spear sticking out of his mask. Blood streamered away in spreading coils. More bolts sped toward Bolan. Two of them thudded against the side of the sub, but the third slashed through one of the warrior's fins.

Recharging his speargun, Bolan knew he'd only get off one more shot before the men were on him. He aimed deliberately and squeezed the trigger. The recoil pushed him slightly out of position, and the haze of bubbles covered his view.

Moving, Bolan slung the speargun over his left shoulder as he drew the Randall survival knife. The broad blade with its saw-toothed spine looked deadly in the murky water.

The first man to reach Bolan had a knife in his fist and attacked him while the second man went for the demolitions strapped to the diving planes.

Dodging the knife sweep, the Executioner grabbed the man's mask and yanked, pulling him off balance and letting water into the mask. Disoriented, the frogman flailed out weakly. As he brought his knife across the man's throat, Bolan got a brief glimpse of the men of Phoenix Force similarly engaged. Then the cloud of suddenly released blood tinted the water so heavily he couldn't see more than a few feet.

The man at the diving planes nearly had the explosive off.

Stroking for him, the Executioner freed the collapsible

grappling hook from his web belt and released the line. Before the man knew he was coming, Bolan hooked the grappling hook to his tank. The guy tried to fight him, but the Executioner bound him to the diving planes along with the explosives.

"She's going down," McCarter warned.

Bolan clicked into the UTEL. "Gary?"

"It's coming," the Canadian replied.

"I've got the communications array all set," Encizo said.

"Touch it off," Bolan replied.

Immediately a small explosion ripped the satellite dish and radio receivers away.

The sub continued to descend. As she did, she started forward, the screw twisting through the water violently.

Bolan was breathing hard as the scuba struggled to keep up with his usage. Normally the tank contained an hour's worth of diving, but he knew the strenuous activity beneath the water was reducing the tank's capacity to only a few minutes. Diving deeper to pursue the sub would take even more time off.

Bodies hung in the ocean, locked into place by their neutral-buoyancy belts. None of them belonged to the Stony Man team.

Finning vigorously, Bolan followed the sub down and forward. His depth gauge put them at thirty feet, then forty. Manning was still locked on to the side of the sub like a leech, working like a madman.

"Stony One, this is Stony Base," Price called.

"Go, Base." Bolan felt the pressure settle in on him, feeling like a huge fist clamping around him, intent on squeezing him to death.

"We're not picking up the transponder anymore."

"That's because the bloody thing became a casualty when no one was looking," McCarter said. Twenty feet away, on the other side of the sub, the Briton held up the plate-sized transponder designed to survive excessive depths. However, it hadn't been designed to withstand the spear that was partially sticking through it.

Bolan glanced at his depth gauge, having to use the light now. They were at seventy feet. Black comets were already in orbit in the warrior's vision.

"Done," Manning said. He flung himself away from the sub.

"Detonate," Bolan ordered.

"Fire in the hole!" Manning cried out in warning.

A series of explosions suddenly ringed the submarine, throwing out clouds of debris and sandy murk. The frogman tied to the diving planes blew up with the assembly. The other explosions took out instrumentation, leaving the sub deaf, dumb and blind, totally dependent on an external satellite feed that didn't exist anymore.

Still, the captain didn't give up. Holding to the present neutral buoyancy and a knowledge of the waters, the man evidently decided to make a run for it. Far enough out to sea, repairs could be made without being picked up or noticed. The screw redoubled its speed.

Bolan swam for the rupture that had been left in the sub's side. The blast had peeled back the sub's outer hide, leaving a gaping hole that was large enough to swim through. The inner hull of the boat was only a little more than an arm's length away.

The water was colder at that depth, and the current told the Executioner that the sub had reached a speed that couldn't be matched by a swimmer if he lost his precarious hold. Only Manning and Hawkins had managed to get on with him.

"Good luck, mates," McCarter called. "Give them hell."

Bolan glanced back and saw the other three Stony Man warriors swimming for the surface. Then he turned back to the men he had with him. His arms were straining as he fought the current. "Gary, can you do something about the inner hull?"

"Yeah. But it's going to be risky being so close to ground zero."

"We don't have a choice." Bolan took out his underwater flashlight and switched it on. He played the beam inside the ballast tank and found that the tank went another ten feet forward. "What if we're in there?"

Manning craned his head around and looked. "Do it. I'll set up a double charge. First one outside, shaped to blast outward. I'll set it so it goes off a split second before the second one, which I'll have on the inner hull. With the water to act as a buffering medium, maybe it'll work."

"You're hoping the first blast draws out whatever concussive force that's reflected from the second detonation," Hawkins said.

"That's what it's supposed to do," Manning said. "Hopefully it'll set up some kind of implosion field. We didn't have all this water around us, it probably wouldn't work. As it is now, it's worth a shot."

"Get it done," Bolan said. He pulled himself inside with effort. Manning and Hawkins followed.

As the Canadian set up the shaped charges he'd need, Hawkins looked at Bolan and played his flashlight over his depth gauge. "We're at sixty-five feet. Going up."

"Must be the diving planes," Bolan said.

"Once they notice, if they think they're safe, they'll get someone out on them."

Bolan nodded. "It won't matter to us. By then we'll be out of oxygen." He tagged the UTEL and tried to raise Stony Man, not sure if he could.

"Here, Stony One," Price said.

Briefly the Executioner explained the attempt that was going to be made, then added, "Can you trace the UTEL?"

"Barely. You're breaking up really bad."

"Same here." The static fuzzed over many of the words. "If we don't make it here, we're going to leave a UTEL in the ballast tank. Maybe you can use it to track the sub."

"I understand. Stony Base out, and God keep."

Bolan knew the mission controller was aware they weren't going to be leaving the sub alive unless they'd achieved some kind of success. His oxygen was almost depleted. His throat and lungs burned, and he was starting to feel dizzy and colder.

"Done," Manning said, rejoining them.

Bolan glanced at his depth gauge. They were at fifty-five feet. The surface was too far away to make it on what they had left in their aqualungs without decent air somewhere along the way. Manning's needle was buried in the yellow. So was Hawkins's.

"Do it," Bolan ordered.

Together, they crowded into the farthest space from the target area they could.

The double explosion was devastating. The concussion slammed into Bolan and knocked his face against the bulkhead. He lost the mask for a moment and found it with difficulty. He played his flashlight over the ruptured area, finding two holes now instead of one.

The turbulence trapped inside the ballast tank was powerful, but not as bad as it could have been. Bolan swam into the lead, grabbing hold of the edges of the new rupture. It was almost manhole sized, and seawater poured into the room gallons a second. Judging from the crates and shelving strewed around the room and now floating on the rising waterline, the space had been used for storage.

Without hesitation, the Executioner pulled himself into the room, propelled by the water as he filled the rupture. Off balance, he flew into the room as if shot out of a cannon, slipping and sliding across the wet floor.

The hatch opened as he pushed himself up. Two sailors, blurred by the water covering his face mask, peered in at him. One of them raised a full-size Uzi and screamed a warning.

The Executioner drew the Beretta 93-R from shoulder leather and fired two rounds. Both bullets struck the men in the face and knocked them backward. He left the Desert Eagle holstered. With the Magnum rounds, the bullets would bounce around a lot off the bulkheads.

Manning followed him into the room, followed by Hawkins. Both of them drew their Berettas.

Taking the lead, Bolan stepped out into the corridor and headed in the direction of the bow. The sub was claustrophobic, dark from flickering tube lights that signaled it had sustained more damage than at first believed.

They raced through two more hatches, dogging them and jamming the wheels with bolts meant for the spearguns to prevent getting caught in a cross fire from any crew that might come forward.

A hail of bullets drove the Executioner to cover just before the next hatch was closed. During the brief instant it had been open, he'd seen the ops center—and Dixon Lynch.

Bolan took the time to recharge his weapon. Noticing the security-camera lens in the upper wall above the door, he crossed the corridor and broke it with the Beretta's butt. If it had been working, it no longer was. He looked at Manning. "Any surprises left to take care of that door?"

The Canadian shook his head. "I used up everything I had on the hull."

Hawkins showed them a mirthless smile. "But not everything I had." He reached into his pack and produced a bar of C-4. "And because I know attempting to take that ops center is going to be an up-close and personal thing, these." He fished out two Thunderflash grenades. "Figured we might be doing a leg of this little jaunt inside somewhere."

"When we pop that door," Bolan said, "there's not going to be much time for thinking."

Both Phoenix Force commandos nodded. Bolan took one of the grenades Hawkins offered while Manning worked the C-4 into the hatch frame. Within two minutes, they were ready to go.

"Explosion's going to be a bit much in here," Manning said. "But there's nothing to do for it."

Bolan nodded. He grabbed two extra magazines for the Beretta in his left hand and pushed the fire selector to 3-round burst. Holstering the 93-R, he fisted the Thunderflash grenade. He waited against the opposite wall, leaning into the steel bulkhead, then signaled Manning to blow the door.

The explosion was deafening, yet still left ringing in the big warrior's ears. Unable to hear, he pushed himself toward the blown hatch. Standing just outside, feeling the wind from the rounds going past him, then the solid thud of at least two flattening against the Kevlar protecting his back, he pulled the grenade's ring with his teeth, counted down and sent the bomb spinning into the room. He drew the 93-R.

The detonation happened a heartbeat later, filling the sub with even more noise and harsh, bright light.

"And two," Hawkins said, lobbing his own grenade into the ops center.

As soon as the second one went off, Bolan followed the

Beretta into the room, going low. The furniture was bolted to the floor, so he tried to remain clear of it.

The ops center was set up in a square, neatly compact and totally functional. At least a dozen men were in the room.

Raising the Beretta into target acquisition, Bolan cut down a pair of gunners with tribursts to the face and throat. He pushed himself up and ran for a mate who was still disoriented from the blasts while Manning and Hawkins poured into the room behind him.

There was nowhere to run.

Gunfire rolled in unforgiving thunder, filling the ops center. Sparks jumped as bullets struck metal surfaces, and smoke and fires erupted from electronic gear as other rounds slashed through them.

Bolan held the mate and knocked the gun from his hand before he could fire at Manning. At least four rounds struck the man in the chest as he was killed by his own men. Holding the corpse as a shield, Bolan fired through the rest of the magazine in the 93-R, then dropped the empty and replaced it.

Hawkins was staggered by a round that passed through his shoulder, but he didn't quit firing.

Bolan burned down another gunner with a triburst. He tracked another man, leading him, then fired through the Plexiglas plotting map in the center of the room and killed the man. He scanned the room for Dixon Lynch, but didn't see him.

Manning put the captain down with a heart shot, catching two rounds from the man's Tokarev against his armor in the process.

Without warning, Lynch stepped from behind a bank of instruments where he'd been hiding and put his arm around Hawkins's throat as the young Phoenix Force commando kicked an empty clip from his pistol. Lynch put his gun to Hawkins's head. "Don't move or he dies!" he yelled.

Bolan and Manning turned, but neither was in position for a clear shot at the man behind Hawkins.

"Put the guns down!" Lynch ordered.

"Take the son of a bitch," Hawkins snarled. "If you don't, he'll kill me anyway."

"No," Lynch said. "You can leave by whatever means you arrived here. Killing you isn't going to matter in the larger scheme of things."

Bolan lowered his pistol, waving to Manning to do the same.

"Take the shot," Hawkins said. "I'm going to count to three, and if you don't, I'm going to move on him anyway. One—"

"Stand steady, T.J.," Bolan commanded.

Hawkins did, but didn't look happy about it. "He's lying."

Lynch grinned. "That's the way. No one else has to die. I know you can't track this sub, and I don't have to kill you to get away."

"No," Bolan said, "you don't."

"Put the gun down."

The Executioner didn't move, and the silence stretched between them.

"Put the gun down," Lynch repeated.

Bolan shook his head. "I don't think so. You're a gamer, Lynch, and you play to win. A tie would be even harder for you to accept than a loss."

"I'll kill him." Lynch pressed the gun harder into Hawkins's throat.

"Then I'll kill you," Bolan said. "We each lose. Another tie."

He raised his voice. "Manning, put your weapon down."

With no hesitation, Manning did.

"Now kick it away," Bolan ordered, "and get down on your knees."

The Canadian did.

"My gun's at my side," the Executioner said. "If you're good enough, you can kill me, then kill my men. If you try to kill anyone but me, you're going to die. Believe that."

Lynch laughed suddenly. "I underestimated you. I won't do that again." Then he thrust the pistol out, already firing at Bolan.

Whipping up the Beretta 93-R, the Executioner fired once, placing a trio of bullets one above the other between Lynch's eyes. The corpse jerked and fell backward, the gun tumbling from the man's nerveless fingers.

"Not in this lifetime," the Executioner said grimly. Then he turned, looking for the communications station so he could start making rescue plans with the Navy units lying in wait. Even when they were attacked with their own weapons, he knew it was the hearts of the Stony Man warriors that kept them strong, not the hardware. A brave and willing heart was the only thing a soldier needed when he took his place against those who would prey on others.

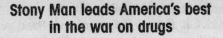

**A violent struggle for survival
in a post-holocaust world**

JAMES AXLER

DEATH LANDS®

Watersleep

In the altered reality of the Deathlands, America's coastal waters
haven't escaped the ravages of the nukecaust, but the awesome
power of the oceans still rules there. It's a power that will let
Ryan Cawdor, first among post-holocaust survivors, ride the crest
of victory—or consign his woman to the raging depths.